The
Bathsheba
Deadline

"This sizzling thriller predicted everything. Everything!"

An Original Novel by

JACK ENGELHARD

DayRay Literary Press
British Columbia, Canada

The Bathsheba Deadline: An Original Novel

Copyright ©2007, 2014 by Jack Engelhard
ISBN-13 978-1-77143-171-2
Second Edition

Library and Archives Canada Cataloguing in Publication
Engelhard, Jack, 1940-, author
The Bathsheba deadline / by Jack Engelhard. – Second edition.
Issued in print and electronic formats.
ISBN 978-1-77143-171-2 (pbk.).--ISBN 978-1-77143-172-9 (pdf)
Additional cataloguing data available from Library and Archives Canada

Jack Engelhard may be contacted through: **www.jackengelhard.com**

Cover artwork: Co-workers having an affair © Mark2121 | CanStockPhoto.com

Previously published in 2007 by Penguin (iUniverse, Inc.).

DayRay Literary Press is a literary imprint
of CCB Publishing: www.ccbpublishing.com

DayRay Literary Press
British Columbia, Canada
www.dayraypress.com

The Bathsheba Deadline

Bestselling novelist Jack Engelhard (_Indecent Proposal_) has produced a heroic work of literature. This is a superb, gutsy novel. _The Bathsheba Deadline_ is a newsroom thriller ripped from the headlines. The present day action takes place in a Manhattan newsroom where three leading journalists find themselves caught in a sizzling three-way love triangle that may lead to murder in the Middle East (Israel). You will never forget Jay Garfield and you absolutely will never forget Lyla. Politics and sex mixed in with the war on terror provoke life-and-death rifts within the editorial staff. Journalists with the power to influence public opinion have lost their neutrality and have taken sides. Readers are taken behind the scenes and into the newsrooms where they are shown how headlines are made and often manipulated to favor one side over another. Media bias usually against Israel? Read all about it in Engelhard's stirring pages. The war for survival in a New York City newsroom mirrors the clash of civilizations here, in the Middle East, and around the world.

Praise received for *The Bathsheba Deadline*

"A rousing thriller about clashing ideals, clashing moral standards, and clashing civilizations. *The Bathsheba Deadline* is a page-turner with much more than just entertainment (although it delivers that in abundance); it is an insightful, courageous look inside the headlines. Bravo, Jack Engelhard."
- Robert Spencer, author

"Engelhard writes with the sparseness of Hemingway and the moral intensity of I.B. Singer."
- Michael Foster, author

"Jack Engelhard is a writer without peer and the conscience of us all."
- John W. Cassell, author of *Crossroads: 1969*

"A towering literary achievement. Jack Engelhard's *The Bathsheba Deadline* is a sexually/political thriller every bit as compelling as his perennial bestseller *Indecent Proposal*. *The Bathsheba Deadline* weaves a tight web of suspense in which the reader is caught, fascinated. We love it, every tense, fascinating minute."
- Letha Hedady, author

"Punchy style reminiscent of everything we may have loved about Papa Hemingway. Engelhard rocks!"
- Daniel Mezei, reviewer

Also by Jack Engelhard

Indecent Proposal: Fiction.
Translated into more than 22 languages and turned into a Paramount motion picture of the same name starring Robert Redford and Demi Moore.

Compulsive: A Novel: Fiction.

Escape From Mount Moriah: Memoir.
Award-winner for writing and film.

Slot Attendant: A Novel about a Novelist. Fiction.

The Days of the Bitter End: Fiction.

The Girls of Cincinnati: Fiction.

The Prince of Dice: Fiction.

The Horsemen: Non-fiction.
Excerpted in *The New York Times*

* * * * *

A new Spanish language edition of *Indecent Proposal* was released in 2013 in both print and e-book editions and made available for purchase worldwide.

The author wishes to express his gratitude and thanks to translator Frederick Martin-Del-Campo for his fine work in this and other projects.

Dedicated to
Leslie, David, Rachel, Sarah, Toni...and Siena!

...and to the loving memory of my parents
Noah and Ida

Immeasurable gratitude to
Jeffrey Farkas

Chapter 1

The logo alongside our masthead reads, IN PURSUIT OF TRUTH. Well, we try. I've got my truth, you've got yours, and Phil had his.

We're all in the same business, only we differ on the facts, which are usually unreliable anyway, for even a dozen witnesses at the scene of the same accident provide 12 different interpretations. But on this we can rely when we do the job of covering the world – blood runs our newsprint. We're motivated by headlines and deadlines but don't shoot us, please; we're only the messengers. We don't make it up as we go along, generally.

We'll know it's safe when parallel lines meet up out there in trans-infinity. Meantime here we are. And do, please, forgive us our sins.

* * *

Phil Crawford was easy to dislike, which is probably why I liked him. I'm a sucker for strays and outsiders since I'm no easy fit myself. Maybe I didn't like him all that much, but he was okay. We did have differences, politically. He wrote a piece, that time back, before it all came out in the open, praising Palestinian suicide bombers, and that caused us some friction, especially when I turned it down for being too obvious.

He said I was the one being too obvious. I let it drop to keep peace in the newsroom. Word got back that he accused me of having a King David Complex.

Where I come from that's a compliment.

So Phil Crawford leaned to the extreme left, a point of view quite favorable in my newsroom, or in any newsroom, but his extreme was too exotic, even for fellow journalists, whose lives began with Woodward and Bernstein, all of them into it, into journalism, for the idealism, the romance of changing the world. This was a generation of dreamers rushing, in their laptops, toward universal blessedness. They want a Brave New World and they want it Now!

Like the rest of them, Phil Crawford talked about the root cause of it all. That was blasphemous in our place of work, the Manhattan Independent, a fine name for a newspaper that was a subsidiary of the Hawkins Newspaper Chain, owned, by the way, by Ben Hawkins, an Americanized Brit who was vehemently Conservative, pro-American, pro-Israel and no man for root causes. "They started it," Ben Hawkins often reminded his staff. "Not us."

Of Ben Hawkins, let's say this. He kept trying to form his staff into his own image. He kept trying and he kept failing.

Journalists are ornery and tough to persuade. Cynicism is part of the job description.

Back to Phil Crawford. I liked him for another reason. We had both attended the University of Cincinnati, and that was enough for me to offer kinship. (I never graduated and "attended" is my everlasting claim.) He was a big guy and almost made the UC basketball team as sixth man. He was tall and trim at the time, though now, years later, he was merely tall, beginning to stoop on a frame going wobbly in flesh turning pink. I'd say he put on 60 pounds between then and now.

He also got himself a wife between then and now. Her name was Lyla, a Hebrew word for night, though she was not

Jewish and neither was Phil. Not even close. His op-eds – he took the usual route from Obits, to Police Beat, to City Hall, to City Desk, to Editorial – were clearly anti-Israel, but that did not make him anti-Semitic, necessarily, exactly what I kept telling Executive Editor Ken Ballard, who kept reminding me that he was getting heat from upstairs.

I often told Ken Ballard and even publisher Ben Hawkins that Phil Crawford was no different from the rest of us. All of us in the news business agree on one thing; everybody is rotten and life sucks. In other words, we hate everybody. We are not prejudiced against any single group, unless you're including all of civilization.

So Phil was merely anti-everything and everybody. A journalist!

You don't start off that way. It's how you end up, human nature being what it is as we, in our pages, keep a running tab of all the crimes, sins, betrayals, misdeeds, atrocities, genocides worthy of a headline, local, regional, national, international. There's never a pause, never a lull, it keeps on coming, and people pay us (75 cents a copy; $1.50 on Sundays) to give them their daily bread of bitterness. Back at UC we'd had a debate as to journalism's true function; was it to give the news, or to change the world? I said give the news; Phil, of course, said change the world, and he was still at it, but with this complaint – he was chained to a desk. He wanted to get out there and be part of the adventure. He wanted the one newspapering job he'd never had – foreign correspondent.

There's nothing truer to journalism than covering a war. If the war is there and you're here – what are you, and if not now, when?

Lyla kept him back. She was willing to let him go but he was afraid that when he'd come back she'd be gone. He was very jealous of her and for good reason, the reason being that she was beautiful. She was beautiful and he was no longer handsome. She was also headstrong and something of a flirt, which he perceived with his own suspicious eyes since we all shared the same newsroom, Lyla as Book Review Editor.

But he'd still be willing to take off for the world's hot spots – especially the Middle East – were it not for upstairs. Ben Hawkins did not want an anti-American/anti-Semite covering Israel. ("Can't we get someone who is objectively pro-Israel for a change?") Plainly, Ben Hawkins did not like Phil. I liked Ben Hawkins. He came up from the bottom, as did I, he disdained contrivance, mendacity, deceit and ruled his enterprises, especially the Manhattan Independent, like a prophet; above all, yes, Pursue Truth!

Ben and I shared a reputation as being "two-fisted" and that was fine with Ben and fine with me. Around the newsroom I was known as Ben's Boy.

Okay, but there was still a paper to get out every morning.

My enemies called me a "rebel" but give me this, there's plenty to be rebellious about.

So Phil...Phil remained desk-bound, and friendless. Outside of me, Lyla and a few others, Phil had nobody. I date this back to UC. Even there he was something of an outcast for all his mysticism. Not that he heard voices or anything, but he had himself plunged into Kolatruda, an end-of-the-world philosophy that embraced parts of Hinduism and Islam. He did say that he was "in touch" with someone. This stopped being funny when he cursed a professor of French Literature, Milos Tremblay – and Milos got sick and died.

Even here at the Independent there were hints of this, this power. Out on the dock, one of our delivery-truckers cursed him out for being such a leftist. Phil cursed him right back and the guy, that same day, got himself wrapped around a utility pole, barely surviving neck and spinal injuries. So it was not good to get on Phil's bad side.

Lyla refused to take this stuff seriously. I once asked her what would happen if she decided to leave him. "You mean would he curse me?"

"Yes."

"You believe that nonsense?"

Okay. I did. I was no believer in the supernatural, but I was not quite ready to dismiss it, either.

I'd been taught to beware the power of a curse. You never know.

Chapter 2

People used to wonder what went on inside Lyla's office after she shut the door. There was no privacy for staffers after the renovation that changed the newsroom from Ben Hecht to Starbucks. (Latte instead of coffee on every desk. Ashtrays? Gone and forgotten like the typewriter.) No more Walter Winchell fedoras, no spittoons. (Kill someone, okay, but light up a cigarette and OHMYGAWD!) No talking, either, except by computer. It was all whispers and when you walked in you thought you were in a hospital, so clean, so quiet, so antiseptic. Not like the old days, when a newsroom's heartbeat was the clatter of Underwoods.

But a few of us, like Lyla, retained three walls and a door. Lyla had built the Books Department from one staffer, herself, and one Sunday edition to a staff of three and reviews each day. She made her department into something big and she lunched with all the big names in writing and publishing, and did it all on her own, by, as legend had it, simply letting her skirt roll up in conference with Ken Ballard, or maybe it was Ben Hawkins himself. Or maybe it was me, managing editor. Or all of us together.

Lyla had killer legs. Lyla had American legs. They don't make legs like these in the Ukraine. It's in the breeding.

Phil lost his focus when someone was in there with her too long. I do not think he objected to me. I was her boss, according to the rules, though she cared nothing for rules.

Lyla was Lyla and whatever Lyla wants...

"What's this?" I said, and for the first time shut the door.

The copy was racy enough for a family broadsheet, but the headline was too much – YES VAGINA, THERE IS A SANTA CLAUS.

"When is this newspaper going to grow up!" she said, shifting in her chair and smiling that devilish smile that always made me gasp.

She was wearing an Armani jacket, clutching a Marc Jacobs bag – ready, I assumed, to join the Alpha ladies who lunch. She was one of them according to the watch or calendar.

She varied from cat to kitten, her green eyes playful with suppressed mischief, unless she was hot on an interview or a story, in which case she was all toughness and business and clear the paths for here she comes. She was one of those (sultry) women who made you wonder what it would be like. Lyla's favorite book was *The Bell Jar*, and thus Sylvia Plath her favorite author, and this was good literature but bad prognosis, all this depression and dedication to defeatism and death. But people will say we're in love. She "read" faces and said I had a strong face.

Where does testosterone end and love begin?

"I thought we reviewed this months and months ago," I said about that headline she tried to pull on me.

"This is a re-thinking, Mr. Jay Garfield." She used my last name when she meant to be snippy. Lyla was a dangerous flirt. She ran her straight long hair, brunette, to a side, like the young Lauren Bacall, and she came at you the same way, full of daring. Like so many women of charm and beauty who came before her, women kissed by the gods, sisters of fortune, she ran at a her own pace in pursuit of something, someone, somewhere, a destination or a destiny, reflected in the quickness of her eyes, never to be reached. (She'd once given acting a spin, out there in Greenwich Village, but couldn't manage "the indignities.") She knew something the rest of us didn't, especially when she planted hands to hips, measuring the size of your balls. She was at her best when she was resolute, but even more fetching when she was vulnerable.

Her message was this: I know you. You will never know me!

She could have me in a flash. But she was the wife of a staffer. Taboo. Seduction was no part of a plan, from her end; it was just Lyla being Lyla.

The girl can't help it and God help the rest of us.

"We're not there yet, Lyla."

"Oh? You've got a problem with that word?"

We've come this far? Is nothing sacred? Not even THAT?

"You know this can't go."

"Copy stays?"

"No promises. We've still got old fogeys at City Desk – you know, men and women, who still believe in decency."

She got up in one move, walked around and faced me. She got up so fast that her skirt forgot to come down. (I peeked. Yes, on a good day life is one cheap thrill after another.)

"It's part of our anatomy," she said. "That's indecent?"

I really was afraid to tangle with this lady. I was in and out of college, learning most everything I knew on the run, and from the Army, and from a self-imposed regimen of a book-a-day, one day Hemingway, next day Virgil. Mostly self-taught. Do not call me intellectual. Lyla was a Vassar lady, bred and raised to be beautiful but tough. I say "bred" thinking of thorough-breds who are supercharged with determination and speed, and that's what she was, a thoroughbred of a woman.

Lyla was in a hurry. What? Afraid she might lose a step and fall behind her generation?

"In my newspaper? Yes. Indecent."

She kept up that teasing smile.

"Don't you know, Jay?"

"What?"

"It's out of the closet."

"What is?"

"Everything!"

8

This is true. Men are kissing men, women are kissing women, and America applauds. It's in our very own Manhattan Independent, front page.

She followed me as I inched for the door. She grabbed the doorknob to halt my progress.

"Getting warm in here?" she whispered.

"Maybe."

"As moist for you as it is for me?"

"Please."

"Something's going on, and you know it," she said.

"There's nowhere to go with this, Lyla."

"Oh, isn't there?" she said, eyebrows raised in defiance. "There's something to be resolved between us."

We were near a kiss.

"Lyla. Play fair."

"Hmm" – and as she reluctantly cleared my path – "maybe we should just play."

* * *

Lyla – now here was a woman who had everything, and so confident, so self-assured, and so empty and so sad. Truly an American woman of the 21st century.

She had everything and she had nothing.

She sometimes said she could see right through me, and I could say the same about her. She was fooling everybody else; not me. What was missing? This I couldn't say, but something was wrong, even with brains and beauty and the most fabulous job in the world. Unlike most Americans (but like most Europeans), she wanted to talk about LIFE, and when it got around to that, between us, she usually ended up near tears. "People are so cruel," is what she'd say.

She seldom talked about her past. I only knew that her father, a judge, had taken his life after being (falsely) accused of accepting a bribe. After something like that – and all that happened when she was just getting into her teens – you are bound to live each day wondering what comes next. She wasn't bitter, only cautious. Her father was her hero and he'd been framed. So her loss of innocence came fast. She maintained a sense of trust, but warily.

After Vassar, she got her first dream job at a major publishing house. She quit after a year because it pained her to reject all those manuscripts that flooded in from anonymous America ("how awful to say no to people who give you their hearts"), and because the literary worthies she met were not so worthy. ("Never get close to your heroes. They'll always disappoint.")

I.B. Singer said he wouldn't cross the street for Dostoevsky. Lyla said she wouldn't cross the street for Salinger. I think she would. For sure. In fact, she once confessed (after a couple of drinks) that Salinger was the scoop of the century. If it ever happened, she wanted to be there, alone, with pen and paper. She was certain that he was NOT working on a novel but on a single word, a word that defines everything. That's what's taking him so long. Beckett had tried that by subtraction and did plenty to cut literature down to size. But he never came up with that single word. To some, Torah is that word. To others, Koran. Salinger must be after the same thing.

Salinger must think he's God, or god-like. God removed himself because the (corrupted) earth could not contain His glory. Well? Ditto Salinger.

* * *

I'd had dreams about Lyla, usually at night, and sometimes by day, and as I typed that day's column or that day's editorial I'd stop and bring her up. She knew this. She'd phone and say, "What are we doing?" Huh? "Oh come on, Jay. I know what you're thinking." Denials did no good. "I keep getting your messages. You, Jay Garfield, are a naughty boy."

Chapter 3

I took my son to Pat's Gym for his weekly sparring but Lyla kept haunting me. Do they know they do this? Joel, what a kid! He was a good kid and I loved being with him, loved being his dad. Something hurt whenever my kid said, "Dad." I mean it breaks your heart when you know one day he'll be a man and you won't be there for him for shelter. Right now he's a kid and there ought to be a law about keeping it that way. I once told him, when he asked me why I was limping (from merely a spar at the gym) that as he gets older, I get older, and this made him very sad. I got him once a week. Myrna, his mom, my ex, never cared much for my training the kid to be tough; rather he should take up ballet or the violin. Myrna and I get along okay, actually much better since the divorce. This happens.

But in the gym you'd think I was the one in the ring, behaving as badly as I was, miming the moves Joel ought to be making, hollering at Joel to use his left hook as the other kid was beating up on my boy. Where's the gusto? Where's the rage? This kid – my kid – doesn't know rage. That's a defect in this world. It's brutal out there. The meek shall inherit the earth? Fine, but we're not there yet. The bullies are still in charge and pushing us around. Slip and slide, son; left/right, roundhouse, uppercut, pow/pow! Next thing, my kid's bleeding from the nose. I was his corner man but it took a ton of self-restraint to keep me from jumping in there and Pat himself had to come over and ask me what's wrong.

I told him – left hook. I didn't tell him, of course, that it was Lyla and everything else.

How long can you put it off? Lyla was going to be trouble. I knew that from the start.

Temptation can drive you nuts.

(Sex is nothing, I'd once read. It's temptation that causes all the trouble.)

A minute into the second round I'd had enough. I jumped into the ring and that ended the fight. Joel, only seven, kept back tears in the locker room and Pat took me aside and told me never to do that again and I apologized, saying I did not know what got into me. But I did. What's a son, at that age, if not an extension of yourself and so that was me in there getting pummeled?

What I did was so uncool and so uncharacteristic. I was a fighter myself, so I knew. I'd hate it if someone did that to me.

The ring is life in microcosm. It's a fight from beginning to end. Babies are born with their fists clenched. That tells you something.

Outside I asked Joel to forgive me and he gave me a big hug and said he understood. I made sure he knew none of this was his fault.

"We'll keep practicing that left hook, Dad."

Driving him back to Myrna he asked if I was crying. I said of course not. Tough guys don't cry.

Later I tried to figure what snapped. Everything, probably, triggered by Lyla. It takes just one thing to make everything come tumbling down.

* * *

Years before I had been fired from the Times, in another nearby big town, for misquoting a movie legend, allegedly. The man said he hated America. He said it all right, but then, after it was published, he denied it and had his people call my people and then there was the threat of a lawsuit (saying that I'd ruined him) and then there was a retraction and then I was fired and blacklisted. Couldn't land a job. Word gets around. Newspapering is a neighborhood. Everybody knows everybody. Ben Hawkins came to the rescue. But the stigma never left.

Here at the Independent I started all over again, from scratch, and finally had it good, pretty good, pretty damned good, but I guess the residue, I mean the residue of poverty, never leaves with memories of watching Mother and Father quiver as the landlord demands his rent – a cliché, but not when he's at your door.

* * *

Some time back I got into a fight with a network anchorman famed for reading the news seasoned with sex appeal. (Naturally, he was number one in the ratings.) He says I started it, I say he did, but in the middle of it all is a woman, Marta Geller, who approached him for his autograph and after he signed his name she spat on it and called him an anti-Semite. His bodyguard moved in and shoved the lady. I shoved the bodyguard and then took a swing at the anchorman and landed a left hook that resulted in a black eye.

A cameraman was at the scene so there is film, 18 seconds of it, to prove that all this was provoked. But the footage that would exonerate me is missing and so is the cameraman and meanwhile I am being charged with assault. The case (at the urging of the anchor) is going forward, before an arbitration panel made up of fellow journalists, but, as I keep showing up on television as the aggressor, the public only has half the story. The anchorman wants me "sanctioned," whatever that means.

About journalism in general, what bothered me most, I suppose, was that we were approaching something new – HALF THE NEWS THAT'S FIT TO PRINT.

Are we there yet? Yes, we've arrived at the place where truth and accuracy keep winding up on the cutting room floor.

Chapter 4

Phil Crawford's Op-ed commentaries finally gained him the attention of the Arab world. Hamas liked what he had to say and they invited him over.

Phil got himself known from our international edition and via that global township known as the Internet.

I was no fan of Hamas. For me (and ALMOST everybody else) 9/11 changed everything, to the extent that I believed this headline:

THE KORAN HAS ARRIVED AND IT HAS COME TO DEVOUR THE BIBLE.

Hamas wanted Phil to come on down and tell the world the Hamas version of events.

Phil had me over at McSorley's around the Village to fill me in.

"That's PR," I said.

"Everything is PR," Phil said, perspiring even though it was April and cool. Up close like this – we seldom did the let's-go-have-a-drink thing – Phil was heavier than I thought, and losing hair by the minute. He never smiled. I do not remember him smiling, ever. He had no sense of humor. He was so very political and so very serious and so very dull and really, what had she seen in him? Well, if love is chemistry it is not always good chemistry.

"Don't give me that everything is PR shit, Phil, not today."

I said that with a tired chuckle to suggest casualness. Phil wanted to do GOOD. People like that are a menace.

"Paragraph by paragraph, picture by picture, everything is slanted. All news is subjective."

"I'm not in the mood for this, Phil. Save it for your seminars."

He wanted to know what I thought, about his going to the Middle East and Hamas – Hamas being all about terror, even landing on our own State Department's list of Most Wanted – if, that is, I'd let him go. The decision was not really mine, not entirely. Stu Greenwald of our foreign desk would have a say. Stu ran his foreign desk like a general and might not take kindly to a soldier from another unit.

Foreign correspondents, after all, were the stars of the newsroom, though they were seldom in the newsroom, their absence, being in the field, part of the attraction.

"Could be a trap," I said. "You know, Danny Pearl."

I did not mention Benjamin Curtis.

"But they know me as a friend."

"Yeah, but you're still an American."

"So?"

"Come on, Phil. That's the real world out there. Here we're just pretending. Besides, you're Jewish."

"NO I'M NOT!"

"Just kidding, Phil. Really, Phil, just kidding, damn it."

I was annoyed at his humorlessness, and that we failed to mention Ben Curtis, who was Jewish and who did die at the hands of Islamic Jihad two years before Danny Pearl. Ben was ours, not on staff but a stringer. They lured him in and, as ransom, demanded an exchange of prisoners that were in both American and Israeli prisons. Both governments were warned to keep it hushed for Ben's safety. That's why it never made the news. I went out there to exchange myself for Ben Curtis. Too late.

Off I went to a West Bank village named Saleem el Shaif. Accompanied by three agents of the CIA and two from the Mossad, I got to meet Abu Bin Sharif, who proclaimed himself to be some kind of Jihad chieftain, and who said the body was not fit for viewing. "Sorry," he said, and that was that, that was Ben Curtis. They had chopped off his head and drank his blood. Before all that they'd festively dragged him through the streets. (Don't look at me. I report, you decide.)

* * *

Phil was drinking scotch, I was having vodka straight up. He was on his first, I was on my second. I needed every finger of it for this company.

I ordered a couple more and tossed them down. Phil kept searching my eyes.

"Can I ask you a question?"

"Shoot."

"What do you think of that Arab-Israeli thing?"

"One side's got it, the other side wants it," I said.

"That simple."

"Yup."

"You never reveal yourself in the newsroom, I mean your views."

Did I agree that it's all about religion? No, I said, "Religion is not the problem. It's the people. They're the problem."

Am I a man of faith? Yes and no. Given all we see and all we know, how can you have faith; how can you not have faith?

It is that simple and that complicated.

I kept reminding myself whose husband this was. I wondered if they still made love. A group of pretty women stepped into the place, passed by our booth and I gave them each the once-over as has been our habit since the caves, but Phil never gave them a glance. So I wondered if they still made love and if Phil had any spark in him other than politics. What keeps a man ticking when politics goes to bed, or when he goes to bed?

I've always hated politics. What's that got to do with the price of tomatoes? Plenty, come to think of it, so I'm wrong.

Phil tried to launch into his pro-Palestinian thing, which had worked on C-Span, but I told him again to cut it out, I knew the pitch.

"They have a right to their own homeland."

Is this where I say they've already got 22 homelands amounting to twice the size of the United States? No, let it slide.

I ordered another round. I wondered why he had such thick, hairy fingers. At some point it must have clicked for her.

I wondered what their home life was like. Lyla hated politics as well. So what did they talk about when they talked? Did they talk? There was nothing between them in the newsroom, which is good – very professional. She never walked by his desk with a pat on the shoulder and they never sat together in the cafeteria and as far as I could determine they never exchanged a smile or did anything to suggest they were husband and wife, which is good – very professional. But still...

"So what's the question?" I said.

"Do I go?"

"I don't know, Phil. I'll toss it around."

My guess was that Phil wanted a straight rejection to get him off the hook. He wanted to go but he didn't want to go. If he made the rejection on his own he'd be a coward, so he wanted me, the paper, to do it for him. I also guessed that Lyla knew of the Hamas invitation. He would not want to be seen as a coward in her eyes. Is there a man who is not a hero in his own estimation? We've all got some Walter Mitty in us and all of us are the stars of our private fantasies and daydreams.

"I really think it's my duty as a journalist," he said, his eyes downcast, his hands fumbling with a soiled napkin. He'd gotten himself a double-chin.

What had she seen in him? She must be fooling around. Back at UC he had excelled, though never with the girls.

How had he landed a woman named Lyla?

But they always do, it seems.

"I gotta head back," I said, nodding for the check, my head beginning to spin.

Phil said that being part Christian and part Jewish, heck, I should be a stickler for love thy neighbor, which defines the entire Middle East conflict. I explained that love is too much to ask for neighbor to neighbor. All we should expect, all I expect from a neighbor, is leave me the hell alone. That's right, forget love; just leave me the hell alone.

Phil had one more question. Why was Lyla in there with me, doors closed?

"My wife," he said.

"Your wife...my literary editor."

* * *

Back in the newsroom, where I rushed to get caught up, though there is no such thing in news, I got a call from Security down in the lobby. A man named Isaiah Mandelcorn needed to come up and talk. This was nothing unusual. They come like this maybe 20 times a day, from off the streets and sometimes from as far away as Des Moines and San Francisco, and they all have a beef, or something that needs to be published. Why were we in Vietnam? Why are we in Iraq? Why are we even in America? Everybody's got an opinion. When did this start, all this griping with everybody chiming in? I guess it started that morning we woke up to find ourselves no longer alone, but part of the world. We used to be so insulated. There's us between sea and shining sea, and there's them. Suddenly (or so it seemed) terrorists without borders, and their tsunami is our tsunami. His Voice is upon all our waters.

Security usually stopped them, those trespassers down in the lobby, though once in a while someone slipped through and once in a while someone really had something to say; maybe one out of 10. Bud, on duty downstairs for Security, whispered, over the phone, that he'd never come across a guy so insistent, so I said all right, I'll come down. So I went down to the lobby and waiting for me was a man maybe six-four in a black suit, black coat, black wide-rimmed hat, white beard, blazing eyes, like he'd just stepped out of the desert Sinai.

He introduced himself as Isaiah Mandelcorn. He spoke gently and with a smile, as though he knew he made a frightful appearance. He was dominating, but affable. He declined to say where he came from, or what organization or cause he represented. He said he was his own cause and his own organization. He did volunteer, however, that he was a member of The Lost Tribe.

"The Lost Tribe," he said, explaining no further and leaving it for me to guess and to imagine its deeper meaning.

He came, he said, with a messianic message. He seemed plenty messianic himself.

"Please," he said, handing me a manila envelope. "Please read this."

I thanked him and said I would read its contents later.

"No," he said. "Please. Now. Later you'll forget."

So I opened the envelope and knew right away what it was. It was a disturbingly articulate response from Rabbi Meir Kahane, the fiery, extremist rabbi who'd been slain, assassinated, years ago. In his "Dear World," Kahane blasted the nations for their sins against his people, the Jews. This was explosive stuff and had never been published within the mainstream press.

"This has to be told," Isaiah Mandelcorn said.

I nodded sympathetically.

"I don't think we're ready for this," I said. Usually, when something unprintable came along, I said I'll think about it, but this man, it was clear, would take no trifling.

"I knew you'd say that," he said. "Israel is not in vogue."

"I'm sorry," I said.

"Don't be sorry. Only let me assure you of this: One day you will see fit to print every word of this document. This must be told."

I shrugged and thanked him again.

"The day will come," he said with utter certainty.

I doubted that – but I did tuck away the document for safekeeping.

* * *

Someone around here is getting entirely too mystical, one step, perhaps, to going completely insane. Was this my Elijah, or a Lamed-Vovnik who'd finally come out in the open?

Chapter 5

Phil was over at the UN after having secured an interview with the new ambassador from Iraq. Phil had many friends on the Arab side and that was a boon to the newspaper. I was at the computer fixing up an editorial about Catholic priest pedophiles and that New Jersey rabbi convicted of murdering his wife and what it all means. We're supposed to know, those of us who write the editorials. All we know is that it's one hell of a world. There's always something going on and it's never anything good and it's never gonna get better. We condense it all into column inches for a public that's conditioned to expect the worst. We say – Here's your world: sorry about that! Have a nice day.

So Phil was over at the UN and there was a knock at the door of my office. She asked if she could come in.

"Of course," I said.

She glanced back at the door to make sure the coast was clear, and she smiled.

She was radiant, her features all lit up. She had on fresh lipstick and it was obvious that she'd given herself a good going over in the powder room. Something was up and it wasn't about news or her Books Department. She was groomed for combat. Lyla was wearing a blue and white outfit that hugged her figure at all the right places. She moved with grace and authority and was always (or so it appeared to me) on the edge between sincerity and mockery. "I came to apologize," she said. I was about to say something, like no need, but she stopped me.

"No," she said. "Please listen."

According to custom, beautiful journalists go straight to television. The rest settle for newspapering. Lyla was the exception. She was here and she was beautiful. So I listened.

She had come to thank me for stopping her the other day from making a seductive fool of herself, for being her rock here at the Independent, for supporting her Books Department when no one else would, for allowing her to expand and find her voice, for helping her shape the newspaper into a literary haven, for giving her a career instead of a job, for putting up with her moods and her temper, and for just being me...wonderful me.

"You're welcome," I said.

After getting all that out, she seemed to relax, but with attitude; still something cooking.

"That could have been a real problem," she said, "you know, the other day." There was a different sparkle to her lipstick.

"Oh yeah," I said, putting on the nonchalance.

She laughed, and when she laughed it was seldom pure but usually within the whisper of tears, and no wonder. She'd had that troubled childhood and now, married to Phil Crawford, who knew what else? She was a strong woman, of course, but that is too glib to say about anyone, because we never know what can shatter or break another person. ("Be kind," said Philo, "for everyone you meet is fighting a great battle.")

"I need to tell you something," she said, and I thought I saw her trembling.

This was what she had to tell me. "I love you, Jay."

We don't need this, I'm thinking – do we? Could lead to dancing.

I gave her a don't-be-silly smile. "Some call it lust."

"So what's wrong with lust?" she said.

True, lust also has merit.

"So this is all about sex, Lyla?"

"Of course not." Then, with a smile that comes along for a man but once in a lifetime: "But it's a start."

She moved back to the front of my desk and began toying with a boxing trophy I had on a bookshelf. This trophy was very valuable to me. She knocked it down for the count.

She apologized, said it was an accident, just like us, an accident. Fate is one accident after another.

She kept talking, but I was not listening, only watching, and admiring, and feeling the bother of temptation.

She was saying something about getting stirred up, how between men it's resolved by boxing, but between men and women it's resolved by sex.

I don't know what got into me, but I took her, right there, upon my desk.

"Oh!" she cried out at the start as if it had all been so totally unexpected.

Chapter 6

With one exception (maybe two or more), nobody smoked, and half the staffers were women here in our New Age newsroom. (Not that there's anything wrong with that...) The conference room, though, where we held our regular editorial meetings, was still largely Old Guard. Minerva Watson, of Arts and Entertainment, Marla Oberman, TV-Radio, Freda Stiles, Real Estate, were the women, the rest were men – I should mention Lyla Crawford among the women but Lyla, being literary and in a loop of her own, seldom attended.

That was powerful – those moments with her. I'd have to get that out of my mind, that I'd made love to Phil Crawford's wife.

This could have consequences.

You never had a chance, she said later, and went on to confess that she had it planned all along and that she had written poems about me, which she'd never reveal, unless we "developed." She shared my sadness, she said, and when I protested, she said melancholy was etched all over my face. Just like Kafka, she said...and if I checked the mirror, I would find the resemblance.

I was not fooling her, she insisted, with my "rumpled manliness." Though it is what attracted her.

Of news and my obsession in keeping up with the latest? She'd forgive this flaw in my character and besides, there is no news. It has all happened before. The answer is in fiction, novels, poetry, music. Read Hawthorne or Proust for the scoop on what was and what is. Joyce is as current as tomorrow's headline. For politics there's Beethoven. This endures. All that endures. The rest is commentary. We are all commentary and find ourselves plunged into nothingness.

For herself, she said, F. Scott Fitzgerald is more alive than her neighbor next door.

In that case, I said, where do I fit in? In that case, she said, a smile increasing the depth of her eyes, you fit in just fine. Just fine.

Yes, forget that, if you can.

WHAT IS THIS THING CALLED LOVE? Is it when she shares your enthusiasm for Beethoven? Or is it when she gives her tush that swivel?

* * *

"How did I end up below the fold?" asked Homer Parkins, our business editor, about yesterday's edition. "Stocks nearly collapsed."

"So did Britney Spears' dress," complained Minerva Watson. "You promised a lower-left teaser, Jay."

Spears stopped the presses with that crotch shot heard around the world.

(Another day in popville, but is this why they hate us and keep coming to upend our entire civilization?)

"Postage rates went up three cents," said Paul Melrose, our man who keeps tabs on regulatory business. "How did that end up in Regional?"

"Nobody goes to the post office anymore," piped in Marla Oberman.

"Yeah, it's too crowded," cracked City Desk's Frank Fitzpatrick, a fan of Yogi Berra.

Most of us around the table agreed that, anyway, Britney Spears was like yesterday, as was Paris Hilton, and certainly Madonna and her Kabbalah and Tom Cruise and his Scientology. That's not news, that's entertainment. We ran them on our

Gossip Page, and always felt cheapened afterwards, dirty, filthy, used. Sometimes you've got to give the people what they want, and this is what they want. A photo of J.Lo's ass usually upped our circulation by 14 percent. But for most of us journalism was serious business. Our duty was to inform, ugly as that is. That is why we warred over Front Page.

All this was ritual.

These daily sessions were like Mafia gatherings where they meet to carve up the world. Our World was Front Page and everybody wanted a piece, each editor staking out rights and claims to his territory. Dividing it all up to make the paper readable, that was part of my job, the other part being to keep the truce. Do we persist with that Big Story (that we'd been running for days), like that hurricane, thousands dead, millions homeless, or, for our headline, do we give it a breather and go with that teenage girl who was hit with a foul ball, and died, right there in the stands. Some stories, weightier and even worthier as they may be, get tired.

My observation was that one untimely death hit home more profoundly than that of multitudes – my Anne Frank Imperative.

Anyway, TV was covering that Big Event wall to wall. We can't compete on that level. We've got to make our own rules.

Or do we go with the Middle East again – and when I brought that up I got the usual groans and jeers.

What it often came down to was philosophy – the philosophy of what this newspaper (any newspaper or TV network) owed its public – the local picture or the big picture? Another observation, from years in the business, and from circulation figures, was that we Americans are parochial. We do not give much of a hoot about what goes on outside, and the farther out you go the faster you lose them. In news radio (where I did a stint while I was being exiled) the dogma, supported by ratings, was that listeners wanted nothing more than weather, traffic and maybe sports.

Yes, Americans are parochial. We don't do *weltschmerz*. We focus on this and that but then it's back to Play Ball. We go from fad to fad.

The average attention span, around here, is 12 and a half minutes, from one commercial to the next.

So this day's skirmish, after an exhausting and sometimes testy hour and a half, was narrowed down to City Editor Frank Fitzpatrick and Foreign Editor Stu Greenwald; Frank going for foul ball, Stu insisting on hurricane, citing the overwhelming disparity favoring his claim. I sided with Frank for the emotional appeal of a single child and was chided by some for going tabloid.

"Sold!" I said.

They were correct in taunting me for going tabloid, but I was going by instinct, which sometimes is all you've got in handicapping horses or Front Page. The hurricane was going below the fold with a headline that also triggered hot exchanges. Shall it be HOLLYWOOD CAN'T COMPETE WITH GOD'S SPECIAL EFFECTS? Or – HOLLYWOOD CAN'T COMPETE WITH NATURE'S SPECIAL EFFECTS? I wanted God, but I gave in on Nature. As to our editorial on the monster hurricane, this line got in: "From the mightiest nations to the lowliest, what powers can we claim, what glory, when a gust of wind can render us desolate?"

Arnold Coffey summoned me after the regular meeting for a private minute or two, and I knew what it was about.

Clive Thomas, our man in the Middle East, had again used the word "only" in his dispatch of eight Israelis slain on a bus in Jerusalem. No human life is "only."

"We're doing them in like all the rest," Arnold Coffey said, meaning the Israelis, meaning rather, what Arnold Coffey imagined to be a media gang-bang upon the Jewish state.

The media pogrom. He was quite proud to have come up with that line and too bad, he said, that it could hardly be used because...well, because of a media pogrom.

Arnold Coffey was a remnant from the previous ownership. He had no real power but reigned as kind of a deposed monarch; indulged for the sake of tradition.

By tradition I mean that, among other perks, he had his own private elevator and personal operator, Otto, to zip him up in plush style.

This elevator was a relic, last of those operated manually. Arnold was claustrophobic and needed someone in there with him wearing a uniform.

"We should be different," he said.

"We try."

"In the end, we all go back to our origins. You'll see." Then: "Yes, Jay, I mean you."

Arnold (like Ben Hawkins, both aristocratic) was likewise outraged at the media's perceived slant to the left. He tabbed the media as anti-American, and this pained him.

I kept as neutral as possible, open to both arguments about the Middle East. Arnold never pressed me too hard. He knew better. He seldom appealed to my Jewish side and I'm not sure if he knew that I was raised more Catholic (from Mom) than Jewish. (Mom was partly Greek Orthodox.) My father attended shul maybe once a year, tugging me along, but Mom schlepped me to Mass regularly, and Christmas was big, though not as big as boxing from Dad's side. Dad claimed that fighting, rather self-defense, was a man's only true religion and he once said something outright sacrilegious, that the Jews of Auschwitz would have been better off believing in Joe Louis for all the good believing in God did them. Dad used to say he wanted me to grow up like King David. ("Now there was a fighter – and a poet!") Lyla liked to remind me that the map of Israel was written all over my face.

This means? This means that try as I might to play it neutral, and cleave to my Christian genes, my roots are in Sinai.

I dare not confess even to myself that, secretly, I share the longings of Judah Halevi.

"He is not good," Arnold said about Clive Thomas, our man in the Middle East. "Remember, the world has divided itself in half. It's us against them."

Then he headed off to his office on the top floor where the old regime still maintained a dignified if distant presence – like a conscience.

* * *

A few weeks back, Arnold Coffey wrote an editorial about the clash of civilizations. That's where I used that headline: "The Koran Has Arrived and It Has Come to Devour the Bible."

The phones, and my ears, are still ringing.

* * *

Mathematicians like Paul Erdős tell us that only numbers are beautiful and perfect (like Fermat's Last Theorem) and perhaps this is true, for words keep failing in this place where nothing makes sense even to scientists and even to those devout practitioners of divinity. We in the news business imagine that some day, one day, we will find the means, through words, to express the human condition and so we pursue the headline that will wrap it all up as neatly and coherently as one and one makes two. Numbers live in a world of unity. Words live in a world of chaos and that is why we fail.

We sit each day, a dozen of us (members of the editorial board), around a big table, and try to put into words the number 6 (corresponding to CREATION), which some mathematicians say is the most perfect, most beautiful number of all, but there is no matching that number, hard as we try. We are limited by linguistics. Still, we are convinced that a perfect headline awaits us and that when we meet it, it will answer everything. Meantime we stagger and have yet to find God in a headline.

* * *

For the Sabbath, Kabbalah founder and mystic Rabbi Isaac Luria of 16th Century Safed (he was also known as Arizal) dressed himself in "four-cornered" white garments to conduit himself to the Tetragrammaton, the four letters of the INEFFABLE NAME. (Numbers again.) Luria also named God's retreat from His creation as Tzimtzum. (Don't ask. We're all learning as we go along.)

* * *

Stu Greenwald's foreign desk office was tucked away at the edge of the newsroom because he smoked, cigars, and once a day I hid away in there with him, sharing his Upmanns. Stu was a big, rumpled, old-timer. He still pecked away at an Underwood and had his woman, Stella, transcribe everything into the computer and Stella always laughed when she saw me coming for I'd arrive yelling Marlon Brando's STELLAAAAAA!

I could never just say Stella. It had to be STELLAAAAAA!

We both lit up, Stu and I.

"I told him no," Stu said about Phil Crawford's approach to attend Hamas. "We don't need Benjamin Curtis all over again."

"He got to me first," I said, feeling relaxed and quite terrific to be in here smoking a cigar. These days everything was against the rules and it was a pleasure when you broke one. We blew out smoke as if telling the whole world to go screw itself. The anti-smoking frenzy sweeping the land, we both agreed, had reared up an entirely new generation of smug, holier-than-thou, self-satisfied bullies.

"I know, and you also said no." Stu had his feet up on the desk, a desk buried from headlines dating back to JFK. He was there, in Dallas. He'd written a book about it; sold 30,000 copies. Not enough to liberate him from newspapering, but a respectable sale nonetheless, and anyway, we all talked about being liberated from newspapering, on the shoulders of that big novel, but, while some made the escape, our hearts beat to the next deadline.

"I said maybe. We can't deprive ourselves of a scoop, if that's what it is."

"Changing your mind?" said Stu, snapping his suspenders and eyeing me through a cloud of smoke.

"No. But we could be passing up a duty to ourselves and to our readers."

"We could also be faulted for sending off a reporter to get himself killed." He leaned back to make a hard point. Most people leaned forward. He leaned back. "This is Hamas, after all."

"That is a consideration, and it's why it's a maybe."

We smoked in silence. I glanced around the room. All those photos. Kings, queens, presidents, prime ministers, Stu right in the middle. There he is with Kissinger. He hated Kissinger. Biggest fraud there is. ("You guys came on the scene too late," Stu liked to say. "Everything's already happened." I disagreed with that Fukuyama philosophy. I liked Solomon's take much better, that "one generation goes, another generation comes." Right, it always starts all over again. We're like the shadow of a passing bird.)

"I don't know if Crawford knows what he's getting into," said Stu, scratching his forehead. "This is real, like the kids say."

"He has done it all."

"Here at home, yeah. But out there? Don't you sense a trap?"

"Could be. But he has been favorable to them. His Op-Eds are practically all in their favor."

"Like Tom Friedman and the rest of them across the street," Stu said with a chuckle.

"So they like him, Hamas does."

"They don't like anybody, those people. They blow people up to get to heaven. Their vision of paradise is a whorehouse."

To make his point he threw something at me that had just come over the wires:

PALESTINIAN BROTHERS MURDER SISTER
FOR DISHONORING FAMILY

"Let's not kid ourselves," he said.

* * *

Immediately after the meeting I was stopped by Peter Brand, our editorial page cartoonist. Peter didn't like me. I didn't like him. This happens. Why I didn't like him I don't know. His wispiness? The knowing smile that was concealed accusation? Was it the mustache, the hair that he wore carelessly but carefully moppish with a trained cowlick to give him a Dennis the Menace flair? I had him measured as sneaky.

"What's this?" he said, pointing to a memo.

"What's what?"

"I didn't want to bring it up at the meeting and cause more trouble for you," he said as he followed me across the newsroom to my office.

"What trouble?"

"This says I need prior approval for all my work."

Peter Brand's editorial page cartoons were famed for being edgy, if you approved; anti-American, anti-Christian, anti-Semitic if you disapproved. Peter Brand's father had done animation for Disney and Peter had tried some of that himself out there but dropped out when he got political, or maybe they dropped him. One editorial cartoon of his charged that 9/11 was a fabrication. No firemen died, he slyly suggested, and, as evidence, asked why "so-called" bodies that were dug up were never displayed?

"The one about the Pope was too much, Peter."

"Jay, can I get personal for a second?"

"Hey, it's a free country."

"That's just what I was getting at; you're a tyrant. You run this place like a dictatorship."

Really? I thought I gave generously to freedom of expression. Not from me will come the chill of censorship. Or so I thought.

When I reached the office Peter tried to follow me in. Gladys, my secretary, signaled that there was a phone call waiting.

"I have to take this, Peter. Must be Thomas Pynchon again."

* * *

From day one it's been like this with Peter Brand and hell if I know when it started and maybe it started centuries ago so maybe there IS something to this business of reincarnation. Else why the attraction or subtraction when two people meet for the first time and for no earthly reason hit or miss? I'm buying this.

Chapter 7

We had arranged to meet at the racetrack, Aqueduct, there in the backstretch, this Sunday morning, eight sharp, so that we might still be in time for some of the workouts. She knew this was my sanctuary, my place to hide from civilization. Eight o'clock was here, but she wasn't. I used to muck stalls when I was a kid and now if I got up in time Kuana Banks gave me a rake. Kuana was a trainer from Hawaii, bred into the business from a Chinese father and British mother. He was a Gary Cooper kind of guy, laconic and terse-spoken in his boots and ten-gallon hat, and was usually successful in concealing the fact that he held a degree in philosophy from the University of Honolulu. Going into the thoroughbred racing business you have to forget all your education and start your learning all over again.

Kuana had a string of 20 thoroughbreds out of the 1,000-plus that were stabled here in the Aqueduct backstretch. Mostly, his were claimers, but he did have a couple of allowance warriors and one two-year-old that had Bold Ruler bloodlines. So once again Kuana had his sights set on the Kentucky Derby, as they all did, all trainers, all of them dreamers, which is what kept them living such long, healthy lives. They lived for the horses, the round-the-clock absorption, the isolation that kept them in a world still undaunted and untamed. The backstretch was immune, sheltered, a universe still unpaved.

I followed him, here in shedrow 36, as he loped along from stall to stall, checking up on his horses and their grooms. Some horses were being bandaged, some were being walked round and round by hotwalkers, some were being hosed down after returning from a work, still breathing heavy. I asked him if on appearance alone he could tell a cheap horse from a champion.

"Yes," he said. "Class shows."

I asked him if the same could be said about people; I mean horseracing was all about bloodlines and genetic consistency. What about people?

"We're less predictable," he said, chuckling. "Don't you think?"

He referred me to Michel de Montaigne and his claim that no man possesses a steadfast and consistent character. Today's hero may be tomorrow's villain or coward. Or the reverse.

"That's where we have it over horses," he said, entering a stall to help with the bandaging. "Or maybe that's where they have it over us."

As he was doing that the owner of that promising two-year-old colt stopped by. He drove up in a beige Mercedes. Some story he had, this Stan Sewald. Made his fortune in Atlantic City. He was a slot attendant in Atlantic City and offered a sick bag lady, playing the nickel machines, a glass of water when no one else would. Except that she was no bag lady but an heiress whose bonanza fixed this slot attendant for life, all for a glass of water.

Eight thirty and Lyla was still missing.

But was that my name being announced over the loud-speaker – to present myself at the front gate? There she was, in jeans and a yellow sweater.

That sweater and those jeans drew some hoots and leers.

Lyla was a knockout.

She was smiling, but timidly, as when we are unsure about our surroundings and whether we will be found acceptable. This wasn't her place. In the newsroom she was queen.

"You're beautiful," I said. It just came out.

"Thank you," she said. "You're not so bad yourself."

35

As we walked, the gravel crunching beneath us, horses being led to and from their shedrows, she took my hand, and asked if it was safe to do this.

"What's troubling you?" I asked.

She was behaving entirely too timid.

"Oh," she said, "nothing in particular. Or perhaps everything in particular."

"Like what?"

"Like us. What's going on, Jay? Is this just a crush?"

This isn't the place for mushy gooey love-talk, I explained, and she caught the drift, and smiled, and, sighing theatrically, said:

"Guess I'll keep saving you for my fantasies."

"Nothing wrong with that," I said.

"As long as we make them come true."

Hmm.

"I guess this is what happens when each morning you wake up to find that the world has turned itself into a giant insect."

Kafka, again. Well, books were her department after all.

"No wonder," she continued, "there's something so hard-boiled, so film noir about you."

Then: "But I also know how soft and gentle you can be."

This (with her) was true already.

I gave her the grand tour, walked her to the track where horses were being clocked by anxious owners, trainers, grooms.

"So this is your secret life," she said.

I wanted her to be amazed at this world that I loved. ("God help me, I love it so." George C. Scott as Patton.)

"It is wonderful," she said. "But why have you been so distant to me in the newsroom?"

"I thought it was you."

"Partly. The eyes. Those newsroom eyes – and then there was Peter Brand."

"Huh?"

"He said something."

She watched the works and said it was thrilling, being so close to the action, the darkly golden thoroughbreds so fierce as they dashed around the track, their heads tucked in as their legs extended stride by stride, their hooves furious upon the ground. She'd never been this close, close enough to see them swagger onto the track and then watch them zoom by.

"What did he say?"

She stiffened. "Oh," she shrugged. "He's such a skunk. He said something about Phil being upset when you and I were behind closed doors."

"Sounds like Peter."

"Yes, Peter Brand sees everything, knows everything."

"Anything else?"

"Just that if there was anything between us he'd be okay with it as long as it didn't disrupt the newsroom."

She said it casual, but it was a bomb.

She turned her attention to three horses that were sprinting for the wire, kicking up dust. I explained that they were just being sharpened, that no racing had been intended but that their competitive bloodlines impelled them to prevail. I told her that, getting her way in the newsroom as often as she did, made her a thoroughbred of sorts. Yes, I wanted to fascinate her about this other-world of abundance that is the backstretch.

"I asked him for a divorce," she announced abruptly.

Huh?

I let out a heavy sigh. My father sighed like that when they came and raided his news shop on Bleecker Street and took him off in handcuffs for alleged bookmaking.

"Don't worry," she said. "I've asked him that before. This time, though, his reasons for saying no floored me. Are you ready for this?"

"At this point, anything!"

She paused in an apparent effort to lessen the drama of what was coming next.

"Did you know that Phil converted to Islam?"

"What's the punch line?"

"He did it six months ago. I wondered why he suddenly wouldn't eat meat."

"We had drinks together. They're not supposed to drink."

"But there it is."

Democracy doesn't care. Islam cares. That was his reasoning. I was surprised that he'd made the switch, but then again, I wasn't. He'd made the deal, found the refuge, years ago, but only now made the announcement, to her at least. Phil Crawford wasn't alone. Converts to Islam were happening all over the place. What else draws these people? Freedom leads to debauchery and Paris Hilton. Islam sets limits. (Let's not talk about jihad, terrorism, beheadings, honor killings and all the rest.)

"He swore me to secrecy, as this might not be the best time to be a Muslim. Of course he didn't tell you. Oh, Jay, tell me this isn't happening."

"So divorce is out of the question."

"Are you kidding? In that culture they murder their wives for even posing the question. Even that much is adultery. I'm trapped."

Would she have to wear the chador, those black robes the women have to wear covering them up head to toe?

"That'll be the day," she said, laughing glumly. "But you know what he did say? He did say this. He said in his religion – HIS religion – it was proper to beat your wife. It was custom."

"Can't you just leave?"

"Not to be overly dramatic, but if I did my life would be in danger."

I shook my head.

"You're not afraid of him, are you?"

"Afraid? No. Terrified."

We paused at the hay bin, a huge shed where the bales were stored.

"So does that end it for us?" she said.

"You mean am I afraid?"

"Yes," she said. "Have I lost you?"

"No."

"You're the only thing I have."

We stopped back at Kuana Banks' shedrow. He asked if we wanted to ride. She'd never been on a horse before and admitted that she was afraid. Kuana gave her that defying smile. He said he'd prepared a special horse for her, named Rocinante. "Well okay," she said, grabbing the helmet from him on fateful impulse. I lifted her up onto the saddle. She looked down and, as if these could be her final words, she said, "If you're afraid to do it – do it!"

Kuana gave the horse a tap and she was off to the races.

She came back exhilarated.

"What was that you said?" asked Kuana.

"If you're afraid to do it – do it," she repeated.

"I like that," he said. Then he turned to me: "I like her."

Then we walked, using our own two legs. She said she finally understood why I loved all this so much. "Horses are so innocent."

"Not so us," she said with a mischievous side-glance.

"Guilt?" I said, surprised, for she never showed that in the newsroom, where she was a walking poster for red-blooded resolve and confidence.

"Only when I think of you."

Likewise, I had to admit, but mostly to myself.

Then she asked if horses lust. In season, I said.

"I must be in season," she said.

We stopped at the hay shed nearby. "Hmmm," she said.

Hmm, I thought.

"Do people really do that thing?" she said, her features steaming up.

"You mean a roll in the hay?"

"I say we give it a try."

We did it in the deep hay, never mind the deep shit we were digging for ourselves.

* * *

Then we separated, back into the real world, and I remembered these words from my father: "Never bet the fillies."

Chapter 8

Ken Ballard, executive editor and my boss, invited me to dinner at Tavern on the Green and said that we sometimes forget that the newsroom is not the only department that makes up a newspaper. "We're so wrapped up in ourselves that we forget those twenty-five other departments," he said.

Like the truckers – who were threatening some sort of action.

"What's this all about?" I asked.

It was about those freelancers that I kept using; men and women outside the Guild. Not just me, but Lyla as well. She used mostly freelancers as her reviewers. As did everyone. I used them when someone walked in with a good story. Like that Stan Sewald in the backstretch whose story about getting rich in the casino fascinated me. He wanted to write it himself and I let him and a good story it was. In fact when it came out our circulation nearly doubled in Harlem and that did us honor, those of us who desired to extend ourselves into the black neighborhoods, a frequent executive-meeting topic about how we can "reach out" and win over this crucial segment of New York that thought of us almost as stuffy and as uncool as the Times. But everybody, every newspaper, used freelancers to an extent.

So why now, why now the controversy? Ken was reluctant to say. Ken Ballard was Main Line Philadelphia. Old money, old values. An aristocrat. Decorum was everything.

So Ken Ballard wouldn't say, for the sake of decorum. So I'd have to pull it out of him. Well, he conceded, his voice a whisper so you had to lean forward, the truckers – whose contract was coming up for renewal in a few months – were demanding more money. Nothing strange about that, except that they were being stirred up by the suggestion that too much budget was being wasted on freelancers instead.

"I wonder," I said, "if any of this was triggered by the Guild," meaning the Guild of Journalists, the members of which liked to think of freelancers as scabs. I offered this as a suggestion, as to state something, as to proclaim something definitive and outright was pushy, in Ken Ballard's Main Line world. To allude, to suggest, to question, all that was permissible – but straight-talk? Never!

"Possibly," said Ken Ballard.

"I wonder then," I said, after a very long pause, "if Peter Brand may have brought these freelancers to the attention of the truckers."

"That's possible," said Ken Ballard.

"Hmm," I said as if I were thinking of something else, because in Ken Ballard's world nothing must be too serious. You must not sweat. "I wonder if Peter Brand stirred up these truckers as a means to get back at me – you know, after I notified him that his cartoons would have to pass through me first."

Ken Ballard let that sit for a while. Maybe he was thinking of his next tennis match, or his next polo game.

"You probably did the right thing," he finally said.

I welcomed his support. But then, after another long pause, he added, "Don't you think?"

"What do you think?" I said, after my own long pause.

"I'd have done the same. Except that maybe he does have a point. I mean about being reviewed. He thinks of it as censorship."

"I think of it as putting out a paper that shows no blacks with thick lips," I said without pausing and with some heat. "Besides, isn't this somewhat mean spirited?"

"Mean spirited?"

That was a very strong word in any yacht club.

"That he would turn another union against us for some personal grudge against me," I said.

"We can't be sure it was Peter Brand, can we?"

"No, but there is that chance." Like hell.

"Tell me, Jay, would you reconsider your position as far as Peter Brand is concerned? You know I never like to meddle in your role as managing editor, so I'm just asking."

"I'd reconsider it," I said, "but I'd still demand to know what goes in before it goes in."

Ken Ballard laughed. "I guess you've spoken."

"Sorry about that," I said.

"No, I admire your convictions. That's good. That's what we want. That's what the paper needs."

That was the end of that, but I was never too comfortable with praise.

Actually, it wasn't the end of that, for upon leaving he said something oh-by-the-way. Like maybe it wasn't smart to be in there with Lyla Crawford, doors shut. There were rumors.

* * *

So this wasn't a good day, and it wasn't over yet. I had promised Lyla that I'd be there at the Book Nook on Fifth Avenue and 48th to attend a reading, which was a monthly event sponsored by the Manhattan Independent and chaired by Lyla, whose idea it had been in the first place, such gatherings among the literate being the centerpiece of Manhattan's book culture.

I usually arrived late so that I wouldn't have to mix and once again I arrived just in time to be late – in the middle of a reading. All 50 or so chairs were filled and the speaker, an author I did not know, was reading from his latest, and this conceit I never understood, once likening it to Lyla as public masturbation.

But I marooned myself in the back and behaved. The reading was long and twisted but I kept my patience to pass the test. Culture is good, if you've got the time. America is in a hurry.

Lyla's infatuation with authors was commendable. She thought of them as her children. She disdained reviewers who were out for blood.

After the reading there was talk about plagiarism, those two historians who'd been nabbed. Lyla joined in by noting that there indeed is nothing new under the sun. She quoted her favorite author, Cervantes, who back in the 1600s said, through Don Quixote: "Those historians who make use of falsehoods should be burned like the makers of counterfeit money." She wouldn't go that far, she said.

In another gathering Lyla had about 10 people say they were novelists who couldn't get published, and could she help. This always happened and at first, going back months, maybe years, she'd been pleasant but it finally got to her, especially when they cornered her and started sermonizing their novels chapter by chapter, so this evening again she said, "Write it, please, don't tell it away," but she was still pleasant.

* * *

I was drawn in among a very attractive group of women, Lyla in the center, beaming, the discussion circulating about our favorite books. I offered *The Last of the Just*, for which I got empty glares. Nobody heard of it, or its author, André Schwarz-Bart, but it was my favorite and my candidate for the Book of the Last Century. When it came to movies I said *The Counterfeit Traitor* with William Holden and Lilli Palmer, but no one heard of that one, either.

Of course, I said, every work of art is a failure. It never ends up the way the artist wants it to be, novel, painting or symphony.

Tolstoy, Picasso and Beethoven would love to start from scratch.

There was one bad moment when Lyla was confronted by a reviewer whose review didn't get in; didn't get in last Sunday's edition of the Independent as promised. The man, a professor, was being loud. Lyla kept her voice low but strong, saying that she refused to trash writers and have any part of literary brutality. The professor kept saying, loudly, that he was being honest. Lyla kept saying, softly but firmly, that he was being brutal – to that writer he meant to review. The professor said he'd never do another review for her again. Suits me fine, she said.

* * *

When the crowd started to thin out Lyla felt safe to snuggle up. She said we had to talk. "I hate when people say that," I said.

"I hate when people have to say that," she said.

It was now dark and we walked a few blocks to her car, up the six flights in the parking garage. Inside the car, after we made love, she cuddled up. But there was news.

Phil was slowly coming out of the closet, about being Muslim, and was thinking of bringing home some of his Muslim friends, friends from the mosque.

"He said I'd have to be covered from head to toe, wear that chador."

She was on the verge of sobbing, her lower lip quivering, like a child's.

"This can't be," I said.

"This won't be," she said, sure of herself and, at the same time, not so sure.

We sat there like that for a while and then I kissed her. Maybe I did love her. Or was beginning to. Or always had.

"We have to do something," she said after she recovered. She lit a cigarette even though they gave her migraines occasionally. She had a migraine problem anyway.

I had already told her that Phil had approached me again about accepting that Hamas invitation. Maybe it was time to let him go. There was a chance that he might not come back. A situation could be arranged to make it sticky for Phil Crawford while he was out there, even with, or rather despite his supposed romance with those terrorists. An Op-ed piece could be planted making him appear unfriendly, undesirable. What treachery that would be!

Chapter 9

Well, this business of making her wear a chador was not a good signal. That's the whole deal, the chador, unlike the hijab that's mostly a head covering and that's making the rounds all around the globe, even into our own newsroom. Yes, we had Muslims on staff and they mixed and matched pretty well, except for the time when someone, Sam Cleaver I think it was, yes, it had to be Sam, anyway, Sam spoke a few words to Ishi's wife, like Good Morning, and that riled Ishi enough to threaten Sam with his life. Sam demanded that I do something about this but there was nothing to be done, Sam's word against Ishi's, and besides, these were nervous times in our newsroom. If I took action I'd have to answer to the Guild where management, like me, and like Ben Hawkins, had few friends. Peter Brand, our op-ed cartoonist, would surely bring me up on charges of bigotry. I didn't need the grief.

Ishi belonged to our headline desk and his wife, Sarina, was a proofreader. Sarina, by golly, only wore the hijab. Once, I think, I saw her in jeans. That must have been a mistake on her part, or maybe on my part. Ishi would not permit something so immodest. Blue jeans changed everything, our entire culture, more so than The Beatles and Elvis and Civil Rights and the Feminist Movement. A generation ago (Marilyn Monroe?) the sweaters were tight and now the behinds were tight and where once they hooked us by cleavage now they turned and gave us their backs. That says something very important I just don't know what it is.

We were still in the car, Lyla and I, parked, after that session at the Book Nook where Lyla had sparkled and shined. She'd been so damned radiant, and sexy, that I fell for her all over again. She was right. Asking Phil for divorce was a bad ticket. You marry a Muslim you marry Islam. Not that there's anything wrong with that...But do I tell her? No. Yet this had come over the wires just the other night:

MULTAN, PAKISTAN. A PAKISTANI MAN CUT OFF THE NOSE AND LIPS OF HIS 19-YEAR-OLD SISTER-IN-LAW AFTER SHE WENT TO COURT FOR A DIVORCE IN A TRIBAL AREA OF THE CENTRAL PROVINCE OF PUNJAB. ABBAS THEN ATTACKED THE GIRL, HACKING OFF HER NOSE AND SLICING OFF HER LIPS.

Fortunately, Lyla seldom read the news or watched the news, otherwise she'd be really spooked.

Her features were bathed in gravity, now that we were talking about Phil and how he had turned his life around – and hers.

I took her hands, to warm them, and then she smiled, and then she frowned. She smiled again, automatically, to prove that she was of good courage, regardless. She had those high cheekbones and sunken cheeks that sunk even deeper when she got to despairing. Actually, that made her even more exotic and more desirable.

I brought up something that I may or may not have mentioned before, about sending Phil off to the Middle East as a combat journalist. That is what he wants, after all. As of last count, over the past year, more than 100 Western journalists had been killed covering the Middle East and parts nearby and afar. The latest were Steven Vincent and Fakher Haider, if, because they weren't conventional journalists, we overlook the fatwa that kept Salman Rushdie on the run but that caught up to Theo van Gogh. Journalists kept getting abducted all over the place, Iraq, Afghanistan, the West Bank, Gaza, for sure. Some were being released alive and in one piece and some were being released dead and in pieces. Anyhow, I could send Phil to a place that was particularly dangerous. Yes I could.

"We couldn't do that," she said resolutely.

"Of course not."

But then, she added: "Could we?"

Some coloring returned to her cheeks and there was a hint, if only a hint, of light fire playing in her green eyes.

"Of course not," I said.

"It wouldn't be right," she said.

"It's something I could never do," I said.

"Same with me, Jay."

"We're not the type."

"But he does want to go, doesn't he?"

"Yes," I agreed.

"I mean he does want to go," she said with emphasis. "You're actually stopping him."

"That's true."

"You're keeping him from ..."

"From being a hero."

"So exactly what is wrong with letting him go?"

Letting him go was not the question. Keeping him from coming back, that was the question.

Lyla was an atheist, thank God. But she knew her Bible, even the part, in Samuel, about King David falling, hard, for Bathsheba, who was married to one of his soldiers, Uriah. So King David sent Uriah to the battlefield with a sealed note that sealed his doom. "Set Uriah," read the note from the king to his general, "in the forefront of the hottest battle, that he may be smitten, and die."

He died. Uriah died all right.

So, is this where I come in and get to play King David, not the good King David, the David that slew Goliath, united the tribes and wrote the Psalms, but rather the David who committed that huge blunder when temptation triumphed over reason? Except for that one misstep, this was a great man, a great king, a great poet, a warrior for righteousness, for Israel, for God. He earned the right to make a mistake or two. What were my merits?

In fact, at this moment, and from this place in Manhattan, I had the same powers of a king if, as managing editor, I chose to dispatch Phil Crawford "in the forefront of the hottest battle, that he may be smitten, and die." Whoa! How quickly this flirtation with Lyla was turning into – oh, here's a word, quagmire. Would this be murder or, well, good journalism? He does want to go, Phil does. He wants to go. That is journalism. Yes, that's what it is. Sure. That's what it is, journalism. Of course. What else would I be thinking? I am a good man. Aren't we all? I am as good as the next man. Wait. That's not saying much.

Lyla brought that up, about Uriah, and I wasn't sure whether she meant that as a warning, as something we should not do, or as a plan, something we should do.

"I don't know," she said when I asked her to explain herself. "I only know we have to do something. Are you with me, Jay?"

"I'm with you, Lyla."

"You don't sound very convinced or very convincing."

"We've got to do something. I get the message."

She was beginning to heat up, regaining some composure. "We can't just wait," she said.

True. We can't just wait.

"You're a man of action," she said.

Yes, I'm a man of action. What action? Uriah got killed and THE LORD WAS DISPLEASED WITH DAVID!

Do I need this? Yes I do. Chalk one up for flesh.

I stared out the window of the car. I was afraid of my thoughts, afraid of Lyla, afraid of Phil, afraid of Muslims...and before 9/11 who knew there were Muslims out there? We thought only we "Americans" inhabited the earth. Where I grew up there were Jews and Gentiles, meaning Christians, pious or lapsed, and as for the rest of humanity, those multitudes beyond the horizon, well, they were extras – like exotically costumed people out of Robert Bolt's Central Casting who show up for background but have no lines.

Of the billion-plus Muslims out there most were surely just plain folks, but the rest sure caught our attention and captured our headlines.

"You want to know the truth?" Lyla said. "I thought you and I would have a nice little affair on the side. I've had hooks on you for some time, and I knew you were not indifferent to me. There were signs. So I thought, okay, I've got a miserable marriage, and I'll go on having a miserable marriage, but to make life tolerable I'll have a lover. It's done, it's done all the time, and this is not the time for moral judgments. We can make moral judgments when it's about other people, but not when it's about ourselves and the lives we've been handed. So wrong or right, that was my revenge. You were my revenge. But it didn't work out."

"What's that mean?"

"You're my lover all right, but I never thought my marriage would turn out like this! I never thought the man I married was not the man I married. What happened?"

"It happens."

I was tempted to ask, but didn't, what made her fall for him in the first place. She should have known. Of course, we never know.

"Am I being bigoted?" she said.

"No, Lyla, this is your life. Have a nice day."

"I mean this Islamic thing – God! Where did that come from?"

I told her about UC and how it all began there, probably, and given how the world had split up between East and West, he'd finally made his choice.

I did not tell her about my earlier chat with Ken Ballard. The rumors he'd mentioned, about us. The newsroom was buzzing, people were whispering. We were becoming an item.

She said, "I feel like I'm living inside a James M. Cain novel."

But I kept taking Phil's side whenever I thought she was going too far. I liked Phil, I think. He was a fine newspaperman, really good, and he never made trouble, not in the newsroom. He never complained when his copy had to be trimmed or when a headline didn't sufficiently convey his report. He was also kind of a lonely guy, not at all sociable, and I had a soft spot for lonely guys, never, frankly, cared much for sociable types, so all around Phil was okay from what I saw of him. At birthday parties or Christmas parties there in the newsroom that wasn't Phil with a lampshade on his head but rather nursing a drink in some corner where I wanted to be.

Once, at a company softball game in Central Park, Phil played center field and nobody hit the ball to him as if on purpose. I felt so sorry for him.

Lyla agreed – about his newsroom behavior. At home, though, he was a different person, an idealist who demanded perfection according to his vision of what is good, good for mankind. Domesticity, the here and now, was secondary to his world-view and his world, not his home, was his chief concern. He was actually a communist, the last communist in America. Maybe that's what led him to Islam. He fumed when she came home with a new dress. Extravagant. Capitalistic. He favored the burning of all shopping malls – temples of capitalistic excess.

At the outset of the marriage she talked back but then gave up, surrendered, choosing frozen silence. (All this, in Lyla's telling, a total shock to me.)

The migraines, she was sure, came as the result of his ranting and rambling and her absorbing it all. She responded by offering fistfuls of silence.

Early on – when she still thought something might be saved – she confronted him about his concern for the poor and the needy.

If you're so worried about them, she said, why is it I never see you give a penny to charity? If you really want to change the world, why not start with you?

This only got him started all over again and taught her to freeze.

(You don't know, I kept thinking as she was telling me all this. You never know how it goes in people's private lives. Phil? This was Phil? This was Lyla's marriage?)

That was before. Now that he'd made the turn, driven by idealism, he announced that only Islam could save America.

"Can you just picture me in a chador!"

I said, "There must be a God in heaven. Otherwise things couldn't get this bad."

"Say that again!"

I did.

"That's startling," she said. "Perhaps even profound."

Then it was her turn to get PROFOUND. She said that suicide crosses her mind now and then.

"Join the club," I said. "Take a number."

"Yes, I know. Suicide crosses every mind."

What was it I read? We're born against our will. We live against our will. We die against our will.

Other than that, life is good.

"With me it's different," she said.

"Why?"

"Because I'm me and not everybody else," she said, finally chuckling and lapsing into momentary good humor.

"I think of suicide," I said, "every time my horses finish off the board."

"You're a lost cause. You're IMPOSSIBLE."

We kissed. She sighed, as only a woman can sigh. We kissed again and she sighed again. She said she loved me and hoped – her only hope was that I hadn't come along too late. There is nothing worse than two people hooking up when it's all over. There is much worse than all that, I said, but it is, I agreed, pretty bad. So – is it too late, between us? I begged her to halt this defeatism. What do I know? I know what comes next in the newsroom, always something coming from somewhere, some disaster, always a safe bet that multitudes will die from the hand of man or the finger of God. But about people like the two of us, what? I know nothing, nothing about what comes next. But she kept going on about how late it was until finally she got me good and depressed. We make plans but nobody knows what comes next, come on!

I never was much good when people got going on gloom and tragedy. I'd had it as a kid from my parents, their very own suffering, which I'd shared just for being around, as kids are, and somewhere I'd made up my mind that I'd be different, so far as obsessing over gloom and tragedy. None of that for me. Things are bound to get better. Oh? I take all that back. That's bullshit.

"I'm sorry," she said. "Gloom is not my style."

That's right. It wasn't.

"Are we ready for another round? Oh – yes you are!"

After that she lit a cigarette and I reminded her.

"Who cares!" she said, inhaling deeply and snapping the lighter shut. "We're all dying anyhow."

Adding: "One way or another."

* * *

A man and a woman – Manhattan sophisticates – making love in a car concealed in a parking garage, how sexy, how romantic, how ridiculous, how sinful!

* * *

An eye sees, an ear hears, and everything is recorded in a ledger.

Chapter 10

On my way to the staff meeting I stopped by Phil Crawford's desk. He was sipping coffee at his computer. I shuddered to think that any day he'd be showing up in that religious costume, but, publicly at least, he was still in the closet. Anyway, he was sipping coffee when I told him that he might soon be packing. His head jerked up, his eyes froze and as I kept on walking I noticed that he'd dribbled some of that coffee onto his shirt. Had I made his day or ruined his day?

If only he knew what was coming. If only I knew what was coming. Of course, he had his own plans.

Shall we still be forgiven even if we do know what we do?

The usual suspects were seated around the conference room table, except for someone named Sam Cleaver, a brash new columnist who'd come to us off a bestselling book about the left, a book akin to Bernard Goldberg's *Bias* and Ann Coulter's *Slander*. Cleaver's book kept to the women's liberation movement, and not altogether disparaging. Still, he was kept off that government funded, national radio network and its segment Clearing the Air.

This prompted Cleaver to submit a scathing rebuke. Titled "Stinking Up The Air," Cleaver's piece charged that liberals were hermetically sealed.

The column was a hit and Sam Cleaver, after a stint on the police beat, was hired on to write three op-ed pieces a week. He was a young guy, 28, lanky, fast-talking, confident, New York-wise. Did I already say brash? Well he was that all right and today he stopped in to offer us a glance at a column that he admitted might be too hot, too sexist, as it wryly suggested that he turned conservative only to please Ann Coulter, Laura Ingraham, Cinnamon Stillwell and Arlene Peck. He had a crush on all four of those articulate Conservative Babes. The Left had no answer for those beauties. (Of Cinnamon Stillwell and Arlene Peck – these two were especially the righteous sound and fury that helped power the Internet into the colossus that was threatening us in print journalism.)

Peter Brand said it was sexist all right and too opinionated and Arnold Coffey said, what the hell, it WAS an opinion, that's what our Opinion Pages are for! So it went back and forth like this and I knew that in the end no one would be happy. That's how we settled our disputes on what goes in and what stays out of our pages; everybody arrives ticked off and everybody leaves ticked off. Sam Cleaver waited by the door for his answer and I told him to give me a minute.

"Maybe two minutes," he said. Cocky son of a bitch. That's why I liked him.

I really needed more time. I had not slept well the night before and those migraines were coming back. Lyla had those and so did I. Lyla kept many doctors' appointments. I had none. No doctors for me. If anything was wrong, and surely something was wrong, I didn't want to know. When the time comes, it comes. Lyla also took many pills, for all the good that did. Valium was my only vice in that department. We just ran the story about the man who invented Valium, the most prescribed drug from 1969 until 1986. Leo Sternbach was the man and he died in North Carolina at the age of 97. A generation earlier he'd made it out of Europe just before Hitler could get to him. Had he been trapped there'd be no Valium, no cure for the shakes, and nervous breakdowns galore.

Sam, Sam, Sam! Of course Sam had written that piece for laughs, even though he was partly serious. So what's next to go after No Smoking? No Laughing? No Sense of Humor? This used to be America. Sam Cleaver was special. He had been my discovery and I was glad to have picked him out of the crowd. He'd gone to college but never finished and that was a plus. He'd have been ruined as a writer (as Hemingway would have been ruined had he gone to college), and I knew that's what he was about, Sam Cleaver, writing, novels. No secret, not to me, that between his journalism he was tapping out fiction on our time clock. Good for him. He reminded me of me when I used to be me.

Sam once asked me what's most harmful for a writer. Two things, I explained; failure and success.

Still, he'd prefer success. Sam was in pursuit of the American Trifecta – Imus to bless you, Oprah to pet you, Page Six to canoodle you.

"Okay," I said to Sam Cleaver. "Go ahead. It's yours."

I waited for the usual sniping to subside after a decision like this and then brought up Mr. Ayayhu Maron who had just been convicted of six rapes in Brooklyn.

"That's got to go," I said, about that courtesy title attached to rapists.

"The Times uses Mr.," said Bull Parker, our City Desk man.

"We're not the Times," I said.

"We sure ain't," murmured Peter Brand.

I heard that. One of these days.

This went round and round for nearly an hour, and was still going. "Is it possible," I said, "that even the Times is misguided about this? Mr.? Mr. Rapist? Come on!"

Ken Ballard blanched when I mentioned – that is, questioned – the Times. The Times was his citadel, his house on the hill.

"Can we really dump these courtesy titles that mark us as a decent newspaper?"

"But we're not dealing with decent people," I said. "Anyway, decent people don't make the news."

This got a wince from some, a laugh from others. The women on our staff had gained equality, even superiority, but had still to gain a sense of grace and a taste for conviviality. (Lyla an exception.) Some arrived still furious over what men had done to them over the past 10 million years, and remained furious as they climbed up in rank. At the same time, the finest writing, especially in journalism, keeps on coming from women.

"I cringe each time we refer to that terrorist as Mr. Arafat," said Arnold Coffey in my support, "even though Mr. Arafat is still dead."

"Check back," said Ken Ballard, "and you'll find that back in the 30s and 40s this newspaper, along with the Times, referred to Hitler as Mr. Hitler."

"That's no justification," said Arnold Coffey. "That makes it even worse."

I called for a show of hands, and lost. Or rather the discussion was tabled for another day. I didn't mind losing this. I took my shot.

I tried again to get a proper definition for the word "climb." Can you climb down? Everybody groaned. Not that again!

As usual at these meetings, nobody was happy. This always happens.

* * *

Jimmy Smokes phoned me on my cell right after the meeting and asked why I wasn't where I belonged, at the racetrack, with him, where he was having a good day. I explained that I work for a living. This, too, he explained, is work – handicapping. Horses, he said, win or lose. People always lose. People are no good. Jimmy Smokes ran the news shop down the street from the Manhattan Independent. The place did good business, but with his wife and son, not him. Jimmy was off to the races.

He was irked to find me so tethered to my job.

"What's wrong?" he said.

"Nothing."

"Come on, man. I know you."

"Nothing, really."

"I can tell by your voice."

"Bad connection," I said.

"Woman troubles?"

"What makes you say?"

"You told me about that juicy married staffer. Now THAT is a bad connection."

"Never. I never said a word."

"Somebody did."

"Really?"

"How else would I know?" he said.

Good question. How else would he know? Who told him? Do the birds really fly the truth?

"Later," I said. "I'm off to a meeting, Jimmy."

"You're always off to a meeting," said Jimmy Smokes.

"How else could I afford to carry you when you're on a bad streak?"

Jimmy Smokes also had bad days at the racetrack. But he had a system. As they turned for the finish line, Jimmy reversed the kibosh and rooted AGAINST his horse.

The trick sometimes worked.

"I know it's that married woman," he said. "Be careful. There's nothing more dangerous than a woman. A woman is more dangerous than a loaded shotgun."

"Thanks, I needed that."

"We need you here at the races, Jay. The horses are asking for you."

"I'll be there, in time."

"Why do you spend 20 hours a day with the news? It's all bullshit anyway."

We call him Jimmy Smokes but I don't know why, don't remember how it started. His real name is Jamil Samil or something. He's from Lebanon, or maybe Jordan, or maybe

Egypt. Who cares? He's a buddy. He's an Arab and again, who cares? We never talk politics. If we did, I'm not sure we'd still be buddies, which is why we talk horses and women. So we never talk politics, and if, by accident, one of us brings it up, the other one says, "Oh shut up," and we're back to horses and women.

* * *

I joined Stu Greenwald in his office after the editorial meeting. I felt jumpy. We lit up our cigars. I said it was time to send Phil Crawford.

"Why now?"

Hamas, now quite fully in charge of Gaza, under new management since Israel had vacated its own Israelis from Gush Katif, committed, some said, a self-inflicted pogrom – Hamas had infiltrated a nearby kibbutz and murdered 14 kids in a playground. Stu knew this, of course, and he also knew that their leader, Sheik Salaman, was willing to talk.

"He's already talked," said Stu. "He talked on television just the other day. CNN, I think it was."

"That was an interview," I said, "and we all know about CNN. I want a STORY. I want someone to live and eat with these guys. Stu, we may be able to make a difference."

I hated to use that phrase, make a difference, but here it fit.

"You mean WE can make the peace?" he said sarcastically. "Tom Friedman over at the Times already tried that single-handed diplomacy-by-journalism."

"Okay, but no one has ever really found out what these people want."

"Come on, Jay, we know what they want."

"So let's find out what can make them stop."

"Phil Crawford is the man?"

"What's wrong with Phil Crawford?"

"Between you and me and these walls?"

"Okay."

"Phil Crawford is chicken."

"But he wants to go."

"But he's chicken, Jay. He talks big here, behind a desk – but out there in the field?"

"He deserves a shot."

Like the rest of us, only more so, Phil Crawford pined for a Pulitzer. "This is his chance," I said.

By my count, every reporter already had at least one Pulitzer. Why not Phil?

Stu let out a puff of smoke and chuckled. "Only he might be getting it posthumously."

So?

* * *

Stu Greenwald was a reluctant intellectual. He'd written, or rather revised, our Style Book and insisted that headlines "must jump at the reader."

Also – "There is no such thing as a slow news day, only slow reporting."

* * *

There's always something else. That's life in general and life (or death) especially in the newsroom. This time it's not about the front page but about Lyla's book review section, which has its own conflicts, wars, blood feuds and bloodbaths. Here too there are grudges, jealousies, rivalries and territorial imperatives. (Dirty fighting even among literary luminaries? Why not? They're people, too, most famously in recent memory Capote on Kerouac: "That's not writing, that's typing.") A good review can sanctify a writer and get him or her on Oprah, C-Span, Don Imus, NPR or Larry King, onward toward the glory of a bestseller, and a bad review can doom a writer. Who wants to get up in the morning after being lashed, shamed and walloped in print and in public? That's what happened to

Trevor Kent and if this man does take his own life, Lyla could be partly to blame.

The review of his book, Kent's – well, it was more of a massacre. This happens, but not on Lyla's pages (Integrity First!), except when she's distracted. That's her only excuse and the reason she gives for being distracted is me and the romance we've got going behind her husband's back, if that qualifies for an excuse, which I don't think it does. The real sin here is that the review was assigned to a man who'd been scratching a lifelong itch for Kent. These two writers were enemies, and Lyla should have known this, or checked it out, but she didn't.

"Now I'm getting phone calls," she says.

It's not Kent who's been calling; it's his wife.

"She's afraid he might go ahead and kill himself."

She'd caught him locked up in the bathroom with a bottle of sleeping pills, among other signs that he did not want to go on living.

I keep assuring Lyla that it's rare for a writer to commit suicide and this prompts her to list a dozen who have, topped by Hemingway.

But not over a bad review.

"Oh yes," she insists.

She hates herself for this lapse in book-review etiquette and is sincerely worried that the worst could happen. She is sick about this.

"I'll blame myself," she says.

I know she will.

Chapter 11

I decided on a dry run for Phil. We met in the cafeteria, where I suggested that he first meet with Hamas operatives here in the United States.

This procedure, if all went well, would pave the way for his trip to Israel and could also serve as a test, in terms of his safety. I figured if he got out of here alive he'd get out of there alive, so maybe I wasn't so keen on sending him out to the heat of battle "that he may be smitten, and die." Maybe it was true that all I wanted was the Big story. Or maybe I wanted both.

This cafeteria of ours, on the fourth floor, was always rancid with the odor of rotten eggs and it was no different today. Our cafeteria cook, a man named Amiel Sheffer, was obviously planted here from a rival news organization and was poisoning us one meal at a time. Phil and I were having coffee. But I wasn't thinking about Phil. I was thinking about Kuana Banks and the racetrack and how badly I wanted to be there, and at this moment, sitting here with Phil, discussing how to go about Hamas, here and abroad, I made the decision that when I retired, or got fired, I'd turn to training horses, thoroughbreds. I'd get a shedrow right next to Kuana's and we'd travel the circuit, Aqueduct, Belmont, Saratoga, Gulfstream, Churchill, Santa Anita – anything but this, these moments with Phil and the business of the Middle East, where only hours ago another suicide bomber struck, this time taking 29 lives in seaside Netanya, a near repeat of the The Passover Massacre, Israel's 9/11.

This, of course, made Phil's opportunity all the more urgent.

Maybe I was recklessly profound after all in saying that there had to be a God up in heaven, otherwise things couldn't get so bad.

A God-less, random world could not be so chaotic.

There has to be a plan.

Chaos is also a plan.

Chaos is journalism. We simply tidy it up into column inches.

"Newark," said Phil. "I know people there. It's a mosque."

Yes, he had done a piece about that mosque, about how it was a religious place and not a setting for terrorism – as first charged by the FBI. I believed Phil. He was my man.

This time, with Phil himself being a Muslim (a topic still too hot to mention), was he still my man, or was he THEM? Am I the bigot?

(Are you a bigot if by their words and deeds they turn you into one?)

"So let it be Newark," I said.

He nodded. I had expected more.

"You all right with this, Phil? Sure you want to go?"

He snapped to. "Of course I want to go." He had that double-chin that seemed to have grown an extra layer overnight and the loose flesh of it began to quiver. "Can't miss a chance like this."

"That's what I thought."

Phil went up for some pie. When he came back, he sat down heavily and avoided my eyes. I said, "There's always some danger, you know."

He smiled a nervous smile. I asked him what was up.

"Mind if I tell you something?"

So here it comes. I knew it had to come.

"Is it personal?" I asked.

"Sort of."

"Can it wait? I've really got to get back."

Phil checked his watch and said, "Oops, yeah."

I knew what he wanted to disclose – that he'd become a Muslim. Like it was my business. Like I should care? Well, I cared about it for Lyla, but not for the Manhattan Independent.

Phil was a pro and he'd do right.

Somewhere a man said, "The worst corruption is a corrupt religion." I think it was that theologian, Reinhold Niebuhr. Don't know the man but I read it some place. Surely, though, Phil Crawford was a moderate within his Islam. There were plenty of those, moderates. Had to be. Otherwise we are in for a very long century.

As I was about to leave, Minerva Watson, who was sitting with her gang at another table, rushed over and handed me a paper, a petition against my smoking cigars with Stu Greenwald in addition to my smoking a pipe in my own office. The second-hand smoke was getting around. There were about 20 signatures down to the bottom but at the top was Peter Brand's. I assured Minerva that I always wear my seat belt while I'm smoking.

Minerva had another complaint. I used to be more hands-on. Now I delegated. I explained that as a big shot I don't do details anymore. That's why God invented other people.

* * *

The trouble with Minerva, well, there was always trouble with Minerva, but I think it all began when I sent around a memo saying we've got to cut down on birthday parties, and Minerva was big on parties of all kinds. I wondered, and still do, how anything gets done around here, or anywhere. It is always someone's birthday or someone's holiday. If it's not Rosh Hashanah it's Christmas or Ramadan, not to mention sick days, weekends, vacations and conventions and oh yes, jury duty. Between all that it's a marvel that bridges get built and news-papers get published.

* * *

Just the other day I casually asked Minerva about her use of the term "sexually active" in describing one of our most sexually active pop starlets. Minerva didn't understand the question. Well, I know politically active. I know socially active. I know academically active. I know athletically active. But sexually active means, in plain language, that she's a slut, right?

"We can't say that," Minerva bristled.

Of course we can't say that, not in this age of euphemistic correctness. A business going OUT of business and laying off 28,000 employees has no problems, according to the PR; it has challenges. Likewise Iraq. No problems, but challenges. People aren't unbalanced. They have issues. There are no terrorists, only militants or insurgents. Defining a thing for what it is can be hazardous to your health. Like our competition across town, across the nation and across the world – keep it fuzzy and nobody gets hurt.

* * *

When I got back upstairs Bull Parker handed me something he had written.

I liked the piece, which was about those pedophile priests, but the approach was original in that it praised Catholics for continuing to be so unstinting in their rebuke of their very own Church. To their everlasting credit, Catholics were "giving the Church holy hell" and were staunchly demanding that the Church set itself right – an unexpected development, according to Bull Parker, in that something contrary was to be expected, such as that Catholics might be tempted to submit to craven silence. This was not happening. They were keeping up their end of the faith and demanded that the Church do likewise. So Hallelujah!

"Terrific," I said.

Bull Parker was too modest to show it, but he was happy – but how terrible, I thought, to be an editor, a god who sits on a throne and decides what words shall live, what words shall die.

* * *

Arnold Coffey then came in, ashen-faced, and said it finally happened. He sat down and I got him a glass of water. Arnold seldom visited my office from his 14th floor sanctum where the old administration still maintained its offices. So I knew something was wrong. "My sister," he said. When the names came in, and they came in almost daily, of Israeli victims, Arnold waited for the AP listing of the wounded and the dead.

This time they got his sister in Netanya.

"Law of averages," he said. "Sooner or later, had to happen."

Homicide bombers were going off in Israel like firecrackers on the Fourth of July.

He asked me if I'd join him in synagogue to say Kaddish. I said sure. I had not been to a synagogue since my father died and I did not want to go this time, either, but it was, of course, again mandatory. We went to the one six blocks away, on 54th down from Sixth Avenue, an Orthodox shul, and we arrived in time for the Ma'Ariv evening service.

We had to walk up three flights because the elevator was out of order and when we got there Arnold was out of breath. He held onto me and apologized for being so weak and so old. Well, he wasn't so old but old enough to have been one of the originals, back when journalism was honest work and not zealotry. He'd seen it all, written it all, and was still here to see everything on rewind. What's happening now happened before and will happen again. Only the names changed. Maybe the work wasn't so honest back then, either, in the age of Annenbergs, Hearsts and Pulitzers, but it was mostly about the STORY, get the facts, write it up, and be done; it was not about idealists setting out to impose their vision of a perfect world.

Arnold made the tenth man for the minyan and for that alone the rabbi said we had performed a mitzvah. These Orthodox were not big on ceremony. Guided by the cantor, who was barely audible, they launched into the Hebrew prayers, most of which sounded like mumbling to the uninitiated. I stood when they stood. I sat when they sat. I didn't follow along with the prayers. I kept reading the English on the left side of the prayer book (Arnold's personal sidur) admiring the terrific writing.

Most of it was in praise – "Offer praise to the Lord, proclaim His name; make His deeds known among the nations. Indeed, the Lord has chosen Zion; He desired it for His dwelling place. For God has chosen Jacob for Himself, Israel as His beloved treasure. Indeed, the Lord will not abandon His people, nor will He forsake his heritage."

Then this: "Praise the Lord. Sing to our God for He is good. The Lord is the re-builder of Jerusalem. He heals the broken-hearted, and binds up their wounds. Praise the Lord, O Jerusalem; Zion, extol your God, for He has strengthened the bolts of your gates; He has blessed your children in your midst. He has made peace within your borders."

Really?

The Israelis, namely the ultra-religious ZAKA emergency volunteers, were now experts at picking up scattered body parts and piecing them together for burial in accord with Jewish law. That's all that remained of Arnold Coffey's sister and even as we sang praises here, over in Israel ZAKA and paramedics were busy matching up her arms and legs that were likely strewn from one end of Netanya to the other.

So given the carnage, I wondered if Arnold was choking on those words of praise. I wondered if he was thanking the Lord, "for He is good."

I was having problems with this. I always had. To fear Him is easy. To love Him is another story.

Or was Arnold finding comfort that "Indeed, the Lord will not abandon His people?" Had He not abandoned them already?

The Bible says one thing, but our headlines say something else.

Passover was no big deal around our home on Sullivan Street in Greenwich Village. For the seder, Dad read a few passages from the Haggadah and Mom, my Christian mother, bought matzah, though we still ate bread. So Dad read those passages about how glorious it was that the Lord, with a strong hand, delivered us from the bondage of Egypt.

So I'd ask Dad what about Auschwitz? I mean how can we remember His deliverance from Egypt and forget His non-deliverance from Auschwitz?

Where was His strong hand then? Where we THOSE miracles and wonders?

Mom crossed herself at such blasphemy. "Child," she said, "such talk is sinful."

Dad smiled because I was only repeating his own blasphemy, about how those Jews would have been better off placing their trust in Joe Louis.

Mom never liked the joke.

Joe Louis and King David – Dad's heroes, and maybe mine.

So I was still the same "contrary son." I glanced over at Arnold when we came to the passage – "How thankful must we be to God, the All-Present, for all the good He did for us." He was reading it from the right side, meaning the Hebrew, so I wondered if he knew what he was reading.

My guess was that it made no difference, the ritual was the thing, the congregating, the spirit of togetherness, the comfort of joining hands in a desperate effort to find God, find Him and ask Him a question or two, like, Dear Lord, What's the Plan? WHAT IS THE PLAN? It was about NOT BEING ALONE, period, my personal take on religion. A Beethoven symphony was all the religion and prayer I needed since, after all, Beethoven's symphonies are King David's Psalms put to music. David didn't know it and Beethoven himself may not have known it, but I, Jay Garfield, I knew it, I knew the secret.

David, Beethoven, and throw in Brahms, was as near as I'd ever get to heaven, in this lifetime.

Arnold, who had been an air force pilot in Vietnam, was not devout, but he was Jewish in capital letters. I admired that about him, his being so steadfast. I knew he had his own doubts. During that business in Europe a generation back, his family had been wiped out in the Ukraine, his father and uncles scorched, his mother and aunts raped and then scorched. So how could he remain so stout-hearted? But as he once said, "How can you believe, but how can you not believe? How can you have faith, but how can you not have faith?" I'm not sure it was Arnold who said that, but someone did, and it kind of summed it up for me.

The cantor was saying the Sh'ma, Judaism's signature: Hear O Israel, The Lord Is Our God, The Lord Is One.

The worshippers followed along, uttering those same ancient words, as did Arnold. My lips didn't move. My heart refused.

"At least this," whispered Arnold. "Acknowledge that something, anything, is above you."

That sounded like Pascal's Wager, that belief in God was the only safe bet. Okay, I'm in, but with reservations, best e xpressed by the 16th century humanist Desiderius Erasmus: "In fact, the other gods [besides FOLLY] are so hard to please that it is safer and wiser not to try to worship them, but rather to avoid them altogether. Men are sometimes like that, so thin-skinned and irritable that hands off is the best policy."

When it came to the Kaddish, the prayer for the dead, Arnold got up and followed the cantor's words in Hebrew, and his eyes turned red. The words of the Kaddish were solemn and mystical. Then Arnold sat down and fixed his eyes upon the Holy Ark, where the Torahs were kept. "Her name was Ruth," he said.

We walked over to Stage Deli on Seventh Avenue and I treated him to a basket of corned beef and fries. Here, where New York is so New York, Arnold brightened a bit. He felt like talking. Arnold had met Hemingway. This was here at the same Stage Deli and it happened when Arnold was 18.

"Hemingway was a newspaperman," he said.

"I know."

"That's not what I mean. I mean he wrote his novels like a newspaperman."

"Like James M. Cain," I said – and glad to have gotten us onto this subject, for a moment earlier Arnold had spotted Geraldo Rivera, or his double, a bad moment for Arnold.

"Exactly," said Arnold about James. M. Cain.

I asked him if Hemingway had said anything significant.

"Yes," Arnold laughed. "He told the waitress to hurry up with his pastrami."

"Was it that interlude with Hemingway that got you into newspapering?" I asked.

"No, that was Ben Hecht."

Arnold also knew Walter Lippmann, James Reston and that whole crowd. But his favorites were Hemingway and Hecht. Hemingway, though, hated Ben Hecht. Why? Who knows?

Arnold fell silent, collecting his memories. "No more Ben Hechts," he finally said. "Today we have Tom Friedman."

Someone at the next table had been listening in.

"Brave new world," he said.

"Sir, I believe you mean craven and cowardly," said Arnold.

The BBC's Barbara Plett admitted that she wept when Yasser Arafat was being scooted off by helicopter to France there, finally, to die. She wept for this mass murderer, did Barbara Plett of the BBC. That's what Arnold meant by craven. He was sorry, I think, to still be around for stuff like this. He was spooked by the rage of the mixed multitudes that were again agitating for the blood of his people, with journalism, his journalism, cheering on.

That got us to talking about Arnold's novel that just came back with another rejection, the note reading: "I also thought the plot was a little too timely and reminiscent of NOT WITHOUT MY DAUGHTER by portraying the Muslim world as being evil." I said, "Arnold, maybe you ought to tone it down a bit, you know."

"Like what? Like forgetting Theo van Gogh? Where's Hollywood? He was one of them, a filmmaker. Where's Spielberg?"

Spielberg, according to "reliable sources," was making a movie about the Munich Massacre, but from the point of view of the Arab terrorists who murdered all those Israeli athletes. At least he was giving them equal time for us to understand their actions, though as we all know, to understand is to justify. So I do not believe this about Spielberg.

Arnold (or was it Sam Cleaver?) had already written a piece titled, THE SILENCE OF THE HOLLYWOOD LAMBS. When, going from book to film, Hollywood changed Tom Clancy's novel THE SUM OF ALL FEARS from Arab bad guys to neo-Nazi bad guys, Arnold (or was it Sam Cleaver?) wrote a piece titled THE FEAR OF ALL SUMS.

"Tone it down?" Arnold said. "Jay, have you been listening to the world?"

"Never mind."

"Oh, I know what you're saying. But I'm just too old to play the game, Jay. Just too old."

I keep telling Arnold it's not that bad. Maybe he's being paranoid. I refuse to believe that it is so clearly US and THEM.

What about Jimmy Carter's new book? "The title," said Arnold, "ought to be changed."

Right now it was selling as *Palestine: Peace not Apartheid*.

Arnold's suggestion for a new title, given what's between the covers? "Jimmy Carter's Mein Kampf."

"Come on," I said.

"So you're still one of the moral equivalency boys."

"Keeping myself steady, Arnold. That is all."

"Let's see you keep your balance when they come knocking on YOUR door."

"Please. That IS paranoid."

"I'm an old man, Jay. I fought the fight, but here we go again. Now it's your turn. Like it or not, you will take sides because there is no middle. I do not envy you."

How would you know that this old man, Arnold Coffey, had once been a war hero?

Chapter 12

She swam six laps in the pool at the Claridge where we decided to hide out, here in Atlantic City, hide out from those "newsroom eyes" that she detested so much, especially those eyes belonging to Peter Brand who had begun a whispering campaign ever since Phil Crawford deployed himself to Newark and that mosque that may or may not be connected to Hamas. (This was one enemy, Peter Brand, who I couldn't keep close enough.)

So we had to get away and Atlantic City was far enough and near enough to be satisfactory. We played some poolside ping pong after she got out and dried herself off. She was wearing a bikini and jiggling like a Victoria's Secret supermodel. She was laughing and saying that I was slamming the ball only so that she'd have to bend down and show her top coming undone. I said this is true.

Back in our room I rushed in. No foreplay. "We're getting so much better at this," she later said, snuggling. She was ready for a nap. "Don't," she said.

I had clicked on the TV and she didn't want that; that was the last thing she wanted. It was all about the Middle East, meaning also Iraq, Afghanistan and all the rest.

In the Sudan, the count was approaching two million Christians slain by Muslim "extremists."

"Please," she said. "Can't we give it a rest?"

I couldn't. I was a news junkie, after all. She wasn't. She was all about books. Her world was fiction. But I had to know. I don't know why I had to know.

"Shouldn't you know what's going on?" I said.

"No I shouldn't."

"Okay."

"For once," she said, "can't we pretend that there's nothing else?"

But non-fiction keeps on happening. Phil keeps on happening. He's over there at that mosque in Newark.

This had me worried. They read us over there, and maybe Phil, for all his being so Muslim, would not be extended the welcome he expected.

"I thought we came here to forget all this," she was saying, still snuggled, eyes closed, trying for a measure of shelter, trying to find a seat in her world of fiction.

My eyes were wide open. Suppose Phil gets into trouble? Suppose people (like Peter Brand) put together this romance and Phil's dismemberment? This could happen to Phil, even in Newark. They could wrap him up, say in a coffin, and ship him off to Ramallah, and do him in there or anywhere. This could happen. Then what? Then we're sunk, if they put it all together, if they deduce that I timed Sam Cleaver's firebrand appearances in the Independent with Phil Crawford's appearance in Newark.

Sam Cleaver, gung-ho Sam, young as he was, was a hotshot reporter all right. He sure got his message across on his op-eds. He wrote hard-boiled and shot straight from the hip. He had something like attention deficit disorder, at least he couldn't sit still. He surely was neurotic and went in for some therapy and got cured and couldn't write anymore. His neurosis was doing the writing when he was good. So he gradually uncured himself, became neurotic again, and here he was, Sam's back, tough as ever. Sam Cleaver was also writing a novel. Who wasn't? He kept sending it off to the publishing wilderness and it kept coming back.

"Please turn it off," Lyla said, beginning to slumber, here in Atlantic City. "No TV. No news. Please. Please, Jay."

Why Newark? they would ask.

Well, because we are after a big story and the big story is Hamas on the West Bank but before all that Phil Crawford – a Hamas favorite – was simply checking in, here, stateside, to provide his credentials, in case that mosque in Newark had any ties whatsoever with that terrorist organization Hamas. It's all about getting the scoop. Really it is. Phil has their blessing, and Phil wants to go. He wants this story. He wants that Pulitzer.

But is it really all about Phil?

What do you mean?

Isn't it really about you and his wife?

Come on.

Come on nothing. Who are you kidding?

I think it's whom.

It's you and his wife, Jay. That's what this is about. You want him dead.

That's not fair. Did you know Phil is a Muslim? Phil himself. Phil Crawford. Phil Crawford is a Muslim.

Didn't know that, but what's the difference?

The difference is that he's one of them.

That doesn't mean he's safe with them – not when you run those pieces by Sam Cleaver.

That's coincidence, and that's freedom of the press, and we publish plenty of stuff favoring the other side, and nobody tells an American newspaper what it can and cannot publish.

But the timing, Jay! Didn't you know, and what did you mean by calling them: them? You got something against them?

Well, those weren't fairies falling out of the sky that did 9/11.

So you are against them.

I honestly don't know.

That honesty is in your favor, Jay. But it's still about you and his wife. Can't you be honest about that, Jay?

"Your mind is racing," she said, rising and leaning up against the pillow. "Now you've got me going. Should we be worried?"

Actually, I should be worried, mostly about her staying with Phil. I didn't want to alarm her about another item that came across my computer. "MADRID – An imam who wrote a book on how to beat your wife without leaving marks on her body has been ordered by a judge in Spain to study the country's constitution. The judge told Mohamed Kamal Mustafa, imam of a mosque in the southern resort of Fuengirola, to spend six months studying three articles of the constitution and the universal declaration of human rights. In his book *Women in Islam*, Mr. Mustafa wrote that verbal warnings followed by a period of sexual inactivity could be used to discipline a disobedient wife. If that failed, he argued that, according to Islamic Law, beating could be judiciously administered. "The blows should be concentrated on the hands and feet using a rod that is thin and light so that it does not leave scars and bruises on the body."

She got dressed for some reason, picked up the phone and rang for drinks. When the guy came up she tipped him ten dollars. I asked her why and she said she was not about to be a slave to money and besides, the kid was cute and probably had a family to support. The kid came right back with more ice and she asked him his name and what his dream was.

"Pedro...I don't understand."

"Well, Pedro, everybody has a dream."

Pedro said he had no dream.

"This is sad," said Lyla. "Very sad."

She tipped him another ten dollars and he left. At these rates he'll keep coming back, I thought, but he didn't.

Lyla was upset. A kid without a dream.

"Imagine that," she said.

I said you cannot feel bad for the entire world.

"All right," she said, "then one person at a time."

No argument from me. Maybe she was right when she accused me of being too much the newsman, always ready for the downside of human nature.

Always ready for the sucker punch.

"You cannot live with that outlook," she said, "that everything is rotten. The newsroom isn't the world."

"But it is."

"There are flowers," she said, "and there's poetry and there's music."

"That's not what comes across my desk, flowers and music."

"Oh Jay!"

"Poetry is your department."

"Then leave your desk."

"I do, but there's always homework."

What with cell phones and computers there is no escape.

Only days before, in my apartment, she'd found two books at my bedside, King Solomon's *Ecclesiastes* and F. Scott Fitzgerald's *The Crack-Up*. Not exactly, she had said, a quick pick me up, either of them. But yes, I said, the beauty of truth extending over the centuries. But depressing, she said. But true, I insisted. Not always, she argued. I said that the Book of Job is journalism in a nutshell.

You need a good spanking, she had said. Oh, there was that between us, kinky. Yes, our lovemaking was often kinky.

She wanted to give anal sex a try. Never. I said that's SODOMY! So what? she said. You think God is watching?

This? Yes! If nothing else, this!

She laughed and laughed and laughed.

So we did still have it on the agenda.

I sometimes thought what it would be like with her. Just the thought was plenty.

"Enough of this," she now said. "We're here to have fun."

She wanted to go down to the casino, do some gambling. Of course our being together, in public, was the biggest gamble of all.

Gamblers. That we were all right.

"You want to go down?" I said.

"Yes," she said. "Yes, yes, yes."

"There's always somebody with eyes, Lyla."

"So let them look."

"I say we head back."

"Back to what?" she said.

True – "The blows should be concentrated on the hands and feet using a rod that is thin and light."

Chapter 13

I do not believe in evolution. Well, I do, but in reverse – devolution. We start off as humans and devolve into apes. It's happening already. I read the headlines. Hell, I write the headlines. (Sometimes.) I don't know why I bring this up, but there it is. Oh yes, I do know why. One of our staffers has two sons and both are in law enforcement, cops, and what they see is nothing but the dark side of human nature, and that's pretty much what we see here in the newsroom. Rip any page off the wire services, or from our own foreign correspondents, or even our guys here on the home beat, and here it is, fresh off the wires – Another mass grave found somewhere out there and survival of the fittest you say? I say it's the unfit who survive and are in charge.

Eugene Ionesco saw it coming in that play *Rhinoceros*.

This staffer tells me that it gets so that they, cops, trust no one except one another. That goes for journalism as well, though it is safe to say no place is safe.

I've got my own guilt.

Anyway, my hunch was that Lyla wanted us to get caught. Yes, she wanted us to get caught. (Why? We don't know. These are women. We don't know what they want, remember?)

So that was my guess. She wants to force my hand, or force Phil out of his Islamic closet. Not me. I wanted no part of this.

Why make trouble now? There'll be plenty of it later – at this rate.

Phil Crawford, still (and always?) her husband, was off in Newark to that mosque as a test before I sent him off to the Middle East – that is, if I'd send him at all. I went back and forth on this, given my unholy intentions, to do unto him as King David had done unto Uriah. Sometimes I said to myself, yes, my motives are pure, purely journalistic. Equally, I said no – who you kidding, man? (Or is it whom?)

I was doing okay. I am with Lyla. This is good. We are in Atlantic City, at the Claridge, to take a breather and to engage, to frolic, in much sex, and this is very good. (How does she know so many new and different positions and techniques? Hmm?) We are in a nice room, all comfy, and this too is very good. But now she wants to go down and gamble, face the public, and we are not married. Whoops. She is. She sure is. She is married to someone else, who happens to be on my staff as a leading reporter/columnist.

I am not famous but I am not generic, either. My name is up there on the masthead of the Manhattan Independent, Managing Editor, Jay Garfield. She's up there, too; Lyla Crawford, Editor, Books. So we are not exactly nobodies and if someone should spot us, well, that could spell trouble, even disaster. Maybe that's her game. Get it over with already!

"I'm going down," she said from the bathroom, applying lipstick and all that business. "You coming? Scared, huh? Chicken?"

She asked what's the worst that can happen if someone spots us. Nothing much, I explained. Except that we'll be ruined.

"That's all?" she said, tossing me on the bed and landing on top of me, laughing, and then getting up abruptly before we could finish what we had started.

She stood by the door. "Come on ya big lug."

Yes, if you're afraid to do it, do it.

Meanwhile, I was on the phone to the newsroom, a bit ticked off for being scooped by the competition over ARAB ROYALS BUY 2 PIECES OF THE SKYLINE. Thus ran the headline about MY skyline, Manhattan, and we were the Manhattan Independent after all. The rest of the story, as it was run by our competition for crying out loud, went like this: "Two Manhattan trophy buildings were bought up by Dubai royals. These are 230 Park Avenue, the gold-crowned, 34-story tower between 45th and 46th Streets, and the Essex House, one of the grand Art Deco hotels on Central Park South."

So maybe that's what's going on – the new terrorism, the new jihad. Why bother CRASHING into our buildings? BUY them all up instead!

[At least we caught this from the wire services: "DUBAI, UNITED ARAB EMIRATES: Some 12 gay Arab homosexuals have been arrested for staging a mass gay wedding. They are slated to undergo hormone treatments, five years in jail, and a salvo of lashings. Public homosexual behavior is against the law in Dubai and the rest of the United Arab Emirates."]

I got somebody at City Desk, about the scoop, and it was an intern named Theo. My man Paul Dexter was out sick. Things always happen when nobody's around.

But about those buildings being bought up by Arab royals, this was not entirely new, this notion, and it came, of all people, from Jimmy Smokes, who ran the news shop down the street when he wasn't at the race track but he was always at the race track. Jimmy is an Arab, and Muslim, and back there at Belmont, when it was running and we were betting, he said, about 9/11, why do that, when they've got all that oil money? So just BUY the buildings – exactly what's been happening, though he was joking, though maybe he wasn't.

Jimmy Smokes, whose real name is something like Jamil Samil, blames himself, yes, personally, for the hijacking of his religion, Islam, and Jimmy Smokes is religious. Even at the track he goes to a corner to say his prayers. So he blames himself. If he weren't at the track all the time, this never would have happened, the abduction of his faith by radicals – jihadists. There is a silent Muslim majority out there, he assures me, good people, plain people, you and me people, but, he concedes, this silent majority is too silent.

"Well?" Lyla said, now opening the door and hot for action. "Come on before I break the bank all by myself."

So down we went and she pulled up a chair at a $25 limit blackjack table. Make way – High Roller Ahead!

"Lady luck," someone said. She didn't want my advice on Basic Blackjack, like don't take a hit on anything over 16, and don't you dare split tens, but she had a nice streak going anyway until the dealer got hot, as they all do, and her $25 chips started going down the tubes. Suddenly a mountain (of chips) became a molehill. Even the dealer, a guy with a Las Vegas face, was surprised at her willingness to accept punishment. I asked her what she was up to and she said it was only money.

Then, a good moment. She actually hit on 16 – everybody groaned – but was dealt a five, which equals 21, most times a winner.

Not this time. The dealer was showing a queen and then...and then turned over a big fat ace, ace of clubs, which equals blackjack.

"I demand a recount," she said but nobody laughed, except the man playing the anchor seat. He was having a good day and was not happy when Lyla got up.

"Hey, don't go," he said.

"I've had enough," she said.

All in all she was out $500 and we walked the boardwalk. That's what people used to do before the casinos came along, walk the boardwalk. They'd walk it in tuxes. I noticed, this time around, that nobody was speaking English, these others walking the boardwalk with us today. No tuxes, no English. I also remembered that the Miss America Pageant, Atlantic City's very identity, the very definition of Atlantic City, was gone, moved to Las Vegas. We ran that story in our New Jersey section of the Manhattan Independent. I thought there'd be an outcry – but nary a whimper. There's a lesson here, though I don't know what, except that the world keeps on ticking regardless and that nothing matters as much as you thought.

Also, the pageant got to be too quaint in a world that offers CAMPUS GIRLS GONE WILD! We don't want girls baton twirling for WORLD PEACE. Just take off your top.

I did not ask Lyla to explain but she did so anyway, saying she wanted to divest, start from scratch, start her life from scratch. She was going to start all over again. Her husband, Phil, was starting all over again as a Muslim. Right? Well then. America was all about second chances. Here's where F. Scott Fitzgerald got it all wrong. What was so bad about her "former" life? She had a job that most women, and men, would kill for. But a job, she said, is not a life.

Anyhow, that was why she did not care about losing at the blackjack table. So what's money?

Money is nothing, I explained, to people who have it, and it is everything to people who don't.

There's a tradition, I told her, that compulsive gamblers want to lose.

"Well I'm not compulsive...and in the end we all lose anyway."

"You've been reading too much."

She does read too much, Lyla. Lately she'd been bingeing on biographies and these were getting her depressed. People always die in the end.

Well – what do you expect?

She said the boardwalk was boring so we took a side street, Baltimore Avenue, and stepped into a bar with a hot jukebox and a lonely striptease going on up on stage. The girl was struggling to make it work. Lyla whispered that she, Lyla, could do better, and I knew she could, but in private. On lap dancing, though, she was weak, and a few days earlier, in private of course, asked me how it worked, and I said that I shouldn't have to explain, it comes automatic with women, as surely Eve lap danced for Adam.

"Would you dare me," she now said, "to go up there and do a strip?"

"Lyla, you're trouble."

"That girl can't dance. She can't even dance. I'm going up and take my clothes off. You should know that all women are exhibitionists."

"Please behave."

"You're no fun, Jay."

Finally, I calmed her down and we ordered and she asked if I'd ever been in a bar fight. Yes I had. Could I lick those two guys down at the other end? Lyla, I said, you're being suicidal.

"Just tell me. Could you lick them?"

"Come on."

We didn't say anything for a while. Lyla got busy, here in this booth, facing nobody except maybe the bartender, slipping off her panties and asking me to do something. Then she got up to go to the bathroom. Those two guys at the bar said something to her as she passed them and from where I sat I couldn't judge whether it was anything offensive and her reaction gave no sign, so it seemed okay. When she came out they said something to her again and this time she stopped and said something back, but again I could not make out what was going on. Still okay.

"What was that?" I asked when she sat down.

Before she could answer the two of them – standard issue bar guys, sleeves rolled high, tattoos up and down – walked over snarling and gnarling and asked me to apologize. I asked for what and they said you know. Next thing I knew I was in a fight, a bar fight, against two of them, but it was even when I remembered what I'd been taught at Pat's Gym.

* * *

We walked back to the hotel without a word. I knew what she was up to, or maybe I didn't. She had some blood on her and so did I. Back in the room we showered together and made love together and, for arousal, slippery as it was, slipping and sliding, and finally bending her over for traction, it was like nothing we'd done before or would ever do again. This was, I guessed, partly what she was up to, but only partly.

Then she joined me in bed.

"You heard it said – men do, women are," she said.

"Yes."

"Well I want to do."

"Well you did."

"That was nothing," she said.

I thought back to the Book Nook when she'd been among her literary crowd. She'd been so radiant, so delicate, so refined. That was the real Lyla. Or was it this? Or both? We've all got two sides, women especially, I think. I did not know what this was, this Lyla. I knew that I was nuts about her, but I did not know what this was. What's next?

Was she trying to destroy herself before her husband got around to doing the job?

"Tomorrow," she said, "I start writing a novel."

"Tomorrow," I said, "everybody starts writing a novel."

("There is no end to the writing of many books," said King Solomon 3,000 years ago.)

"It's an idea you gave me – remember? A guy, formerly an immigrant but now fully Americanized – this man loses his citizenship papers. He goes from office to office, clerk to clerk and no one can help. Red Tape. He loses everything. It's even worse than identity theft. A man without – suddenly without a country. You should have written it yourself. Too late. It's mine."

"You ought to have no problem getting it published."

"I hate my job."

"You love your job."

"I'm going to start all over."

"From scratch, right?"

"Maybe," she said, "I'll become a nun, or a prostitute. It's a toss-up."

I asked her what she told those two guys.

"I told them you thought they were gay."

"How nice."

"Nice to know you're around to protect me."

How long, I said, was she going to stay in this mood?

"What mood?"

"You're being tough."

"That's my problem. I'm never tough. I let people roll right over me. I've never done anything bad."

"Well you're being bad right now."

"You won't respect me in the morning?"

"I wish you'd stop."

"I need another shower."

On C-Span Harvard kids were being lectured by a high professor and a Supreme Court Justice. Question: Do you believe in evil?

Young female student: "I don't think there is such a thing as evil."

"She's young," Lyla said, stepping beautifully naked out of the shower.

Later, I continued channel surfing. Some people search for it in drink: I search for it in news. Somewhere out there, perhaps in the Green Room of CNN or Fox, sits the Messiah. Heck, isn't that why we all keep watching and waiting, waiting and watching? This word just in: The Messiah has arrived. The bad stuff's all over. Along some of these channels, well, according to them, the Messiah is already here, you just have to believe in him, or Him, and if that's the case it's worse than I thought. This is as good as it gets?

If the announcement does come – where? When the Messiah arrives what platform will he (He?) choose to make the announcement and proclaim that it is now safe to keep our car doors unlocked? My first guess is Oprah (everybody in the WORLD gets a new car); second, Rush Limbaugh. Then, David Letterman for the Top Ten Ways To Acquire Eternal Salvation, and finally (with a good business manager), over to Jon Stewart on the Comedy Channel, to get the kids in on this. Salvation is so fun.

On CNN marchers against our war in Iraq are telling America to drop dead. On Fox, Hannity says they're not about Iraq, these people; they're about hating America.

I nod. I agree. They hate America. Americans hating America. How does this happen?

When did Hollywood decide to go sour, or is it yellow?

Then Bush comes on and says how thrilling it is that the people in Iraq are voting. We're making progress and I begin to wonder, what do the people of Iraq mean to me? I must take a side. I cannot be for the war and against the war all at the same time. Yet that is my position, firmly. I care about the people of New Orleans. Tell me we are making progress there, and then I'll cheer. Our most liberal columnist, Marshall Kenricks, keeps writing this: "After we pull out, the Sunnis will still be the Sunnis, the Shiites will still be the Shiites." There is something to that, but still, I cannot abide the DOWN WITH AMERICA crowd. Everything is NOT our fault or as Ben Hawkins, publisher of the Manhattan Independent and my boss, keeps saying, "They started it," and that is still true.

Anyhow, politics is not an exact science. Science is not an exact science.

But what would the world be like without an America? Where would people go? I'm thinking this out loud and Lyla says, "Please shut the TV."

Yes, I am hooked, hooked on the news. Lyla hates this. She hates the news and she hates that I'm hooked.

"What is it about you guys?" she says. She asks if it's genetic, about our need to dominate the TV remote control.

"Yes," I say. "It is written in our DNA."

She runs over and shuts off the TV.

Then she says – "One day we'll have to decide whether this is love or adultery."

Chapter 14

Peter Brand came into my office wearing that all-knowing slithery grin. He asked if I'd checked out his editorial cartoons while I'd been away those three days, three days, he said, that corresponded with Lyla Crawford's absence. What a coincidence! I got the message. He was doing me a favor, he said, by giving me a heads-up about the rumors.

"People talk," he said.

Another favor he was doing concerned the truckers, who were angling for a raise at the expense of the money I lavished upon freelancers. He was doing his best, he said, to keep them in line, talking to them as one union man to another. I told Peter that I appreciated his efforts. This was not what I wanted to tell him.

Today's cartoon, for my review, was about that Bronx teacher who had been molesting a student for three years.

Peter's strip depicted the classroom as a brothel.

A bit strong, but okay. Why was I afraid of Peter Brand? I was afraid of Peter Brand because Peter Brand was the world.

So I said okay to Peter Brand.

Peter Brand was one half of the world; Phil Crawford the other half. Where does that put the rest of us?

"Thank you, Sir," he said, clicking heels.

I'm thinking about children here, how we breed them to molest them, and there, where they breed them for (Moloch) sacrifice.

I shouldn't be thinking. News is news and nothing more. Like a surgeon. Not supposed to think. If he thinks he'd never be able to use the knife.

Same with news. Must not think, must not feel.

On the contrary – bad news is good. Sells papers, ups the ratings.

Yes, bad news is good news in this business. What a business! We keep waiting for the world to explode, piece by piece, and it never fails. The world never fails us.

I was, in fact, in the middle of writing a column titled "Disgrace Is Good," about all the people who profit from shame, from Al Sharpton to Monica Lewinsky to Paris Hilton to – oh the list is too long. Then I realized what time it was, yes, Happy Hour. Each day I put aside an hour to listen to complaints, so that's what I called it, Happy Hour, and today's main gripe came from Sam Cleaver, hot-shot Sam.

My own gripes with the proofreading desk would have to wait. This typo got in the other day in our Society pages: Mrs. Heather Lynn Baelfort had been "abusing herself." The copy was meant to read "amusing herself." They keep blaming it on technical malfunctions, over there in Proofreading. I am convinced that they are out to sabotage me. Also, someone down there does not like Mrs. Baelfort, period. A few weeks before all this she was identified as the Grand Damn, instead of the Grand Dame, of New York Society. She is bound to sue us one of these days. I wouldn't blame her. Sam himself once got this into our pages during a mob trial – "a well-hung jury." He claimed to have been set up by Re-write.

"Sam, Sam," I said when he sat down, though even sitting down he was still moving, arms, legs, he had everything going. He was a born reporter.

"Why do you always repeat my name?" he asked.

I explained that it's praise, pretty near a blessing, if you know your Bible, as when the Almighty referred to Moses as Moses, Moses. That is an endearment.

"So what did I do wrong today, Sam?"

He hands me this column he wrote with the headline – MAUREEN DOES TIMES SQUARE.

Come to think of it, I have got to get fresh blood for our headline desk. People only read the headlines. There is no time for the rest. There is so much going on. The Internet. Yes, the Internet keeps outpacing us. By the time our paper gets out there, we're only catching up. Newsprint doesn't move once it's done. The Internet keeps moving and it's never done. There's a great big web universe and blog world going on out there, terrific writing going on too, and I will have to start finding space in the Manhattan Independent for Tom Gross, and for Phyllis Chesler, once a feminist and still a feminist but on the outs with her sisters because she saw, and named, the hypocrisy.

"You're trying to get me fired, aren't you," I said to Sam Cleaver, after I read the piece, in which he aimed back at Maureen Dowd of The New York Times. Maureen, in her new book, titled, *Are Men Necessary*, pretty much took on the women's lib movement, saying nothing's changed since the 1950s. Girls are still girls. Sam agreed with her, of course, except that he was getting personal, writing about her love life, which we, in the news business, don't like to do too much, that is, we don't want it out there what's going on in our bedrooms. I should know this first of all.

Anyhow, Sam wanted to know if I'd let it ride, that Maureen column of his, and hell yes, why not? If I get fired, I get fired. The Manhattan Independent will survive and so will the rest of the world. Take television, please. No more uncles. Tom Brokaw, gone. Dan Rather, dumped. Peter Jennings, dead. Ted Koppel, hasta la vista. Does anybody care? Nobody cares. Has anybody noticed? Hardly. The world is still the same, rotten, but still the same. Yes, a generation goes, a generation comes, and the earth endures.

"What does objectify mean?" asked Sam.

"Objectify means whatever you want it to mean," I explained.

Here was the problem. Sam's new novel had been rejected again. That he'd started off with a bestseller meant nothing anymore, and besides, his first book had been non-fiction. This was fiction and in fiction you are swimming in different waters with different sharks. You're being tested against Cervantes, Tolsoy, Camus and Hemingway. Tough sharks.

So what happened was this – the novel had been read by an editor over at New Lit Publishing Company and this editor, Natricia DeFarr, had "enjoyed" the novel and was giving it "serious consideration" up to the point where Sam had begun "objectifying" women, "so unfortunately, we must decline. Sorry. Good luck elsewhere." (Why is it that when people wish you good luck they usually mean bad luck?)

"You're not playing by the rules," I told Sam, as, I remembered, I had told Arnold Coffey who likewise had a novel going, and going nowhere.

"There's an agenda out there," said Sam. "If you don't adhere to their political correctness they put a fork in you and you're done. There's a blacklist, Jay, that's what's happening."

"I know," was all I could say about something that was too close.

"Wasn't she, this bitch of an editor, OBJECTIFYING me?"

"Yes she was. But she's in a position to define the word." They owned the entire dictionary, I agreed, and the agenda. We all slant the news, but they also own the slant. That is why God (or Al Gore) invented the Internet, to bypass the mainstream in journalism and in literature. Something like this went on in the Soviet Union so what they did, these writers, was develop an underground of journalism and literature, and that is still going on today, but in the United States. In the Soviet era bypass literature went by the name Samizdat, where people passed along pages of forbidden writings under the table. In our era, to get past the PC Police, we go by the name Internet.

So it is true that holier-than-thou buffoons, crackbrains, lit-dandies and wench doorkeepers retain the keys to our culture, and keep it locked for themselves.

Sam had one other contact with this editor DeFarr who said she'd been "undone" by what Sam had written about women. Undone? Get the smelling salts? Sam had previously shown that passage, from his novel, to Lyla and Lyla had laughed, thought it was terrific and hysterical and even correct, not politically, but correct.

"Writers, real writers," said Sam, "keep getting stonewalled. Hey, is there anything you can do, Jay?"

I'd be no help. We were, after all, that newspaper on the Right. What friends did we have out there among the literary worthies who sit fat in their big chairs?

The only advice I could give Sam came from my father's side of my upbringing, the Talmud, I believe: "It is not for you to complete the task, only to persevere."

Sam asked if this is what it's come to – They crave diversity, but their diversity, not yours.

"Please don't get me in on this," I told Sam. "I've got my own troubles with women."

Sam smiled. "I know."

"You know?"

"Come on, Jay. Everybody knows. Lyla, Phil Crawford's wife."

"Who told you?"

"I'm an investigative reporter, Jay. Remember?"

"Who told you?"

"How come you're not calling me Sam, Sam anymore?"

"Who told you, Sam?"

"I think it's whom."

"Whom told you, Sam?"

"Everybody."

I said I'd take him out back and beat it out of him – unless he spilled.

"Oh, yeah? I was the toughest kid in my block," said Sam.

"I can beat you up blindfolded, you young pup – come on, seriously."

"Peter Brand. Happy?"

"Delighted."

* * *

Sam offered this advice before he turned and shut the door behind him. "Deny, deny, deny. That's what I always do."

Not always. Sam had a reputation, according to which he had already run through half our staff, or rather half our distaff. I doubt that this included Lyla. I'd never ask, of course. If it was anything, it would have been a one-night stand. He was much too young for her, though, come to think of it, not all that much younger. Anyway, it wouldn't be like Lyla and, from what I knew, I was the only one from the moment she married Phil Crawford, Islam's new convert. But you never know.

* * *

Out in the hallway I bumped into Lyla and for both of us it was like touching the third rail. We were both nervous about being out in the open, even though it was business she wanted to discuss. She was off trying to secure an interview with Gore Vidal, who had that wonderful line that you must never pass up a chance to have sex or appear on television – shading, I supposed, Warhol's 15 minutes of fame.

Anyway, Lyla wanted to know what I thought about Kurt Vonnegut's latest outburst, saying, as he did, that suicide bombers were brave and heroic. Should it go in her Books section or somewhere else, like our NEWSPEOPLE section? (At least we weren't talking about us for a change, the two of us, or rather the three of us.) As for me, I said, I'd let it drop. Leave Vonnegut alone. Maybe he had a bad day at the track. I'd always been a fan of Vonnegut's, but more as an entertainer than as a writer. He was still bitter about our firebombing of Dresden. Too bad. Yes, as our publisher Ben Hawkins would say, "They started it." We left it at that, for the moment, Lyla moving on, though not before shifting to a smile and whispering, "Jay, you're cute."

* * *

Later on she phoned to have us meet in the archives room, a musty place that always smelled from a million tons of news-print because that's what was in there, everything from day one. Lyla needed something important from there that only I could give. That's what she said. We met and nodded to Mrs. Pepper, the 80-year-old librarian, and then walked deeper into a storage room that was completely dark, a room abandoned so long ago that no one thought to fix the lights. "Are you kidding?" I said. She unbuckled me and unzipped me. "Hurry," she said as she lifted up her skirt and pulled down her panties. Then she said, "Oh, Gawd."

Chapter 15

"Who?" I said.

"Phil Crawford," said Gladys.

He'd been leaving me e-mails. He had filed no stories, which surprised me, but his e-mails were about his making progress in gathering information.

He'd moved in with a Muslim family in Newark and was attending prayers daily in the mosque. (In response to the muezzins, they pray five times a day, or, namaz.)

He was phoning from his cell phone, and he sounded ticked.

"What's up?" I said.

Those op-eds we were running were hurting him, he said. They read everything, and they take it all very personal. I thought back and recalled that yes, there were those pieces from Sam Cleaver and from Charles Krauthammer. But also, there was no escaping the Internet, or what is clearly Bypass Journalism, and the writing coming from there was often stronger and more in-touch than we'd been getting from conventional print commentators.

Okay, so I did run all those conservative columnists – but these were offset by a number of columns written by Arab professors and, naturally, abundantly favorable to the Arab cause.

"They don't see it that way," said Phil, sounding nervous.

"Phil," I said, "we can't let people dictate to us."

We also ran a Page 3 photo of Hamas gunmen hiding behind 8-year-old schoolchildren as they, Hamas, fired away into an Israeli home. No other newspaper picked that up.

I wrote up the caption myself – HEROES!

Was I beginning to take sides? Or were all the others crooked and me, I was just trying to make it straight?

"You there?" I said, beginning to worry.

"Here's the deal. I've established good relations, but those are all at risk. Hell, Jay, even I'm at risk."

"What does that mean?"

"They think I'm a plant."

"A spy?"

"Call it what you will."

"So come home."

"But I've been getting close."

Right here, in his agitated condition, he conceded that he was a Muslim.

"I'm a Muslim, Jay."

I faked surprise.

"Congratulations," I said.

"That's not the point. The point is that they trust me. Or that they did. Until they started reading the paper."

"They read lots of papers, Phil."

"But I'm here!"

So he was all right.

"I'm here and they're starting not to like me. Just hints."

"Like what?"

"I can't say. Well, one interview I was supposed to have got canned, and the family I'm staying with, a nice Muslim family, they've asked if I can find another place to stay."

"There are hotels in Newark."

"That's no way to get inside this story."

"I admire that, Phil. But maybe you should get yourself out."

Pause.

"I hope this is a safe line."

"If not…"

"I do think my e-mails to you are being monitored."

"Possible."

"This cell phone may be tapped."

"They can do that?" I asked.

"I don't know."

"But they're your people, you say."

"I'm also a newsman, Jay. They don't trust anybody."

"But they trusted you."

"Up to a point. Listen, here's where we're at. There's one worshiper here whose cousin works for Hamas. He told me that in secret, of course. So I told him that I was invited to go out there, to Ramallah, and he said, if I did go, there better not be any inflammatory articles in the Independent or else Hamas would do me like Danny Pearl."

This is true.

"Jay?"

"Phil, how can I make a commitment like that?"

"The mullah here is prepared to give me a letter of safety – that's what they call it – if I can promise we'll play fair."

"I think we do."

Another pause.

"What's that crackling I hear?" Phil said.

"Static?"

"Hope so."

"This letter of safety," I said. "What's it do?"

"Once I get to the West Bank and hand it over to Hamas, it's supposed to be like a seal of Good Housekeeping, like a guarantee that I'm okay."

The word kosher came to mind. A guarantee that he was kosher. Not quite fitting, a word like that, not for Phil, not for Hamas.

"So you've done your job," I said. "Come home."

"I still need that word from you so I can get that clearance."

"You can't be serious. We're not Al Jazeera." (Was it true that George W. Bush had made plans to bomb Al Jazeera? That was the rumor. Someone had leaked a memo and memo-leaking was becoming the in thing in Washington.) That Phil could ask a question like that, was he that far gone? "You're asking us to censor ourselves? Phil, that's not like you."

"These are different times, different circumstances. I thought you wanted this story, Jay."

"But not like this, at the expense..."

"I'll see what I can do. I'll hang here for a few more days. Gotta run."

"Wait a minute. Are you in danger?"

"I gotta run."

If he gets himself killed in Newark, I'm thinking, Lyla is all mine. So is hell.

* * *

I told Stu Greenwald, later on, that maybe Phil Crawford was not such a coward after all. Stu offered me the usual cigar, but this time I declined. I had a bitter taste in my mouth.

"The Middle East is exploding," said Stu.

This meant we agreed, that this was the best time and the worst time to send a man over there; even if he got out of Newark in one piece.

(Editor to writer in a *New Yorker* cartoon: "This is ridiculous! How can something be the best of times and the worst of times, Mr. Dickens?")

"Why do you say that?" asked Stu, snuffing out his cigar. I didn't tell him about that petition. He'd snarl. Tobacco police. What's next?

Stu used to say: "There once were spittoons around here and no women. Those were the days."

I repeated the conversation I'd had with Phil, this time emphasizing the fear in his voice – even in the words he was attempting to restrain.

"So we've got to get him back here," said Stu, showing a trace of alarm. "My gawd, we've already had one Ben Curtis!"

"He wants that clearance paper."

"We can order him back."

I explained that I did try; phoned his cell but no answer. E-mail? Monitored. Very likely. Phil had reason to be suspicious.

"Did you know Phil is a Muslim?" I said.

Stu's jaw fell to the floor.

"Is this a joke?"

"He told me so himself." I did not reveal that I had known it for some time, from Lyla.

"When did this happen?"

I told him the story, going back to UC.

Stu gave himself plenty of time to let it all sink in. We agreed that idealists, do-gooders, are the most dangerous people in the world. Stu said:

"So what does it mean? I mean he's still a journalist, for shit's sake. He's a Muslim but he's still a journalist. We've got other Muslims working around here."

That was true. This was New York. We had Muslims wearing their particular garb and we had Orthodox Jews wearing theirs. This was New York.

"I'll keep trying," I said.

"Somehow," said Stu, "we've got to get him back. Quick."

* * *

"Told you so," said Vernon Pickins, walking into my office after his usual three knocks.

Yes, the results were in and Vernon's Gay Talk column was a hit. We'd only been running it for three months against much opposition, principally from the boss, Ben Hawkins, conservative down to his toes, though he was not alone in dissenting. Oh no, there were others – plenty. Mainly religious groups. But I insisted, and I won. So did Vernon Pickins.

Look – I argued – that's what's going on out there; we cannot hide. Vernon, though, still did not know how I felt, how I really felt. Vernon was gay, openly gay, as I was openly straight. Originally, when he brought up the idea for the column, to be run once a week, I suggested (stupidly) that maybe we should just call it Happy Talk, you know, not be too obvious.

"Come on," he had said. "Either we do it or we don't."

Far as I knew, we were the only ones doing it, and we were the conservative paper of record, supposedly (except for the staff).

Now he showed me the results of his survey. Sixty-four percent yes. The rest, no or no opinion.

I've always wondered about people who have No Opinion. Are there really such people? No opinion? Really?

"Are you pleased?" said Vernon.

"Yes."

"Jay," he said, sitting down. "The truth."

"Huh?"

"How do you feel, I mean really feel, about gay rights?"

"Here it is, Vern. You don't bother me in my bedroom, I don't bother you in your bedroom. Okay?"

"What about the gay marriage issue?"

"I hate issues. You know that, Vern."

"Jay, are you with the cause or against the cause?"

"I am with no cause," I said. "I am against all causes."

That is true. Do your business and as long as it does no harm to your neighbor, knock yourself out.

"Wish I could figure you out," said Vernon.

Same here. "Vern," I said, "I don't need the demonstrations, the parades, the marches, and what's this about gay pride?"

"Well we are proud."

"You're proud to be gay?"

"Yes, Jay. I'm proud to be gay."

"Well," I said, "I'm heterosexual and I am not proud. That's just what I am, no big deal. You're something else, again no big deal."

"I like that," he said. "I think I like what you're saying."

"I mean, you stick it there, I stick it here – so? Of this we're proud?"

Sex is not a natural thing, no matter who is doing it to whom. All variations of it are strange. God is watching as we're twisting and turning and saying to Himself, "Behold, this is so strange. I did not get this quite right. Yes, I did say Be Fruitful and Multiply – but not like this! What I meant was, well, I meant make babies, but that should only take a minute, including the cigarette. Next time, after I destroy this world and make a new one, start all over again, I will be sure to delete sex from the equation. This time around, my mistake. Yes, I saw that Paris Hilton tape."

I cautioned Vernon about getting too explicit in his columns. Too often he referred to his following as a KINKDOM.

He smiled. "I think we're friends."

I really do not know where I stand on the monumental ISSUES and CAUSES facing our culture, and maybe I should, running this newspaper, and maybe I shouldn't, for the same reason. The death penalty, abortion, assisted suicide, school prayer, yes, gay rights, really, I am not that smart. I do not have the answers. Sometimes I do, sometimes I don't. I keep changing my mind. On Monday, yes, on Wednesday, maybe, and catch me on Friday for any or all of the above and the answer is no. I am not that smart. I am very firm in my convictions whatever those convictions are at the moment.

* * *

Lyla reached me by phone from the other end of the newsroom.

We made a date to meet later in that bar at the Warwick Hotel. She loved the Warwick for being so classy, an oasis in the middle of turbulent Manhattan. Her thinking was that it was safer to be seen together out in the open, as two people carrying on would be loath to show themselves in public. We worked together after all – so what's wrong with that, in case Page Six got wind. Anyway, if you're afraid to do it – do it!

Other than carrying on behind her husband's back, we had no secrets.

We had agreed, earlier, to find a place for ourselves and she did find one, one of those lofts in Greenwich Village. We'd make that our sanctuary.

Meantime, there'd been another phone call from Phil Crawford, who was showing signs of panic out there in Newark, at that mosque that was supposed to serve as his rehearsal for going out as a combat journalist in Israel, or rather the West Bank, or Gaza, whichever still belongs to Israel at the moment. So Phil got me on the line for a second but kept breaking up. Not this, please. Not now. I wasn't ready for the consequences.

I thought I heard him say HELP and then I heard him say DEAD. "What's dead, Phil?"

Then, click. So what's dead, him or his cell phone?

Chapter 16

Still no word back from Phil Crawford out there at that mosque in Newark and here I am, wondering what died, him or his cell phone, all of it my doing, if it's him and not his phone that went flatline, my doing in collaboration with Lyla, of course, and what a dirty word that was, collaboration, and what a headline that would make, and this wasn't even the plan. Over there in the Middle East, that is where we wanted him smitten, or something. But all that was still negotiable. I was not ready for such a step. I was having doubts by the minute, flip-flopping. I had enough deadlines to meet running this newspaper and did not need that other one. Things could be worse, my Christian mother always said, to which my Jewish father always said – yes, just wait.

Right now Lyla was outside my office waiting impatiently. I could hear the spiking on the warped carpet and I could imagine her pacing on a spree of some hot news and driving Gladys batty. When Lyla got hot on a story or on anything – fuhgeddaboudit! Gladys, my assistant, since we are not allowed to use the word "secretary" anymore, was not too charmed by Lyla, and this was nothing she expressed, just something I sensed. Maybe it's the way Gladys never referred to Lyla by name, just "that book editor." That book editor is here to see you, Mr. Garfield. Or, will you take this call from that book editor, Mr. Garfield? I wonder if she suspects. According to Sam Cleaver, hotshot Sammy, they all suspect, thanks to Peter Brand, the source of our editorial cartoons and gossip-mongering.

Besides Lyla out there on *shpilkes*, as we say in Manhattan, I had an appointment with Ben Hawkins, publisher and my boss, about an hour away, and what could that be about?

I tried to keep my business with him to a minimum. I admired the man, respected him, but men who are very rich are like Greek gods, volcanic.

Meantime, I was finishing up a meeting with Norma Lincoln, our science editor, and we were having our weekly dispute, nothing major other than Darwin versus God, with Darwin, according to what's going on, leading by 31 lengths. (Yes, Secretariat winning the Belmont by that margin, 1973.) All of it goes back to a discussion we had, which led to a dispute when I asked her if she prayed to Darwin every morning, and we were still going at it as, right now, I asked her when, in her next column, she'd propose IN DARWIN WE TRUST. "That's not funny, Jay," she kept saying, and I said I was serious, for you science people have turned Darwin into God and Darwinism into a religion, no less rigid, no less fundamentalist, no less RELIGIOUS than all the rest. There is no bending, no yielding, no give. It's Darwin or the highway.

"Don't tell me," Norma said, "that you actually believe in intelligent design."

I explained it like this – "You don't believe in Intelligent Design? sayeth the Lord. How about I give you another tsunami, huh?"

Norma did not think that was funny, either, and left the room saying "to be continued," and that's for sure, as this contretemps was splashed all over our pages.

Fortunately, Norma Lincoln was not gorgeous, only quite attractive, but gorgeous enough for Lyla to be jealous.

"What took so long?" she said, stepping in softly, smiling, but with some heat.

So we'd been going round about something else and I told her, again, that it was foolish, and beneath her, to go chasing after J.D. Salinger. It started, about three months ago, when an author friend of hers, a guy who did reviews for her Books Section, Donald Whittings, confided that he was in touch with Salinger, and might just be persuaded to be approached, by Lyla, for the Manhattan Independent. I knew, from the start, that this was bullshit. Had to be. So she kept on having meetings with this Donald Whittings to get it all arranged, the biggest scoop of the century, so far. "SALINGER SPEAKS, To The Manhattan Independent. Breaking Story From Lyla Crawford." Meanwhile, she was on the verge of giving Donald Whittings the go on the "chase" for Salinger, and we both knew articles and books on this had already been done into the thousands. But this was genuine, she insisted.

Actually, I wouldn't be all that amazed. Salinger, we know, liked them brainy and beautiful, and that Lyla was, in spades. But this Whittings character, what's his game? He'd written, and gotten published, something like 20 novels, and that's too much. One should be enough, yes, like Salinger. One of his books, Whittings, ran 900-plus pages, and that's longer than the Bible, and, it's been my conviction that if a writer can't get it done in 500 pages or less he's got nothing to say. There ought to be a law. After 500 pages a writer is just repeating himself, unless it's God writing the Bible, or Darwin, of course.

"You're obsessed with this," I told Lyla about Salinger.

She leaned into my desk, getting all feminine and I knew I'd have to touch something before she left, even though we were soon to hook up at the Warwick.

(MANAGING EDITOR AND MARRIED BOOK EDITOR NABBED IN WARWICK LOVENEST.)

"I am," she confessed. "I've had a crush on Salinger since I first read *Catcher*. He's mine!"

I asked her if she'd have sex with him.

"In a New York minute," she snapped.

Listen, I explained. Salinger hung up a do-not-disturb sign 50 years ago. Leave the man alone. Leave the mystery alone. Maybe there is no J.D. Salinger. It's like Big Foot, the Yeti,

Atlantis, the Bermuda Triangle, the Loch Ness Monster, Noah's Ark, the Ark of the Covenant, the Holy Grail, the Shroud of Turin, the Jersey Devil, Jimmy Hoffa, Howard Hughes, Greta Garbo – all of it unfathomable and best left to the imagination. Imagination can be fun. The rewards are endless.

"So who wrote *Catcher*?" she said, hands on hips, then sitting down, crossing her legs, skirt riding up – Lyla being mannerly, naughty, feverish all at once.

"Charles Darwin."

"What?"

"Oh, I'm just thinking about the talk I just had with Norma."

"You're thinking about Norma?"

"No, Darwin."

"Are you losing it, Jay?"

"Yes, and you're the reason."

She smiled. "I would hope so."

She turned, swiveled that tush, just enough, and stepped for the door, waiting. I got up to escort her and just happened, accidentally, of course, to frisk her. She smiled again, differently, warmly, gave me a peck on the cheek, and then, switching to her game face, her work face, her newsroom face, assured me that she would not make a fool of herself but would, possibly, go ahead with ON THE TRAIL OF J.D. SALINGER whether I approved or not.

Oh once it starts they own you all right.

* * *

En route to my visit with Ben Hawkins here came Arnold Coffey stopping me for a second at the elevators. Arnold – I liked this man very much. I wished I could be as Jewish as he was Jewish, or as Christian as he was Jewish. He used to run this place until Ben Hawkins' people bought out his people. But he still owned a share and still kept his offices high up, our conscience. The talk of the town (and the world) was that Spielberg movie, *Munich*. Arnold finally saw the movie and gave me his review. "This man Spielberg and that man Kushner who wrote part of the screenplay, listen, they are okay with a Jewish State as long as it is not Jewish and it is not a state." Then: "We don't need anti-Semites. We've got plenty coming from our own families and homes." Then the elevator came.

* * *

I kept on walking the long corridor to Ben Hawkins' office but that moment with Arnold Coffey got me thinking in chills. The man so was upright, so decent, uncorrupted, still, even after all these years in newspapering, a trade that corrupted everyone. We were part of the problem. Not so Arnold. I doubted that Arnold, even back when he was young, dashing and daring, would trade in his decency for a fling. As for me, I was okay with a fling. My conscience could handle that, the sex part, no problem there, or hardly any, for as Lyla said, we were using each other and for a multitude of reasons but mainly to distance ourselves from a world gone loopy, so this was our revenge, sex, maybe love, unholy as it was – but that other part, the scheming to rid ourselves of her husband by sending him off to places where there is killing and dying, the Middle East in other words (or anyplace nowadays), that was troubling and I could barely recognize myself in this picture.

I wondered how King David wrestled with himself over Uriah, for here was a godly man, a man of God, David, a king who read the Torah mornings, evenings and bedtime (was indeed the top Torah scholar of his age and perhaps any age) and modeled himself after his forefathers, Abraham, Isaac and Jacob, except that God spoke to these forefathers and would not speak to David, so, from Jerusalem, David sent e-mail messages via the Psalms – "Why stand Thou so far off, O Lord? Why hide Thyself in times of trouble?"

Surely David read the prophets that preceded him and knew that slaying Goliath, as he had, was no feat compared to conquering temptation, and what, were there no nice Jewish girls in Jerusalem at the time – single? He could have had them all. (As did Solomon at home and abroad.) No, Bathsheba, that's what he wanted, and some prize she must have been, married and all, her husband, Uriah, off and away in combat.

But David knew the score and the sin was not the fling but the murder, by proxy, that followed. The hanky-panky, well, it wasn't even adultery (in the strictest sense) because all married Israelite soldiers off to battle gave their wives conditional bills of divorce in case they, the soldiers, were among the missing and stayed missing. So it was not the "adultery" that got Nathan the Prophet all riled up, got him wagging his finger at David with the rebuke – "Thou art the man!"

No, it was the murder of Uriah the Hittite, Bathsheba's husband, that got David to confessing and atoning, "I have sinned against the Lord." The Lord forgave David, though not completely. Their first child died, but along came Solomon, but after that, with the sons that preceded and that followed from other wives, it was a royal mess; rape, murder, rebellion, all in the family. Absalom's revolt against his own father, David, resulted in Absalom's capture and death, and then this from David upon hearing the news: "O Absalom, my son, my son Absalom! Would I had died for thee, O Absalom, my son."

I imagine David the King "stricken in years and he could get no heat" baffled as to which son to name his heir. Enter Bathsheba. (Accompanied by the prophet Nathan.) But now she too, no doubt, is stricken in years. She is not the babe, the pin-up queen, the glamour girl, the Julia Roberts of her day, he had lusted for years ago when it was KINGS GONE WILD. Suddenly (or gradually) Bathsheba is a wife and a mother, and she wants what's best for her boy, Solomon, and David gives in. Even on his deathbed she still has him wrapped around her pinky – and besides, so it WAS WRITTEN. Solomon was to follow.

I picture David as a kid up against Goliath, and later on the run from Saul, and still later in grief over Jonathan ("Thy glory, O Israel, is slain upon the high places. How are the mighty fallen." (Go ahead, for poetry, match this!) I picture David finally King, the mighty warrior upon the battlefield but in conflict between his flesh and his spirit. I picture David carrying the weight of a nation as, unable to sleep, he walks his royal balcony and beholds Bathsheba taking her bath.

("Place Uriah in the front line of the fiercest battle and withdraw from him, so that he may be struck down and die.")

I picture David at once humble and vainglorious, only a little lower than the angels but not an angel.

Stricken in years and for all the years that came before, I love him. I love him as much as Jonathan loved him. I love him for his poetry, his faith, his strength, his weakness. Where do I come in? I am the grasshopper in this scene but as Lyla keeps reminding me, I do have powers. I can assign reporters here, there, everywhere. They are my soldiers. I am their king. What is Lyla? Lyla is Bathsheba. What is Phil Crawford? Phil Crawford is Uriah the Hittite. What am I?

Yes, what am I? All my heroes were, well, heroic. Most I'd never met or even seen, except on grainy film. I knew them, admired them, from their conquests, their myths, their legends and from our collective memory – Jefferson, Lincoln, JFK, Babe Ruth, Joe Louis, Joe DiMaggio, Ted Williams, Mickey Mantle, Maurice Richard, Beethoven, Hemingway, all of them flawed but knights to me. A man must answer to his heroes and I have no answer – and I still haven't heard back from Phil Crawford out there in Newark and, if something happened, what answers do I give to myself? Hemingway would understand, but what do I tell Beethoven?

I was keeping Lyla in the dark about this, about her husband's abrupt sign-off, but eventually she'd have to know if our game was already played out, prematurely.

This trick I was working on was not so original even after David. Prince Hamlet was also sent off with a sealed note that was to seal his doom.

Even in my wickedness I could not authorize something original.

* * *

I made a quick tour of the newsroom just to make sure that there were no fires to put out, and there was indeed something going on at Sam Cleaver's desk, between Sam and Minerva Watson. I hate to interfere so I just listened. It was about those three British citizens that had been abducted by Palestinian Arabs in Gaza, a humanitarian worker and her parents, and just now they were let go and, "We were treated wonderfully by our captors," says the humanitarian lady.

"Sure sounds splendid getting kidnapped," says Sam to Minerva. He is smiling that crooked, wise-ass smile of his. Minerva is not smiling, and Sam continues, "I'll bet you can't wait to get yourself out there, get yourself good and kidnapped by your Palestinian friends, and get treated WONDERFULLY. What a treat that must be for you HUMANITARIANS." Minerva must have had her say before I got there, puffs up and storms off.

"Give it up," I tell Sam.

"They all say they were treated wonderfully after they were kidnapped. This whole world's gone Stockholm Syndrome. We're just living in it," says Sam.

* * *

Vernon Pickins was just walking out of Ben Hawkins' office as I was about to walk in. Vernon, our openly gay staffer who wrote an openly gay column for us here at the Manhattan Independent, was not surprised to see me but I was surprised to see him. I did give him a raise. Maybe it wasn't enough. Was he going over my head? Doubtful. Well, none of my business. Backstabbing was common in the newspaper world. Actually it was common in every world. But here in newspapering we were all crazed with ambition and never satisfied. Yesterday's scoop was today's fish wrapper. We were never happy with the assignment, the story, the beat, the editing, the headline, our place in the hierarchy – overworked, oversexed, under-nourished, under-appreciated, underpaid. But Vernon Pickins was not the type to backstab. As for the rest, we were not beyond duplicity or above pettiness and we were quick to expose such flaws on everybody else but one day it could be our turn. (Across the street, at the Times, they're laying off 500 people and that is the trend nationwide, though we at the Manhattan Independent have not yet been touched.)

"Hey, Jay," he said.

"Hey, Vernon."

"Think about this. Two biggest stars of the 1950s, icons the girls swooned over, were both gay. Rock Hudson and Tab Hunter."

"Guess I'll be reading about that in your next column, Vern."

"You bet."

He was right. Rock Hudson and Tab Hunter, both gay, and Sandra Dee, paradigm of all that is wholesome and virtuous, had been raped repeatedly by her stepfather since she was eight.

* * *

Ben Hawkins was on the phone when I went in and talking, apparently, to someone overseas, and even more apparently, to someone in the Middle East. He was saying, yes, he under-stood some Arabic, and laughing, so it was all quite mirthful and not just business, though business as well, to be sure, and I would not be surprised if this business concerned the Manhattan Independent. There had been rumors and, after all, Murdoch had already sold a piece of Fox News, something like five percent, to an Arab sheik and this Arab sheik already had some say about what went out over the airwaves. A banner that spoke of "Muslim Riots in France" was hastily changed at Fox to "Civic Disorders in France" after a phone call from the sheik.

There was chatter that we could be next, but I doubted that about Ben Hawkins – but at one time I had also doubted that about Rupert Murdoch.

Ben's TV was showing the BBC and a man there was saying that against those Kassam rockets being hoisted from Arab Gaza, Israel had no right to defend itself.

"Let's talk," said Ben Hawkins, getting off the phone.

Ben Hawkins was easy to describe. He was simply Winston Churchill all over again from bushy eyebrows to that pleasant scowl, and even a cigar that he kept puckered and mostly unlit. Ben Hawkins had vanquished England. Press Lord, the tabloids called him, and he owned the tabloids. But how can you keep them down in London after they've seen New York? But here, he'd gone legit, respectable – made the Society Pages. His five billion helped. He ran an empire, newspapers, radio stations, TV networks, and owned a big part of a motion picture studio. He had a piece of Comcast, Diller, Bronfman. He failed to buy into the casino business in both AC and Vegas. An investigation of him by the authorities had turned up something. There were rumors. (He owned all that but who owned him?)

He remarried, ditching the old one for the trophy. He was worth 10 billion before he ditched the old one. He was in his 70s and he was not handsome. He was tall and his face was full of folds and wrinkles and the remains of a terrible case of acne, but though he was not handsome he was magnetic. He had no back class, but his grit gave him style. He lacked the pedigree of Secretariat but got himself moved up to Stakes competition like a hard-knocking Claimer who just keeps on coming.

"I'm here," I said.

"Got to do something about those performance evaluations, Jay. What's the problem?"

The problem was that I did not believe in performance evaluations as a means to measure performance. The act of one employee evaluating another employee was demeaning and had no place in a newsroom, especially a newsroom, where we prided ourselves in our professionalism. Yes, I continued, I know it's going on from corporation to corporation, but I refuse to go along. Just because the rest of them are doing it doesn't mean we have to, and just because the rest of them are doing it is exactly the reason we shouldn't. (What's next? – EMPLOYEES MUST WASH HANDS?)

I will not have one staffer sitting in judgment over another staffer. What if there had been a dispute between these two, personal. Would that be fair? What if those two were after-hour drinking buddies? Would that be fair? What if a man had been wronged by a woman and what if a woman had been scorned by a man and this one was to "evaluate" that one? No, I told Ben Hawkins. I am against this.

"Suppose I insist," said Ben in a tone that was not insistent. There was a trace of humor, indulgence, twinkling in his eyes.

"I'd have to insist right back."

He wasn't laughing. He wasn't smiling. He was testing me. How far could he push me? How far could I push him?

"So the rest of corporate America is wrong. Is that what you're saying?"

"Yes – or rather, each to his own."

I added that the phrase "corporate America" would not play well in a newsroom. Those are the people we go after.

Now Ben laughed.

"But every other department within this operation has that, performance evaluations, except your newsroom."

"Dandy."

"Jay, I shall relent on this, for the time being."

"For the time being then," and we shook hands, for the time being.

Chapter 17

I checked us in at the Warwick, on 54th Street, under my real name, Jay Garfield, and that, in itself, was low risk as even before I had it going with Lyla I'd come here to cool off and regroup from the deadline to deadline madness of the newsroom. So that was okay. Lyla had freshened herself up in the washroom up a flight of stairs and was already seated at the bar, Randolph's, apparently named for William Randolph Hearst, who had commissioned the building of this place in 1926 for Marion Davies and her Hollywood crowd. Cary Grant and Elvis had slept here and I could see why.

That had not been the plan, checking in. Drinks only, and then see what happens. She changed her mind when we took the walk – Autumn in New York – and said it would be wasteful to spend such a beautiful day outdoors. Yes, she had said, check us in and we'll see what happens. Was I chicken? Well, when a woman says that there is no choice but to heed. No, I am not chicken, and if we get caught they will have to prove that we were NOT doing company homework. Maybe I was giving her a performance evaluation.

I joined her at Randolph's and we had our own comfy sofa. She was wearing skinny black pants, low at the waist, purple sweater that brought out the purple of her eyes. Dangling from her neck were beads of many colors, three strands of costume beads, purple, green and red. She had on a pair of high-heeled boots (not too high) and over the shoulders she was draped in a black and purple tweed jacket. She was as fit and as ready as any Manhattan woman of this time and of this place. (She'd never admit to being trendy, but she was.) She was smiling and had a different do, her hair rioting all over the place, by design, and supremely attractive. She was happy, quite carefree, and altogether in bloom. Lyla knew her moments.

That's another thing. Women are always ready. We just don't know the plot. We go one scene at a time. They've got the whole play written out.

"You look nice," I said.

"Ain't so bad yourself," she said.

We ordered, and after some first-round jitters, I said, "What is it with you women?"

"Huh?"

I told her the story we were running in our WHAT WERE THEY THINKING! section, about a lawsuit here in Manhattan that was going forward against a clergyman who was being charged with disturbing behavior. (Rabbis, priests, ministers – so what else is new?) Yes, another sex scandal, but with a twist. This clergyman goes and tells this woman that if she has sex with him "doors will open and men will come." (So to speak.) This man tells this woman that he's her only hope and – get this – that he is the messiah.

Now she is suing.

"You mean she fell for all that?" said Lyla, laughing.

"So what is it with you women?"

"We go for the power, Jay. We're vacuumed in by power."

"But to be so stupid?" I said.

"Men make women stupid," she said.

"I thought it was women who make men stupid."

She raised her glass. "Here's to both. All of us stupid."

No shop talk. Her rule. Certainly no politics. We talked books for a while, or rather arts and entertainment – Is the novel really dead? Are the movies really dead? Is everything really dead except the iPod? What about my treatment for a screenplay that I am calling Prop 24/7? That's going into the future, but not too far, maybe tomorrow, when Congress will pass a law that all of us, throughout the land, are required to read advertisements and watch commercials nearly round the clock. Every home and every person is monitored, and prison for those who tune out. I still have to work it out but it is grounded on what's really going on, with all the technology that lets us bypass commercials, so that corporate America is losing billions, as is our government treasury in taxes.

"We're nearly there," said Lyla. "Everywhere you go, ads, commercials. Everything is sponsored. What's next? I like where you're going with this treatment."

"What treatment?"

"Make the time."

"Between you and the newspaper – what time?"

She smiles warmly and squeezes my hand. The room number is 610.

* * *

After all that, we were back at Randolph's and we were both very tired but very happy, the wrong time to break the news. But is there ever a good time?

"You mean click?" she said.

"Yes, click, click."

"That happens all the time."

"I could swear he used the word dead."

"He meant the cell phone, Jay."

I could not convey how panicked he sounded – or was it me? Anyway, Lyla was taking it well and wasn't even taking it at all. Brave girl, Lyla, or perhaps it made no difference to her, dead cell phone, dead husband, same thing. But that is not fair. Must take into account his abuse of her, if only mental, since he'd switched to Islam – and wasn't everybody these days? All over Europe, and even over here, this is happening. Phil Crawford is not alone. They go for it because it sets boundaries.

"I also have news," she said.

"Good news?"

"It's about Phil."

Phil called her regularly (truly news to me) and told her more than he told me. He had made himself useful to them in Newark by serving as a driver. Muslim women were forbidden to drive. (Boundaries.) They had to be chauffeured. So that's what he was doing. Yes, he'd been kicked out of that Muslim home in which he'd been rooming, and this I already knew, but the reason he was in no hurry to get back – the reason was more than what he told me. He told me that he was hanging in to get himself certified by that letter of safety (that seal of approval to attest that he was a pal of the Palestinians once he got out there to the Middle East), which was true, but not the whole truth.

"He wants to be a hero," Lyla said, and in one move tipping over her martini.

"So does every guy," I said.

She took a sip from my drink, vodka, dabbed her lips. Her eyes flashed.

"But he's afraid of being tipped off as a coward. He's afraid I might think that of him."

"He told you so?" I asked.

"Maybe not in so many words. Or maybe in so many words, I can't remember. But it was clear. He's afraid I'll think of him as a coward."

True, there is nothing worse, for a man. If he is a coward, that is bad. If he is not a coward but people think he is, that is just as bad.

Women, bless them, can do anything they want.

"So that's what's behind it all?"

"Not that simple."

"Oh," I said, leaning back and sensing my temperature rise. What now? Always something. So what now?

"Nothing really to worry about," she said. "Not yet."

Just wait.

"Please. What?"

"He asked if I've been seeing you."

I gulped.

"Go on."

"That's it, really," she said as she thanked the waiter for a fresh glass, and then turned her eyes from me to gaze across the room lazily and indifferently.

"You're okay with this?"

Back to me...

"I said of course I've been seeing you. We work together! I have to see you. You're my boss." She smiled wickedly. "I guess."

I drained my vodka and ordered another. I knew that if she ordered yet another martini this would turn into another round of sex. That's the signal. She did.

"How did he take it?"

"Fine. Just fine. Well..."

"Well what?"

"Who knows?" she said.

Right. Who knows? Who knows what he's thinking, what he's guessing. The husband is always the last to know, or maybe not.

"My guess," I said after a while, "is that Peter Brand is our snitch."

"But of course," she said laughing, putting on a bit of a show in case spies were watching and we were seen as being too intimate.

"Yes of course," I said. "For all we know they may be in touch every day, Peter Brand and Phil."

"To be sure," she said, now leaning in and being very intimate. Go figure this one out, I thought, this chick. She's afraid that we will get caught and afraid that we won't get caught. "For all we know Peter Brand has his eye on us this very minute. That's what's got me slightly riled. I won't live in fear, like a Taliban, like those women he's chauffeuring around, those Muslim women. I know what happens." (She'd been reading Phyllis Chesler, an original feminist who saw a different light and who, years following the breakup of her marriage to a Muslim, wrote an account titled "How Afghan Captivity Shaped My Feminism.")

For some reason I felt compelled to offer up Phil's point of view, the legitimacy of his suspicions.

"You don't get it," she said.

"But I do."

"But you don't," she said, snapping shut her powder compact.

"Please."

"Even if there was nothing between us, even if there was nothing between me and anybody, he'd still have me tethered. That's their way."

Fascinating how she had begun to refer to her husband as they.

I had forgotten how threatening all this was to her. Maybe I was being too cavalier. I was in this for much simpler reasons. I was in this because that's what we do, that's what men do, we fall for women. We fall for them despite the danger and sometimes because of the danger. We've done this since the beginning. Women are the only alternative we have. Well, that's how it works for me.

But I still thought she was carrying this too far. I argued that, after all, didn't he have a right to be jealous? Married to a beautiful woman, no man feels safe. Every guy has his eyes on her, and some women, too. (Even here at the Warwick, with scented competition pretty strong, she had heads turning her way.) So maybe he was acting so overly possessive not for any Islamic motivations. He was merely behaving like any guy who had to keep on winning the girl he had already won.

After all, when it comes to women, all men are jerks. We are all stupid and we are all jerks, when it comes to women.

"Please," she said, a wrinkle showing in her brow, "you protest too much, in his favor."

"So he's trying to impress you, and..."

"No, he's trying to prove to me that he's no coward."

I asked her why? Had something happened?

She sighed a troubled sigh, as people do when it's a long story.

"So make it short," I said.

* * *

"Once," she began, "before we were married, we were walking along forty-eighth, late, after something on Broadway. *Phantom of the Opera*, I think it was. No, I'm sure. How could I forget? We were heading for the parking garage, and got jumped. There were two of them. We didn't know what they wanted. Our money, our lives, or just me. I was scared, of course. I mean I was terrified. But not as much as Phil. He ran. That's what he did, Jay. He ran. They touched me up a bit, but all they wanted was my purse. Thank God that's all it was. But no thanks to Phil. He ran. Then he came back, after they were gone, and he said he was running to find a cop."

"Maybe..."

"Oh hell, Jay! He left me standing there, alone. He ran, and he's been trying to make it up to me ever since."

"How come..."

"Because I'm stupid, that's why I stayed with him and got married. I decided that maybe it was true, about a cop, his trying to find a cop. I knew it wasn't true. I knew he ran because he was chicken, but I was in love, I guess. I guess I was in love. How could I love a man like that? He had me bamboozled. We read the same books and I was young and naïve, and I thought anyone who read the same books must be my other half."

She thought it would be all wine, cheese, Proust and Brahms.

"Another reason," she said, "was that I did not want to come off like that bitch in that Hemingway short story, you know, "The Short Happy Life of Francis Macomber." That was partly real, you know, I mean based on characters Hemingway knew in real life, cowardly husband and the wife whose derision pushes him to an act of reckless heroism, and death." She began staring, reprovingly, at a group of rowdy businessmen up along the bar, which was out of sync for this charming place. Lyla, artistic Lyla, was put off by talk of business and politics and of men who worked those trades. "So I didn't want to come off that way," she went on. "Maybe I married him out of pity, because he WAS a coward. What do you think?"

She married a man of politics. That was his business. Go figure.

"What do I think?"

"Yes, you."

"About what?"

"Oh everything," she said huffily, arching her shoulders.

"I think..."

"Oh I really don't want to know what you think, Jay. You're much too reasonable. This is no time to be reasonable. This isn't the time."

She got up to go to the bathroom and all eyes followed her, especially those businessmen at the bar, and though I didn't like it, I couldn't blame them. She was sensational.

She came back all fixed up with fresh make-up and a fresh smile. Where was that switch that turned on this electricity?

"You know what I think?" she said.

"I'm afraid to ask."

"Let's do it again."

"Until we get it right?"

"Hmmm."

* * *

Later, we had a spat when, over two sips of wine, she wondered what it would be like with another lover. Besides me? Or, in addition? Oh, she said, she was just kidding. Don't you fantasize? No, I said, not since we, together, found eternal bliss moments at a time. Well, this was only the wine talking. Please forgive me, she said, I was just being silly. Don't be angry. Please. Forgive me. Don't. Don't be angry.

But I was. Is that all this is? Are we all disposable, interchangeable? Are we all generic? I thought we were king and queen.

If this is not high romance, then it is nothing. If this is not David and Bathsheba, then it really is nothing. If only I could write a single Psalm.

We were cool for several days.

Where I grew up, on the streets of Greenwich Village, all of us poolroom and stickball and standing-on-the-corner bums, it was understood that only boys liked sex. Girls went along just for the reflex of biology. I am beginning to wonder. Girls (except for the hookers, of course) needed to be perfumed, flowered, sweet-talked, baby-talked, persuaded, implored, deceived, hoodwinked, tricked, swindled, blarneyed and baited in order to get them to submit, and all that just for first base. But I am beginning to wonder.

With them it's all about the foreplay and the romance and who's got time for all that?

Anyway, we were cool for a few days.

Chapter 18

The cameraman's name was Waji Halid. I got that, finally, from Paul Baker, a private eye I knew from my days as a columnist. Waji Halid was a Saudi. My nemesis THE ANCHOR, Kevin Rod Rodgers, whose on-the-spot coverage of the Middle East and Hanan Ashrawi was extensive, used Saudi mercenaries as his bodyguards, and also, obviously, as part of his staff, like this photographer, or photojournalist, Waji Halid.

Waji Halid, however, was being kept on the run by the NETWORK, which now had him all over the globe. I took it to mean that they were hiding him from me, him and those 18 seconds of missing film that would prove, finally, that Kevin Rod Rodgers, the anchorman, had started that brawl outside Pat's Gym. Rodgers still wanted me to stand trial before an arbitration panel. A date for my pending disbarment was being set and drawing closer.

* * *

"But we can't let this go on," Executive Editor Ken Ballard was saying in the newsroom.

He knew the story. We'd been through it a hundred times. We – journalists – are not supposed to be the story.

"Why does he keep after you like this?" asked Ken Ballard.

It did go back, even before that exchange of words inside Pat's Gym and that scuffle outside Pat's Gym; it went back to when I was a columnist for the Moorestown (NJ) Herald and found out that, early in his career, before becoming a big time anchorman, Rodgers had been funded by Saudi Arabia. He was a foreign agent, in other words. Other "journalists" did this, too. They were on two payrolls. In Jerusalem, journalists from all over stayed snug and smug at the American Colony Hotel, a marketplace for story angles seldom favoring Jerusalem. (Why go to the territories where Hamas ruled? It's dangerous. Get it from someone who has a story, true, half-true, untrue, but a story.) The Manhattan Independent used to have stringers that were obviously shilling the Arab line, and even "fixing" stories that never happened, or that could be arranged. (Such as the Mohammed al-Dura caper, the classic of manufactured footage to manipulate emotions, worthy of an Academy Award.) So this wasn't new between me and Rodgers. He was one of them, though now he was number one across the network dials. Sure, he was out for some time with that black eye I gave him, but still, number one.

"I agree," I told my patrician superior Ken Ballard, "that it can't be tit-for-tat."

That was agreed to all the way upstairs.

Ben Hawkins, from the very start, said we cannot get ourselves into a hissing war. We must remain aloof, dignified. We are not on television. We preen for word processors, anonymous, the byline our only claim to fame. Anonymous we are and anonymous we must remain for the sake of tradition and decorum and professionalism.

Newsmen, dedicated to print, the written word – we are assigned to be the flies on the walls of civilization.

We arrive in the newsroom or at the scene uncombed, unkempt, no make-up, in T-shirts and blue jeans. We are disdainful of the imposters.

Television news is inferior but if the price is right off we go...

"Are you sure," Ken Ballard was saying by the coffee machine outside the newsroom, "that this is the best policy?"

"You mean avoiding the arbitration panel?"

"Might it be best to just get it done?"

"I can't fight back, Ken, with one hand tied behind my back."

Ken Ballard shook his head. "You're being railroaded all right."

I could have said that each time my face appeared on the air, our circulation jumped. Yes, scandal is good.

But that would be the wrong thing to say to Ken Ballard. Scandal is never good, not on the Paoli Local.

"I'm sure it'll work out," Ken Ballard said, tapping me on the shoulder and then moving along.

That meant he wasn't sure.

I did admire him. Old money. Protestant purebred old money. The last of the Americans. Overrun, overwhelmed by the Immigration Act of 1965, they were finally a minority. They still ruled, but with much less authority. Simply because of the math. For the first time in history there were more of them than there were of US. The melting pot finally cooked them. But they took it like the gentlemen that they were.

They took it from women, from gays, from blacks, from Latinos, now from Muslims on the home front, but they seldom answered back. They never answered back. That would be so rude. But if anybody had a gripe, they did. Their world had disappeared. One morning it was all gone. They got their hair cut by José, Vince had retired, they bought their newspapers at Ahab's news and cigars shop, not Hank's, Hank sold the place, they bought their gas from a man in a turban.

They bought books from booksellers who spoke no English and there was no more gabbing with cabbies.

The last soda fountain at Woolworth's was the end of Ken Ballard's world.

* * *

Up the elevator to the top floor I made a slight pause for indignation. Ben Hawkins wanted me again. I thought we'd had it settled, this performance evaluation business.

"Drink?" said Ben Hawkins at the bar in his office. His office took up half the floor. There was a photo of him and the Queen, but he wasn't knighted.

I said vodka straight up would be fine. "I'll do the same," he said, and sat down on the couch at the opposite end of his semi-circle mahogany desk that had no papers on it, as if he did no work. He did plenty, of course, kept his world in his palm, but made it a pact of honor to keep off newsroom business. But we knew he was watching, and knowing this made us vulnerable to a rightward tilt, though we'd deny it, including to ourselves. His unwavering patriotism toward his adopted America (even before 9/11), and his steadfast support of Israel made him a bit of an outcast in the corridors of journalism. (Though 9/11 redeemed him a great deal. He saw it coming.)

"Don't let them get to you," he said, with only a slight trace of an accent. "You came up from the streets, like me. I know you're a fighter."

So this was about my troubles with anchorman Kevin Rod Rodgers, or rather his troubles with me. Ben Hawkins didn't need the grief. I didn't need the grief. The Manhattan Independent sure didn't need the grief. But let's get ready to rumble. Ben Hawkins made me think of my father. This was the man who brought me in from the cold. I liked him, I liked Ben Hawkins.

He laughed. "I know I'm supposed to be upset each time they show that on the TV, you knocking him down. Not good for the paper."

"Sorry about that," I said.

"But I gotta tell you – each time I see that prick Rodgers go down, warms my heart. Nice left hook, by the way."

"Thanks," I said. "Rodgers is very stylish and very smooth."

Rodgers had not been stylish or smooth when he had toppled over. The camera picked that up, too.

The camera had picked up everything except Rodgers' bodyguard throwing the first punch – and before that shoving that lady Rodgers had mistaken for a fan.

Ben Hawkins was saying, "I do hate that son of a bitch and all that he stands for. I know his kind. I knew them back in England. Sweet to your face and sour to your back."

He knew my end of the story – those 18 seconds.

"I could buy that network, you know. I could buy it and fire that pussy." He seemed to delight in the thought. He smiled as a prizefighter does when he returns to his corner after scoring a knockdown. Ben Hawkins had a pugilist's swagger about him in any case, fists punctuating his words, and once every couple of months we put on gloves at Pat's Gym. "But that's talk for another time."

"Meanwhile," he continued, "I know it's been our policy to prevent you from responding in our pages. Let me take that back. That's been Ken Ballard's policy, and you know how he is. We've gone round and round on this, Ken and I, but you know I try not to interfere – directly. So it's been Ken's decision, and a proper decision it is, if proper is what we're all about. Well of course it is. We're not tabloid. That was his argument against using our pages to fight back. He said that would be too much like tabloid. I do agree. I guess I agree. Do you?"

"But there have been times when I've wanted to let it rip."

"Same here. This has not been a fair fight."

I caught him up on the latest.

"So we have a name of the cameraman?" he said in reflection.

"Yes."

"We know where he is?"

"All over."

"Right. You said that. So we've got to chase him down. Are you paying this private detective?"

"No, he owes me a favor."

I did a feature on Paul Baker, when I was in Features, and it was so favorable that it brought him booming business.

"But this private eye of yours, he's local, right?"

"He doesn't have the means or the contacts to chase down our cameraman all over the world."

"Well I do," said Ben. "Here's the deal. I'm going to find that Waji for you, and when I do, when you get those eighteen seconds, then we'll set you free to fight back."

I thanked him and he walked me to the elevator. "I'm not doing this for you," he said when the elevator came. "I'm doing it for the paper. It's all for the good of the paper."

"That's what it's all about," I agreed.

He slapped me, father to son, across the shoulders.

"We'd never want to do anything that might harm this newspaper, right?"

"Right," I said. But nearly doubling over like a man who's been hit below the belt.

* * *

When I got back to my office Lyla was on the phone. "It's that book editor," said Gladys. I kept replaying HARM THE PAPER...HARM THE PAPER...HARM THE PAPER.

"What's wrong?" said Lyla.

"Nothing. Why?"

"You came back from upstairs like something's wrong. What's wrong?"

"Nothing."

"Are you okay?"

"Yes," I said.

"Am I okay?"

"Yes."

Pause.

"Are we okay?"

Chapter 19

There really is no place to get away from it all. Run but can't hide. The newsroom, in fact, is where the world comes looking for you. We keep building walls but never tall enough. No fence is high enough to ward off the mobs. Even fortresses won't do. They tunnel under them. (Gaza, for instance.) Ever since that Danish newspaper published those cartoons that mocked Mohammed (peace be upon him), igniting those riots (ISLAM GONE WILD was a headline I approved, reluctantly) we've had to increase Security, which means three more rent-a-cops down there in the lobby, minimum wage, maximum age, around 80 years old, the typical Security Guard, and one of them is a woman and pregnant. Had I said no to that it would only spark another protest. Everybody's protesting, every-body's pissed, everybody's been wronged, everybody's got a gripe, a grievance, a complaint, an indignation.

So? So I was at the racetrack with Jimmy Smokes, *aka* Jamil Samil or something equally Arabic – and it is interesting that when two people become friends, racetrack buddies especially – who cares, I mean about religion or world events. The next race is all that counts. Jimmy was having a good day. I was hav-ing a bad day. I knew I would from the start when on my first bet my horse came in second and they all did likewise thereaf-ter, they kept coming in second race after race, seconditis it is called, like a disease, and I wonder why it usually happens like this. The opening race is a tip-off of what's to come and I wonder if that says something deeper, say about life in general.

Never mind.

Between races I could tell that Jimmy Smokes had something on his mind and I even knew what it was – whether I intended to run those Danish cartoons, in the Manhattan Independent, that were triggering those riots all across the Arabic firmament, deemed anti-Islamic, those cartoons, for taking liberties with Mohammed, peace be upon him. I had not made up my mind. Jimmy, I think, was embarrassed for all that rioting. It reflected badly on his people, and upon him personally. Jimmy wouldn't bring it up and neither would I as that is what kept our friendship friendly – no politics. So we would not even mention Hamas, either, that group of terrorists that had just won the right to represent the Palestinian Arabs (which I knew would happen all along) with a mandate to destroy Israel and everybody else. Jimmy Smokes was Palestinian. (Well, everybody's got to be something or other.)

The difference between then and now, I think, is that in the past people only whispered their hatreds. There used to be shame. Today it is out in the open and we say okay. That's fine. We understand your need to rape, behead, enslave and murder your neighbor. Perfectly understandable. You're pissed and it's our fault. We are sorry and we are ashamed. We deserve everything you've got to give. (Though even the Nazis usually went about their genocide by metaphor, like Final Solution.) I knew Hamas would win because as the prophet (Isaiah) said, Woe when day is called night, night is called day, bitter is called sweet, sweet is called bitter.

So here we are in a world plunged in darkness and in bitterness, and under such cover, how convenient for Hamas.

During a pause in the racing action, Jimmy said this, and it surprised me. He said, somewhat distractedly, "It's tough being an Arab."

Okay. So I said this. I said, "It's tough being a Jew," even though I was but part Jewish, but still tough.

That is as far as we ever went politically.

We were betting Gulfstream. Jerry Bailey, the greatest jockey of his generation, was retiring and on this, his final race, he was going off at one to five, and I never bet those odds, ridiculous, no value, but I did here and now, for a keepsake, and sure enough, he came in second – and to a 50 to one long shot. Damn. I tore up my ticket. To hell with the souvenir. To hell with Jerry Bailey.

I drove Jimmy back to his place in the Village and before he stepped out he said, "Life is not fair."

I wondered if Jerry Bailey was all he had in mind.

* * *

I managed to save the day, partly, from a $200 win at Aqueduct, when a hot new rider brought home the first half of a nice exacta.

This jockey is sure to replace Bailey as numero uno and his name is John R. Velazquez, peace be upon him.

* * *

I stopped off at Pat's Gym to do some sparring and between the ropes was up against a kid who'd just turned pro, Hectorio Marquez, so he was good and good enough to give me a black eye, but I lasted in there with him for three rounds and that is something, and Pat told me so himself, impressed. "Not bad," he said. You'd think one black eye is enough, enough for one day, but then came another when I got back to the newsroom.

"Phil Crawford keeps trying to reach you," said Gladys, and right there with her, outside my office, was cartoonist Peter Brand, smirking it up.

"Finally," I said.

"But there was so much static…"

"I'm not even sure it was him," said Peter Brand.

"You spoke to him?" I said.

"I spoke to somebody."

"There was so much static," said Gladys.

"So we're not sure who it was, is that what you're saying?"

"You worried about something?" said Peter.

Yes, I was worried that Phil Crawford was dead and all of it my fault and soon people would know this. When you send a non-Muslim to a mosque he could come back dead. But wait. Phil is a Muslim – all of a sudden. He is one of them. Yes he is. He converted. He made his choice. But he is also a journalist and that is not compatible. I know he's at risk. He made that plain during our last conversation, and maybe, worst case, he's at risk no more.

"I'm worried about you, Peter," I said.

"I'd worry more about Phil Crawford," said Peter, turning and trampling off to his drawing board.

Peter Brand surely belonged to Hamas, or al-Qaeda, or Al-Jazeera. Terrorists wear suits nowadays. They've gone corporate. They walk among us.

I sat down at my desk, ran over some copy, like the one about our school kids here in New York that need to answer, correctly, only about a third of all questions for their finals – yes, only a third – so that here they come, a generation of illiterates to be handed the keys to America and all of it thanks to our Board of Regents who have chosen dumbing down as an imperative. I gave it this headline DUMB and DUMBER but had other things on my mind, like Phil Crawford. Was he live or was he Memorex?

In walks his wife, my lover, Lyla.

"You won't like this," she said. "I know you."

"What?"

"I know you."

"What won't I like, Lyla?"

She sat down, skirt riding up as usual, and what legs! God! Women!

Chapter 20

She was right. I did not like this. But she told it so casual, like what is the big deal? Grow up. It was about her pursuit of J.D. Salinger.

Rather, it was Donald Whittings' pursuit of her, of Lyla, Whittings being that writer (of sorts) who claimed to have access to Salinger.

"He swears he can get me that interview," said Lyla.

"With Salinger."

"With Salinger."

"Who has spoken to no one for 50 years – but now you?"

"Why NOT me?"

Salinger, it turns out, wants to know more about her, such as her credentials as a journalist, fine, but also her credentials as a woman. As a woman?

"What's wrong with that?" said Lyla.

"You? The feminist?"

"Oh don't give me that," she bristled. "Feminism is about power. That means mind, and body."

"Salinger wants your body."

"Oh stop this, Jay. It's not like that, not quite."

"You silly thing! You're being taken for a ride, Lyla. This isn't Salinger who wants your mind or your body. It's that Whittings – and talk about a phony!"

"You've got him all wrong. I knew you wouldn't understand."

"So what happened?"

"Promise you'll understand."

"What happened?"

"Promise."

"No, what happened?"

She finally gave it, and like this. Salinger (according to Whittings' bullshit) wanted a photo of her face and also the rest of her.

"Nude?"

"Not totally," she said unsteadily. "Only the top half."

(In a survey we took from here at the Manhattan Independent, most men, 68 percent, admitted that they undressed female anchors, the BBC's Katty Kay topping the list.)

"So you took off your top, for Whittings."

"No, for Salinger."

"You took off your top."

"For the sake of journalism, Jay."

"Oh he's got your number, that Whittings."

"Don't be ridiculous. This is win-win."

"You mean nude-nude."

"I wasn't nude. Just the top."

"You took off your sweater."

"Exactly. Just that – and bra."

She asked, smiling, if it was getting warm in here, and yes it was.

"Now there's a picture of you topless," I said.

"For J.D. Salinger," she insisted, "and in the name of journalism."

"No, for Donald Whittings, and in the name of gotcha sucker."

So naïve. She said I was so naïve. So very naïve. Don't I know? Don't I know what goes on in the name of journalism or in the name of anything? People do strange things to get ahead, or maybe it is natural things that they do, yes, natural, according to nature. You think Barbara Walters, Diane Sawyer, Katie Couric, Lesley Stahl, Paula Zahn, Christiane Amanpour and all the rest – you think they made it on brains alone? What world was I living in? Hanky panky goes on all the time. To get to the top a woman has to go down.

About Salinger, yes, even in his dotage he did pick out women from photos, images from magazines, television, the movies. This is known.

When it comes to sex – oh when it comes to sex the bigger the man the bigger the pervert. Women, too.

"What if he wants more, this Whittings?"

"You mean Salinger."

"No, I mean Whittings. There is no Salinger."

"This is as far as it goes, Jay."

"If that's what you say."

"Please trust me."

"I did."

"Now you don't?"

"I don't know. You said I don't know what goes on, and I guess I don't. I guess I am naïve."

"Maybe that's why I love you, Jay. I'm sorry if I hurt you. This won't happen again, I promise. Do you still love me?"

"Did he touch you, this fraud?"

"He is not a fraud. He's a published author."

"So was Hitler."

I knew – I could tell more was coming.

"No, he did not touch me. No one touches me but you."

She forgot to mention her husband. But that's another story. Such a smart woman to fall for something like this. That is also another story.

But how could she fall for this?

"Did he want to touch you?"

"Yes."

"Of course."

"You're angry."

"Disillusioned."

Was she starting to cry? Yes, I think she was.

"I didn't think you'd be so – so shocked. Well, I guess I did. Maybe I did, knowing you."

I should not be so shocked. Sex keeps happening. As long as there are men, and women, sex will keep on happening. Even Sam Cleaver tags me as clueless on this. If only, he keeps saying, if only I knew what is really going on even in this newsroom. People are sleeping with people. He himself has slept with half the staff though he won't name names. I can't even guess. The women seem such ladies. I can't imagine this. I have done some of this activity myself, plenty, but always outside, well, except for Lyla. Yes, except for Lyla, for Lyla was different. I thought she was different. I used to think she was different. If she is not different, I am not different. We are like everybody else. If we are like everybody else, we are not only committing a sin, we are committing a joke. When this ends, and it will end, one way or another, it had better end as a tragedy and not as a comedy.

"I'm telling you everything."

"I don't think you are."

"Okay, he said my nipples weren't aroused enough."

"So."

"Jay..."

"So."

"So he touched my nipples."

"He touched your nipples."

"Just to get them aroused."

"Were you aroused?"

"Only because I thought of you."

"Then?"

"Then nothing."

"Nothing."

"He took the picture and I put my clothes back on."

"Your clothes."

"My bra and my sweater."

"Suppose SALINGER wants more?"

137

"Jay, no more. The rest belongs to you."

"But your top belongs to Whittings – whoops, Salinger."

"No, all of me belongs to you, Jay. Do you still love me?"

"Lyla, I am starting to grow up awfully fast, and when it comes to being naïve..."

"Do you love me? Do you still love me?"

* * *

Marie LeClair runs our letters-to-the editor department and when she came in, in tears, Lyla had to leave and just in time, for I'd had enough. Marie had come to us from Montreal, the Montreal Gazette. She had written a fine book about the differences between Canada and the United States and what got me was her chapter on hockey and how hockey was to Canada what baseball was to the United States. I loved her section on Maurice Richard. I lured her away with promises to move her up quickly at our international desk but to get her started, I sat her on letters-to-the-editor, never thinking that she was too fragile, too sensitive for such an assignment.

"I cannot take this," she said. "I did not know it was like this."

I knew what she was talking about. She'd been e-mailing me copies of those letters that kept coming in and so many of them were ugly and getting uglier. There was raw hatred out there, kindled from the Left, some from the Right. If you did not agree with them you were a fundamentalist, a right-winger, a bigot, and they wanted you hanged. They wanted everybody dead who disagreed with them – and these were (self-styled) humanitarians.

I was thinking, seriously, of a special section to be named HATE MAIL. Not a bad idea. Maybe. I just might do this.

Funny thing. The Manhattan Independent was really not a right-wing newspaper. But compared to The New York Times, we were. Abu Ghraib, which the Times carried 100 times, was no big deal for us, nothing more than back page except when it first broke, and that, I suppose, made us right-wingers, plus my own editorial, which I signed, and in which I wrote that females have no right being in combat ("Girls Just Wanna Have Fun") – and that sure stirred them up, the armies of feminism and all the rest. Oh, the letters! Ben Hawkins offered to surround me with bodyguards.

"We can't print all this garbage," said Marie. "So much hatred."

"You be the judge, Marie."

"Who are these people?"

"Believe it or not, they are the people who are so full of love."

"You mean hate."

"No, I mean love. That's why they hate so much. Please, don't try to figure it out. I can't."

"So it's up to me."

"Yes."

"Thank you, Mr. Garfield. But this is all so very disturbing."

"You'll get used to it," I said.

"I hope not."

* * *

Sometimes we did respond when a letter came in halfway articulate. Someone wrote in that it is outrageous how the State Police profile. We (actually, me) replied that next time you need help, do not bother with the State Police, call Noam Chomsky. Besides, if there'd been profiling (and sweeps of wiretapping) before 9/11 there'd have been no 9/11.

* * *

Sam Cleaver came in to test-run his latest – HOW DID WE SURVIVE JIMMY CARTER? Jimmy Carter, he wrote in there, was the worst person in the entire world.

"Do you agree?" Sam said.

"Stiff competition for that title, Sam."

"Right," said Sam, "but I nominate Jimmy Carter."

Sam was running a once-a-month feature titled, simply, BAD PEOPLE. The list was long and kept on growing.

"Get out of here," I said, "before I change my mind."

"We need to grow you a new set of balls."

"You're asking for it, Sam."

"Sometimes I think you're getting in touch with your liberal side."

I got up as if to sock him and he edged out the door laughing with – "Okay, okay."

* * *

Sam Cleaver is young. He is a man on fire. I like that about him, his rage against injustice. He will take on anything, anybody. I hope he stays that way and does not submit, as the rest of us have to one degree or another. He thinks he can make a difference and that journalism is the answer. But I am beginning to worry. I am beginning to see signs. We all wear down after a while and this is what he said to me the other day, "Sometimes I wonder what's the use."

* * *

Karen Moskowitz said she'd heard a rumor that I did not like her review on that Clint Eastwood movie about a female boxer. Karen was our movie critic though she was not critical about this one. I said girls don't belong in the ring. Had I seen the movie? No. Well then, how can you judge if it was good or bad? Well, it had to be bad. Why? I just told you. Girls don't belong in the ring. Oh, she huffed. You're impossible, Jay Garfield. Okay, where do girls belong? In the kitchen, I suppose? Now there's an idea, I said.

Chapter 21

Finally, Waji Halid slowed down and I got his address. Waji Halid had been recalled from his posting in Rome and was now attached to the network's Los Angeles bureau, inside info I got from my private eye pal, Paul Baker. This happened so fast, this transfer, that it could only mean that Ben Hawkins made a deal with the network, or a threat, a threat of somehow putting it into play on the Big Board, a Carl Icahn maneuver.

I also had a phone number, 310 area code, and phoned that number. A man answered and paused when I asked if he answered to the name Waji Halid.

"People call me Wayne," he said.

There was no accent and I knew that since 9/11 people whose names were Mohammed now, sometimes, called themselves Moe. Hence Wayne for Waji. But he had no accent.

He said he knew why I was calling but that there was nothing he could do for me. He knew the whole story up to anchorman Kevin Rod Rodgers' slander that I had slugged him unprovoked when, in fact, 18 (missing) seconds of film would prove otherwise. I was glad that we did not have to start from zero and go round in circles. Actually, he sounded downright friendly – a fellow newsman! I'd been prepared for evasions. People who report the news do not like being part of the news, the spot I was in, and now perhaps Waji Halid.

Still, I said, it was important that we talk, and not by phone.

"So come on over," he said.

From LAX I took a cab to Brentwood. His digs were 555 Barrington on Barrington Avenue. I had the cabbie drop me off several blocks short of that address to measure the place, and got off at San Vicente Boulevard. I stepped inside a drugstore to get some Life Savers and everybody inside was a movie star. The guy at the counter was ten times more handsome than Robert Redford; his bad luck that no Paul Newman had come along to steal those scenes in *Butch Cassidy and the Sundance Kid*. But he was terrifically square-jawed and handsome and you just knew that he was just biding his time for the next casting call, as was everybody else around here, including the women and their babies. "Don't touch that," one mother said to her infant. "I love you." She said that in one sentence without pause – "Don't touch that I love you."

I walked the half mile to 555 Barrington and this wasn't New York. No fat people, no ugly people, no smoking. Nobody smoked. They jogged. People were jogging all around me. I tried to find a place to tamp out my pipe but the sidewalks and the streets were so clean it wouldn't be right. (If all the beautiful people head for New York and LA, where do all the ugly people go? I still say Philadelphia.)

The streets were so clean that you could eat off them and in New York people would.

Even with my pipe unlit I got glares. People were playing tennis as I walked along Barrington Avenue, robot-like, the smiles, the easy manners, something Stepford about it all. On the sidewalks people greeted each other with smiles and chatter, all of them young, trim and trimmed, like cutouts. Much Barbie. Much Ken. I was a stranger, so naturally I got nothing, but there were some worried glances cast my way. Most likely I had New York written on my back, gritty New York. No gritty in Brentwood. They, in LA, seek perfection, we, in New York, pursue power.

I found 555 Barrington. That was the name of the place and it smelled of tulips and other flowery fragrances that I cannot describe, being from New York. The place was surrounded by palm trees, gardens and a swimming pool. Must be very expensive living here, surely beyond the means of a network cameraman. They made good money, cameramen, but not like this. No, there must have been an inheritance or a payoff. My guess was payoff.

Wayne was waiting for me in the courtyard. He was wearing designer jeans and a purple designer polo shirt. He was smiling and greeted me with a handshake.

"Welcome to LA," he said.

He was almost exactly my height, six feet on the nose, dark hair cropped short and only his eyes were Arabic.

"I'll take you to a nice place," he said.

We chatted along the way. He was Saudi but became an American citizen when he turned 28; he was now 36. He had started off with Al Jazeera television but quit, or got fired, when he began sending in footage of Arab atrocities as well. This was not popular at Al Jazeera. So he moved here and was quickly embraced by the NETWORK. He'd been to all the world's hot spots, been shot, wounded, arrested.

I liked the son of a bitch. It seemed to go both ways.

"I like your paper," he said.

He read it regularly when in New York (also online), and I knew he was telling the truth when he mentioned Peter Brand's cartoons and Lyla Crawford's Books section. He liked Peter for his daring, and he liked Lyla for her weekly book column for promoting lesser-known writers and their lesser-known works. He was writing a book himself, about his experiences as a combat photographer. I took that as a hint and told him that I'd bring it to her attention when it was done.

We ended up in a restaurant called Toscana.

"That's Halle Berry over there," Wayne whispered.

That's the kind of place it was.

We sat down and shared pizza with all the trimmings.

So?

So yes, he shot the whole thing. He saw the whole thing and his camera saw the whole thing.

"You were in the right," he said. "I'll tell you more. You were heroic."

This was pleasant to hear, and astonishing.

He said, straight out, that Kevin Rod Rodgers, the anchorman, was a bully. "I don't like him," he said. "He's a phony from the word go. He treats his staff like dirt, me included."

Those 18 seconds?

"They've got them somewhere."

"You don't?"

"They confiscated them as soon as I brought them in, I mean he confiscated them. He's playing a game. He wants you. You're pro-Israel, aren't you?"

I said I'm pro truth, and immediately hated myself for being so pompous and self-righteous.

"So am I," he said. "I'm Arabic, but I think of myself the same way, like you, pro-truth."

I liked the son of a bitch.

"You have no copy?"

Here he paused and his face clouded up.

"No, they took everything."

I wasn't so sure. Something was lacking in that response, but we were getting along too well for me to risk a challenge.

How did it happen? I mean how did it happen that he got himself transferred so fast out of Rome?

He smiled.

"Somebody turned some wheels."

That had to be my man Ben Hawkins. Hell, had he really threatened to buy the damn Network! He would? He could? Yes he could. Bless his name.

So who was paying for all this? This was no dump, 555 Barrington.

He shook his head and smiled sheepishly. "The network took care of me."

"You mean they paid you off."

"Okay."

"So you wouldn't talk."

"Something like that," he admitted.

I was almost uncomfortable by such a surge of honesty.

"That's Catherine Zeta-Jones over there," he said to change the subject, and most likely to cover his own discomfort.

I told Wayne that his silence about the incident was hurtful. He assured me that there was even more to be silent about. That flash about CNN, that it manipulated the news from Iraq for ten years to flatter Saddam, was no scoop to him. He knew all along what CNN's Eason Jordan, CNN's chief news executive, finally confessed in a New York Times op-ed. What remains to be told, said Wayne, is the Arab intimidation faced by newsmen trying to cover the Arab-Israeli conflict, or any conflict throughout that region. He grinned when he said, yes, he was an Arab himself, but that "we're great at deception. Deceiving ourselves, deceiving the world."

He coined a phrase – MEDIA JIHAD.

This almost outdid Arnold Coffey's MEDIA POGROM.

"That's Michelle Pfeiffer over there," he said. "And Julia Roberts."

"Thanks...they sure are beauties. But..."

"I know," he said. "What do you want me to do?"

I said if he would speak out, that would be helpful – the two of us being so pro-truth.

He let that absorb.

"Then I'd lose my job," he said, his eyes wandering the room, the room in all its glitter. He'd lose all this...Halle...Michelle...Julia...

He was caught up in all this. There's no business like show business. They've got beauties around these parts all right but nothing compares to New York women, their walk, their talk, their confidence, their arrogance – different broads different breeds. They're not auditioning. Maybe that's the difference. They've got it made. That's the attitude and it sure is an attitude.

"What about the truth?" I said, pushing but afraid that I might be pushing too hard and lose him altogether.

"If I speak out, if I defend you, I'm finished."

"I understand," I said, ready to leave the table.

"Don't think badly of me," he said.

Back there at 555 Barrington he had a wife, American, and three kids. That was also truth. If he spoke out, he'd surely lose his job and 555 Barrington, and most likely be blacklisted. I knew all about that, how that could happen. Nothing official, but word spreads along the grapevine. So it was between me and 555 Barrington, which to preserve? No contest.

He offered me the hospitality of his home. I said I had the next plane scheduled. He nodded and began gulping and seemed on the verge of opening up. He wished me luck but I knew that there was something unspoken going on. As we shook hands outside Toscana, he reminded me not to think badly of him. He also reminded me – speaking of the TRUTH we both loved – that in the world that he once covered, the Middle East, and would never do so again, for the sake of his integrity, "Truth is for sale."

Hmmm. Truth is for sale.

* * *

Wayne handed me something on the sly as we parted, saying that it was for me to know, for a better understanding of him and his predicament.

"This is what goes on," he said – and I read it on the plane, munching peanuts, an online printout from the media watchdog group HonestReporting.com:

"Daniel Seaman, director of the official Israeli Government Press Office (GPO), has touched off a media scandal by accusing some international news organizations of gross bias in favor of the Palestinians. The GPO is responsible for issuing press credentials to all foreign journalists.

"In an interview with the Israeli newspaper 'Kol Ha'lr' (translated by the Israel News Agency), Seaman claims that journalists coordinated their reporting with terrorist leader Marwan Barghouti. 'He used to call them and inform them about what was about to happen. They always received early warning about gunfire on Gilo. Then they shot for TV only the Israeli response fire on Beit Jala. Those producers advised Barghouti how to get the Palestinian message across better.'

"Seaman singled out four correspondents who have recently been removed from their assignments in Israel.

"To put things in perspective, HonestReporting readers should recall the words off Fayad Abu Shamala, BBC's correspondent in Gaza for the past ten years, who spoke at a Hamas rally in Gaza: 'Journalists and media organizations [are] waging the campaign shoulder-to-shoulder together with the Palestinian people.'

"Seaman says that Palestinians who work with the media attend a course in media manipulation at Birzeit University, and exercise control over information flow. He says: 'The Palestinians let the foreign journalists understand: if you don't work with our people we'll sever contact with you, you won't have access to sources of information and you won't get interviews.'

"Seaman gives further examples of Palestinians manipulating the media coverage: 'The IDF announces that it is going in to demolish an empty house, but somehow afterwards you see a picture of a crying child sitting on the rubble. There is an economic level to that. The Palestinian photographers receive from the foreign agencies 300 dollars for good pictures; that is why they deliberately create provocation with the soldiers. They've degraded photography to prostitution.'

"Seaman also says that 'today we know that the entire Mohammad al-Dura incident was staged in advance by the

Palestinian Authority in collusion with Palestinian photographers, who worked for the foreign networks.'

"Seaman says: 'At the direct instruction of the Palestinian Authority, the offices of the foreign networks in Jerusalem are compelled to hire Palestinian directors and producers. Those people determine what is broadcast. The journalists will deny that, but that is reality.'"

Ach Zo!

* * *

When I got back – finally, that was Phil Crawford on the phone from Newark and that mosque that was supposed to prepare him for his Gaza vacation, among Hamas.

"Come on home," I said, really meaning it, too.

I need him dead just so I can have Lyla? How stupid is that? Who is Lyla anyway? She strips for J.D. Salinger and there is no J.D. Salinger.

She did surprise me with a gift later on, a thousand dollar pipe that somehow ended up on my desk with a note, "Keep it hot – Lyla."

"Okay?" I said to Phil Crawford.

"Not so simple," he said.

"Why?"

"Complicated," he said.

I am starting to panic. "You're trapped or something?"

"It's about that cartoon," he said.

"You're kidding."

"These people don't kid, Jay."

"You have got to be kidding."

"Why did you publish that cartoon, Jay, and with that headline?"

Chapter 22

Four in the morning and that's Phil Crawford on the phone and then off the phone. Says he can't talk but that he'll be calling back in a few minutes.

"Just be ready," he says.

Huh?

He sounded scared. Well, if he's scared, I'm scared. I sent him out there to Newark, to that mosque.

Be ready for what?

Obviously, things are not going well.

Well, if he's dead, I'm dead, and Lyla, too. She set this up. Did she? Or did I? We both did. Or maybe he did, Phil. He wanted that assignment. He wanted it all along. He asked for it, combat reporting. That's the romance of journalism. When you come back you're a hero, if you come back, and so many of us don't, the latest, the latest casualty being Bob Woodruff of ABC-TV. He's recovering and that's good.

(I'd done combat reporting and yes, women do gaze at you differently.)

This was supposed to be a test, Newark, before I dispatched him out there to Gaza or someplace like that to be placed "in the forefront of the hottest battle, that he may be smitten, and die." Like David did to Uriah for Bathsheba. Like I'm doing to Phil Crawford for Lyla. This wasn't supposed to happen in NEWARK (NEWARK!) and now, really, it wasn't supposed to happen at all as I keep gradually returning to my senses.

I was asleep when the phone rang and it took two Valium to get me knocked out in the first place and maybe that is why I usually, make that always, wake up suicidal, like what is next on the world's agenda and what does it all mean for my newspaper, the Manhattan Independent, and me personally. First words when I wake up? Life sucks. This is a bad routine, I know, and it wasn't always like this. I don't know what happened.

Lately it's been the insomnia. When the phone rings four in the morning it's never Happy Birthday. I've had this trouble since 9/11, always afraid since then (when I was at the race-track) that the world's blowing up and me? Asleep. I tend to worry that one day we'll miss the big story. The world started with a bang and sure to end with a bang, maybe the same bang, implosion. The Manhattan Independent is my newspaper, all of it my responsibility, what goes in and what doesn't go in and sometimes what doesn't go in worries me nearly as much. The world doesn't sleep, so what am I doing?

That's the news business since 9/11 – waiting for the other shoe bomber to drop.

After that phone call from Phil, I showered, got dressed, and waited. I ate some corn flakes, drank coffee, then, for some reason, went back under the covers.

I had never done this before, committed murder, if that's what this was. Nope, first time. First time, at least, to get some-thing like this rolling, all in the name of love. All the brutality, all the chaos, all the killing, all of it in the name of love, really. They love their prophet so much that everybody else has to submit or die. But that's been going on for centuries, all this love.

When I drifted off the TV was on with an Al Pacino movie and here's an actor who started off terrific (*The Godfather*) and keeps getting better. It was that movie, the one I fell asleep on, where he's blind and wants to die. I'd seen it a dozen times and it always gets to me, about a man so tired, so weary of it all, that he just wants to call it quits. Enough! Reminds me of Burt Lancaster and his later films, or later "work" as they say, and how he grew, through those films, so majestically and acceptingly into his old age. In that *Rocket Gibraltar* movie he's rich and famous and surrounded by an adoring immediate and extended family but he's stricken in years and so tired, even of the good life, that he just wants it to end, and end it he does in a trick finish. For some reason I understand this, this being so tired.

I fell asleep to Pacino but around 5:30 I woke up to some porn. I had a porn channel going. I watched in amazement and admiration as these two (later four of them) were going at it and there was nothing to get turned on about for these people were not having sex, they were working. All work is honorable, no? So these were professionals. Yes, the job was sex, having sex, but still, a job, work. They were as professional as any carpenter, any engineer, even journalist. I do what I do. They do what they do. It's a living.

That is how I watched this, professionals on the job. How admirable to be so good at what you're doing.

I once covered a convention of them, porn stars, at the Sands casino in Atlantic City and they were no different from a convention of accountants.

There was carousing, of course, but mostly shop talk.

At some point in this porn flick, another couple arrives, and it is amazing what four people can do, I mean naked and without any tools or equipment except God-given.

The phone!

(Phones used to ring, now they play Beethoven's Ninth.)

That was Phil saying to get in my car, drive over to Newark and meet him at the train station and don't ask any questions. I zoomed the car over highways and turnpikes and was there in 53 minutes (I timed it) and there he was, Phil, at the Newark train station, waiting outside, pacing, and jumping in even before I had a chance to come to a full stop. Drive, he said.

Phil was unshaven or maybe growing a beard and he'd lost some 20 pounds, bags of pinkish flesh sagging from his face, and his belt was tied in a knot to hold in all the bulk he had dropped. His eyes were bloodshot. Still in Newark, we drove past a marketplace and that made me think of a shuk, those shuks they have over there in Arab countries, mobs of fruits, vegetables, people, as for the moment, this moment, Newark was indeed the Middle East, like Dearborn, Michigan.

We really are at war but what a strange war. It's a war we've forgotten even while it's going on.

I'm thinking James Joyce again. There in *Ulysses* (of a century ago) he writes: "He passed Grogan's the tobacconist against which billboards leaned and told of a dreadful catastrophe in New York." Obviously that was about something else – still, though, spooky, especially when right after that he adds: "In America those things were continually happening." Hmmm. Abu Ghraib. We should be better. We should? Why? Maybe we should be worse and then they'd leave us alone.

Out on the open highway, that's when we started to talk.

"Why?" he said. "Why those cartoons?"

Yes, we had published those cartoons that had run in a Danish newspaper (mocking Mohammed) and that had crazed that other half of the world. Riots were still going on. So we had published them in the Manhattan Independent, on my say so, because, well, because we are Americans and Americans are not afraid, or rather, we never used to be, I mean, we used to be Teddy Roosevelt and George S. Patton and Gary Cooper; that's one, and two, that is our motto at the Manhattan Independent, IN PURSUIT OF TRUTH.

"Nobody else ran them," Phil said.

"That's shameful."

"You insulted them, I mean us."

Us meaning us as a newspaper, or him as a (new-born) Muslim?

"Doesn't take much."

"That's what did it," Phil said.

He had won their (grudging) trust, over at that mosque, until those cartoons appeared with the banner, ISLAM GONE WILD. Though even before that they were suspicious of him. He was a newsman, after all, and in the religion he had adopted loyalty belonged to the Koran and not to freedom of the press. The Koran was the only truth and besides, someone caught him taking a piss without wiping himself afterward; a sign that he was not fully converted and true.

"Okay, Phil. But why all the suspense?"

He was certain that his phone was bugged, his rooms were snooped and – and that they had placed a bomb in his car, sure to go off the minute he turned the ignition. Then there was this. The woman he'd been chauffeuring around – the mullah's wife since women were not permitted to drive – tipped him off if rather obscurely when she advised him to be careful. (Did he have something going on with her?)

I found the next exit and turned us back.

"Where are you going?" Phil said, somewhat in panic.

"Back."

"Jay, what are you doing?"

So I explained. If his car is indeed booby-trapped, someone else is bound to get in (like the police) and get blown up.

"Why should you care?" said Phil Crawford.

"You don't, Phil? You don't care?"

"Let's just go home."

"You really don't care."

"I just want to get back. Forget the car."

The car was up on the sixth floor of the Municipal Parking Garage and I snaked us up and when I got out to start his car, Phil ran for cover.

I got it started all right. Phil came back – he'd run down to the fourth floor – but still wouldn't get in, into his own car, actually a company car.

I'd have to get someone to pick it up, later.

Back on the road, together, he apologized for his fear and I said nothing wrong with fear, I was plenty scared myself.

"But you did it," he said. "I didn't."

"Never mind."

"You won't tell my wife," he said. "Will you?"

I didn't answer.

"Y'know, Jay, it really felt like a set-up, you running those cartoons."

I didn't answer.

"As if it were personal, you out to get me."

"Oh come on."

"I did get that letter of safety. I still want to go, Jay. Forget Iraq. The big news will come from Palestine."

"You mean Israel, Phil. There is no Palestine."

"Hamas is now in charge."

"I know that, Phil. Hamas was always in charge."

"I don't know what you mean."

"Well I know what I mean."

"Are you ticked off at me, Jay?"

"No."

"I still want to go out there, to Palestine."

"Israel, Phil."

"We'll see what happens, okay?" said Phil.

"Yes, Phil. We'll see what happens."

Chapter 23

Hot-shot Sam Cleaver is in my office and he's saying, "Boy meets boy, boy loses boy, boy gets boy, but loses the Oscar for best picture. Crash."

That's the column he's writing.

"What else, Sam, Sam?"

"So I'm on this train –"

"Will this take long? I've got a paper to run."

"So I'm on this train going to Atlantic City for a night of blackjack –"

"Were you alone, Sam?"

"What's the difference?"

"Who, what, where, when, why – journalism 101."

"Okay, I'm with this girl."

"What girl?"

"Jay, you're being impossible."

"What girl, Sam?"

"I can't say."

Surely someone from the newsroom, or someone famous, possibly married. There was talk, always talk about Sam Cleaver, Sam Cleaver and his women. But the story was about something else. So he's on this train from Penn Station going to Atlantic City and it's a quiet train except for the hooting of the train's whistle and off they go, excited about the gambling ahead. Behind them, Sam and his girl, seated right behind them, are a man and woman, likely married, and they're talking, and the talking gets louder and louder, and the talk is in

German.

"German," says Sam.

The train keeps speeding, wheels clanking, horns whistling and wailing and the talking gets louder, in German. "Jay, I got the willies."

"What?"

"I fell into a trance, like we were being taken to a concentration camp."

"You should include this in your novel."

"Can you imagine how this felt?"

"What about the girl?"

"She felt the same way. She said we have to move, and we did. We changed seats."

"The new people behind you spoke Spanish, right?"

"Of course," said Sam. "But that's all right. It's not German. I mean German's all right, but not on a train. I mean, that could have been a cattle car."

"Good story, Sam. Did this really happen?"

"Oh come on. Yes it happened. Over the weekend, while you were in Newark."

"You knew I was in Newark?"

Sam laughed. "There are no secrets. Isn't that what you keep telling me? I even know what happened."

"What happened?"

"Phil thought his car was booby-trapped. So he called you to check it out but you were afraid, so he started it up even at the risk of his life."

"Sam..."

"Yes, Jay, I know it's bullshit. I know you and I know Phil Crawford. So it's the other way around. But that's the story he's telling."

"What's the difference?"

"Stop being so easy, Jay. You've got to stop this. Wake up. Fight. God – you're my hero."

"I pick my spots."

"Quite a story, huh? Spooky."

"Who's the girl?"

"You will never know."

"There are no secrets, remember?"

* * *

Minerva Watson, our ranking feminist, caught me in the cafeteria where I ran in for a quick slice of apple pie, which is always taking a chance, for here it is not wine that is subdued for aging, but food. Minerva objected to a column I wrote about the Olympics, first, writing as I did, that ice dancing is not a sport; second, why is it that it is always the boy who lifts up the girl, never the girl lifting up the boy?

"This proves?" she asked.

"You figure it out at the next meeting."

I do know this. She could bring me up and file charges, even for a joke. Yes, that's how it's become and that's how it is.

Likely, she's taking notes, building a case, Minerva along with Peter Brand.

In the john, next to the cafeteria, I spot a sign that says, actually says, EMPLOYEES MUST WASH HANDS. Don't know what got into me, but I flipped. I ripped it down and then called on Max Bracken, who heads our maintenance department, to ask him when this started (I have my own private facilities), and he said about a week ago. On whose orders? Corporate. Somebody in corporate.

"Well I want those signs down."

"All over the building?"

"All over."

"Yes, sir."

People have to be told? Animals know this, to wash up after they're done. My cat knows this. Humans are the last to know and this is evolution?

I think I'm getting edgy. I think I should start taking Valium even in the morning, before I start the day, not just later.

157

Later I'll go to Pat's Gym and punch a bag and if Pat can line it up, punch a person. That always helps.

It's not just that, it's not just this, it's everything. I miss my father. I loved my mother but I miss my father. He was such a straight guy and then they arrested him for bookmaking. He was no bookie. He ran a news shop in the Village (also some groceries) and there was gambling going on in the back, just neighborhood guys playing pennies and nickels. But someone had it in for Dad and they busted him, for no reason, and, come to think of it, same thing happened to Lyla's dad, a judge, destroyed on the false charge of accepting a bribe, so perhaps, subconsciously (we seldom discussed this) that brought us together.

Dad was in jail for only a week and he was cleared, but the indignity stained him, forever. He was such a proud man. Proud of his patriotism, proud of his decency.

That doomed him, that one week, marched off publicly in handcuffs. He was the most giving and charitable man on this earth. He knew his customers and gave half of everything away for free. He'd say, "You will pay me when you can afford it or when you get that job." The neighborhood loved him. He made me do all that reading. Baseball, stickball, hockey, sure, even hanging out, okay, but one hour each day, reading. "You must read everything." I started reading The New York Times when I was eight and learned how news stories are developed, from the lead (actually LEDE) on down, the lead most important. He'd say, "Everything should be summed up in the first paragraph, even the first sentence." Nothing is so complicated that it cannot be summed up in one phrase, sometimes a single word, even America. "Give me one word that sums up America." I could not think of that word, not at that age. Think, he'd say. Okay, "Liberty."

"That's my boy!"

I miss him. There is no one else to talk to.

* * *

158

An old-timer joined us in the newsroom as a headline man. He was a rumpled sort, what people would call a has-been but he was merely a recovering poet and novelist. He was a leftover from the Greenwich Village-San Francisco beat generation with six books to his name, three of them a collection of his poetry. Now he was down and out in Manhattan and I hired him. Everybody else was against it, Ken Ballard, our executive editor, and even the big boss himself, Ben Hawkins. But I hired him.

He was a Charles Bukowski type and Lyla liked him for that reason alone. This guy had LIVED. This guy had lived and lost. How could you not love him? He had actually done some boozing with Bukowski, or so he said, and I believed him, and he had known Kerouac, and I believed that too. He knew Kerouac's List of Essentials (on writing) primarily, Rule #10 – No time for poetry but exactly what is. Or Rule #17 – Write in recollection and amazement for yourself. Or back to Rule #4 – Be in love with your life. Or Rule #13 – Remove literary, grammatical and syntactical inhibition.

Maybe he knew all that from reading Kerouac or maybe he knew it from those nights of jazz with Kerouac at the Village Gate. He turned out to be good at headlines but was terrified of the computer. He refused that contraption. He kept asking for a typewriter. (I relented.) He was a remnant of another age, lost in this spaceship known as the 21st Century, hurtling too fast toward destination unknown.

He once said: "Suppose you wake up one morning and in that haze discover that everything your enemies said about you is true?"

That takes some pondering.

I checked up on him regularly and in fact I liked to pump him about the old days, the Bukowski days, the Kerouac nights.

Will we ever see that again – the creative energy of that age? Free association? Anything goes as long as nobody gets hurt?

"We were young then," was all he'd say.

His name was Paul Westman and he'd given up on writing but wanted to stay in the game.

So this day I walked over just to chat. His desk was in a direct line to Lyla's office and though the glass around her office was mostly tinted you could still see in. I glanced up now and then and thought I caught sight of Phil in there, in there with Lyla, and this was unusual. No it was Phil, I was quite sure, and it was Lyla pacing. Then I thought I saw something else. I thought I saw her slapping him – one good slap across the face.

Nearby staffers took note and exchanged quizzical shrugs.

I wondered if this was any of my business and of course it was, taking place as it was in the newsroom. I knocked and after a pause Lyla said, "Come in."

Lyla was back behind her desk and Phil was sitting there, across from her, quivering.

"What's going on?" I said.

Neither of them said anything, but both were steamed.

"Come on," I said. "People saw."

Still nothing.

"I can't let this kind of stuff go on in my newsroom."

Lyla finally spoke up. "He raped me."

Phil said, "It's none of his business." Then, to me: "Jay, this is a family matter."

"He raped me, Jay."

Phil got up. I thought he was going to hit me, or Lyla.

"A husband can't rape his wife."

I said this wasn't the place for that kind of discussion.

"He raped me, Jay."

"This woman," said Phil, "is my wife. I'm entitled."

"Under what law," said Lyla. "Islamic law?"

"Any law...but yes, Islamic law." Then, turning back to me: "Sorry, Jay, to get you mixed up in this."

I felt horrible for Lyla, but pretty rotten for Phil. He was not a violent man. He was, I always had to remember, an idealist –

an idealist who had turned to Islam for its ideals. He was wrong to do what he did, but right to demand, or rather expect, that a wife provide her services, otherwise it's not a marriage and they were still married. Yes they were! Sometimes this was too easy to forget, that Lyla was a married woman and not to me.

I thought this through from a distance, distancing myself from my relationship with Lyla. This was different. This wasn't about me.

"Phil," I said, "you've got to come to terms with the old and the new. You're married to a modern American woman."

I went on to say that I respected his beliefs, his ideals, but that somehow some way an accommodation had to be made, that it was unfair to put Lyla in the middle, between America and Mecca. Phil sat back down and started shaking his head. Then, softly, he started to cry, like dry heaving. I was moved. Lyla wasn't. "I don't know what to do," Phil said and kept saying.

I asked Lyla to leave the room so that I could talk to Phil man to man.

"He raped me, Jay," she said as she left.

I gave Phil some time to compose himself and went over all that again, about two worlds colliding around Lyla.

"I love her, Jay."

"But you can't force yourself on her."

"You think it started when I converted? She stopped caring long ago. I'm so sorry to mix you up in this."

Why, I wondered, was I comforting him, when it was Lyla who was the real injured party? Because – after all, I was the silent partner. Besides, I could never fully dislike Phil. He meant well, I know he did. He meant well. He meant no harm to Lyla or to the world. Quite the opposite. He wanted to do good, and that was his problem. He wanted to change the world through journalism and now, through Islam. "Maybe you just have to give her time."

Phil grabbed some tissues from her desk to wipe tears and sweat. I lit my pipe. Screw them! "She'll never accept," he said.

161

"Neither me nor the change in my culture."

I asked him how he'd feel if Lyla came home one day and announced herself a born again Christian. New rules.

"What do you mean?"

"I mean new rules. Why your rules over hers?"

He nodded. "I see your point."

I thought that I had gotten through.

"But that's not how it works," he said, firmly.

"Yes it is."

"No it isn't, Jay. You don't understand."

"What?"

"You just don't understand. I mean, it's too late. I'm in, and whatever I'm in, she's in."

I let my pipe do some thinking. "You're gonna lose her."

I did not much care for the new Phil that was beginning to emerge. "That can't be. Once a wife always a wife."

"What century was that?"

Phil got up – and he seemed to have a new way of walking, sort of strutting, in a way that you feared. Where had he picked that up?

"None of you will ever understand," he said, and as he started out the door, he said, "Don't think I don't know."

Lyla came into my office, stomping. She asked, sarcastically, if we had that man to man talk. She admitted that she'd smacked him. She admitted that she'd not had sex with him in months, even before US, and what about US and what about my being so kind and so reasonable with the man who had raped her? What was that all about? That makes it a gang bang.

"Oh come on."

"Have you changed sides, Jay?"

"Lyla, this won't work between us if we make him an enemy and besides, he is not a bad person."

"Then you live with him and his mullahs."

Chapter 24

Sam Cleaver accepted an invitation to defend our newspaper's (alleged) slant to the Right and Sam being Sam corralled me into sharing the moment (moral support) over there at Beth Sinai Synagogue where crowds were waiting to take us on and take us on they did. Everybody was there and in fact the Jews were in the minority. It got ugly when we defended Israel and just as ugly when we defended the United States of America. Numerous groups were here on a platform of "humanitarian" causes and "solidarity" business and if words could kill we'd be dead.

In the car, as we headed back to the newsroom, Sam Cleaver, well, Sam was hurting.

"Don't let them get to you," I said. "I don't want to lose you."

"What do you mean?"

"Something like this can really shake you up."

He kept staring out the window as I kept to the road. He was a sensitive kid; brash but sensitive. If you want love, newspapering is the wrong business.

"Okay, they got to me. I wonder if I'll ever be ANGRY again. A bit sobering when you consider what's out there – wow!"

"Not safe to go out."

Mingling with the public, even the readership, was never smart. I hated that part, always did. You're supposed to think of your readers as high-minded.

You should have only one reader in mind, someone like Joan Didion. That's the only way to keep sane and keep it going.

"But this – how they also hate America!"

"That's becoming my revelation, too."

"Why is it," he said, "that intellectual left-wing liberals are the most mean-spirited of all? The extreme right-wing kooks, them we know, but..."

He must have sensed my own unease. "Don't worry," he said. "You were even-handed." He gave me a sly side-glance. "But do you have to be so even-handed? I mean, get real."

"Meaning?"

"Not everything has to be editorial – on the one hand this, on the other hand that."

"I gave my opinions."

"You're on both sides of the street, Jay. You really want a Palestinian state – a twenty-third terrorist state?"

"Mine is not to judge but to report."

"Some people might call you too even-handed."

"As a good newsman should be."

"Some people might call you gutless."

"Gutless?"

"Well..."

"I won't answer that one, Sam."

"What about the real Jay Garfield? You're tough in all the right places but not on politics."

"I can't let that be and still call myself editor."

Sam Cleaver pondered that, shaking his head. "One day you'll grow balls again, Jay. You'll have to."

* * *

I was driving during that conversation and I was irked, about everything. Sam asked what good it did to be cussing out every red light.

I said I take every red light personal – thank you, God, this too?

* * *

Lyla was saying, grimly, "This can't go on. You know this can't go on."

"I know."

"You know? No, you don't know. You took his side."

"Lyla, please. You know the spot I was in."

We were in the Village, walking, just walking. We had a place, that place I had leased on Sullivan as it meets Bleecker, our hideaway.

But there'd be none of that today.

"This means," I said, "I won't be able to touch your nipples?"

"Stop it," she said, almost smiling.

"Don't your nipples need arousing?"

"Jay!" But this got a full smile, if reluctant.

She was doing some window shopping and even stopped into some of the shops, the boutiques. Amazing, even when troubled, they shop.

"You were in love with him once."

"Don't remind me."

"Women."

"Men."

I had to admit it; something had to be done. Whatever sympathies I had for him were dashed in Newark, and later that scene in her office.

She wanted to visit an art gallery.

"I'll wait outside."

"You're a barbarian."

"Too late for art."

"What does that mean?"

"Art has nothing to say, not to me. Music, yes. Not art."

"You really are impossible. All the girls in the newsroom say that about you anyway."

"Oh."

"But they still have a crush on you."

"Oh!"

"You know they do."

"No, I don't."

"Well, I'm jealous."

We stepped into a bookstore instead where someone was giving a reading, poetry, the audience, rapt. I had no idea what he was talking about, this poet.

Later – "What? No poetry, either?"

"Too late for poetry."

On Bleecker Street, that great street, a man rushed up to her and hugged her, and she hugged him back, and they almost air-kissed, as people do in LA and even here in Manhattan at certain uptown gatherings, but not the Village, Greenwich Village. No, please. But they were friends, this man and Lyla, Rafe Gorgan or something, his name, publisher, his job. They chatted, mostly about books, the latest from his imprint. He was big time.

Lyla introduced me but I declined to shake his hand. Lyla tried again but I declined again. He said he knew me by reputation.

"You're known as the last of the two-fisted newspaper editors," he said with a smile.

"Okay," I shrugged.

"I do admire you for offering so much space for the arts in your newspaper," said Gorgan, "especially books."

"Thank you," I said.

"Without people like you –"

"There'd be no people like me."

He laughed. Lyla smiled, tightly.

"So nice to see you," he said to Lyla as we began to drift separately.

"Same here," said Lyla, and we were alone and together again.

She asked what that was all about and I told her that this Gorgan had turned down Sam Cleaver's novel, so screw him.

"You were rude, Jay."

"I should hope so."

She pecked me on the cheek. "I guess I'm proud of you for sticking up for Sam. You're a good man, Jay."

"Huh? What brings this on?"

"Let's go to the apartment."

We marched on, lively.

"Will I be able to arouse your nipples?"

She laughed. "I won't live that one down, will I?"

"Will I? I mean arouse your nipples."

"No, we have to talk. Behave."

Over there in our hideaway she did not get sassy or sexy but poured us some wine so we could talk, around the table, and this was the talk she had in mind, serious, that she was thinking of getting pregnant, with me, of course. I poured down the entire glass in one swig and poured another one. Pregnant? She was not sharing her bed with Phil, her husband, then it would have to be me, and then, pregnant, he'd kill her. Yes, he'd kill her.

He was that far gone and he'd kill her. So it was written in some sura or another.

"When did you decide this?"

"For quite some time. Yes, I want your baby."

I let that sink in. I likewise assumed that if everything turned out all right – which it rarely does – then we'd get married and THEN we'd have that baby.

Not NOW.

"My clock is ticking," she said, "and – and I love you. I love you, Jay."

"But you know –"

"Yes, I know."

"He'll kill you."

"Not if we do it first."

"Lyla, if you only knew how relieved I was to see him back and in good health. Well, more or less."

"Well I wasn't RELIEVED. You saw how RELIEVED I was."

"Sorry, you're right."

"This can't go on, not like this."

So? She was planning to have a baby. How was this supposed to work? She takes that pill.

"Suppose I won't?" she said.

"Please, Lyla, I'm not ready for this."

"I am, very ready. I want that baby."

"Can't we just make love like normal people?"

She said yes we could, but without the pill. She knew I could not perform with my protection, so there was only the pill, and I'd have to trust.

How will I know when she is or ISN'T using it, that pill?

"You won't."

All this was heavy. I sat down on the sofa and she joined me, cuddling up, with Brahms, his first piano concerto, the first movement that drove us both crazy. Some music does this, most of Brahms, all of Beethoven, and lately, more and more, Dvorak. Dvorak, here's a guy, a composer, finding his stride, after all these years. But you have to die first. First you die and then become rich and famous. That is how it works most of the time. Did Beethoven know he was Beethoven?

"What about now?" I asked, as she started with me and the breathing started coming fast.

"I'm not telling."

"You mean I don't know and I'll never know when you've taken the pill?"

"You'll never know," she said.

"You mean every time," – as I carried her into the bedroom – "I'm taking a chance?"

"We're both, Jay. We are both taking a chance. Doesn't that add to the mystery, the excitement? Isn't this fun?"

Chapter 25

Not again! Suddenly, those bells go off and here we go, another fire drill. Once a month this happens, or is supposed to, and what a waste of time. Elias Francone, our director of Security, has been getting sloppy (thank goodness) so now it's maybe once every two or three months that the announcement comes on and circulates, booming, around the building. Ben Hawkins, our publisher, got this started, those fire drills, in response to 9/11. "None of us," he told me, "is safe, ever again."

Least of all a newspaper that's got our reputation (correctly or incorrectly) for being so Conservative. We've made enemies.

So here comes the announcement – "Everybody, vacate the building at once."

As is typical among New Yorkers – yeah, yeah, yeah. So we stay, most of us. We pay no attention and proceed with our work. Of the 680 employees here at the Manhattan Independent (210 on Editorial) about a third pay heed to the alarm and go scurrying down the steps. Ben Hawkins is never happy about this slacking and neither is Elias Francone, a stickler for safety. Safety First is his motto. But we are New Yorkers. We have been through everything.

Then this: "Everybody leave the building at once. This is not a drill. Repeat. Not a drill." In addition, something like an air-raid siren goes screaming through the speakers.

This is different.

Elias rushes into my office. "Jay, this is the real deal. Got a phone call. There's a bomb in the building."

(I swear that's a line out of a hundred movies.)

"Didn't we just have this same thing a couple of months ago?"

"I'm not here to argue. Leave! Now!"

True, I may be managing editor but on matters of SAFETY his word is final.

"Okay, in a minute."

"No. Now."

Off he goes and this time, yes, the building clears and the computers are lonely and must fend for themselves. (This is where we find out, as some say, that computers are capable of thought and action.) I'm wondering. I'm wondering if this has anything to do with Phil Crawford and those people he got to know at that mosque in Newark, from which I had to help him escape. If he had to escape, that should be a sign that things did not go so well over there and this – this is an answer. Or maybe not. Coincidence. Yes, coincidence, for he did get that "letter of safety" from some imam for a trip to Gaza or some other Palestinian territory under the rule of Hamas, a story he's hot to get, and so are we, even if I likewise have a second motive, which I care not to think about too much, please.

That sure would be a Pulitzer for Phil and a coup for us if we got Hamas to spill, and maybe Phil is the man, upon his return dead or alive.

I do recall his fear – Phil's – that they, his mosque buddies, may have placed a bomb in his car over in Newark, which is why I had to check it out first, only to find it safe, but not safe enough for Phil. So after I brought us both back to Manhattan, I had that car of his checked out by our company mechanics and guess what, no bomb, but, there had been tampering. Yes, they had tried something, so yes, I could not rule out some connection between that and this.

All this I find quite baffling, re: Phil Crawford's turn to Islam. One minute they're his friends, next minute they're not. One minute they trust him, next minute they don't. Is he their "useful idiot?" I know he is a sincere Muslim. He's made the conversion everlasting and of course there is no other choice as once you're in you're in and so is everybody around you, thinking here of Lyla and oh brother what a mess she's in, I'm in, we're all in. Oh hell.

What I've been doing – and am doing through all this, this bomb scare – is reading Sam Cleaver's novel, the manuscript that keeps getting rejected all over the place, and I have finally gotten to it because Sam needs to know if maybe they are right, all those book editors that are relentless in their sneering, sniffing and scoffing. Can it be that they are right and that he is wrong? Can one man stand up against the rest of the world? (Well, Abraham did. Smashed the idols and gave us nothing less than monotheism. Gave us God!)

I am reading it off the computer and am hooked. This is wonderful writing and it's about a Jewish scientist who is about to be sent to a death camp by the Nazis. People are trying to save him and get him to America. This scientist has found the cure for cancer. Yes, the cure for cancer. Finally, they get him on the ship "St. Louis" along with hundreds of other evacuees and this ship goes from port to port and gets turned away from port to port, and this includes the United States. NO ENTRY PERMITTED.

The ship is sent back to Europe, back into the arms of the Gestapo. Our scientist dies in Auschwitz. Up in smoke goes this man and his cure for cancer.

Well, not exactly uplifting, a story like this, but so powerful and so well-written and actually, so true, for Sam based this novel on a real person, Hermann Strauss.

This happened.

The "St. Louis" also happened.

Sam put it all together, and with rhythm, with tension, with class, with style. Who knew he had this gift? Well, I knew.

So I am so deep into this that I have forgotten all about the bomb alarm and later, when it's okay, that is, when the building has been vouched from corner to corner, end to end, wall to wall, even by the NYPD (hmmm, this really was serious) I am finally aware that Sam Cleaver is in my office, smiling. "You trying to be a hero or something?" he says. I tell him what kept me.

His features turn yellow.

"Should I sit down?" he says as he sits down, already humbled. (To a writer, the verdict on his work is more terrifying than a bomb.)

"Sam. Sammy, Sammy –"

"Please, Jay, tell me. That bad?"

"Horrible."

"You hated it?" he says.

"Just awful. All those publishers are right, as always."

"Jay, if you're teasing me I will never forgive you."

"I am teasing you, Sam. Do you forgive me?"

"Tell me the truth. This novel means everything."

"I loved it, Sam. Fabulous story. Wonderful writing. No wonder you couldn't find a publisher."

Good writing dies young.

He fills me in on something else he found out in the research – not fiction, but fact. One of the original Nazis and Hitler's Luftwaffe commander, Hermann Goering, had a cardiac condition and needed medical attention to stand fit for trial at Nuremberg for crimes against humanity. A doctor from Cincinnati was assigned the task, and this was no ordinary doctor, rather a cardiologist named Dr. Nathan Silver, son of rabbinical giant Rabbi Eliezer Silver. Doctor Silver had been attached to Patton's Third Army as a medic (where he saved thousands of American lives in the field of battle) and after the war this was what this Jewish doctor had to do – save the life of a Nazi. Years later, when asked why – why not let this monster die, or even kill him, Silver, who ate powdered eggs throughout the war to stay kosher, plainly said: "I am a doctor."

(In the end, Goering was sentenced to death, but committed suicide in his cell.)

After the war, Dr. Nathan Silver took up family practice in Cincinnati and never spoke openly of his exploits, his heroics, with Patton.

He was so simply, so humbly, so honorably, a doctor.

"Jay," says Sam, "can we talk some day? I mean really talk. We never talk."

"We always talk."

"You know what I mean."

"Who has the time?"

"I need to get things out, Jay. I don't understand anything anymore."

"That's my line."

"Some day we'll talk, all right?"

"Sure, Sam."

"I'm losing my footing, Jay. I need to be heard."

So does my boss, Ben Hawkins, who steps in as Sam Cleaver steps out.

"Don't do that again," says Ben Hawkins, red in the jowls. "Ever. I need newspapermen, not heroes."

"Sorry, Ben."

"Suppose this wasn't a false alarm?"

"Won't happen again."

"I get death threats every day. Don't you?"

"By the hour."

"All it takes is one."

"I know."

As he's about to leave, he pulls a Columbo. "Oh by the way, what's this about J.D. Salinger?"

Whoa! I thought this was our secret – Lyla, Donald Whittings (that phony) and me. But you've got to move fast to get ahead of Ben Hawkins.

"It's crazy," I say. "Just crazy talk."

"If we could get a scoop like that –"

"Ben, Lyla is only dreaming."

For some reason he just stands there, at the doorway, staring at his shoes. "I hear," he says, "she has another dream."

"Ben –"

"There are whispers, Jay. Be mindful of Peter Brand. This newspaper needs you."

Yes, and I need this newspaper.

* * *

Lately I've been having trouble with women and I don't mean Lyla, necessarily. Lyla is another story altogether. By trouble I mean it's like I've been asleep throughout all these years when women went to war. I thought the war ended. Wrong. It is still going on. Of course I don't mean women who bake cookies (God bless them), I mean women motivated by rage to get ahead – out in the workplace. God bless them as well, if only they'd calm down. It is not all our fault and it is not all my fault.

Minerva Watson thinks it is.

We rotate our editors to run our BUZZ (gossip) column and this month it's Minerva's turn and we are all aware of this scandal that has hit our competitor across the street wherein one of its gossip stringers was caught (allegedly) operating as a shakedown artist, demanding money from the rich and famous. Pay up, goes the scheme, for favorable press, and if you don't you shall pay with your reputation, which we shall tatter.

That's only one (corrupt) reporter in all this, and of another newspaper, but now questions are being raised about the rest of us.

Is that how it also works at The New York Times, at the Manhattan Independent? Is that how it works, period?

No, not from my experience.

"Minerva," I say, "I just need to be sure we've got nothing like this going on."

"I resent the accusation," she says.

"This is not an accusation."

"Of course it is."

Well, it goes back and forth like this and there is no give in her and I know she wants a scene, an event, a cause. She has formed a group here that only about half of our female staffers belong to and it's called "The Women's Caucus" and they meet now and then to invent and discuss grievances and surely my name has come up more than once. I once referred to Gladys as my "secretary" (unforgivable!) and in that column I wrote about Maureen Dowd I said, "You go girl," and that got me a loud memo. If Katie Couric, I wrote in another piece, is our answer to Edward R. Morrow, that only attests to the further (rapid) decline of our culture – and that sure riled them up! (Lyla, naturally, does not belong to this group. She is too confident and secure and loves being a girl.) I am now known as "the last of the macho editors." I do not mind the sound of that, for some reason.

"I want it in writing from this entire gossip staff, and stringers, that nothing like this is happening at this newspaper."

"Or else?" says Minerva.

"Or else I start firing people starting with you."

I realize, as I go stomping to my office, that I am angry, more than this deserves.

"What's wrong?" says Gladys as I settle in to do some editing at the computer but it is all a blur.

"Gladys, do you mind being called a girl?"

"Oh dear Lord," she says, "at my age I wish you would."

Chapter 26

"How did it go?"

This was Ken Ballard, executive editor, poking in a friendly face. For a guilty second, I didn't know what he meant.

"That business with Sam Cleaver over there at that synagogue?"

"Disaster," I said.

"Figures," he said. "How did Sam do?"

"Above the shouting, not bad."

"Did we lose or did we win?"

"Everybody lost."

Ken Ballard chuckled but then turned serious. "We shouldn't be public figures and part of that spectacle. We mustn't become part of America's shouting match." All that, he said, was business for the likes of Hannity, O'Reilly, Franken, Dobbs, Matthews. From the Left or from the Right, makes no difference. "They know the tricks. Leave it to the pros." Depart from speakers' corners and run from the microphone. The pros know when to smile, wink, frown, and this is no knock, but admiration. It is their trade, not ours.

(True, the public discourse is down to shouting and barking.)

The one word to describe Ken Ballard is this – decent, and unlike Ben Hawkins (and myself?) he is no Conservative. He just can't stomach the Left.

Ken Ballard belonged (along with me) to the old school that held no trust for the public in the flesh. Our place was the newsroom or out there covering a story and after that, go home or get drunk, but, do not engage. TV and movie people belonged out there, not us. You will never persuade people who are absolute. Other than his pals and partners in golfing or yachting, Ken didn't like people anyway, except as news to fill up our pages. We loved our readers as readers but as people? Charles de Gaulle loved France, but he hated the French.

* * *

We ran two guest opinion pieces side by side, the one supporting total amnesty and full citizenship for those 12 million Mexicans here without documentation (illegals), the other supporting a kick in the pants and heave-ho, running with this headline, PRESS 1 FOR DEPORTATION, so naturally 10,000 people were outside with pickets accusing us of being anti – well, anti-everything. (Even though, editorially, we offered both sides.)

At the staff meeting everyone was here including Lyla, yes, Lyla (who seldom attended) and of course Minerva Watson and Peter Brand, among all the rest.

"That was perfidious," said Lyla about that headline and even about that entire commentary that favored throwing them out one by one, those here illegally.

Being so literary and artistic, Lyla was, by breeding and upbringing, usually on the liberal side of any argument but that she should take me on, here in front of everybody – that was a surprise. "Really, Jay," she said, "what were you think-ing?" I said I was thinking of running a newspaper that permits freedom of expression. "Well," she said, "if I were Latino, I'd be insulted."

"Latino?" said Marshall Kendricks, a reporter who was married to a woman from Cuba.

Lyla blanched. "I'm sorry."

"So what is it?" asked Stu Greenwald, head of our foreign desk.

"American," said Marshall. "Period."

Peter Brand said, "Jay, that was bigoted."

"This entire continent is America," said Minerva Watson. "Mexico is America. Even Canada is America."

"I guess that makes me a gay American," said Vernon Pickins.

"I guess there's no solution," I said. "We can't call anybody anything."

Blacks do not like being called black and some even object to African-American. Hispanic is a bad word and now, so is Latino. For American Indians, the default position is now Native Americans, though some Native Americans want that reversed back to American Indian, since that is how it all start-ed with Columbus who discovered America by mistake. Some Jews find the word Jew offensive (especially in dictionaries) and Muslims find most everything offensive. Liberals shy from being designated by that name and have taken up Progressive. Even the word Christian has come to define an individual as being inflexible, intolerant, Bible-thumping. We keep adding new people but are running out of words.

"Our Style Book does need to be revised," said Ken Ballard, who (blessedly) is never provoked at being called a WASP.

"We're supposed to be one nation under God," said Arnold Coffey.

"What is God?" said Norma Lincoln, our science editor.

"Oh, please," said Arnold.

"What is a nation?" asked Lyla.

I quoted James Joyce from *Ulysses*, where he has Bloom saying: "A nation is the same people living in the same place."

"We're not Ireland," said Vernon Pickins.

"We're not an island, either," said Peter Brand.

"We sure won't solve this in one sitting," I said.

"But you were wrong, Jay," said Lyla.

"Okay, so why bother having an opinion page if we can't offer opinions?"

"There must be limits," said Marshall Kendricks.

"That is ridiculous," said Sam Cleaver. "I'm amazed at this discussion. You want us muzzled?"

"Marshall," I said, "I'm surprised, and at you, too Lyla. THERE ARE NO LIMITS! This is America. For gosh sakes this is America!"

"Whose America?" said Minerva Watson. "What do you mean by America?"

* * *

Paul Westman says that the greatest book of all time is not Don Quixote (as consensus has it), but Ecclesiastes. "I credit King Solomon, son of King David and the author of Ecclesiastes, as having produced the truest quotation of the ages, which is – 'There is nothing new under the sun.' Listen, I have gone through every page of the archives around here, going back 10, 20, 30, 40, 50, 60, 70, 80 years, and it's all the same, the same then as it is today."

My man Paul has also read practically every book under the sun, and still nothing has changed.

Take Judah Halevi of the 11th century and from his book, *The Kuzari*, there is this, in poetic form, about an ongoing conflict: "Between the armies of Seir and Kedar (Christian and Muslim), my army is lost. Whenever they fight their fight, it is we who fall, and thus it has been in former times in Israel." Indeed, that passage from some 900 years ago, of Islam in strife against the West, could serve as a headline and stop the presses today.

I stop by Paul's desk every now and then to take a breather. He is my oracle, my wise man, my reminder of a time that existed before my time, the age of Hemingway and Kerouac and Bukowski, and he knew them, knew Kerouac and Bukowski, not Hemingway, and how odd that on most lists that number the greatest novels of the 20th century, Hemingway is absent. Paul Westman – what a waste to have him writing headlines after such a life, a life of poetry and fiction, and now here he is, washed up, but still thinking. But what a waste.

"So why do we go on?" I say.

"Hell if I know."

"But there must be a purpose."

"We just don't know what it is," says Paul. "That in itself is mystical."

"You're mystical, Paul?"

"I believe we have a soul and that later there is a better place."

"Never thought of you as religious."

"A poet must be religious. Poetry is about something higher, about faith, about trust that someone is listening and if it is not your fellow man, it must be God."

Poetry, he says, is prayer.

"Harold Bloom suggests that three books of the Bible may have been written by Bathsheba – Genesis, Exodus, Numbers."

"That's ridiculous," says Paul. "She knew more, than, than all the Greeks? Not Homer, not Socrates, not Plato, not Aristotle ever came up with a single notion to match the Ten Commandments, not even a Day of Rest, a Sabbath, such a revolutionary concept that we now take for granted, as if it were always so. No it wasn't. Bathsheba came up with this? Harold Bloom should stick to Shakespeare, a plagiarist."

"Shakespeare a plagiarist?"

"Nothing new under the sun, my boy."

* * *

First, she made us do a stop at MoMa (Museum of Modern Art) to get me civilized and after that, getting all civilized, we walked across the street to the Warwick Hotel for drinks at Randolph's Bar, and here, past the first wine, I asked Lyla what that was all about, back at the staff meeting when she rose up against me, and, smiling, wickedly, she said, "I am not an appendage, Jay. I am a total person. That means contradictions. Hasten, please, to Walt Whitman."

"I know what he said."

"I thought you don't DO poetry."

"I'm big on Allen Ginsberg. HOWL."

"Well, well. I am proud of you. So, about Walt Whitman."

I gave her the quote – "Do I contradict myself? Very well I contradict myself. I am large. I contain multitudes."

She leaned over and planted me a kiss. "Besides," she said, "we mustn't be too obvious. I was trying to deflect. People are watching."

"But did you really think I was being perfidious?"

"Well, yes."

"I really am having a bad year with women."

"No you're not. You've got me."

"That is a problem, not a solution."

The waiter came over to ask if we wanted seconds and Lyla declined and I took that to be a signal.

"Jay, people are watching us."

"Where?"

"Everywhere. The newsroom is on to us. Maybe that's why my migraines are coming back."

"Something I don't know?"

Yes there was. Her Muslim husband, Phil, wants her to quit her job.

"Quit?"

"As editor of the book reviews. There are no books besides the Koran."

"Oh hell."

"His exact words."

"So?"

"I don't know. When does the violence begin?"

"Lyla, I'll do what I can to send him off as soon as possible."

(That, too, must not be too obvious.)

"Back to our plan?"

"We were never off the plan," I said.

"I thought that incident in Newark had scared you off. It did me, for a while."

"Likewise. But now I'm okay."

"Please, Jay, do something." She reached over for my hand and squeezed till it hurt, though her more than me.

At the table next to us a couple in the bloom of romance was laughing the happy laugh of carefree lovers.

"That's not us," Lyla said.

"Sometimes."

"We're like hostages. Love does this?"

She excused herself to go to the bathroom. I waited. As I waited I thought of her predicament and this was some fix she was in.

No books except the Koran.

Well, well, well.

It has come to this.

The Sharia (Islamic law) has begun. How do you spell Shariah? The Times uses the h at the end. We don't. We have our own Style. However you spell it, here it is. Can I bring myself to do this, really do this thing? The law would favor Phil Crawford – or rather, his kin, his survivors, his mourners. If the newsroom is on to us, as she alleges (and as I've noticed) then it would be deemed murder, even if not by my hand, but something like a contract, sending him off to a place from where he'd surely never come back, or maybe not so sure, but likely. Hamas is Murder Incorporated of the Middle East. They may buy his conversion to the Koran – but he is still an American. What is an American? Oh, please, not that again.

Americans go by many names, including Mohammed. That's okay. We are large. We contain multitudes.

There ought to be enough room for everybody.

If only it were that simple.

It is not that simple for Lyla, or for me.

She was taking her time in there, in the bathroom, and I was beginning to worry. Well, women do sometimes take all that time.

We don't know what they do. We still do not know what they want.

"Why," she asked when she came out, but not sitting back down – "why do we seldom marry the person we really love. We usually marry someone else."

"You look pale."

"Please take me to the hospital."

She'd been throwing up in the bathroom – the migraines. I know how it is once they go on the attack.

In the cab to St. Vincent's Hospital she said she knew when it was time to go, when even those Fiorinal pills won't do the trick. The Emergency room was packed, busy as always, though not busy enough when the Twin Towers fell, as there were so few survivors, and after checking her in, we waited. "I am not quitting my job," she said. "I refuse to be afraid of him. I'm counting on you, Jay. Be my hero. Oh, I'm babbling."

"We'll be okay."

"I feel like I'm going to throw up again."

She rushed for the bathroom, here at the hospital, and when she came back her beautiful face was drained of its glory. Her hands were ice cold.

"Stay with me."

"I'm here," I said.

"I'm frightened."

"Come on."

"You're my hero, Jay."

Something else was troubling her. The school system was out to ban Mark Twain for the language (the N word), plus Hemingway and a dozen others who wrote about their place and their time – the truth of how it was, political correctness versus literature. At risk – the storehouse of our historical treasures and literary heritage. "Censorship," Lyla said. "Imagine, back to this, book banning, book burning. Will we ever learn?" Lyla was on some committee to ban the ban. She was hot on this as, to her, it reflected a big step back into the dark ages, and this day, on this day, she was supposed to present a petition to the Mayor.

"Not in this condition," she said.

What amazed her – her friends, her literary friends, some favored the ban. In other words, they favored political correctness above truth.

I walked over to the Receptionist's desk and asked how much longer since this IS an emergency.

"When there's an opening."

Lyla asked what she said.

"When there's an opening."

"Shouldn't you tell them who you are, Jay? You're one of the most powerful men in New York."

"In a few minutes. Hang in."

"Jay?"

"What?"

"We're good people, aren't we?"

"Of course."

"I read where ninety reporters have been killed covering Iraq."

"So?"

"So what's one more? Wait. This came out wrong. I don't want him to PERISH. We don't need THAT upon our heads. Can't you make him just vanish – vamoose?"

"Do you really believe he has the power to curse?"

"I never believed that before. Now I do. What do you call this?"

Just then her name was announced and a nurse came out to bring her in. An hour later she was back, happy.

Happy?

"I'm pregnant," she said.

Chapter 27

Well, millions of women get pregnant every day; that is pretty much how the world turns. So I was not going to worry about this. It would take a while until she began showing and then, of course, we'd have to make decisions of the variety does she live or does she die, if Phil, her (Muslim) husband finds out – finds out, that is, that the child is not his but mine. So I am in this, too, of course, very much so, entirely so, and soon he may have to go, yes, go, to a place like Gaza, never to return, if it can be worked out. That is the plan.

Another plan, for the time being at least, is to have her – well no, hell no, that was her reaction when I mentioned it, that she ought to relent, just once, so that he can claim the birth. Never, she said. She would never permit that monster, yes monster she said, to penetrate her ever again, and again her word, penetrate. Even if her life depended on it (which may well be the case) this, she said, will not happen. There is no love between them anymore, since he turned Muslim and began to enforce Sharia rules, turning himself into an altogether different human being, so, no love, no sex. (No love on her side, though who knows what he's thinking.)

No, sex with Phil would be rape, as before, when she finally put a stop to the business. (How long will he let this go on?)

Meanwhile, Phil was on assignment to find The Mood On Campus, which put him on the road and kept him off Lyla's back figuratively and even literally (for the time being). I'd expected him to follow up on Tom Wolfe's I AM

CHARLOTTE SIMMONS but Phil Crawford was no Tom Wolfe. I was hoping for more on the sex and beer angle, rapists on the prowl, especially after that lacrosse scandal at Duke, but Phil's approach was virtually all political and happily (reading between his lines) slanted left.

Over at Brandeis U, which had been founded in the name of Justice Louis Brandies, a Zionist, the switch to Jihad U was near complete. Wahhabi academics were being brought in as lecturers. Playwright Tony Kushner (of MUNICH fame) was being awarded an honorary doctorate, whereas in an earlier generation the same Tony Kushner ("It would have been better if Israel never happened") would have been writing approved copy for Nazi Propaganda Minister Joseph Goebbels ("The Jews are our misfortune") when not busy turning out commentary for Julius Streicher's Der Sturmer.

But as for indoctrinating Lyla into his newly-adopted Islam, Phil Crawford was no fool. He knew he could not do it all at once, if he still wanted to keep her, so he'd do it by increments. Yes, he wanted her to quit as editor of our book review section as any book outside the Koran was blasphemous. He was insistent on this, but not quite insisting. Not yet. He'd give her time. How much time? This we do not know. I don't know and Lyla doesn't know. Only Phil knows, and maybe he doesn't know it either, if he is (as is easy to suspect) under the spell of some imam or mullah. They give the orders.

* * *

This morning, fresh and cool and dappled out like Spring itself, Lyla was in my office to discuss her upcoming interview with French philosopher heartthrob Bernard-Henri Lévy, known in France merely as BHL, being so famous over there, and now trying to duplicate his fame over here with a new book AMERICAN VERTIGO. He'd already been on C-Span and exchanged quips with Jon Stewart, and, like so many women, Lyla wanted him, too.

"Of course I have a crush on him," Lyla conceded.

She wondered – her skirt riding up and me reflecting how do they do this and do they measure how much they like you by the inch, I mean how many inches they let their skirt ride up? – so she wondered why I was not more like him, more like Bernard-Henri Lévy, who was so public and outgoing, and me, so private, nearly a recluse. I run this big Manhattan newspaper but am never on TV, never with Imus or O'Reilly or Hannity or Kati or Matt or Diane, always cloistered here in the newsroom or at the racetrack, when the world out there NEEDS ME to do some stand-up wisdom.

Just the other week, though, the host of some radio station here in Manhattan asked me a few brief questions and since I couldn't run from the microphone fast enough I was compelled to answer. The question came in two parts, first, was the Manhattan Independent really a Right Wing newspaper, to which I said no, the Manhattan Independent is a newspaper, period, and if we appear to be Right Wing it is because we give the Right Wing a voice, equal to the Left Wing, which I guess makes us Right Wing, like Fox. It appears, I said, that giving conservatives equal space and symmetrical coverage is considered unfair and biased. I guess, then, we are Right Wing.

Naturally, there is no Middle Wing, except for 250 Million Americans who reside in the fly-over states between the Left and the Right. These people in the middle never have a voice except when it comes time to vote, and even then they do not have much to say as the only choice is between the Left and the Right. These people who live between Washington, D.C. and Los Angeles all live in Cincinnati, or that is how I have it figured, as Cincinnati so typifies the America that never (or so rarely) makes the news. These people just work, play, pray, raise children. I lived in Cincinnati for a time so I know what I'm talking about. I lived there, in Cincinnati, when I was in exile from newspapering. I worked for a Carpet Company, yes

I did. That really was exile – until Ben Hawkins saved me and brought me back to life.

The next question from this radio interviewer was this: Do I believe in God.

Do I believe in a personal God? Depends, I said, in what kind of day I am having at the racetrack. When I win, yes. When I lose, no.

(On July 20, 1944, Hitler's own generals put in motion their plan to assassinate Hitler. This took place at a meeting of the high command at Wolfsschanze – Wolf's Lair – where Hitler was going over maps and documents related to Germany's invasion of Russia. The plot to do in the fuehrer was initiated by officers of the Wehrmacht, led by Oberst (Colonel) Claus van Stauffenberg, heir to an aristocratic lineage. At this conference, Stauffenberg sat to the right of Hitler and placed the suitcase containing the bomb next to Hitler's legs. Stauffenberg then left the building and waited for the explosion, which came moments later. Four officers were killed, hundreds injured, and except for some shrapnel, Hitler slipped unscathed. Hitler survived to murder millions more and considered his near-death experience a miracle – divine intervention.)

"Of course," Lyla said, "I've got a much bigger crush on you. You're much better looking and far more sexy."

Then that smile, oh that smile, and another inch upwards.

"Trouble is," she says, "you're not French."

"Trouble is," I say, "he is French."

She laughs.

I get up and tell her I've really got to get going. Important meeting.

True, I have a meeting set up with Sam Cleaver. I'd been putting him off for that "long talk," but now, it's time. Sam is desperate.

I am worried about Sam. He is the best we've got. He is that young idealist I used to be – and look what happened to me. I don't know what happened to me. Maybe it is good what happened, maybe it is bad. I do know that all the idealism I started off with, well, that's shot. Must not let that happen to swashbuckling Sam. Or maybe that is how it is with all of us, merely the consequence of growing older – or just growing up. We begin to comprehend and make peace with our limitations and the limitations of those around us. In a nutshell, we quit dreaming.

I think Sam is right on the border with this and wants to make it stop. He wants to dream on, but something is happening.

Lyla says, "Okay, you were on the radio. Huh! You should be all over TV. You're so handsome!"

"Give Mr. Bernard-Henri Lévy my regards."

"Well, do you? Do you believe in God? Bernard-Henri Lévy doesn't. He's an atheist."

This much I know about BHL. He is a multi-millionaire; inherited a fortune, owns palaces.

"Lyla," I say, "he can afford to be an atheist. I can't."

* * *

True, Lyla has a meeting and I have a meeting but something is happening. Something always happens when we're together, even for a second. There's that look she gets and her voice goes soft, whispery, her features turn to shades of crimson. "My meeting can wait," she says. "Can yours?" Actually it can't. I've got horses picked out. But I also have Lyla picked out, don't I? So, taking separate paths, we head for the Archive room, which, far in a darkened corner, is becoming more and more our Slam Bam Thank You Ma'am room. Lyla doesn't mind – when she gets horny like this.

In fact, she likes it better without the foreplay, sometimes.

So we meet back there and, breathing heavily, she says, "Be imaginative." I lift up her skirt, pull down her panties, turn her around, and it's show time.

Back in my office she is already on the phone from her office. "That was powerful," she says. "How about you?"

"What do you think?"

"I don't have a crush on that Frenchman anymore," she says. "There's only you, Jay. Only you."

* * *

Minerva Watson stops me to say there's a surprise party for me getting started in the conference room. Seems I had won some journalism award from some group for something I did. I tell Minerva I have other plans and besides, I don't do celebrations.

* * *

"Oh come on," she says. "You have to." I reiterated that I do not do celebrations. I don't celebrate anything, not birthdays, weddings, anniversaries, awards, retirements, holidays and not even weekends and not even New Year's – what are people so happy about? Another year? This is good? Minerva says winning this award is good not just for me but also for the paper. I must attend. Yes, this is good.

Well, I explain, when something good happens something bad happens right away later so what the hell!

"How awful!" she says, turning.

No wonder I love the horses.

Chapter 28

Over here, upstairs at Bally's in the racing parlor, where 100 monitors, row by row, telecast the races live from a dozen tracks across the country, and where you can place your bets by machines or by going up to the windows, Sam Cleaver and I were tucked in side-by-side making our selections (at least I was), mostly at Belmont, and I was having a pretty good day at the races. Sam was not having a good day all around. "I'm done," he said.

"So go down and play some machines," I said.

"I mean I'm done, Jay."

"Stop this, Sammy."

"I'm done with newspapering, Jay."

"To do what?"

"Write."

"That's what you've been doing."

"You know what I'm talking about."

Of course I did.

He wanted the fanaticism of Salinger, of Flaubert, of Proust, of Hemingway, in their devotion to the purity of the novel. He held no admiration for The Renaissance Man, a man who could invent the wheel and chew gum at the same time. No, Sammy reserved his esteem for people who were skilled and relentless over one task alone, like Ted Williams at the plate, like Bobby Fischer in chess, like Paul Erdős in mathematics, like any thoroughbred who was bred and schooled for a single duty, obsessive and ruthless.

"That's what I'm after," Sammy said.

"Purity."

"That's right. The rest is horseshit."

"Newspapering is horseshit," I said. "Huh?"

"You know what I'm talking about, Jay. You know what I know. You see what I see."

"But you can't just quit."

Newspaper writing corrupts, said Sam, and that is true, if that is all you write and read as meanwhile you pursue the ART of the NOVEL. Hemingway (Sam reminds me) started off as a newspaper reporter and then went on to say that newspaper reporting "blunts the instrument" for true writing, the writing of fiction. "Who said that?" I ask Sammy. "Hemingway." I shake my head. "See, he was right. Never heard of the guy."

"I'm not kidding, Jay."

No he wasn't.

Sam does not appreciate horseracing, hasn't a clue what the fuss is all about, and sits here, without a racing paper, glum, watching the horses go by blur after blur. The Racing Form is my second bible. I am hot for every race, a student of every horse. I keep on betting and Sam keeps moping. There is no integrity in journalism, he says. It is all bogus. Why? Because the world is bogus and we do the stenography. Only in fiction is there truth.

I agree. I tried it myself when I was young, his age, and am still only about ten years older than Sam, maybe 15 years older, and wiser. Wisdom sets in when you find that the only pleasure in true writing is the writing itself. The rest is horseshit. Sam keeps finding that out, that, in fiction, you must write only for yourself. Nobody is out there waiting except to break your heart.

"That won't stop me," says Sam.

Good. Nothing stops a real novelist, and the novel Sammy's got going is real, the one about the Holocaust and all those Jewish lives that were lost at our expense. Cures for cancer and a hundred other diseases went up in the chimneys of Auschwitz, and we were silent, and silent again when the ship St. Louis came around and got turned back. Sam's focus is on the St. Louis and on a scientist patterned after Hermann Strauss, a beloved teacher at Berlin University, and a world-class researcher who, on the verge of the big breakthrough for cancer, was tortured at Theresienstadt and took his own life en route to Auschwitz.

"Nobody cares about that anymore, Sammy."

"That is the cynicism I'm talking about," said Sam.

"You're not even Jewish."

"Jesus was Jewish. That's good enough for me."

"The Holocaust has been trivialized, the word itself."

"So maybe it's my task to bring it back in style. Maybe that's my purpose. Maybe that's why I'm here – and I don't mean the races."

Sam (for his novel) was particularly fascinated in the true story of Talmudic giant Rabbi Eliezer Silver who, at the outset of the Holocaust, was not silent but founded Vaad Hatzalah, an international rescue committee, and at Silver's urging some 300 rabbis from around the world, back in 1943, marched to the White House in an effort to get FDR to save the Jews, but FDR was out on more important business. Silver (as Sam keeps learning from his research) traveled throughout Europe to personally save as many sons and daughters of Jacob as he could. He could not be stopped even in churches and nunneries and orphanages and relocation camps where he was told to move on as there were no Jewish children kept here, to which Silver loudly sang out the Sh'ma (Judaism's signature liturgy – Hear O Israel, The Lord Is Our God, The Lord Is One) and suddenly a hundred voices sang up and joined him word for word in the Hebrew. Sh'ma Yisrael Adonday Eloheinu Adonay Echad.

"I can't get past this story," said Sam. "This is my story. This is my novel. I can't stop."

193

Rabbi Silver did his traveling, on ships, trains, planes, jeeps, all in the uniform of his son, Nathan, cardiologist, medic and captain in Patton's Third Army. As Dr. Nathan saved thousands of fellow American soldiers on the field of battle, in his role as physician, his father, the rabbi, is credited with saving more than 10,000 Jews, mostly children.

Meantime, seems that I have just won the late Daily Double at Belmont. I cannot share this with Sam. Sam is in another place.

He shows me this, a printout from some website carrying the words of J. D. Salinger:

"An artist's only concern is to shoot for some kind of perfection, and on his own terms, not anyone else's."

I am not indifferent to Sam. I just don't want him to quit. He has indeed been getting cynical and bitter and this cannot be helped when faced with the same news, the same realities, day after day. He has joined this heartbreak hotel and wants out. Why, for instance, are we just now paying attention to the genocide in Darfur? Perhaps it's because our attention has been wickedly focused on Israel, and perhaps that is as much our fault at the Manhattan Independent as it is the fault of The New York Times.

"I'm not trying to save the world," says Sam, "if that's what you're thinking. I'm only trying to save myself."

"That's why I go to the races, Sam."

"You've got your tricks, then, and I've got mine."

For some reason I'm remembering Walter Blum, now a retired steward but once a first-rate jockey, in fact the best gate-man in the business – he'd burst from the gate as though he were on fire – and then the interview when I was just starting out, as a racing writer, and Blum asking me what I wanted. I wanted him to take me through a race paragraph by paragraph. Blum says: "What is a paragraph?" I'm thinking, this man can't be that stupid. Then he agrees to take me through a race furlong by furlong and I say, "What is a furlong?" He must be thinking, this man can't be that stupid.

I tell this story to Sam, maybe he can use it in his novel, but Sam is not amused.

"I'm quitting," he says.

"Why?" I say. "Tell me again."

"I just don't feel like going on."

He is blank to the cavalcade of jockeys in their colorful silks astride the shoulders of locomotive thoroughbreds.

He hears no bugler and sees no drama in the rush of four-legged athletes bursting around the final pole in their head-long dash to the finish.

"Can't take the heat?"

"Have it your way."

"They got to you, huh?"

"You mean that Beth Sinai business? Maybe. But it's all the rest, too. I mean, what's the use?"

"Of what?"

"Of trying. Nothing changes, Jay. Nothing changes."

That is so true. Nothing changes.

"Why not just take a leave of absence," I say. "Take a sabbatical."

"That would only be shortchanging you and the paper. I have no desire to return. I need a clean break."

Newsmen do not talk like this, so defeated.

That's what journalists have in common with trainers. Always tomorrow, another story to cover, another horse to run.

"Sammy. You didn't know there's all that strife out there in the big world?"

"But it's all crap. None of it counts. None of it means any-thing. It just keeps going round and round, the same people, the same frauds, the same things."

"Consider that an education – but no reason to quit."

"But what's the use? You tell me, what's the use?"

"Somebody has to tell the people what's going on."

195

"I'm supposed to report what I think," Sam says. "You made me a columnist, remember? And if I really wrote what I really thought, Jay, it would not be fit to print."

"Give it a try."

"Not in a newspaper."

He is right. There are rules. No such rules for a novel. There the writer is free, unshackled. He may not get it published, but he gets it done if only for himself. If there is hypocrisy in our business, the newspaper business, there is equal hypocrisy in every other business. The pity of it, for Sam Cleaver, is that right now he belongs. He is part of our club and our club is quite exclusive. Not everybody can get in. Thousands come to us swarming fresh from journalism schools fit and ready to CHANGE THE WORLD. But few make the grade. Sam made it and even made a name for himself. As a novelist he'd be starting from scratch. That too is a club. Who does he know that can get him in? What are his connections? Does he truly believe that good writing is the ticket? Yes he does, but he is wrong. There is plenty bad writing getting published and plenty bad writers selling big. But you have to know somebody and it sure helps if you've got your own show on TV where you can promote your own book, even if your own book was mostly written by someone else, ghosted. That's one trick and there are many others but the one trick that is most unreliable is good writing, which means nothing.

This Natricia DeFarr turned him down despite his good writing as did a dozen other publishers on the same novel that Sammy keeps writing and re-writing in pursuit of Salinger's "perfection." (If Lyla really does get that interview with Salinger – huh! – maybe Sammy will hear it directly from the writer's mouth.) There was a man who once wrote a book about chief terrorist and video star Osama bin Laden, and this book did poorly, when suddenly, in one of his videos, Osama mentions this book, and zoom, the book tops the bestseller lists. That is luck.

Luck is everything, and maybe Sam Cleaver will be lucky.

"The human condition sucks," Sam says, "and if I do not write what I think, then what am I? I am a fraud. So there is no choice but to quit."

He has a point. The kid has a point.

"Do you," he goes on, "ever write what you think? I mean what you really think?"

As managing editor, I do write a regular column, under my own byline, and certainly I write a great number of editorials.

This is something to seriously ponder. Do I ever write what I really think? Terrific question.

"I've seen you waffle."

"What do you mean?"

"The truth?"

"Isn't this what this is all about?"

"You're sure, because this may get personal."

"I am holding my breath, Sam."

"Okay, here goes. I'm afraid I might end up like you."

"Wow!"

"Please, don't be mad."

"I'm not, but I do need an explanation."

"Over there at Beth Sinai, you took the middle road, and even in your columns and even in your editorials you're always taking the middle road. How can you call that truth?"

"Truth is not my business. Facts are my business."

"Bullshit, Jay. You're afraid to stand up and announce yourself."

"No, I am adhering to a newsman's credo. Give the facts."

"You call that writing?"

"No, I call that journalism."

"I call it being chickenshit, Jay."

"Okay."

"I think this impartiality of yours even translates into your personal life."

"How do you know about my personal life?"

"I don't know much, but you have a tendency to – okay, to equivocate. That's not what I call living. That's not what I call writing, and that's not what I want."

"Maybe you're right."

"Maybe I'm wrong. Sorry. It's just that I'm so fed up. It's all bullshit. People are bullshit. Everybody."

"That's still no reason to quit. Give it another chance. We need you, okay? I've said it, Sam. The Manhattan Independent needs you."

"Won't work."

"Why?"

"Because I don't care. I don't care, Jay. I don't care anymore."

So, I figured, I've lost Sam. What a waste!

One last try.

"Take two weeks off, paid, write your heart out, and then we'll talk again. Okay?"

Only when the limo dropped us off back in Manhattan did Sammy consent.

"Okay," he said.

* * *

When I got back there was trouble. There's always trouble when you leave and come back. Frank Fitzpatrick, City Desk, came in and showed me an obit of someone who was still alive. Fortunately it got caught in time, but someone had written this obit, and then another, and even a third and a fourth on our computer system, apparently as a joke, a hoax, or as a means to wax revenge, really, quite a clever way to kill, that is, kill people still very much alive. Was it someone in the building, even a staffer, or someone outside the building hacking in?

We could get sued something awful if any of these "obits" get in.

"I'm worried," said Frank.

So was I, and I wasn't sure what worried me more, inside or outside. If inside, who could it be? If outside, could be anybody.

"Obviously," I said, "from now on every obit gets triple checked. Don't need this."

Something else I did not need was a visit from our chief of Security, Elias Francone, who shut the door behind him.

Was I aware, he asked, that since 9/11 every inch of this building is monitored?

"Of course," I said.

"Every room," he said, "has cameras."

"Yes. So?"

"Even Archives," he said. "Even the Archive room."

Oh hell! That's where Lyla and I –

Elias placed a cassette gently on my desk. "Please," he said, "be more careful. Much more careful."

"How far did this go?"

"Just heed my word, Jay. Take very good care."

Chapter 29

Gaza was in the throes of ochlocracy, mob rule, civil war approaching among the Palestinian Arabs, so there was no choice but to send one of our people to cover the story before it simmered down. We don't like it when things simmer down. Then there's nothing to report, except for the sweepings, and we may as well pack in our credentials as journalists. No, we need the action and we need to be there when it's happening.

Of course, Phil Crawford was the man. Yes, I'd made up my mind, finally. I already had the memo out to Ben Hawkins, publisher, Ken Ballard, executive editor, and Stu Greenwald, foreign desk. Technically, I did not need their permission. But it would help in case something happened to Phil and word got back that I'd had a secondary, or perhaps even a primary, motive – for example, Lyla. Phil wanted to go, and I sure wanted to send him, anywhere, fast, before a whisper got to him about that "home movie." I still did not know who saw that tape. Maybe no one saw it except for security chief Elias Francone, and, of all people, cartoonist Peter Brand. (That would be curtains.)

I hadn't seen it myself, that tape. I had it hidden in a drawer. For sure it was porn, a Jay Garfield-Lyla Crawford production, filmed right here in the Manhattan Independent's archives department. No, I couldn't bring myself to watch this. I did not even tell Lyla. I needed to sweat this out myself. Lyla did ask, in passing, why Elias was being so friendly to her all of a sudden when, ordinarily, he was quite rude, to everybody. I shrugged it off as par for my gender. Letches are us.

So – that was my decision, or maybe it wasn't. Things just happen. You think you're in charge, but no, things just happen. We float along. Our destinies are out there some place and we're just keeping appointments. Phil was being dispatched among the feuding Palestinian Arabs, his friends, really. His papers were in order, all of that done during that practice run in Newark. All that remained was to tell him. So I told him. I said, "Phil, when I get back, we'll talk."

He knew what it was about, and quite thrilled. This would be his first shot as a combat reporter, and perhaps, a Pulitzer.

Better yet, he would be a hero to Lyla.

Islam, Phil's new religion, wasn't working for Lyla. He kept trying to convert her but it just wasn't working and got worse when he tried the strong-arm approach, as when he insisted that a wife is "property." Yes, property. That's how it is. "Over my dead body," was Lyla's response and Phil's response to that was quite menacing. He just stared at her, hot in the eyes, as if to be saying – it may come to that after all.

Now – if he returned as a hero, maybe she'd learn to love him and love Islam. If he returned not at all, of course, that's the plan. That was our plan. I like to think otherwise, that this is entirely legit. We need that coverage out there in the Middle East and Phil Crawford deserves this chance to be the next Homer Bigart or even Edward R. Morrow. Good night and good luck. So, really, I was doing him a favor.

I did not believe this for a minute.

"Why wait?" said Phil, by phone. "Why can't we talk now?"

"I'm off," I said.

"Where?"

* * *

Yup, off to the races again. Not my fault. Blame Jimmy Smokes. "Oh come on," he said. "Barbaro can be the next Triple Crown winner."

This colt, Barbaro, had won the Kentucky Derby two weeks earlier, and won it spectacularly. Next up, the Preakness in Maryland, and following that, the Belmont in New York. Affirmed had been the last champion to sweep all three, our last Triple Crown winner, and that was back in 1978. That's how long it's been, and now, perhaps, the wait was over, so here we were to witness it all firsthand. Jimmy Smokes said that this was business, on my part, not pleasure, so I shouldn't feel guilty and view this as another goof-off day at the track. This was history if all went well, and I had a duty, yes a duty, to be here in Maryland my Maryland. Okay, I'm easy.

For some reason, I wasn't my usual giddy self upon the approach of a big day at the races. Usually I'm brimming with anticipation. What could it be? Well, it could be my former wife Myrna slapping me with a restraining order, or something like that, against having access to my son, my only son, the son that I love, for bringing him home that one day with some blood on his nose from a sparring session at Pat's Gym. He was fighting a kid his own size and his own age, but it did not go according to plan, not my plan.

No damage was done, except for that bloody nose, but that was enough for Myrna. So now I was off-limits (court order) for three months.

I told Pat about it a week later and Pat shook his head and said, "Women." Pat was a grizzled old-timer but before he was grizzled and old he was a boxer, a near champ. He started the gym some 40 years ago, back when boxing was mostly Italian, Irish and Jewish and blacks had to fight two opponents, the other guy and bigotry. Pat knew them all, including Floyd Patterson who'd just died. Pat had never been married and Pat never left the gym. He slept here, too. Still, to this day, he'd never allow a woman in or near the ring. That Clint Eastwood movie about a woman boxer, *Million Dollar Baby*, was sacrilege.

"Where's your son?" he asked the day I arrived without my son.

"Home," I said, and then explained.

"Over a bloody nose?" he said. "That's a badge of honor."

"Tell her, not me."

That's when he said, "Women." He couldn't figure them out, which made him a member of a very big fan club.

What else was on my mind? That son of a bitch Kevin Rod Rodgers, the anchorman who was still after my scalp, was going ahead with a suit before an arbitration panel made up of fellow journalists, something like a tribunal, all because I'd socked him when he hit a woman after she called him an anti-Semite. Now, finally, I knew who had the film proving me in the right, Waji Halid, but Waji, or Wayne as he now referred to himself, had to keep it under wraps for fear of his job as a photojournalist, or maybe even for fear of his life.

Wayne had those extra 18 seconds of tape that Kevin Rod Rodgers refused to air (before 40 million viewers), film that would exonerate me, and that's the proof of how news is manipulated. It's personal, sure, but it's also universal, and so flammable. French television had summoned the world's outrage against Israel by filming a shoot-out that pinned the blame on Israel for the killing of 12-year-old Mohammed al-Dura.

The film showed the boy – all this at the Netzarim Junction in Gaza – ducking into his father's arms for safety, but to no avail. This imagery made the news for days, weeks, months, years, and sparked the intifada, a five year war against Israel, supported by most of the world, certainly most of the press. Two details, however, never made the news, except here and there, and in small print; first, given the positions of both forces, the Israelis here, the Arabs there, the boy, according to all scientific evidence, could only have been hit by Arab gunfire.

Germany's main public-TV network, ARD, had found five minutes of missing footage to make that case, or even to prove that the entire incident had been staged, and was offering to show those five minutes to anyone in the press who would buy – but nobody was buying, and so it goes. The blood libel persists. Not a single network or newspaper was willing to recant, to show what really happened, except for the Atlantic Monthly, which cracked the case.

Even here at the Manhattan Independent, well, we were slow ourselves to disprove the fabrication. We ran that incendiary photo over and over again along with everyone else. Ben Hawkins, in a momentary reversal of personality, wanted to wait until all the evidence was in, fearful of having us painted as instinctively pro-Israel. Finally, we headlined the truth. But it made no difference as people believe what they want to believe and it is far more convenient to hate than to love. So that's how it goes all right, half the news that's fit to print or broadcast, and it can hit me, you, anybody, everybody. Or, as Ronald Reagan's secretary of labor Ray Donovan put it after he was cleared from accusations of misdeeds in office, but following months of brutal character assassination in the press: "Where do I go to get my good name back?"

I guess that puts me in the same boat and I guess I could go after Rodgers for slander but without those 18 seconds they keep hiding from the public I've got nothing, except my word against his, and why bother anyway. I haven't the time or the inclination to bother with lawsuits. His word, that is, his voice is much louder than mine. From his perch he reaches some 40 million and big as we are, we can't compete with network television.

* * *

We were outside, taking up seats in the clubhouse section at Pimlico, and Jimmy Smokes turned and said, "You're not really here, are you?"

"I'm thinking."

"But not about the horses."

"I'll come around."

The card was already up to the sixth race. The 12th race was the big one, the Preakness. The crowd on hand was numbered at close to 150,000. NBC was running the telecast but there was coverage here from all over the country and all over the world and it was mostly about Barbaro. This could be the one. Except for the bluebloods and the rest of us who care for the sport day after day, most of America's eyes are turned elsewhere, except for the Triple Crown races, thoroughbred racing's High Holy Days. This is when America becomes a family. We do have a common culture and every so often (usually a sporting event) we collect ourselves in front of the national fireplace, television.

"What's the problem, Jay? Talk to me."

Hell, I told him. I told him about that cassette that caught us making love in the archive room.

"Oh, shit," said Jimmy Smokes, language he never used, being a true Muslim.

"Exactly."

"How could you be so stupid?"

"Thanks, Jimmy."

"Don't you know we're being watched – all of us?"

I didn't want to remind him how it started, all this surveillance, like 9/11, like Islam gone wild. No, that's not how it is between Jimmy and me.

Me, part Jewish, and Jimmy, fully Muslim, and yet he may be my best friend, along with Kuana Banks.

"Sorry to rub it in, Jay. But that was reckless."

"Now you tell me."

"Amazing."

"What?"

"Temptation," said Jimmy. "That's why we cover up our women."

"That's no answer. That only says that men have no control over their emotions. We fear our own impulses and blame women for our weakness. That's pathetic."

"Better we drop this."

"Right."

Naturally, we had seats reserved for us up in the press box, but we were happier out here with the people and the horses, in the arena of all this excitement. Jimmy was Lebanese. He and his family escaped Beirut when Beirut was in chaos, and there, in Manhattan, he'd raised his own family, married well, did well in that news shop that he ran, or rather the news shop that his wife ran since Jimmy was mostly at the track. He was a happy man, fully American, though when 9/11 happened he ran to me with the lament that all those people, the hijackers, were his twins. Would he always be stereotyped? I assured him that Americans keep no grudges. There were no riots or burning of mosques even when Sirhan Sirhan murdered Bobby Kennedy. But still, even to this day, Jimmy spooked easily – and he feared mobs, like the mobs that had trampled Beirut. So he wasn't totally comfortable out here with the wall of sound after each race, even when he shared the winning ticket, as he did after the 10th race.

I had failed to scoop out the winner, but Jimmy Smokes had the winner alone, plus the exacta and the trifecta.

"*Allahu Akhbar,*" he said, or rather exclaimed.

Jimmy went to the windows to collect his bounty, and he'd be awhile since there'd be paperwork for the taxes, as that's the penalty for anything at or above $1,200 on a two dollar wager. I sat there without glancing at the racing paper and, suddenly, without enjoying the fanfare, the pageantry, the festivities, Jimmy came back and asked if I'd picked out any-thing for the next race and I said I'd get to the handicapping when I was ready.

"What's up?" he said.

I said nothing. I wouldn't know where to begin.

"What's up, Jay? Tell me."

I still said nothing.

"I guess I should explain," he said.

He explained that the expression Allahu Akhbar was common among his people and simply means God Is Great and it is even common among Christians and Jews. It was a mistake to utter those sacred words at the racetrack and for that he was sorry, not to me, but to Allah. It just came out, impulsively. He'd never done it before and he'd never do it again. But, Allahu Akhbar is simply a recognition that there is a god above. Okay?

It is also a common expression, I explained, when people strap themselves with explosives and run in to murder a class-room full of children.

Allahu Akhbar is what they say – and then there's blood.

From Ma'alot to 9/11 and points before, between and thereafter, that's what they say, and to the survivors it's not invocation but abomination.

"Jay, you know I can't apologize for this, but please, let this not come between us."

I left him there to make a bet, any bet, just to be doing something else. I just picked a number. My head was spinning.

"It's been corrupted," he said when I got back. "You know it's been corrupted and you know it's not me."

The race went off and I won, but I couldn't shake off the gloom. Jimmy smiled and patted me on the back.

"Snap out of it," he said. "Come on, Jay."

I thought of Arnold Coffey and the sister he had lost in Netanya all on account of that "expression" and all the rest of it together.

I thought of Lyla and what she was facing – a wife is property, a wife must be obedient. Allahu Akhbar. God Is Great.

Jimmy Smokes was to blame for none of this, except by association. Was I expecting him to pay for the sins of his brothers and sisters? We had made a deal, some time back, to never touch on politics or religion. We knew there'd be no end, and no friendship, once we got it started, so we let it go and preserved the deal by renouncing all the cultural garbage that occupied loftier minds. We were just two guys, two horseplay-ers, gamblers, New Yorkers.

"Are we okay?" he said.

The big race was coming up and the crowd thundered at the approach of Barbaro stepping gallantly from the tunnel and onto the track – as if forgetting that there were eight other horses along the parade passing the clubhouse and the grand-stand. With minutes to go before loading, jockey Edgar Prado jogged Barbaro lightly along the backstretch to limber him up and get him used to the footing.

Barbaro's record was 7 for 7; he had never been defeated, and that, of course, included the most prestigious race of them all, the Kentucky Derby. The loading at the starting gate went without incident. But a moment before the starter was to give the signal for the race to begin, one horse broke free prema-turely. That was Barbaro, and this was stunning. This colt was overanxious, raring to go, a good sign, or something was terribly wrong.

He had cantered only a few steps from the gate, so no real harm was done, except for doubt and concern among his connections and the millions who had given their hearts to this colt. The assistant starters led him back into his stall and all seemed well when the gates opened and nine strapping thor-oughbreds dashed hell-bent for the lead, Barbaro in contention but not among the leaders. Then something happened.

A furlong (220 yards) from the start jockey Edgar Prado pulled him up, stopped him as much as anyone weighing 120 pounds can stop a race horse weighing 1,200 pounds going full speed. Now the jubilant throngs grew hushed and fell to a roar of silence, as we watched this second-coming of Secretariat hobble on three legs – and intelligent enough to know that he must not step on his right hind leg, which had snapped. The leg had snapped and Barbaro was done. The van came instantly, and the van was soon covered with a tarp when Barbaro was coaxed in, crippled, but just as quickly the tarp was removed to keep the public from being horrified at the thought that Barbaro was being lethally injected, or put down as the saying goes in racing.

No, Barbaro would be saved, and perhaps live onward to produce a thousand foals.

I wrote up the story as a sidebar, right where I was sitting, and got it done in 14 minutes, and it kept me occupied, the writing, and even pleased me that I could still write on deadline, something I had not done in years. The writing, the business of it, kept me a safe distance from my emotions. Kuana Banks came over and we shook hands and then we hugged and this big Hawaiian, a trainer with his own stable of horses, wept without shame. He read my copy and said that this was correct. We weep for horses because they are surrogates of our innocence lost.

Chapter 30

Over at Pat's Gym of all people to walk in, why it's anchorman Kevin Rod Rodgers, here for a workout, with his bodyguards.

"It's a free country," he said after I asked him why this place of all places. I thought he had quit, following our public brawl.

Pat shrugged.

I had a three-round bout scheduled with a kid named Hector Pelez, but here was a better idea.

"Say," I said to Kevin Rod Rodgers, number one in the ratings. "How about you and me?"

"You and me what?"

"Gloving up."

"What would that prove?"

If he wins, well, I lose, and he continues to taunt me. If I win, he quits slandering me, threatening me with sanctions imposed by the journalistic community, and most of all, releases those 18 seconds of film that prove that my hitting him was justified in that I was protecting a woman from his goons and from himself. This woman, Marta Geller, had called him an anti-Semite right here outside Pat's Gym and one of his thugs, acting on his behalf, struck the lady, so I struck him right back, yes, Kevin Rod Rodgers. What was missing? Those 18 seconds of tape showing the attack against the lady. This tempest between us was getting so big that even our rival, the New York Post, was beginning to pick it up – Page Six. (Which always scooped our own BUZZ section.)

"Just you and me," I said to America's smoothest anchorman.

"That's silly," he said.

"You're probably right, but that's how it used to get done."

"I'm not a fighter."

That's true. His goons did his fighting for him.

"Only when it comes to women, right?"

His bodyguards quit grinning and began moving in.

Pat stepped up between us.

"All set?" he said.

As he walked me to the ring, where he'd be my corner-man, my second, he said, "Sorry."

"Not your fault, Pat."

He said something about never mixing print people with broadcast people. The two just don't mix. I said it was more than that. Pat was among the chosen few who did not know (or care) what was going on around the world outside the ring. Pat never read The New York Times or even my newspaper, the Manhattan Independent. Occasionally he read *The Ring Magazine*. Boxing people and racetrack people were about the same on this score.

They were blessed.

My sparring partner, Hector Pelez, was Mexican. Even with my headgear he began working my head and I rocked to every punch. He had a heavy hand, a boxer's hand. He had a future. I felt sorry for him. He wanted to let loose but he was a good kid and kept to his instructions about this being a light spar. But after he clocked me with a salvo of punches he looked scared, just as Joe Louis was once scared – scared that he had killed the other guy.

By round number two I had found some rhythm and got in some good combinations and even slipped him one to the chin when I glanced my right above his advancing left.

He backed off and nodded in a show of respect.

But by the end of the third and final round he had me

211

pretty much where he wanted. I was huffing and puffing. Still, I had done well. I was cut up, but I had done well.

I was alive and that's something. (Or maybe not.)

* * *

Later, I went on the prowl for the anchorman. I found him in the big gym. He was doing knee bends and then jumping jacks with a group of men and women, all of them in Spandex and bouncing around to the beat of some rap from 50 Cent. He saw me and kept on prancing. I showed him my fist, as we used to do in the schoolyard, which meant let's get ready to rumble. He saw me all right but turned his head. I stood there and watched, and wondered why I was so pissed. Besides me, who else was he slandering? What other 18 seconds were being omitted?

Possibly it was Mailer who said to get the truth you have to read between the lies. Actually it was Mailer quoting, of all people. Trotsky: "You can tell the truth by a comparison of the lies."

Sam Cleaver, and others, like Arnold Coffey, had wanted me to headline CNN's admitted complicity with terrorists but I played it on page eight.

Maybe I was trying to be a good guy, or maybe I was afraid that all of us in the media shared the same hypocrisy.

When Eason Jordan came clean and admitted (in an op-ed in The New York Times) that CNN had omitted newsworthy but damaging facts about the Arab world in order to keep its reporters safe and maintain its bureaus in Baghdad and other such places, maybe he was speaking for all of us. We all lied by the sins of commission and omission. Sometimes, to make a story fit, make it fit our agenda, our bias, we cut the part that tells the truth. All of us were guilty of deceit, corruption, perversity, manipulation.

If only I could knock all that out with one punch.

* * *

There at our favorite hangout, the bar at the Warwick, Randolph's, I told Lyla that I was shipping him out, Phil, her husband.

"That's settled," I said, "except for letting him know."

I thought she'd be thrilled.

She sipped her martini as if I hadn't said much of anything. She dabbed her lips and put on a fresh coat of lipstick. She had soft lips, curved delicately.

I knew she had other problems. Mark Twain and Ernest Hemingway were being neutered by the school system for being politically incorrect and a movement was going forward to have offending passages "corrected" and perhaps have Twain and Hemingway dropped from the curriculum altogether. Lyla had formed a committee to stop this but was up against some powerful forces. She was a powerful force herself. She had the Manhattan Independent (her weekly column) to wage her fight. I'd put my money on Lyla – or maybe not, given all the correcting being done in our culture so that soon enough we'd have no culture.

Maybe that's why my news wasn't so big.

She was wearing a beige outfit and a sweater that hinted at her nipples. Or maybe it was just me who took the hint.

No, Lyla was a stunner. Those eyes, sometimes green, sometimes blue, were always switched on for action.

"Does Ken Ballard ever say anything to you when you show up in the newsroom like this?" she asked – referring to my swollen lip.

"He just laughs."

"Should I have seen the other guy?"

"No, he was much younger, Mexican and a pro."

I asked her why she was changing the subject.

"Is this the right move?"

"Isn't this what you wanted, Lyla?"

"Is it?" she said.

"Oh come on."

She is pregnant (from me) and this we both know. We were caught flagrante delicto, and this only I know. Phil Crawford has to go.

"I'm just not comfortable with this, Jay, that's all."

"Cold feet?"

"I guess. Just tell me that you're sending him for the sake of journalism and I'll be happy."

"That's what I keep telling myself."

"So?"

"Yes, the story is out there and Phil is the right man."

"Could we live with the consequences if –"

"Oh stop this, Lyla. I've made the decision."

She smiled.

"I like it when you take charge."

"You're something."

"You're not doing this just for me, right?"

"I'm doing it to get a story and even a Pulitzer for Phil."

"Even if posthumously," she sighed and glanced about the room.

Oh, there was this. Seems there was some sort of school where newly-Islamed wives were taught obedience, how a woman of infidel lineage was to behave when she married into a Muslim household. Phil wanted her to take the course. This was after he'd had his imam over to the house and Lyla refused to cover herself up and remain silent and obedient. Phil was angry. He'd been mocked in the presence of his leader. She'd been impudent. Ordinarily, there was punishment for such disrespect toward a husband. But Phil was willing to let it slide – since she had not yet taken the course. Lyla now kept a knife in her purse.

"Can you get me a gun?" she asked.

Why hadn't she told me any of this before?

"I thought you'd stop loving me. I'm nothing but trouble."

"Your troubles are my troubles."

"I love you, Jay. Can you get me a gun?"

"That's a terrible literary transition, Lyla. You should know better."

"Okay, forget the I love you part. Can you get me a gun?"

"Don't be silly."

She wouldn't be needing it anyway. Phil was going and if God, not Allah, was on our side, he would not be coming back.

* * *

After her third martini, her features dazzling up in the candlelight, she asked if I felt like making love, and then she answered her own question saying, of course, that's all men think of – we know what men want, oh yes, that we know. We know what men want all right. That's no mystery. Men are so transparent and never advance beyond adolescence. Is this true that men undress practically every woman they come across? Is this true or some nasty rumor?

"This is true," I said.

She laughed.

"What are your thoughts right now?"

"I don't feel like playing this game."

"Right now. Come on. What are your thoughts?"

"I'd rather show than tell," I said.

"Oooh. You're naughty."

"After all, you know what men want."

"Shall we get a room or go to our place in the Village?"

"Room," I said.

"Hmmm. That much in a hurry, huh?"

"You seem prime yourself."

"How can you tell? Oh never mind. Get the damn room."

In the room – "Don't be gentle," she said.

* * *

For 26 days in a row the Middle East had been our top

215

Front Page banner and even consumed the rest of the sheet.

Most of it was about Hamas, now in charge of Gaza and also in charge of murder, rape, kidnapping, chaos, anarchy.

That's where Phil was going.

"I thought we're a New York paper," said City Desk's Bull Parker, and he was right.

So I gave in and ran more pothole stories.

But it was getting treacherous out there and our pages were also filling up with reproaches against Israel and the United States. Everything was our fault. Now that 9/11 was receding into the historical past, the backlash had it that America had it coming. The root cause crowd, spiked by the academic left, made the case in classrooms, newsrooms, journals, television, that WE were the terrorists and that 9/11 was justified payback for involving ourselves in one part of the world but ignoring another part of the world. We shouldn't be in Iraq but we should be in Darfur.

Poor Ben Hawkins, our patriotic publisher. He hated this stuff. He had me carry a piece by Robert Spencer, who'd just come out with another bestseller, *Onward Muslim Soldiers*, which profiled the New Anti-Semitism, here and around the world, as being powered by the influx of Muslim/Palestinians, who, according to Spencer, were indeed taking over. Ben Hawkins was a huge fan of Spencer's and of another fighter against the (alleged?) encroachment of Islam, Fr. Keith Roderick. "These guys," said Ben, "they've got the facts, and the guts. If only we had such balls."

("Real men," Ben liked to say, "seldom use the word alleged.")

Even our own sacrosanct firemen were becoming targets. For some time – given their selflessness and heroism at Ground Zero – they'd been paradigms, certainly untouchable. As others ran from burning buildings, they ran in. But then we headlined that story that quoted a certain council member as saying they deserved no raise as, after all, they spend only five hours a month fighting fires; the rest of the time they play cards.

Minerva Watson said she wasn't happy doing arts and entertainment anymore. She said she had opinions. I explained that we were all filled up in Editorial and Op-ed and what were her opinions anyway? How unjust America was to women, gays, African Americans and Muslims? I said when I find room I'll let her write a column or two and she said, you know, certain people control everything. I asked which people. She said, "You know."

Chapter 31

Phil Crawford had done a fine job covering the mood on campus – we ran it as a six-part series – and drew raves from executive editor Ken Ballard and even got himself a nod of approval from publisher Ben Hawkins, who never liked Phil Crawford, neither the writing (generally) or the man. Phil was too far left for Ben, practically, as Ben saw it, a communist. Did Ben know that Phil had converted to a different religion? I wasn't sure.

"Congratulations," I said.

We were in the cafeteria.

"For what?" asked Phil.

"You're off to Gaza."

He stared at me and then looped over the table and shook my hand.

"I'm not totally surprised," he said. "I'm elated and grateful for the chance, but not surprised."

He'd already made arrangements. In fact he'd already been in contact with a Gaza mullah, actually a tribal chief more or less, named Sheik Salaman (who was wanted by the Israelis for dozens of terrorist attacks). This sheik knew all about Phil's hazardous experience in Newark and was apologetic for all the mistrust, for it was clear that Phil Crawford was a friend of Islam, indeed, a Muslim himself, and hence would be most welcome in Gaza.

"You know the risk," I told Phil.

He said this was a prize catch, Sheik Salaman.

"But this I have to ask," he said when he came back from getting a plate of stale apple pie. "Please try to hold back the anti-Arab slant."

"I didn't know we had an anti-Arab slant."

I further asked what newspaper he'd been reading, and what newspaper he'd been writing for?

"If something gets run, like something from Spencer's Jihad Watch, or Cinnamon Stillwell, then I could be in trouble, again," he said.

True, Robert Spencer's Jihad Watch was tops in monitoring that other half of the world, and Stillwell was writing more powerfully by the day. This was some fighter, Cinnamon Stillwell (I started catching her along the Internet, and dropped whatever reservations I'd once had about women as writers), and I was tempted to offer her a spot here at the Manhattan Independent. I just might do that if Sam Cleaver doesn't get back right quick. Stillwell (and he'd hate to be told this) was his equal in nailing injustice.

Yes, a man could get himself killed if his newspaper ran with something other than praise for their prophet. Anyway, out there he'd be among his fellow Muslims in Gaza or wherever. Phil was one of them. Any doubts about that were dashed when he said that the Arabs were right in blowing up civilian Israelis in cafés and buses. The Arabs had a right, a duty, to do this. My qualms about sending him out there (whatever my personal motives) were gradually being put to rest.

"I've got to say," Phil said, almost timidly, "that I'm not nuts about our new policy."

Our policy, at odds with other newspapers and wire services, was to call a terrorist a terrorist. We used the word "terrorist" instead of "militant." "Militant" was in vogue throughout the news media to keep it neutral between those who do the killing and those who do the dying, as long as it is only our newsprint that keeps running and not our blood. But here at the Manhattan Independent we chose a trend that departed from moral equivalency. This decision was reached after hours of heated editorial debate.

"That really puts us out on a limb," Phil Crawford was saying over his coffee.

He asked which side I had taken in the debate.

I told him – terrorist.

"They don't think of themselves as terrorists," Phil said.

"Who does?"

"They really want justice."

"Phil, please."

"I know these people. They want peace."

Everybody wants peace. Hitler wanted peace. First, though, everyone else had to die. Then there'd be peace.

How many Cambodians had to die so that Pol Pot could have peace? (Twenty percent of the population.)

"Every story has two sides," said Phil.

"I don't think so."

I was starting to dislike Phil all over again. I warned him that if he was going out there to crusade he may as well stay home and cover city hall.

"Jay, you're not changing your mind, are you?"

* * *

The cafeteria began filling up and Dan Boyle walked by without a nod. Dan Boyle was shop steward for the drivers and there was that, I remembered, to deal with, this new friction that had been brewing with his union against our management, about my use, or rather overuse, of freelance writers, so that suddenly drivers, at $32 an hour, were being underpaid for all the money being "wasted" elsewhere. We used to be friends, Dan Boyle and I, fellow street kids, but I'd been properly snubbed, and I blamed Peter Brand. He'd stirred them up, riled them because I had ordered him to show me his cartoons before they got published.

For the same reason, the same Peter Brand was clocking me, me and Lyla. If Phil knew anything about us, it was Peter Brand who knew it first.

As the cafeteria kept humming up with the bustle and warmth of people who had worked together for years, I had to agree with Ken Ballard; a newspaper is more than just the newsroom. In fact, of all the people filing in and waiting in line for their grub, few were editorial. Most were from Production, the engravers, the pressmen, then the mailers, people from sales, graphics, circulation, classified, advertising, human resources, security – a universe of which editorial was just one planet.

If the drivers had it in for management but once in a while, the mailers were constantly on the verge of walking, and for cause, the cause being technology. They did the assembling and the collating when the newsprint came off the presses but much of that was gradually falling to technology. Mailers were being thinned out, and they belonged to another union, one of 11 (drivers were Teamsters), resulting in a constant standoff between unions and management, so that every day was a miracle, a miracle that the Manhattan Independent and its daily circulation of 480,000 made it to the news shops and doorposts day after day.

Drawing on my street-kid origins, Ben Hawkins frequently used me as a go-between when it was time to negotiate or to head off a crisis and there was always a crisis.

But I did not mind mixing it up with the men and women who worked in overalls. I liked to smoke my pipe out in the docks, where the papers were being bundled and loaded. I liked to kid with the guys, some of whom I sparred with, right there on the platform, and when Main Line patrician Ken Ballard caught sight of that one day he kept on walking, shaking his head and mumbling, "True to form."

In the newsroom, I got along. I'd say most of the staff respected me. Some even liked me. I liked them, most of them.

I strolled the newsroom regularly just to keep in touch and see what people were doing and this wasn't done anymore. In this culture there was no walking and talking there was only e-mailing, even to the man or woman at the next cubicle. So I must have nettled a few people for being overly hands-on.

The new kids on staff – they were a different breed altogether. Taking the cue from Woodward and Bernstein, they were here with an agenda. Woodward and Bernstein had brought down an entire government practically all by themselves, so if it was done before (through high idealism) it could be done again. Armed with idealism uber alles, these kids skipped the usual humanities and social services (like teaching) to take up journalism as a means to repair the world. I suppose, in those FRONT PAGE Ben Hecht days, people were drawn to newspapering to cover fires and burglaries – get the story and then go out and get drunk. Now it was all about changing the world, making it a better place. No smoking.

* * *

Peter Brand came along to show me his latest editorial cartoon and to warn Phil Crawford against joining the ranks of Danny Pearl and Benjamin Curtis.

They'd both been murdered out there, for the sake of peace.

"Watch your back," Peter Brand said.

"How did you know?" asked Phil.

Yes, how did Peter Brand know about this Gaza assignment I was offering Phil? I'd been careful to contain it within the family.

"I know everything," said Peter Brand.

Oh?

"Well," said Phil Crawford, "I better start packing."

* * *

Women, really!

222

It's Sunday and we're strolling along Bleecker Street in the Village and Lyla is being especially fleet and upbeat, and, from a street vendor, we get ourselves hotdogs, heavy on the mustard, and keep the pace till Washington Square Park where we find a bench, sit back and take in some of the open-air poetry and guitar strumming, and then, with a big smile, she turns and asks if I have it – Do I have it, she asks.

"Have what?"

"Do you have it, Jay?"

"I don't know what you're talking about, Lyla."

"Do you have it?" she says.

"Maybe I do, maybe I don't – what?"

"You know what I'm talking about."

"No, I don't."

"Yes, you do."

Okay, finally, here it is. She knows about the cassette. She knows we were caught in the archive room. She knows we're porn stars.

How does she know?

She won't tell.

How long did she know?

She still won't tell.

Is she troubled by this?

"Not at all," she says. "Not one bit."

How come?

"Maybe I want to get caught."

"Why so?"

Because, she says, she is tired of the subterfuge. Besides – what a turn-on!

She insists that we get drunk, bring the cassette up to our apartment, and get turned on like nobody's business.

But the cassette is in a drawer back in the newsroom.

"So get it and be quick."

"No."

"Oooh. Mr. Macho Man is scared."

"Yes."

"Jay. The world is going to hell anyway. What a dump! Who is there to judge us?"

True.

Then she says: "Come on, you're part Christian. You know we're all sinners. So let's sin. Let the sinning begin!"

"But..."

"Never mind your buts. Bring the cassette. I've never been so horny."

"Suppose we get caught?"

"Suppose," she says, "they come back to finish the job and there we are when the walls come tumbling down? We're sunk either way. Go. There's no time to lose."

Chapter 32

So Phil Crawford, Lyla's husband, was finally out there in the Middle East covering the war for us at the Manhattan Independent, the war between Israel and everybody else. (As foretold – Israel shall dwell alone among the nations.) Phil kept sending in sometimes two and sometimes three reports a day – and then it stopped, couldn't even reach him by phone. "When do we start worrying?" asked Lyla. Worry?

Worry?

Yes, another war! What happens when everything is a cliché, déjà vu all over again? Is it you or the world that keeps repeating itself? It is all so familiar. Didn't we do this already? Anyway – what, me worry? First, reporters frequently go underground to get the story within the story. So that's where Phil was, probably, underground in Gaza and in touch with Hamas. Second, we'd been through this before with Phil, and others, the loss of contact sometimes for days. Third, Phil Crawford was one of them, a convert to Islam. (Phil's copy was generally okay, so far as not being too slanted, and required only the usual amount of editing from a reporter who so plainly had taken sides; the photos, however, of alleged Israeli atrocities, had to be scuttled for being so obviously staged, as, for example, the same old woman in a hijab wailing the loss of three different homes.)

Arnold Coffey, who once ran this shop, this newsroom, before Ben Hawkins and his people bought out Arnold Coffey and his people, though Arnold still maintained an aristocratic presence as he still owned a piece of this newspaper and was, besides, the model of dignity and integrity and a fixture of respect and esteem – so Arnold pauses in the hallway and says: "Mel Gibson gets stopped for drunk driving and what's the first word out of his mouth? The Jews." Arnold insists that bigotry, anti-Semitism in particular, is hereditary, even genetic. It is nature. Hmmm.

Meanwhile, back at my desk, I start to worry. Maybe Phil is a goner after all. Two other journalists covering the same story in the same place, Gaza, have been kidnapped. But here is the surprise: It is not big news. Another day, another kidnapping. If there is one thing they have succeeded in doing, these crazies, it is to cheapen the value of human life, their lives and even our lives. We've begun to accept. We've become conditioned to their terms. Anything is possible. So it really isn't a surprise. (Even 9/11 has been reduced to a squabble, among ourselves, over how to honorably replace the Twin Towers, with hardly any reference to the outrage itself.) How do you fight an enemy that doesn't care for life? They care nothing for us, that's for sure, and nothing for themselves.

(To arrive at this you don't need to be a Conservative but merely a Liberal with eyes wide open.)

Logical question then – WHEN DO WE START WORRYING?

Meaning, do we worry that Phil is dead, or do we worry that he's alive? How committed are we to this plan, this scheme of ours to do him in? We keep going back and forth. We keep dithering. We're amateurs. Lyla teeters between alarm and near-jubilation over what we're doing. As for me, I'm starting to wonder if I'm destined to one day fess up like Gunther Grass who, alongside his Nobel Prize for Literature and his years serving as Germany's (and the world's) conscience, finally spilled the beans, okay, the sauerkraut, on himself by admitting that he was not some lowly maintenance worker for the Third Reich, but an actual Nazi, part of Himmler's Waffen SS killing machine.

All that after some 60 years of silence, which proves once again that you can run but you can't hide.

Truth is patient but inevitable.

One day I may choose to write my own memoirs and what will I write when I approach this chapter – the Phil Crawford chapter?

Or rather, the Lyla Crawford chapter –

I am, in fact, writing an editorial on Gunther Grass under the headline – "What Did You Do In The War, Gunther?"

So here I am, here am I, getting all so righteous and judgmental when I'd prefer that no one do likewise unto me.

Can anyone stand the glare of his own pathways?

Veeery Interezzzting that Gunther's publisher is rushing out his memoir – *Peeling the Onion* – to cash in on the notoriety.

Scandal is good.

Gunther himself, meanwhile, is not remorseful, or not as remorseful as he should be. My hunch is that he is proud of this, yes, pleased and proud, though he'd never admit as much, of course, but pleased that he got it all out, and proud that, old as he is, in his late 70s, behold, once he was a MAN, in his own eyes and in the eyes of the world, this cockeyed world that today, more than ever, fails to distinguish between victim and villain. (Was he confessing or was he bragging? Was he repenting or was he boasting?) As long as you make news, you're a celebrity. We ogle and embrace celebrities regardless of how they've earned their fame and infamy.

I know this. I'm in the business. I make celebrities every day. (I am part of what used to be called the press and is now called the media and even worse, though we at the Manhattan Independent are painted Conservative, we are thrown in with the MSM, or mainstream media.) Here's a man, John Mark Karr, an absolute cipher, a nothing, a nobody, and like magic he's front page here at the Manhattan Independent and everywhere else for confessing (falsely, as it turns out) that, some 10 years ago, he murdered six-year-old JonBenet Ramsey. On the flight from Thailand back to the United States he's surrounded by what appears to be – admirers! This (alleged) murderer, this creep, chases the President of the United States off the front pages. He merits this attention because he may have done something horrible.

Why do people confess to crimes they didn't commit? What is this?

Don't ask.

* * *

Minerva Watson says, "This party you can't miss."

I inherited Minerva from the previous managing editor, Guy Simpson, and why she's editor of our Entertainment page is still a mystery.

She is so grim. The women's liberation movement turned out some pretty good people, but not Minerva. She still wants to get even.

Goes back, oh, five million years.

That's a long time to keep a grudge.

What party?

"Bertha Humphries is retiring."

Minerva could at least knock before entering my office. Gladys never stops her. I guess she just isn't quick enough.

So who is Bertha Humphries? Oh yes, been here 44 years as a proofreader – and they said it wouldn't last. I remember her as a woman who kept to herself and kept to her job and stayed in for lunch. If she socialized, it wasn't with anyone in the newsroom outside her department. (Proofreaders are worse than lawyers in that nothing is fit to print.) She was unmarried, or maybe a widow. We had maybe 50 people like Bertha Humphries, the fount of our operation but without glory and only scant appreciation and recognition, or, if any of that came, it came too late for them and for us.

I was at fault for not knowing everybody. But who has the time? In all these years, I'd had but one conversation with her. I asked if she enjoyed reading – books, that is, outside the job. "You mean," she said, "do I keep searching for typos?" Yes, that was exactly what I meant. She reflected and then smiled and then conceded that, yes, reading for pleasure was difficult when you were trained to read for flaws. That was the extent of our relationship.

We're all in there, in the Conference Room, and drinking watered-down wine from paper cups. There's mingling and the usual chatter and unease, as is routine when we party, all of it, the stiffness, the plastic smiles, the herding, according to formula. Ken Ballard, executive editor, is first to speak and express his gratitude for her loyalty and long years of service. Publisher Ben Hawkins follows with a joke that there never was a typo that got past her desk. People laugh, not because it's funny but because it's Ben Hawkins. Then it's my turn and best I can do for the occasion is – "We'll miss you, Bertha."

I am sincere. It's "the little people" that keep us afloat.

I add this: "We're family. Come back and let us know how you're faring in your new life of leisure."

We all know this won't happen. People never come back. Once you're gone, you're gone. You're family only as long as you're still punching the clock.

Bertha gets a watch, and it's over.

Forty-four years gets a watch.

She's on display so she smiles but won't reveal the pain of losing a household that sustained and nourished her over more than four decades.

This – the workplace – is where we really live, now in America.

Well, at least we didn't dump her the way CBS dumped Dan Rather and before that Walter Cronkite.

But it's not a CBS thing – ingratitude. It's a corporate thing. Or maybe it's how the world turns.

Say what you will about Dan Rather, but he did put in his own 44 years, and then poof. Gratitude? No such thing.

There's always someone to take your place. Life goes on.

Ingratitude is a fate that awaits us all. We think we belong, but we're only visiting, passing through, hitchhiking from cradle to grave.

* * *

The big debate – as we're gathered for our editorial meeting – is about Tom Cruise. Where does he belong?

Sumner Redstone, the boss of Viacom and Paramount, fired him and wants him off the Paramount lot like yesterday. Is this front page? The firing is hot and new, but Tom Cruise is old – his Scientology, his couch jumping on Oprah, his dispute with Matt Lauer over prescription drugs (Scientology says no). That's gotten old. He's made two billion dollars for Paramount over the years, as Hollywood's number one male star, but recently, he's also made a fool of himself. (How do you forfeit two billion dollars worth of goodwill in one swoop? Insult the women of America.)

I like the story for front page but only for this reason, that with all the machinery that goes into making a corporate decision, decisions made in exactitude by marketing and accounting and computing, all of it down to the digits, sometimes it's a whisper from a wife to her husband (pillow talk) that is most formidable and sets the agenda. I love this! The New York Post broke it first but we can own the story, with more digging, if we can prove that Redstone wife's, Paula Fortunato, put the hex on Cruise for his heckling of Brooke Shields and other women who resorted to prescription drugs for postpartum depression.

So (as we'll pick this out from the Post but take it further) Fortunato told her husband, "I never want to see another Tom Cruise movie again."

Down goes Cruise!

To keep it democratic, I asked for a show of hands about giving this front page, and was outnumbered and outvoted as never before.

"Perhaps too tabloid," reckoned Ken Ballard, politely.

"I'll say," said Peter Brand.

"But it's your decision," said Ken to dampen Peter Brand.

"Thanks," I said, but still offended, and wondering if I was losing the editorial staff, and if so – why?

Or was I being paranoid over Phil Crawford? Or was I correct to assume that Peter Brand had my number and was turning everyone against me one by one?

I had made him an enemy, Peter Brand, by insisting that all his editorial cartoons go through me first. This, I had to do. His drawings and musings on our editorial page had crossed over from controversial to plain anti-Americanism and anti-Semitism. African Americans had their own legitimate beef against Peter Brand. Marie LeClaire got stacks and stacks of those letters and I got a hundred e-mails a day protesting Peter Brand, but it was my own wariness that got me to call stop.

"Front page," I said.

If Tom Cruise does not sell box office tickets like he used to, it was my guess that he'd still sell newspapers. It's the same reflex that has us ogle the scene of an accident.

Outside, after the meeting, Peter Brand brushed past me with such fiery contempt in his eyes that I shuddered, as if evil itself had breezed in.

But was it the cartoons, or was it something else, something deeper, that made Peter Brand my nemesis?

* * *

That's Sam Cleaver on the phone.

"You survived?" he says in that sandpaper voice of his.

"Survived what?"

"Without me."

That's Sammy all right, same cocky Sam, full of balls and starch, though I also detected a touch of gloom in his voice. Yes, I survived, even the Manhattan Independent survived his sabbatical, or whatever it was that spooled him off in disgust at newspapering, opting instead for the life of a novelist. I missed him. He was the kid I used to be. He's back from Miami where he hooked up with a woman, Karen Sweeny, twice his age (when you're 28 everybody is twice your age) who took up duties as his mother, lover and editor. He was still at work on that novel but missed, he admitted, the urgency of journalism. "When can we get together?"

I suggested later on in the week.

"How about right now?"

Yes, that's Sam Cleaver.

"I'm downstairs at Nick's. I've already ordered your Salad Special and vodka. Hurry before the vodka gets warm."

I hurried.

He was still dressed for Miami and he even brought the sun. He featured a tan over his pugilist's face. He still had the nose of a fighter who had gone one round too many. But his quick eyes and his rapid speech – all that was New York. We hugged and got down to business. Would I take him back? "Gladly," I said. But only for special assignments? "Whatever," I said. He laughed. "You're too easy."

His woman joined us. She'd been out shopping or something. Karen Sweeny was a California-bred hippie, the daughter of Berkeley sit-ins and love-ins.

"Tell him," she said.

But Sammy wouldn't tell.

"Sam had a nervous breakdown," Karen said.

"Not exactly," said Sam.

"Exactly," said Karen.

He'd been hospitalized for an irregular heartbeat and for a medical term that defines anxiety, stress and panic.

"All those rejections got to him," said Karen.

His novel had been turned down by 36 publishers, and still counting. He had taken up despair and boozing and there was an attempt at suicide. "Not so," said Sam. "Then what do you call what happened?" said Karen. "That was an accident," said Sam, and went on to explain that there was a difference, a huge difference, between wanting to die and not caring if you lived or died. Karen insisted that there was no difference.

I defended Sam on this, for I'd had these moments myself of not caring if I lived or died – and that is not suicidal, necessarily.

"Yes it is," said Karen.

I liked Karen. She had her own story. Some other time.

So it was Karen who got him to come back home to journalism. Maybe this was where he belonged from start to finish. That's tough. It's a rude moment when a man faces his limitations, as we all do. ("It is not for you to complete the task, only to persist.") Sam would never relent, being Sam and a true writer, and he'd continue to pursue his dream, but at a different pace, rating himself for the long distance rather than the sprint.

Sam's fiction was too commercial for literary and too literary for commercial. This is how they team up to trap you and destroy you. I knew that, out in Miami, he had tried to get a job at a local newspaper just to stay in shape and, as a sign that he was going bonkers, described himself in the application form as "a failed novelist." More on this when he sent out his novel with a different title, once as SOLID WASTE and again as USE THIS DUMPSTER FOR TRASH ONLY. (Sometimes, it is true, a title can spell the difference between failure and success.) He'd also resubmitted it to hyper-feminist editor Natricia DeFarr with the title TITS and ASS.

Karen began – "I'm not asking you to –"

Sammy groaned. Obviously they'd been through this and plenty – about his not forfeiting his dream.

The challenge for all of us is to accept our limitations but still retain the dream – a paradox, but what isn't?

Sam will need some healing. He'd been humbled and had willingly placed himself in the hands of a nurturing woman. He was being too compliant. This will change when he catches up to the rhythm of the newsroom and the chaos of Manhattan. I was glad to have him back, even like this, like starting over. He will be all right once he quits being sore at the world of book publishing and finds other sources of injustice, of which there is no end. He will be fine once he gets back to chasing deadlines. Journalism – that too is writing, even if it is not writing of the purest form. Newspapering tells the same story as fiction, only without the flourishes. ("No time for poetry but exactly what is" – Kerouac.) Writing comes from rage and indignation. Sam Cleaver had that in buckets.

A writer who is happy with his life and with the life of others has nothing to say.

"You will be accepted," she said, clasping his hands. "You will be recognized."

"After I'm dead or while I'm still alive?"

My God! He is only 28! Life plunders you that fast?

Chapter 33

Stu Greenwald asked the same question – when do we start worrying? Two weeks now, and not a word from Phil Crawford out there in Gaza. Two (abducted) newsmen had just been released with a touch of Stockholm Syndrome as, upon arrival back here, they announced that while in captivity they'd been brutalized, had converted to Islam, at gunpoint, but that should not deter other journalists from hurrying on down to report on the "plight of the Palestinians," assuredly a "beautiful people." (Sam Cleaver, back in cynical stride, wrote it up as HOW I SPENT MY GAZA VACATION.)

"Nothing to convert," I told Stu, the rumpled chief of our foreign desk.

"Huh?"

"You didn't know?"

"Know what?"

I told him. I was sure that he knew, from me or from someone else. Obviously, he forgot, so I told him again.

"So he's a Muslim," said Stu, reflecting with an unlit cigar, the cigar getting frustrated. "But maybe the wrong kind."

"True."

"He could be Sunni when he should be Shiite or maybe the other way round – like Protestants and Catholics in parts of Ireland. Not enough to simply be Christian."

"Light that damned thing up already. I won't tell."

"I've been uncomfortable about this from day one," Stu said, not about the cigar, but Phil.

"Why?"

"Phil Crawford? He brings along too much attitude. I always thought so."

Stu had covered every story on earth since Cain slew Abel, so his instincts were usually right on. He never cared for the notion of Phil as a foreign correspondent. They're a different breed, these guys – extraverted, brazen, dashing, romantic, and they won trust, even among crooked executives and slimy warlords, by their swagger and sense of humor. Phil was none of the above. He was introverted and humorless. Stu had voted against the Gaza assignment and so had Ken Ballard, so whatever happened to Phil Crawford was on me.

Women ought to come with a price tag; like, in terms of grief, how much for this one?

* * *

Lyla got me to Serendipity to meet a friend who would need no introduction, in other words, a surprise. She wouldn't give his name.

"I knew you wouldn't come otherwise," she said.

"When does this amazing person show up?"

"Soon, and I want you to behave."

"Don't I always?"

"Not even in bed."

Already this did not sound good. What now? Before this we'd been naughty over at our apartment in the Village where she'd asked if I took Viagra as it was a marvel how I could keep on going. (Who wouldn't be a pushover for a line like that?) No, I did not take Viagra. "So," she'd said, "you're a hunk." I wondered then, and even now, if she was comparing me against other lovers of the past and maybe even the present. I was quite sure that I was her one and only but we can't be too sure, ever. I wondered if women, especially women as sexual as Lyla, kept a mental ledger in which they kept score. Was it about size, duration, location and what were they thinking even during the performance – that Johnny had been bigger and better? In lovemaking, men succeed or fail. Women always succeed. Doesn't seem fair.

Or was it the foreplay? STATISTICS PROVE that sex itself is less important to women than cuddling. (Real Women scoff at this.)

With Lyla (at least between us) everything was foreplay. She was always ON.

Lyla waved to a man who was introduced to me as Donald Whittings. He was tall, dark, maybe handsome but surely professorial and, as it turned out, a tenured scholar of early and mid-20th century American Literature, which was all I needed to remind me that this was the man, for all his collegiate aplomb, who ran with J.D. Salinger groupies. Finally, we meet, and finally I know that I've been roped into hearing him out on Salinger.

"He has met Salinger," says Lyla with devotion.

"He is willing to talk and sit for an interview," says Donald Whittings.

"What's the catch?"

"Jay, please."

Someone has just kicked me under the table. Anyway, Lyla can get that interview for us at the Manhattan Independent as long as it goes in unedited, that is, word for word as spoken by Salinger. I nod. Money? "Jay, please!" says Lyla. But Whittings is not so offended. "That's for later," says Whittings, and concedes that business is business, and that yes, of course he'd expect a cut for the introduction.

"How much?"

"Jay!"

Whittings doesn't flinch. "Fifteen percent."

He estimates that the cost to the Manhattan Independent will be around a million dollars BUT AFTER ALL, look whom we're getting!

(Would I pay a million dollars if I could get the real J.D. Salinger to stand up? Yes.)

"Why us? Why Lyla?"

"He reads her and loves her writing."

This, even Lyla can't quite swallow. Lyla writes well, but Salinger, so picky, has even belittled Ernest Hemingway.

"There's got to be more."

"Well, yes," says Whittings. "He's seen her picture and he's got a crush on Lyla."

Now this makes sense. This I can buy. From that photo that runs alongside her Sunday column, everybody's got a crush on Lyla.

This also makes sense – that Salinger won't live forever (it's getting late) and it's time for a testament.

"What made him slip off and go silent for all these years?" (More than half a century.)

Salinger never got over all those rejection slips when he was first starting out. He took it personal. Maybe that's when he began to detest "phonies" and, skittish as he was (and is), and perhaps paranoid, magnified that grudge against editors to include everyone else. Then – the war. We don't know how it changed him when he liberated that Nazi death camp as part of the U.S. 4th Infantry Division. We can only imagine. Hint: He told his daughter – "You never really get the smell of burning flesh out of your nose entirely, no matter how long you live." Also, he was hospitalized for combat stress reaction. In all his writings (except for his depiction of a traumatized soldier in "For Esme with Love and Squalor"), there is hardly a word about all that, about what those Nazis did, and just maybe that's where his indignation has its origins, and maybe again, that's the root of Holden Caulfield's scorn.

(My own fascination with Salinger – alongside my reverence for his work – can be traced to an upbringing we share; Jewish father, Catholic mother.)

If all that is too psychological, there's his view of writing as a holy summons. The writer (of fiction) is God's messenger. Salinger, then (in his own estimation) is one of those 36 Just Men "upon who the world reposes." Against myself, I am becoming less of a skeptic and more of a believer.

I would hate to be proven a sucker later on. (This has happened before and I had promised myself never again.) How do I take this to Ben Hawkins? He'd go for it – even a million dollars – if the whole business could be certified, ratified and guaranteed. He is a gambler. For sure we'd triple our readership and get coverage here and around the world with money coming in quicker than it went out (plus the universal esteem upon the Manhattan Independent for such a scoop). Clifford Irving was paid a fortune when he offered LIFE the book on another recluse, Howard Hughes, and then, oh hell, that turned out to be a fraud with Irving paying it back, all the money he had left over after a spree, and then, and then, why then he went directly to jail, did Clifford Irving. Scary.

"Will we be able to take pictures?"

"No," said Whittings. "Salinger wouldn't approve."

(Near to that was Salinger's response about turning "Catcher" into a movie: "Holden wouldn't approve.")

"No?" I said.

"Jay," said Lyla, "a man like Salinger sets his own terms."

"No, Lyla, for a million dollars we set the terms."

"We're getting ahead of ourselves," said Whittings correctly. "All that will be resolved when it's time to negotiate."

I said that I'll think it over but that most likely I'll bring it up with Ben Hawkins, when I think he's in the mood to roll the dice.

One of us could end up like Clifford Irving.

* * *

If I'd meant to be truly impolite I'd have asked Whittings why Salinger had chosen him above all other knights, but later for that and anyway, if it had to be somebody why not him, why not Whittings? He was as good as anybody to carry the message, or to be the message-broker, or to be to Salinger what Max Brod had been to Franz Kafka, above all, faithful to the work. Salinger knows what time it is and (perhaps – wishful thinking?) that it's time to end the truancy. Bob Dylan, in that documentary, in that book, in that *Rolling Stone* interview ("I own the 60s,") has dashed out of his own self-imposed exile as if there's no tomorrow.

(The line of 20th Century – and of 21st Century – absurdity and alienation runs from Kafka through Camus to Salinger; the dots easily connected. Salinger may have used Mark Twain's voice but the word was clearly Kafka's in expressing detachment, from Gregor Samsa-K and Joseph K to Holden Caulfield. From Prague to Manhattan we keep trying to fit but our papers are always NOT IN ORDER and we keep being sent to the wrong line.)

* * *

I was over at Pat's Gym sparring a few rounds with another 18-year-old up-and-comer from Mexico who, accidentally, I am sure, hit me in the balls and as I doubled over I wondered why Pat so often put me in there with these contenders; for my sake, he'd say. So I was doubled over and hit the deck. The kid apologized repeatedly but it was all a blur for a few moments as getting it right there is a crushing sensation. You can't breathe and you really think it's all over. You'll never breathe again. Next round I got him back with an uppercut-roundhouse combination and even had him against the ropes when Pat stepped in, just like that, to say it's over – but why? I had it going.

"Someone here to see you. Urgent."

I glanced around and here was Gerard Fabre, Ben Hawkins' French-imported chauffeur, friendly, smiling, but impatient. (He moonlighted as a chef – dreaming.) I stepped out between the ropes and he said there's no time to shower or change; Ben Hawkins needs to talk. I wrapped a towel round my neck and in my sweats joined him outside where Ben was waiting in back of the limo. "Something's come up," Ben said, and we drove off. Ben was in his tux and en route to some charity function at the Grand Hyatt.

Turns out that a third newsman had been kidnapped in Gaza and this guy – this guy was murdered, evidently by Hamas. Ben knew this from his contacts in the oil world. (Ben had money invested in that business.) But this murder was being kept under wraps, by consent of journalism throughout, so as not to prejudice the Palestinian cause. We were to be part of this conspiracy until we had all the facts.

But it didn't end there, as there was perhaps a fourth journalist being held captive – and if so, that may well be Phil Crawford.

"We can't be sure," said Ben, "but it's a good guess, according to my sources."

We sit tight, said Ben, until we know more.

I knew enough. I'd been hit in the balls all over again.

Chapter 34

Kuana Banks, that big Hawaiian (the product of a British father and Chinese mother), loped along his shedrow, stopping at each stall to bring in the feed or to help the grooms bandage up the horses, some of which were going out or coming back from their works. The early morning breeze was quickly turning to summertime humidity, but this was the backstretch where the air always tasted fresh and moist and smelled of dew, country, backwoods.

I joined him step for step.

He laughed, that soft laugh of a big man, a big man fully confident in himself and in his surroundings. I envied him his inner peace. He practiced no religion except horses, training them to run and not to behave like people. He could quote Sophocles, Thucydides, Euripides, Virgil, Petronius, Dante, Bocccaccio, Rabelais, Cervantes, of course Shakespeare, but he favored the drawl of horsemen, and silence. Kuana could sit with a friend for an hour and say nothing and still you felt that you'd conversed and been enriched.

He laughed, saying, "So it's always about a woman."

There was a rumor that he'd once been secretly married to an A-list Hollywood starlet. She came at him with a knife as he lay sleeping. Black belt that he was, he felt the cold tip of it on his chest before it went in any further and managed to turn rapidly aside and grab it away from her before real damage was done. He had married her, apparently, before she became above the title billing, and apparently he had gone broke financing her. When her career took off, so did she. Kuana, the few times he spoke about it, thought it was funny.

Among us, his friends, there was constant guessing and betting as to who this starlet was. He'd never tell, though once he did show us the scar.

(Sharon Stone?)

I told him everything.

"No wonder you look like shit," he said, mixing up a pail full of feed and warning a hot walker to hold that shank tighter.

He handed me a rake and I mucked out a couple of stalls and began to feel better and wished that I could stay here, right here, right here in this backstretch, in this stall, and remain here forever and forget about the rest, about everything. This was the place. The world did not come here with its jamboree of Udays and Qusays. There were even walls and fences to keep the horses in and the rest of the world out. I kept on raking, took pride in it, and began to feel tranquility. (Imagine this – real work!)

In one stall I kept raking and raking and was so lost and so happy in what I was doing that a groom came by and said, "I think that's enough."

Then I hotwalked a horse, around the barn, and took pride in that I knew that they were always approached and walked from the left, never the right, otherwise they'd bolt. They were creatures of habit, and they were so big and so beautiful. On the track, in the afternoon, they were four-legged locomotives, but here, in the backstretch, they were babies, big babies, but babies who had to be doctored, nursed, disciplined, petted, walked, fed and burped. They all had nicknames and most of them had favorite snacks. Some liked candy. Some liked carrots. Some liked beer. Then, on a patch of grass directly outside the barn I hosed down a horse that had just returned hot, sweaty and depleted from a work on the track. The horse stood there obediently as I hosed him down and he appeared to be grateful. I felt a wonderful sense of achievement. I'd never felt like this even when I thought we had put out a particularly good Sunday paper.

"Is this the same lady you brought here a while back?" Kuana said back in his tack room as he conducted business; paperwork and phone work. I liked watching him. He was a general, grooms, hotwalkers, exercise riders, jockeys, surely the thoroughbreds, all of it his army. This was war. (Kingdoms used to be won and lost on the outcome of a race.) I liked knowing that his headlines were about Todd Pletcher and Bob Baffert, and not about Osama bin Laden and Yasser Arafat, who was still dead.

He'd been reading off the Condition Book to an owner who wanted his horse to run within a couple of weeks, if a spot could be found.

"Lyla," I said.

Kuana had been best man at my wedding to Myrna. (He did not like her from the start and saw everything before it happened.)

"You sure pick 'em," he said on the negative side, but remembering Lyla's, "if you're afraid to do it – do it," on the positive side.

In his beat-up truck we drove the three minutes to the track where his exercise riders were working two horses against each other. Kuana set his stopwatch. He liked the times and he liked the way they came back, eyeing the legs, always the legs, and asking the riders how much the horses had left galloping out past the finish line. They called him "sir," an ancient protocol still observed.

"I don't think you were meant for the big world," Kuana said when we were settled in the track kitchen for some toast, eggs and coffee.

The place was packed with jockeys, trainers, grooms, vets, hotwalkers, agents, a wild west of boots, stirrups and ten-gallon hats. Every man had a horse right here that is destined to be a world-beater, the next Secretariat, just watch him this afternoon. Morning at the racetrack, the place brimming with expectation and of thrills and triumphs yet to come, was most likely what JFK had in mind when he spoke of Morning In America.

I told him everything again.

"I don't see the crime," Kuana said.

As far as he could tell, everything was legitimate.

"He is, after all, brutalizing the woman, no?"

Yes, I said.

"So? The son of a bitch deserves to get killed."

Was he kidding? Despite his black belt, or because of it, Kuana had no rage or violence in him and being of several breeds himself, he had no prejudice, either, and this was known, respected and admired. Back in Cincinnati (where we first met), when he ran a few at River Downs, only Kuana could walk all-black Avondale when those riots broke out. He stood a commanding six-feet-two and as has been said of another dignitary (Herzl?), he is fit to meet with kings.

"I guess I'm kidding," he said, "but you? What's with the guilt?"

My motives, I explained.

"But you didn't send the man. He wanted to go, right?"

Right. He wanted to go. He insisted on going.

"He was once a coward, right?"

Right.

"He was cowardly in the eyes of his wife, right?"

Right.

"He needs to make it up, right?"

Right.

"There you are. You can't deprive a man of a duty to re-establish his manhood."

True.

"Then there's this," Kuana said. "That's his business, or rather, his occupational hazard. He's a journalist and a journalist goes where the story goes."

But the story, I explained, goes in a place very dangerous.

"That's part of the job. You went, didn't you? I remember you did."

Yes, I also could have gotten myself killed, and nearly did.

"Who says he's going to get killed?" Kuana said.

I said, given this new information, I would not take bets on Phil Crawford's life.

"Why not?"

"Not with what I have in mind."

"Aha," Kuana said.

"I told you what I could do."

This made him stop and think.

"Something like murder by proxy," Kuana said.

I said that might be the headline. Murder By Proxy.

"She wants him dead," Kuana said mulling it over.

"She's not the type, but he's killing her."

Kuana shook his head. "This Muslim thing, you saw it coming, huh?"

"Way back at UC."

I had only spent two semesters at UC before going Army.

"My guess is that she was through with him even before. She came on to you, didn't she?"

"Yes, but..."

"I know. I know how it goes. Some of it was her, some of it was you."

"That's how it goes," I said.

We were onto our second cup of coffee.

"Maybe it will come out the way you both want it, he'll just disappear into the Muslim woodwork out there in the Middle East."

Not likely.

"What's the worst that can happen, if he does perish while he's out there on assignment for you?"

"Nothing – until they tie me in with his wife."

"Then what can they do to you? You didn't kill him."

"Yes I did, and so did Lyla. We'll both be ruined."

"Ruined, how? What can they prove?"

"That it was all staged."

"But it's still legit. He's a newsman."

"That's the crux, Kuana. It's legit and it isn't legit."

Kuana lit up a cigarette. The signs that said NO SMOKING did not dissuade Kuana in this place where men were men and so were the women.

"Fact is," he said, "he's been terrorizing her."

I had not thought about it quite like that, applying the word terror. But he was, he was terrorizing her.

"That's a bit strong," I said, defending Phil. "That may be overstating it," I added.

"I'll tell you this," Kuana said. "After what happened, I don't have much sympathy for them."

This surprised me, coming from Kuana.

"Really?" I said.

"I'm not as isolated here as you think, Jay. I know what's going on. In each century there's a new wave, a new idealism on the march. Check your history and you'll find that it's usually Christianity pushing forward, or Islam. One or the other is on the move and right now Christianity is passive and Islam is inflamed. They want it all. It's them against us. So I have no sympathy for them and I have no sympathy for this guy."

"That's not bigotry, Kuana?"

"No, that's clarity. He is a wicked man, this Phil Crawford, is he not?"

"Depends," I said. "Depends what side you're on."

"Well, he's made his choice, you've made yours. Nothing to feel guilty about. He's got what's coming. Remember your Talmud."

Yes, those who are merciful to the wicked will one day be wicked to the righteous.

* * *

Kuana had other business so I walked the backstretch for the sounds, sights and smells of America when it was young and frontier – unpaved, uncluttered, un-littered. Horses clip-clopping on gravel – what makes this so pleasant for me? Was this my own recovery of the past? Was this a remembrance of another life? I thought about Myrna (for some reason) and wondered how I had blundered into a marriage like this. I wondered if, with Lyla, I was blundering all over again. We do not want to be redundant, now do we?

You can't handicap them, either. No charts for them. Though it was mostly my fault with Myrna. Her claim, and justified it was, was that I remained married to newspapering. This was an entirely justified accusation. Probably it is true that on the rebound we choose the same one all over again. (On and off the track, with fast horses and fast women, we make the same mistakes and never learn. We never learn.) Myrna was a writer, a novelist, a poet somewhere in the same league with Lyla, and Myrna, who came over from Russia when she was 11, had the same figure and the same dark eyes as Lyla.

Myrna had published three novels and two books of poetry, all of which got fine reviews and all of which RESONATED.

How the split happened? It just happened. There was no single moment. Mainly, I'd say, her friends were not my friends, her life was not my life.

If there was a reason, a real reason why it all came apart, it was her disdain for newspapering. She declined to read newspapers, even the Manhattan Independent.

I took that personal, especially when she'd glance at a column I had written and then toss it aside; no comment.

It wasn't literature.

Ironically – so very ironic – Lyla was about the same. Lyla also hated news.

Poets, Lyla believed, should run the world, and in a sense, I said, we are, meaning journalists. Maybe we are not poets, but we are historians. We do history one page at a time. Of course we know too much and really know nothing and nothing changes, even with all this flow of information. Deadlines go, deadlines come, but the earth endures forever, sayeth the preacher, and all of it flows into our newsroom, yet the news is never full but flows back to its source to return and repeat.

* * *

"Don't take it personal," said Ken Ballard.

Which always means DO take it personal.

I read the memo, after Ken left, being officially notified that my budget for freelancers was being slashed, cut in half. Freelancers were people like Norman Mailer and John Updike and Gay Talese. They (thanks to Lyla and her courageous lobbying) gave us literature! We'd be just another newspaper without them. This had been Lyla's baby that I had nurtured along into the teeth of a mutinous staff.

Was this a message? Was this about my tiff with anchorman Kevin Rod Rodgers, or was it about Phil Crawford – still among the missing in Gaza, and on my watch?

Did people know? Did people suspect?

Had that tape made the rounds?

Someone – Arnold Coffey or maybe it was Stu Greenwald – had asked if it was true that Lyla and Phil had split even before Phil went off to Gaza.

Why ask me?

Oh – just asking.

The note said that the cut was a gesture to the drivers and the regular newsroom staff, all of whom regarded freelancers as scabs.

Nothing personal. Strictly business.

Or strictly Peter Brand.

* * *

We don't stare at a blank sheet of paper anymore. We stare

at a blank screen. I had this editorial to get out about the war but forgot how I felt about the war and in fact I forgot how I felt about everything. All circuits down! I guess this is writer's block (first time for me as a journalist), or maybe it's help me I'm falling, or maybe it's finally an appreciation that it's all useless and that if less is more (in writing as well as in architecture), imagine the bounty of NOTHING. If less is more, NOTHING improves the writing to perfection so why not leave the screen blank, as God intended. Why not publish and distribute a newspaper with no words at all and let the reader fill in the blanks. Why not? This makes such good sense. What makes my opinion more worthy than your opinion and who says I'm right and you're wrong? Where is it written? That's right, it shouldn't be written. All the writing's been done. There's nothing more to say. There's nothing to add, only to subtract.

Beckett started cutting everything in half and Hemingway preached (against Thomas Wolfe and William Faulkner) that what's left out is more powerful than what's put in. With all the infamy going on out there, local, regional, national, global, it's no wonder words fail. We've simply exhausted vocabulary and run out of language.

If I wanted to recall how we (at the Manhattan Independent) felt about this, that and beyond, sure I could check the archives, our own archives, or the archives of The New York Times, and then, with the Times in hand, take the contrary view, for that was our position editorially, no when they said yes, yes when they said no. We act as if we have the answers (the Times especially) but we're only guessing. William Goldman (screenwriter par excellence) said the same about Hollywood; nobody knows anything.

Malaise, depression, confusion – there must be another name for it when you can't remember why you're doing what you're doing.

How absurd to think that anything you say, anything you

write, can clean up this mess.

"Maybe," Lyla said later on as we walked along Bleecker Street in the Village, "you're just upset about the situation."

We were off to do our wine and French bread routine.

She – we – preferred to leave Phil's name out of this. There'd be plenty of that to deal with soon enough.

We called it THE SITUATION.

As we approached our place a black cat rushed out in front of us.

"You're not superstitious," she said, laughing. "Are you?"

Superstitious? Me? That would be bad luck.

Did I really believe that Phil had such powers, the power to curse? (Were we already in the web spun by his curse?) Ridiculous. But I was not so ENLIGHTENED as to dismiss the supernatural. I knew stories. (Go then and explain the Witch of Endor.) Gambler that I was, I did believe in the general principle of good vibrations versus bad vibes. That's why you tipped the stickman at the craps table. If you don't believe in God, you must believe in Luck, except that luck is random, and that's no way to live. With God, you have the Bible to mark your path. Without God, you've got Geraldo Rivera.

(Lyla wasn't one to talk, either, when it came to fearing the hex or the jinx. She had terrible premonitions – certainly about Phil – and she'd usually get it started with me by saying, "I really shouldn't be telling you this," but then she would. She had a tendency to expect the worst and I guess it all started with her father when she found him in the bathtub, the bathtub full with water and blood, exactly as had been foretold in a dream. As for me, from my years in combat, soldiering and reporting, I knew that there was something else out there that fixed our destinies as it was too strange why some men lived, some men died by the chance of the same bullet. Boxers are more religious than the Pope.)

Back in our hideaway she cooked us spaghetti and we ate it with the French bread and some red wine and if Truffaut were still around (he died much too young), we'd be living in a French movie, black and white, no subtitles. That's pretty much how we saw it anyway when we escaped to the Village and placed ourselves in the mercy of forgetfulness.

We made love and it was all right (I guess) except that I was no stud this time around. Writer's block hurts all over.

I clicked on the TV.

"Please turn that off," she said.

"In a minute."

She sure hated television, the news part of it, and never, or seldom, watched it when she was alone. Television was bad news. Television not only reported bad news, it was bad news, and if not for television there would be no bad news. That's how she had it figured. No TV, no terrorism. No TV, no fires. No TV, no rapes. No TV, no murders. No TV, no pedophiles. No TV, no Bin Laden. TV was responsible for it all. TV was the villain. TV was more than the messenger. TV was the author. TV wrote the script. That's how she had it figured.

She was afraid that one day the TV (or the man in the TV as our grandparents suspected there was a man in the radio) would show something horrible... about us. One day that would happen. She feared that very much and spoke of it often, as if the speaking of it would give it the kibosh. "I wish," she said...she wished we were living in Cockaigne, tradition's land of luck and plenty. This, instead, was Dante's limbo. She sat down at the edge of the bed brushing her hair. This I found to be a calming exercise for her and for me. The left side, the right side, then the back, getting those stubborn shags out, then the entire business of brushing all over again. I marveled at how the world came to a stop when a woman brushed her hair.

"Please turn that off," she said. "Please. You are so positively addicted! Off it, for me."

I was about to do so when a news flash came on announcing that an American reporter had been snatched by Hamas or a subsidiary group – the fourth within a month. Two had been released, one had been assassinated (the beheading finally made public by his captors for our viewing pleasure), and now this, this fourth American correspondent, was "a guest" somewhere in Gaza. No ransom demands as yet and no identification, as yet, of this journalist. "Must be," said Lyla.

"I don't know."

"Oh, Jay. You know it's him."

"Could be anybody."

"I told you," she said, "about watching television."

Other than her blaming TV, I wasn't sure how she was taking this (I had my own mixed emotions) – but she went to the kitchen and dropped something, or maybe it fell, a plate or a glass, and it cracked, it shattered against tile loudly and violently, and I still did not know if this, this accident or tantrum, this breaking of the glass, was an expression of fear, rage, frustration, or maybe mazel tov.

Chapter 35

The e-mail tolled for me, just as Lyla thought it would. Word came that the abducted journalist was indeed Phil Crawford, her husband. I was to fly out there to Gaza and report to some group affiliated with Hamas in an effort to save him. Lyla suspected that it was all a trap. They were really after me, these people, and Phil himself may be a decoy or even – well, Lyla suspected that Mohammed nee Phil, may even be manipulating the scheme. Why?

"To get you," she said.

"What did I do?"

"Don't be cute."

"Can't help it," I said.

No, really – why me?

"You run the Manhattan Independent."

"So?"

"They regard the paper as anti-Islam, as an inflammatory voice against the caliphate."

True, we ran those Danish cartoons and supported the Pope when the Pope made those remarks about Islam being a religion of the sword. I signed my name to an editorial blasting Islam after Theo Van Gogh was murdered. That surely got their attention, and Lyla, in her book review section, praised Robert Spencer's *The Truth About Muhammad* and also praised Oriana Fallaci in remembrance of Fallaci's wake-up call to Europe against Islam gone wild, where again we used the headline

"The Koran Has Arrived And It Has Come To Devour The Bible."

All that is no way to make friends and influence a billion and a half people.

But also true that we gave equal time to Muslim voices. Phil himself got in his licks, as did cartoonist Peter Brand.

I wasn't quite ready to buy Lyla's conspiracy fears – but we must never dismiss a woman's intuitive Ides.

"Ach zo," I said.

That was William Holden's great line in *Stalag 17* when he found out who'd been planted as an informer.

William Holden. How did Hollywood find such men? They will never come round again. Who killed Jeff Chandler?

"Don't go," she said.

We were leaving Lincoln Center after a performance of Brahms' First Piano Concerto. Brahms never surpassed this. Nobody did. This music, this Brahms, touched Lyla so deeply that sometimes she needed hours of silence and contemplation before she could recover. She'd wept during the performance. We can't replace him either, Brahms. Seems that in the Arts they arrive only once.

Give some credit to the rough men who founded Hollywood. Watch the young William Holden and you wonder why they stuck with him, nurtured him along when, in the beginning, he was mostly arms and legs and a face that would take years to fill in. Who knew he'd turn out to be, well – William Holden! They did. They knew. Likewise Clark Gable, Jimmy Stewart, Gary Cooper and all the rest. They must have known something, these tycoons who had started off manufacturing buttons and bows in the Garment District. From there they went west and manufactured stars.

Maybe it's destiny. BUT – "Nothing is written," protests Peter O'Toole in *Lawrence of Arabia*. There's another one. Peter O'Toole.

Some roles can only be played by one performer – O'Toole

as Lawrence, George C. Scott as Patton, Pacino as the young Godfather.

"Please tell me your plans," said Lyla.

I'd rather not even though we were in this together. I didn't need the scene.

We were at the Starbucks in Times Square. Lyla was big on their coffee. Why, I don't know. Real Men don't drink Latte.

I'd been reading the book *Caesar* by Adrian Goldsworthy and Lyla had been after me to hand in a review, only I never wrote reviews foremost because I can't finish anything anymore. I start but can't finish because I know where everything is going and even if I don't know I don't care. That goes for books, where I'm doing well if I get through a third of all the pages, and even movies (except the classics) and even baseball, where I seldom make it to the final out, and as for football, I hardly ever make it through halftime before I snooze off in front of the TV. All this is recent. I used to be a glutton for all that and could finish up the entire helping of *War and Peace* and even polish off Joyce's *Ulysses* but that was then, when I considered myself in training, when I hungered to know everything. Now I know too much. Yes, too much. I'm still in training, even as managing editor here at the Manhattan Independent, yes, still in training, still know nothing and still – still, I know too much.

(These days I just scan and it is my new theory, as a newspaperman, that most readers just check out the headlines and maybe the lead. There's simply too much of everything.)

"I gave you the book to inspire you," Lyla said.

"I should be Caesar?"

"Heroic," she said, adding that, "You're already a hero in my eyes and I want it to remain so."

A hero accepts the tragedy of his command and is able to send up a thousand men to take a hill knowing that 800 will die – and still sleep well at night.

This hero must never teeter, never falter, never turn back,

never regret, even if he knows that he miscalculated and was wrong from the start. He's made the decision, and that's that, final. A commander must always be bold and even recklessness is never a vice. (Is the managing editor of a Manhattan daily this sort of commander, and are his war correspondents his troops? Even if he did wrong, this editor-king, this Caesar of the newsroom, this King David of Manhattan, he must keep strong and never regret.)

Right here in Starbucks I was taken by an epiphany that women are stronger than men. We know how to fight, true, but women know how to endure.

I wondered if we were going to finish off this evening as we always do – sex.

"I wonder," said Lyla, smiling that wicked smile, "if we're going to finish off this evening as we always do."

There – we'd begun to think alike.

"I don't think I'm in the mood," she said.

"Same here," I said.

"Liar."

"You, too," I said, and we laughed.

Good. We're laughing. We're putting our troubles aside. Phil? Phil who? He's Mohammed anyway. Nothing wrong with that except that we don't know if his kidnapping is legit or a trap to get me out there and get ME killed. It's becoming dangerous to speak out against the Religion of Peace. Robert Spencer knows this. Ayaan Hirsi Ali knows this. Oriana Fallaci knew this (before she died) and Salman Rushdie knew this first and from Rushdie we all should have seen what's coming. No prophet arose to warn us that the fatwa against one man, Rushdie, was the first anvil toward a jihad against the rest of us.

Another writer, this time in Muslim Bangladesh, is in a run for his life for speaking in favor of the USA and Israel. His name is (was?) Salah Uddin Shoaib Choudhury and he refuses to hate in this world that is rapidly devolving into Sodom where hatred was a virtue, and where they stoned you to death for providing shelter, mercy and compassion for the widow and the orphan. Hatred was a virtue back there in Sodom, and here we go again! Hello? Wasn't anybody home when history began repeating itself with a vengeance? This already is Sodom, half the world, and they're coming for the other half.

(Am I losing my precious editorial detachment? This is a worry.)

"So let's go back to our place and just read," I suggested.

What did I say? She bristled.

"Next," she said, tightening, "you'll suggest we just be friends."

This didn't help when I said, "So what's wrong with being friends? We're friends already."

"No," she said. "Oh you're so naïve. Lovers can't be friends. Love is conflict. Love is combat."

Back at our place in the Village she played the Brahms we had just heard and here again she fell into a swoon and I was beginning to worry about all this melancholy going on. After this she insisted that we talk religion, which I never care to do as this only causes trouble. Lyla was raised Presbyterian, but barely, as she liked to say. Religion never motivated her family and she stopped believing in God after her father, the judge, was wrongly accused of accepting a bribe and then, in despair, took his own life. That's when she lost her faith, whatever there was of it from the start. Now, however, she needed to know, as if I knew, because religion was so much a part of everything these days. Me? I was raised part Catholic, Mom, part Jewish, Dad. That should make me an expert on both and yet I claimed no expertise on Catholicism or Judaism.

We were sipping wine. Lyla was in a negligee after she had stripped down to bra and panties. Actually it wasn't much of a bra as her nipples showed through and sharply upwards and the panties weren't much either because – well, because. Not quite the atmosphere for a talk on theology. Was this a test? Okay, I'm strong. I can resist temptation. Watch me. In either case, I had to dial in my reserves.

"Yes, I believe in God," I said.

"How could you," she asked, "with all that's going on?"

"Chaos," I said, "that too is a plan."

I reminded her that of Shakespeare we have no authentic version of Hamlet, the texts vary, and yet of the Bible no one questions a single word from the moment at Sinai.

"So the Bible is absolute?"

"Absolutely."

"I envy you," she said.

Do I believe in an afterlife?

Yes.

Why?

Because what's the alternative?

"I do envy you, Jay."

Then: "Sinai? You really believe all of it is the word of God? God spoke, Moses wrote?"

"King David believed that, so that's good enough for me."

As a favor to me she had already read (11th century) Judah Halevi's "The Kuzari" ("Sinai – the one and only authentic event in religious history") and this book, more than any other, led her to think again. This is true, I admitted, that religion (in excess) intoxicates people and is the crux of all, or most, of the world's problems, but then again, maybe it's not religion, it's just people being stupid and needing something, always something, as a reason, as an excuse, to go bonkers, for if there were no religion to drive men berserk there'd be soccer, for example.

"Oh shut up," she said. "Let's fuck."

Oooh!

* * *

Paulette Hammerman was here in my office. Over the phone she had sounded like your worst nightmare of a high school English teacher, tall, flat-chested, age-non-specific, weak-eyed, prudish, humorless, and here she was, finally in person, and again, tall, flat-chested, age-non-specific, weak-eyed, prudish and humorless, exactly as I had imagined. Paulette was director of the Society for the Protection of Journalists (SPJ) and her errand was Phil Crawford.

"We are very concerned," she said, as if it were my fault.

Well –

She was joined, a moment later in my office, by a man named Lester Lax, also with SPJ.

He also said "we are very concerned" and added he'd heard that Phil Crawford had been reluctant to go, out there to Gaza, but that I had forced him.

"Nonsense," I said. "Phil was raring to go."

This was true, of course. I could hardly hold him back.

"That's not what we've heard," said Paulette.

I asked where they got this information – and why did I know the answer even before it was given?

"Peter Brand, your cartoonist," said Lester, "led us to believe..."

I tuned out about here but could only think, aha. Ach zo.

Soon the room filled up with Stu Greenwald, head of our foreign desk, Ken Ballard, executive editor, and finally Ben Hawkins, publisher.

The word – given to Ben Hawkins – was that the abductors wanted me, by name. There were no other demands. I was the demand.

"You don't have to go," said Ken Ballard. "This is an issue for the government, not this newspaper."

True.

"He's right," said Stu Greenwald. "If you go, Jay, we could lose both you and Phil."

True.

"I wouldn't expect him to go," said Paulette Hammerman, "but that leaves us with nothing for a response."

True again.

Paulette Hammerman and Lester Lax had good reason to

be concerned and well beyond this, this particular case, as journalists were going down all over the place, most recently Anna Politkovskaya in Russia, for a total for 40 journalists murdered in Russia over the past five years, not counting (most famously) Daniel Pearl of the Wall Street Journal and so many more across the globe. Journalists were in season.

"We can't let this go on," said Lester Lax.

Absolutely.

"It's never been this bad," said Paulette Hammerman.

That is a fact with stats to back it up. Not only journalists, but anyone with an OPINION was at risk. Soon they'd know what you were thinking. Combat reporting had always been hazardous but mainly in the combat zone. Now the entire world was a combat zone. Full-time journalist and part-time blogger (excellent on both counts) Cinnamon Stillwell sent in an opinion piece (which I'll be carrying in the Manhattan Independent) noting that "all across the Western World, a worrisome phenomenon is spreading. Fear of incurring Muslim wrath is leading politicians, journalists, artists, professors, teachers and business owners to censor themselves." She cites the Pope himself who had to backtrack for his opinion and a French journalist named Robert Redeker forced into hiding for expressing himself in Le Figaro.

"We're in a spot," said Paulette Hammerman back to the subject at hand, and on me with a certain gaze that I remembered from somewhere.

She wore glasses that had gone out of style with Himmler.

The discussion turned generic, mostly about this world growing ever more violent and ever more inhospitable to us, the messengers. What was our role, to be advocates or observers? Was it possible to be a reporter without a point of view? Should we be mere messengers or indeed soldiers for truth? Here at the Manhattan Independent, for instance, we referred to Hamas leaders as "terrorists" (sometimes even "thugs") and over there at The New York Times these suddenly became cuddly "lawmakers" and "legislators."

Little things mean a lot. Here, terrorist, there, militant. We say "disputed territory," you say, "occupied territory."

Earlier, Phil Crawford had sent in copy with the dateline "Occupied Jerusalem" and I caught it and nixed it just in time.

That is not a fact. That is a point of view, and people do it all the time, passing off POVs as facts.

How is it a "cycle of violence" when only one side does all the suicide bombing?

You say Mozart, I say Beethoven.

I cleared my throat. They forgot I was in the room.

"Yes, Jay, what do you think?" This came from Ben Hawkins but, abruptly, all eyes were on me, as, after all, this was really about whether I was going or not.

"The decision really is yours," said Paulette Hammerman.

We'd never make a couple, even if we were the last two on earth. She kept glancing around the room taking note, disapprovingly, of my boxing trophies, my Krav Maga martial arts belts, those photos with me and Joe Frazier sparring, and there I am wall-to-wall at one race track or another and never in the winner's circle with the fancy people but in the back-stretch with people like you and me.

"Yes," said Lester Lax. "It's your life on the line."

You say Gordie Howe, I say Maurice Richard.

"Not to mention Phil Crawford's," added Paulette Hammerman. "He's the one really in danger at the moment."

She couldn't keep her eyes off me, this Paulette. Maybe it's love.

"Sorry to be so blunt," said Lester Lax.

About here it got testy, my guys, Ken Ballard and Ben Hawkins, annoyed at these other two, who seemed to be putting it all on us.

(Stu Greenwald had already left, possibly in disgust.)

"Why is this an editorial issue?" said Ken Ballard. "This is about a crime that's been committed. That's not our line of work."

Yes, the State Department, the FBI, the CIA, all of them were on the case as summoned by this group, SPJ.

"We're on top of this," said Paulette Hammerman. "We made all the calls and contacts immediately."

"As did I," said Ben Hawkins. "Only I resent the implication that somehow we're at fault, and that another journalist here, Jay Garfield, must pay the price."

"No blame intended," said Lester Lax. "But these are the facts."

"What facts?" said Ben Hawkins.

"One of your reporters, Phil Crawford, has been abducted, and these hostage-takers demand Jay Garfield." Thus spoke Paulette Hammerman.

"Those are the facts," said Lester Lax.

You say Loretta Lynn, I say Patsy Cline. Did you say Michelle Pfeiffer AND Jessica Lange? Sorry, you can't have both. One or the other.

All right, then. I'll take Michelle. No problemo!

"It still comes down to what you people intend to do," said Lester Lax.

"You mean what Jay Garfield over here intends to do."

"Okay," said Paulette Hammerman.

Paulette Hammerman – still giving me the naked eye – followed up by declaring that this newspaper was known for its hostility toward justice in the Middle East.

This is code for dump Israel – and quite surprising to be coming from an organization that is supposed to be neutral.

"I won't dignify that with a response," said Ben Hawkins. But then: "What's your evidence?"

"I apologize," said Paulette Hammerman. "Really, I'm sorry."

"We give everyone an equal shot," said Ben Hawkins. "If we are CONSERVATIVE, and I'm not saying we are, it's only to pick up the slack."

"I do regret the remark."

"Please don't speak to me about justice" – Ben warming to a boil.

"I take it back, really I do."

Really she did, except that the horse already left the gate.

"Would you go," asked Ken Ballard, "knowing what you're walking into?"

"Honestly, I don't know," said Lester Lax.

"That does not qualify as honest," said Ben Hawkins.

"All right," said Lester Lax, "no, I would not go. But then, I did not start this fix."

"Jay?"

That was Ben Hawkins.

Brooklyn was never the same after the Dodgers left town.

"Jay?"

I got up and headed for the door. I said: "You people keep talking. I'm already packed."

* * *

Lyla has been dreaming that only one of us would be coming back from Gaza – most likely Phil, her Islamic husband. I told her to quit dreaming and to quit believing in omens. That's sinful. Fact is, I'd been having pretty much the same dream. I must assume that the world is not big enough to contain the two of us, so it's either me or Phil Crawford, and how about that for symbolism?

* * *

After that meeting with the people from the Society for the Protection of Journalists I went back to my office, took no phone calls, no e-mails, nothing, just sat down in that big red chair my former wife Myrna had bought me as a gift when I first went to work, some eight years ago, here at the Manhattan Independent. She called it a "power chair" fit for an editor who was going places. At the time I was not yet managing editor.

Power, I was learning, was not so desirable after all. By its very definition, you made decisions that touched the lives of people all around you and even beyond. To be Caesar, to be King David – you had to have the stomach. I'm reading from that book, "Whenever he felt that it was in his interest, Caesar was utterly ruthless." Well, good, good for Caesar. In my case, here was another cliché so true; be careful what you wish for, though, really, I had wished for nothing more than to be an honorable journalist. I had started off, back in southern New Jersey, covering fire, police, city hall, zoning boards and boards of education. These were small towns and when I got to Manhattan I thought it would be nearly the same, only bigger. I had not counted on a clash of civilizations, with me right in the middle of it all. The man who said all politics is local left the building much too soon.

Most of us never got the memo that the world was about to go bonkers.

I had covered wars, been in the heat of combat, but never expected bloodshed to spill over into newsprint.

Gladys, my assistant, knocked softly and asked if I was okay. I said yes and she said I came back from that meeting awfully glum and still appeared shaken.

"I'm okay," I said, but she left unconvinced.

I kept thinking about that meeting and realized, as never before, that the world had taken sides, the microcosm of it all right here in the newsroom among my peers. People were changing colors, right in front of me, turning green like those people in that town imagined by Eugène Ionesco, where one-by-one the inhabitants succumbed to the brutality of the invading rhinos, and became rhinos themselves.

* * *

"You rang?"

That was our theater critic, Lance Collier, and yes I had summoned him some time ago but forgot why.

"Sit down," I said.

"I'm sitting, Jay. You seem distracted. Should I come back some other time?"

Lance was Our Man from Princeton, Ivy League from head to toe, on loan (it always seemed to me) in his tweeds and elbow pads from those academic lecture halls where no deadlines but only tranquility prevailed. He'd written an excellent book on F. Scott Fitzgerald, the focus on Fitzgerald's "Crack-Up." In his analysis of that work he traced Fitzgerald's despair back to King Solomon's "Ecclesiastes," matching them up, side by side, as if nearly a single work, or the work of a single mind though 3,000 years apart, but still, bridged by the same pessimism and sense of futility for everything under the sun.

(Fitzgerald: "I would cease any attempts to be a person – to be kind, just or generous...There was to be no more giving of myself – all giving was to be outlawed henceforth under a new name, and that name was Waste." Solomon, King of Israel, 3,000 years earlier: "So I hated life, for I was depressed by all that goes on under the sun, because everything is futile and a vexation of the spirit." Did Fitzgerald know that he was borrowing or do the same truths get refreshed generation to generation?)

"Frank Rich," I said, now remembering why I'd called him in for a talk.

Yes, Frank Rich. This man had been the theater critic for The New York Times but was better known as The Butcher of Broadway. In his day he had scorched nearly every play under his withering eyes, sending thousands of writers, actors, directors, producers, stagehands and angels into the pit of eternal damnation. Most were never heard from again, so all-powerful was this executioner for the Times.

Finally (and for whatever reason) he got switched to another beat and now he could speak his mind, and so on a morning radio show – Imus, I believe it was – relaxed and entirely happy with himself, he confessed that most of these plays, on second thought, weren't all that bad. Some were even good and maybe excellent. But he destroyed them and why? Well, because he felt like it and because he could.

Then, after saying all that, he laughed, and everybody laughed along with him, never mind all the people he had ruined and all the dreams he had dashed.

So? I had noticed that Lance here – Lance had been following the same trend, or so it seemed to me judging from his latest reviews.

"I'm certainly not about to tell you your business," I said, "but just be mindful that you've got people's lives in your hands."

Like Frank Rich, he could shut down a production by the might of his poison pen. He could do it, ruin it all, by reason of a bad tooth, a headache, a fight with his wife, a traffic ticket, a crying baby on the train, or just for fun, to watch people squirm, or for revenge, but most likely for the power and to prove himself above the playwright. (Likewise book critics, but that's another story. No, it's the same story.)

In one review, Lance had poked fun at the female lead and not about her performance but about her appearance and that sounded like Frank Rich all over again.

I did not like doing this, imposing myself in another man's arena of expertise. The theater was not my business BUT this newspaper was, was my business.

"I'm only asking you to think again before you go in for the kill," I said.

Lance – gentleman that he was – took it well, MY criticism of him, and agreed that he may have been hasty here and there and yes, he'd think again. An overindulgence of theater (as an overindulgence of virtually anything) does lead a man to be slothful and jaded and for all that he may well have been guilty. He was glad, he said, that I had brought it up again.

"Again?" I said.
"Jay, we went over all this earlier this morning."
"We did?"
"Jay, are you all right?"

* * *

Jimmy Smokes (Jamil Samil) is a practicing Muslim, only he practices it mostly at the racetrack when he can get off (for good behavior) from running the news shop, which he doesn't run anyway. His wife does. She's fed up with him and his gambling and his ignoring the business (and quite lucrative it is), except that she loves him, Seena does. From selling newspapers, candy and tobacco, Jimmy Smokes is practically a millionaire, nickel here, dime there, adds up, although really, he's got that humidor room in the back that stocks cigars worth $400 a piece. That too adds up, especially when big men park their chauffeur-driven limos along the curb and walk in to buy a dozen of those cigars, and that really adds up.

Jimmy Smokes and Seena refuse to conform to the stereotype. They are wild and crazy Americans.

(What is it about news shops and barber shops that make us long for the way we were?)

"Try this," he said, pouring a new pipe tobacco blend into a plastic bag. "Mostly Turkish, but I've spiced it up knowing your taste."

"You know I don't like it too sweet."

"Of course I know. Stop insulting me."

His wife laughed. Some of the customers didn't understand what went on between us, and sometimes I didn't, either. That's why we never (okay, rarely) talked politics, and frankly I'd prefer to not talk politics with anybody, or religion, or anything, really, except baseball, football, boxing, and horseracing, of course, and oh yes, writing. All of that yes, but not politics or religion. Please – that's why we go to the ball game.

Jimmy and Seena had a 19-year-old daughter named Galeel, a knockout, and she asked how I was, using those eyes.

In some places she'd be lashed for this.

After she left, Seena told me that her daughter had a crush on me. Actually, Seena told me that all the time and I took it as a joke. Seena winked and told me that she wouldn't mind it if her daughter hooked up with me and I took that as a joke as well. As it was, this daughter was dating a guy from NYU's school of film, non-Muslim, this kid, and no objections from either Jimmy Smokes or his wife. If only, I kept thinking, it could be everywhere like this.

(Who needs this? From a prominent Muslim leader here in the U.S.A.: "Islam isn't in America to be equal to any other faith, but to be dominant. The Koran should be the highest authority in America, and Islam the only accepted religion on earth." Really, who needs this? Not me, and not Jimmy Smokes either, along with his wife Seena.)

"I hope you two degenerates have no plans to go to the track," said Seena, and then to her husband: "Remember, we have inventory to do, and that man is coming."

"What man?" said Jimmy.

"The accountant."

"Jay isn't going anyplace," said Jimmy Smokes. "Right, Jay?"

"Right," I said.

"That's not what I heard," said Seena, "and Jay, you'd be foolish to go."

"He's not going," said Jimmy. "He's not that stupid."

"Truly," said Seena, "you must think this through."

I explained that I had thought this through and that there was no choice.

"Do you really believe you're on a rescue mission?" she said.

"He's probably dead already, this Phil Crawford," said Jimmy.

"They are going to kill you," said Seena. "Trust me, I know

these people."

"Never mind how," said Jimmy. "But believe the woman. She knows these people."

Yes, I'd heard. There were stories about members of her family, some in Syria, some in Lebanon, some in Jordan and Egypt, and what happened to them when they refused to go along with the prevailing orthodoxy and instead spoke up against the fanaticism. Seena was about all that was left of that family, so she knew, firsthand. (Seena had been raped over there but kept it quiet to spare herself an Honor Killing. Jimmy Smokes once blurted this out and immediately regretted telling me this and swore me to forget, so I forgot.)

The question was this: How much pipe tobacco will I need to keep me smoking in Gaza or wherever they'd be taking me – a few ounces, a few pounds, a few tons? Or, perhaps the No Smoking frenzy has reached terrorism central along the caves of Afghanistan, Pakistan, Gaza, Ramallah and all points where they practice decapitation but also good grooming, safe sex and preventive hygiene. Does the man facing his firing squad rate a final cigarette, or has that custom been dropped for the condemned man's well-being?

In Jimmy Smokes' "Sinatra Room" (all Sinatra all the time, naturally) we lit up and spoke about everything except what was happening. Jimmy needed someone to help him write his book about the adventures of a news shop, yes, adventures – all the crazy people who came into the shop with their eccentricities and their stories, like the man whose wife had dementia and when they came in she, the wife, teetered around the store and grabbed and routed all the candy she could and even squeezed to smithereens hundred dollar cigars, along with no effort by Jimmy or the husband to subdue her. No, this was her thrill. The customer paid for it all – sometimes amounting to a thousand dollars a visit – and this, to Jimmy, was the ultimate expression of love, that a man would be so merciful toward his wife.

"Is Sam Cleaver still available?"

"Sammy only does fiction."

"So what is this? Look around. This is fiction."

True, that's the only way to make sense of everything large and small. We'd covered this before, about Sam or anybody writing Jimmy's book, and I never had the heart to tell Jimmy that every life is worthy of a book and that everybody wants it done, but by someone else, and for free. Lyla gets it all the time, people saying, "Wait till you hear MY story!" (Like yours is nothing.) Sam hears it from family, friends and strangers, and even I get offers to tell someone else's story, guaranteed to become the biggest bestseller of all time.

I've got my own secret novel in reserve. It's about – oh hell, who cares!

"You should listen to my wife," said Jimmy Smokes. "She's worried about you."

"Let's not talk about this."

"I know you've got your mind made up. Nothing anybody can say, right?"

"Who do you like in tomorrow's feature at Belmont?"

"When do you go?"

"Other people are making all the arrangements. The government is also involved. About a week, maybe more, maybe less."

"Can you take torture?"

"Whoa!"

"Well we have to talk about this. We have to talk."

"We don't have to talk."

So we didn't talk.

On my way out I refused the ceremonial farewells. No hugs, no kisses, but a strange blessing that even got Jimmy to do a stricken double-take.

"Allah be with you," said his wife Seena.

Chapter 36

I liked to watch Lyla in action, I mean when she went forth to mix it up with her people, the smart set. These were the ladies and gentlemen who supported the symphony, dance, theater, film (as opposed to "movies"), the art galleries and surely books, the book world. Today's meeting was 14 flights up on 72nd near the East River in an apartment (that can't be the right word) that must cost a million dollars a year to rent, unless it was bought for $20 million. These people had money.

The men were fat and bald, the women were tall and thin and quite attractive, but only Lyla glittered. Even dressed down for business in her Donna Karan suit, Prada bag and shoes, plus some frills and flowers, she sparkled as ever the Manhattan princess. Her hair was cut to run wild for that touch of carefree and careless nobility. There was no mistaking her stage presence, her preeminence. I loved this, watching her perform.

Lyla introduced me all around as her editor, not her lover, though I would not have been surprised if some people did the math.

I don't do well in these soirees and always find myself attached and in conversation with the help, the people handing out the snacks.

"The wrong people," Lyla kept whispering as she pushed me to a forced march among the Right People.

Finally, the meeting came to order and about half of them (the other half sided with Lyla) got up to denounce Ernest

Hemingway and Mark Twain for their repeated use of the "n" word – and what's to be done? Banish them from the schools. Lyla was already on record as being forcefully opposed to this measure and had used her considerable influence, in her weekly column and in meetings with the mayor's office, to stop this warfare on literature.

I was not a member of the "committee" but as managing editor of the Manhattan Independent was asked my opinion anyway and said that I was against censorship of any kind and that what we had here was a case of literary cleansing, same as ethnic cleansing, which is always a terrible business, downright sinful, and that doing the right thing sometimes ends up being the wrong thing, like this. Lyla declared that racism was America's shame but that it ought to be obliterated state by state, city by city, person by person – not book by book. Also, how can we recover our past and be true to the present if we harness the written word to the culture of the moment? "Warts and all, that's life, that's literature," she said, "and when we begin placing literature on the witness stand how far are we until we call it book burning?"

Later, at the Cornelia Street Café, we agreed that we had both been terrific but had probably made no progress. The world keeps fluctuating between freedom and suppression, still, even in America. For every act of freedom along comes a movement to suppress, tit for tat. Lyla was horrified that her people – yes, the Right People – were so quick to insist on censorship. That's taking liberalism too far, and it's not even about liberalism but about political correctness gone berserk.

"The right people, huh?"

"I knew – I just knew you wouldn't let go of that," she said.

"How come you're looking so good these days?"

That was not my only question. Why was she drinking while pregnant?

"I'm not," she said.

"Oh?"

She'd lost the baby.

"Forgot to tell me?"

"You have enough troubles."

"Shouldn't the father know?"

"Jay, listen."

"I'm listening."

"I mean really listen."

"Go."

"Right before he left..."

"I know what's coming."

"Yes," she said, and it wasn't right before he left, not only then, but had been going on throughout, and by force. He was her husband. He knew his rights. Wives were property. She had kept it to herself, apart from me, afraid of what I might do and also afraid that I'd stop what we had going. So it had all been deception when she assured me, so honorably and bravely, that none of that was happening between them and now I understood her rage against him and blamed myself for not understanding it earlier. I could not blame her. This was not information you shared with a lover. I should have known and actually I did, I suspected. I never asked. Maybe once or twice I did, roundabout, but preferred to stay blissfully stupid and unaware. I should have cared about her suffering and maybe didn't want to face up to that, either. In that case there'd have been no need to ship him off to Gaza. I'd have done the job right here, with my own hands. She knew that, too, and what good would that do, so she kept silent and suffered coming and coming.

In other words, she could not be sure whose child it was.

"I had an abortion. Are you angry?"

"Yes, but not at you."

"Oh, Jay," she began.

Who said big girls don't cry?

* * *

This made me think: Lyla said she knew exactly how to get even. "I know just what to do." But she wouldn't tell.

* * *

A group of men came in to brief me. I think they were from the government, most of them anyway. They identified themselves one by one but I failed to keep score. They were dressed like undertakers with faces to match. So they kept on briefing me, these men, but I had stopped paying attention, some time ago. Some time ago I lost something, somewhere, even lost myself as we do when we know events are beyond our control and we humble ourselves to the inevitable. We know what's coming, so let it come.

They kept pausing to ask if I had any questions and I said no, no questions, and this surprised them and even annoyed them. I wasn't playing the part, the part assigned to me, that of a sacrifice. I did not seem to care much about Phil Crawford, nor for myself. Phil Crawford, I was assured, was alive. My job was to bring him back and if possible bring myself back as well. A sheik named Salaman was calling the shots, according to what's been learned, and he, this sheik, wants nothing more than to talk to me – about the coverage he'd been getting in our newspaper. After that, Phil would be free to go, along with me, if I behaved.

One of them, one of these men, gave me a pill, just in case. He started to explain but I waved him off.

This, too, annoyed them.

"We seem to be intruding," one of them said.

"Please," I said, "can't we just hurry this up?"

That really annoyed them.

I guess they expected a performance.

Someone asked if it is true that I am part Jewish. I said yes, yes I am, and they shared glances, suggesting that this was REAL trouble.

"You know of course…"

"Yes I know."

Paulette Hammerman (though she wasn't an official part of this delegation) came in to sit in as an observer and she observed that I was being terribly blasé about the risks facing me and strangely cavalier about the perils to Phil Crawford. The men were glad to hear this as apparently that is exactly what they had been thinking. One of these men kept taking notes and scribbled especially fast when Paulette used the words blasé and cavalier. Okay, call me blasé, call me cavalier, but don't call me Ishmael. (See, I must do something to regain editorial neutrality. I am becoming the man Sam Cleaver wants me to be, no passive messenger but a soldier for truth. Is this good? I don't know.)

Any questions?

No, no questions.

But there must be something.

No, there is nothing.

We are here to help you.

Appreciated.

There are steps you will have to follow once you get off the plane at Ben Gurion Airport.

Surely.

The phone rang. I had to take the call. It was City Desk wanting to know what was more important, North Korea setting off another bomb or Madonna adopting another African baby. Which one of these goes above the fold? Soon, days from now, I wouldn't be making these decisions but for now let's go with North Korea and refrain from getting entirely too cynical as we all know that to sell newspapers the choice would have been Madonna. Give the people what they want. No, not yet. There is still time to give the people what they need and let's not go there yet where we let cynicism and the love of gossip rule our news judgment.

"If all this is too much information at one time," one of the men said, "well..."

Well – it was too much, really it was, but it would all come together, eventually, like a Sibelius symphony.

But in my own style and on my own terms. I had told Ben Hawkins, my boss, that I needed nothing more than the plane tickets to Tel Aviv, I had no need for rituals except the facts (such as my life for Phil's in payment for my sin) but this had to be done, this briefing, if for no other reason than the insurance. I'd been dropped by my own provider (suddenly high risk, I guess), so the Manhattan Independent was picking up the tab.

* * *

Ben Hawkins drove me to the airport; quite a personal touch. When he dropped me off he said this: "God be with you."

Chapter 37

Figures to be a delay, over at El Al, possibly 24 hours. Something mechanical, according to the announcement.

But we all know what it really means.

People around me are groaning. Not me. What's the rush? I'm off to Gaza to exchange my life for another man. There's no hurry.

Over there in the corner, all in black but extravagantly cheerful, those are the Lubavitch. They're always at the airport. They hasten me over and ask if I am Jewish. Today, yes. Today I am fully Jewish. My Christian mother would approve. When they asked him to identify himself (before they beheaded him), Daniel Pearl testified, "My father is Jewish, my mother is Jewish, I am Jewish." Include me in. These Lubavitch, they're always looking for customers. They strap tefillin on me and along with them I recite the Sh'ma, plus King David's Psalm 23, and here it gets me, at the end: "Surely goodness and mercy shall follow me all the days of my life, and I shall dwell in the house of the Lord forever."

Amen.

Yes, Amen.

So I'm at an airport Motel 6 waiting for bomb sniffing dogs to give the all-clear for my flight to Israel and I'm watching a Seinfeld rerun. Not the news. (Lyla would be pleased and proud.) That's right, I am not watching the news because frankly my dear I don't give a damn. I'm switching off. Clark Gable, in his prime as a movie star but drunk while driving, ran over a man and killed him, or maybe it was a woman but, in any case, he, Gable, never went to jail, right, the studio fixed it so that someone else did his time.

Actually it was a studio exec who was persuaded or implored to take Gable's place in prison – something like, "Hey, George, you're not going to like this but..."

Or maybe, "George, how would you like to spend the next ten years of your life in prison – as a favor?"

I mention this only because, at the moment, I could also use a surrogate. Only kidding.

I only peeked at the BBC. We all watch the BBC for only one reason and that's hoping anchor Katty Kay will one day take off her top.

I am beginning to worry about something. I seem to know the news, all the latest from here and all around the world, even without getting it transmitted from conventional sources. I don't have to be told. I already know. Maybe that's what happens to us after we've been in this business too long, we develop a third eye, a third ear, an antennae that has us subliminally plugged into every frequency. (Remember Dan Rather, mugged on Park Avenue back in 1986, and "Kenneth, what's the frequency?" There's more to this than we've been told.)

Sometimes I know it before it happens. I swear. I am no genius, no prophet, but everything is SO PREDICTABLE!

I know what's coming.

Just call me a newsman, that's all.

We all know what's coming.

Why do I feel like I'm in a foreign country already? (Are we there yet? Maybe.)

The cabbie had Ricky Martin blasting on the radio. Can't beat the Latin beat. I'm beginning to appreciate that music.

Interesting how I've begun to appreciate Seinfeld. Never took to that show while it was young.

Anyway, I'm in for a Seinfeld marathon here at Motel 6 and am all down and cozy under the sheets when –

Sam Cleaver?

"You've been stabbed in the back."

A dispatch had come through, to the newsroom, with Phil Crawford's byline, meaning that he was alive and well, or that someone using his name was alive and well, but let us assume that it truly is Phil Crawford back on the beat. (He'd been silent for so long.) Is this good? Yes. In this case my assignment is to substitute myself for a living, breathing hostage, instead of a body. After all, in all this time we'd been in a quandary as to whether Phil was still with us, with them, or with Allah and those 72 virgins. (Still virgins after all those guests?) But here's the catch. The dispatch was sent in with "Occupied Jerusalem" as the dateline and that's how it's set to go for the next edition of the Manhattan Independent. Occupied Jerusalem.

"Double cross, Jay."

Phil had tried this trick numerous times and I'd always been there to stop it, along with Ben Hawkins in firm support.

No American newspaper so blatantly denied Israel its sovereignty. We'd be the first.

"Ben has switched sides?"

"Sure looks like it," says Sam Cleaver.

Ben Hawkins, as I've always known, is loyal to newsprint, but he is also loyal to his other investments – oil! – as I've come to suspect. (I had seen him in his office with those titled men, some even in their silken robes.) True, Ben Hawkins owns the Manhattan Independent, but, as I keep asking, who owns Ben Hawkins? Now we know. Sooner or later he'd have to make a choice between what's good for the newspaper and what's good for himself. Apparently, the deal is done. Apparently, oil is thicker than newsprint.

Inside the building Ben is big but likewise he is part of the global economy where other men, from desert kingdoms flushed with the resources and the reserves that we require to keep our system lubricated – these men are even bigger than Ben Hawkins, bigger in money, bigger in power, bigger in influence. They've got barrels of money invested in this country. They've pumped billions into our real estate, into our universities (talk about shaping the minds of our young!) and have even spread their wealth into the ranches that produce thoroughbred champions. (This is personal.) If he owns pieces of them, these sheiks, they own chunks of him. Along the corridors of the newsroom we used to wonder (the whispers, the gossip) if we were about to be traded, or if, perhaps, we were already an American newspaper operating under the influence of foreign ownership. We still don't know.

Yes, Ben has partners.

Partners ask for favors – even insist, upon the towers of their seniority.

This was the favor. Give us Jerusalem.

Ben gave. Ben gave up Jerusalem.

Ben gave them my father.

"Plan B?" says Sam Cleaver.

Ben gave them my father.

"Plan B?" says Sam Cleaver.

But Ben had brought me in when I had been cast out; saved me from exile. He'd been a friend. But as we are taught, and AS IT IS WRITTEN – never count on this. Draw too close and you will get scorched. Do your work but expect no lasting friendship from the men who run the show. They will use you (as you use them) and when it's all over, when they are done with you, consider yourself finished. No scenes, no tears, no refunds.

"Come on, Jay."

Yes, Plan B. Lyla had come up with it and now it was for Sam Cleaver and Arnold Coffey to deliver. I'd been reluctant.

Occupied Jerusalem?

Reluctant no more.

* * *

Plan B, yes.

That would take some doing to get it past Ben Hawkins, Ken Ballard and all the rest, including the copy desk. But I knew it would get done, to the discomfort of Phil Crawford and his companions. They wouldn't like it, no, not at all. Meir Kahane was poison to them (Phil told me so himself) and finding Kahane in our newspaper – Phil's newspaper! – would surely place Phil in jeopardy, equivalent to setting him "in the frontline of the fiercest battle and withdraw from him, so that he may be struck down and die."

Lyla had the initiative. Sam Cleaver had the balls. Arnold Coffey had the authority to get Plan B (and Phil Crawford) executed.

All that remained was to get it published by the time I arrived in Israel and thereabouts. I had no doubt that this would get done.

Was I feeling guilty? Always – but modified by this headline; SAUDI COURT SENTENCES RAPE VICTIM TO 90 LASHES.

Phil Crawford would approve. He'd already told Lyla that American women (Lyla herself?) were asking for it in the way they were dressed or rather undressed.

They'd find it online, like this:

WORDS FROM THE GRAVE
OF A SLAIN WOULD-BE PROPHET
Written Months Before His Assassination In 1990
By Rabbi Meir Kahane

Dear World:

It appears that you are hard to please. I understand that you are upset over us here in Israel. Indeed, it appears that you are quite upset, even angry and outraged. Indeed, every few years you seem to become upset over us. Today, it is the brutal repression of the Palestinians; yesterday, it was Lebanon; before that it was the bombing of the nuclear reactor in Baghdad and the Yom Kippur War campaign. It appears that Jews who triumph, and who therefore, live, upset you most extraordinarily.

Of course, dear world, long before there was an Israel, we the Jewish people upset you. We upset a German people, who elected a Hitler and we upset an Austrian people, who cheered his entry into Vienna and we upset a whole slew of Slavic nations – Poles, Slovaks, Lithuanians, Ukrainians, Russians, Hungarians, Romanians.

And we go back a long, long way in history of world upset. We upset the Cossacks of Chmielnicki, who massacred tens of thousands of us in 1648-49; we upset the Crusaders, who on their way to liberate the Holy Land, were so upset at Jews that they slaughtered untold numbers of us.

We upset, for centuries, a Roman Catholic Church that did its best to define our relationship through Inquisitions. And we upset the arch-enemy of the church, Martin Luther, who in his call to burn the synagogues and the Jews within them, showed an admirable Christian ecumenical spirit.

It is because we became so upset over upsetting you, dear world, that we decided to leave you – in a manner of speaking – and establish a Jewish State. The reasoning was that living in close contact with you, as resident-strangers in the various countries that comprise you, we upset you, irritate you, and disturb you. What better notion, then, than to leave you and thus love you – and have you love us?

And so we decided to come home, to the same homeland from which we were driven out 1,900 years earlier by a Roman world that, apparently, we also upset.

Alas, dear world, it appears that you are hard to please. Having left you and your Pogroms and Inquisitions and Crusades and Holocausts, having taken our leave of the general world to live alone in our own little state, we continue to upset you. You are upset that we repress the Palestinians. You are deeply angered over the fact that we do not give up the lands of 1967, which are clearly the obstacle to peace in the Middle East.

Moscow is upset and Washington is upset. The Arabs are upset and the gentle Egyptian moderates are upset.

Well, dear world, consider the reaction of a normal Jew from Israel.

In 1920, 1921 and 1929, there were no territories of 1967 to impede peace between Jews and Arabs. Indeed, there was no Jewish State to upset anybody.

Nevertheless, the same oppressed and repressed Palestinians slaughtered hundreds of Jews in Jerusalem, Jaffa, Safed and Hebron. Indeed, 67 Jews were slaughtered one day in Hebron in 1929.

Dear world, why did the Arabs – the Palestinians – massacre 67 Jews in one day in 1929? Could it have been their anger over Israeli aggression in 1967? And why were 510 Jewish men, women and children slaughtered in Arab riots in 1936-39? Was it because of Arab upset over 1967?

And when you, dear world, proposed a U.N. Partition Plan in 1947 that would have created a Palestinian State alongside a tiny Israel and the Arabs cried and went to war and killed 6,000 Jews – was that upset stomach caused by the aggression of 1967?

And, by the way, dear world, why did we not hear your cry of upset then?

The Palestinians who today kill Jews with explosives and firebombs and stones are part of the same people who – when they had all the territories they now demand be given them for their state – attempted to drive the Jewish State into the sea. The same twisted faces, the same hate, the same cry of "idbah-al-yahud" – "Slaughter the Jews!" that we hear and see today, were seen and heard then.

The same people, the same dream – destroy Israel.

What they failed to do yesterday, they dream of today – but we should not repress them.

Dear world, you stood by the Holocaust and you stood by in 1948 as seven states launched a war that the Arab League proudly compared to the Mongol massacres. You stood by in 1967 as Nasser, wildly cheered by wild mobs in every Arab capital in the world, vowed to drive the Jews into the sea.

And you would stand by tomorrow if Israel were facing extinction.

And since we know that the Arabs-Palestinians daily dream of that extinction, we will do everything possible to remain alive in our own land.

If that bothers you, dear world, well – think of how many times in the past you bothered us.

In any event, dear world, if you are bothered by us, here is one Jew in Israel who could not care less.

* * *

Arnold Coffey and Sam Cleaver and the rest of them were correct. One day I'd have to step out from the safety of my nonpartisanship, my dithering, my equivocating, and take sides. There is no neutral, not anymore. There is no middle. There is right and there is left. There is us and there is them. All that is heavy traffic and bystanders beware.

The Arabs were not alone. The Jews, along the mainstream, were not in love with him either, this Meir Kahane of Brooklyn, New York. In Israel, where he'd served time in the Knesset and later in prison, he was persona non grata for advocating "population transfer" of the Arabs and for favoring Greater Israel. He was pilloried for being divisive, fanatical, radical, racist, sexist – and all around trouble-maker and hell-raiser. Not OUR KIND, Kahane, and not your father's rabbi.

Maybe he was all that, but we have it from Heschel that a prophet is defined as someone who knows what time it is.

Kahane, give him that; he knew what time it was.

* * *

This is crazy. I'm on the plane and we're up and flying. I know where I'm going. I have an appointment with killers so there's a terrific chance that I'll get killed. Okay, but what's been flashing through my mind? You'd expect me to revisit my past, take inventory of my successes and failures, opportunities lost and found, people who drew me up, dropped me down, regrets (I've had a few), women – oh the women! Or, you'd expect me to pray, and maybe I will, later. But during the flight I keep thinking about the Kentucky Derby, the one coming up next May, and that if I get killed out there I won't know who won. I've got TICKETS!

My son – I gave him my (last?) weekend. I dare not think of him and deluge myself in tears.

I told him to be righteous and strong.

"Just like you, Dad, right?"

That's what I mean.

* * *

Here I am at the Kings Hotel in Jerusalem. Two men brought me over, Avraham and Ibrahim.

Over there at Ben Gurion International Airport in Lod, Avraham said, "We are going for a long ride."

Ibrahim said, "Welcome to Palestine."

Avraham said, "You mean Israel."

Ibrahim said, "For the time being."

If they were enemies, why were they together?

Strange country – verily, "Two nations are in thy womb."

They were in unison when they dropped me off.

"Wait," said Avraham.

"You will be contacted," said Ibrahim.

"Shalom."

"Salam."

Who are these guys?

They will come for me when it's time.

I've been assigned room 301 and that's strange. That's the same room (for whoopee) Lyla and I usually share at the Warwick, 301. More strangeness. There's a bible on the table by the bed and it's open to the pages that tell the (sinful) story of David and Bathsheba. Another coincidence or, truly, am I being followed by the prophets? (According to legend, David asked the Lord if it would be possible to skip that part in his bio; bleep it out. The Lord said, No, it's all going in, warts and all. I have spoken.) In this land of prophets there's every chance that they're still around and, through their connections, are still keeping us afloat, even though we merit a second Flood. The man standing next to you, waiting for the light to change, may well be Elijah. This is Jerusalem. Three major faiths drink from this well. People turn messianic just by breathing in the air. (Apparently I am no exception.)

So what's on TV here in Jerusalem? What's going on along the dials? CCN, sure, the BBC, of course, Fox, Al-Jazeera and even more exotic programming from Jordan and beyond. But what's this? Son of a bitch what's this? Lo, it's Seinfeld! I didn't miss a thing. Nothing happened between New York and Jerusalem. Except for a time zone here and there, we're all in the same boat without a paddle.

Lyla was worried that I'd fall for some Sabra chick. I reminded her that Philip Roth couldn't get it up in Jerusalem. God is watching.

(Is this good? Do we really want to be judged and written up warts and all? Our only shot is if we're graded on the curve.)

Here's the thing. I've come to believe that we're all set down here (on earth) to accomplish but one task, one task and no more. Some of us are here to start the personal computer revolution, like Bill Gates, others are summoned to invent the intermittent windshield wiper, discover the remedy for polio, like Jonas Salk, and the pet rock, whoever that was, but he came, he saw, he gave, and then thank you, done, goodbye, obit.

287

(Most obits are about the person's one and only achievement.) I know a man who had this one heroic moment and none thereafter – thereafter he lived nobly but humbly. Some of us are invited to make one (good) movie, like Orson Welles, sing one (enduring) song, like Tony Bennett. That's what I believe, that we're all assigned a singular task and the lucky ones know what it is, the rest of us don't.

Maybe I already gave at the office, or perhaps this is my destiny, first to sin, then to repent.

Sirens, I hear sirens, and then a commotion out in the lobby. There's panic among some of the guests but among the staff it's just another suicide bombing. I rush over to Ben Yehuda pedestrian mall but the police and the ZAKA paramedics are already there, and, with all my combat experience, this is like nothing I have ever seen. I have never seen human heads rolling down the street and I have never seen doctors and nurses chasing after arms and legs in order to fit them onto the same body. I have never seen so much blood.

I kneel down to help a woman who is still together but is bleeding from the mouth, barely conscious. I hold up her head to prevent her from choking on all that blood and find myself yelling for the medics. I think I am being calm but am probably hysterical. The medics arrive and carry her off to the ambulance, but, her cell phone is still on the ground, and it is talking, and saying: "Miriam, are you okay? Hello, Miriam? We just heard something on the radio. Just tell us you're okay. We love you, Miriam. Please, say something. Hello! Hello!"

This is all taking place outside a gift shop and the lady from the store says, to herself, or maybe to me: "This is what we get for trying to make peace with them."

So quickly it's all over. The living all in one piece go into those vehicles, the living but in pieces go into another vehicle, and the dead go where the dead go.

Then come the hoses to wash up all the blood and life goes on.

Someone says: "In an hour the young mothers will come with the baby carriages." They do this to show that this (Israel) is their vine and fig tree and none shall make them afraid.

Still at the scene but after the worst is over, a group of men form a minyan to recite Birkas ha-gomel, a liturgical thanks to the Almighty for being spared the peril.

Back at the hotel I take a long shower and then, toweling off, can't recognize myself in the mirror. Who is this? My eyes are vacant. My coloring is gone. My lips are white. My expression is fierce. Who are the people who would do this? What do they want? This is not about land. This is about nothing. This is about the love of murder and the joy of bloodshed. It must be true, then, that "he shall be a wild ass of a man; his hand shall be against every man."

The phone.

"Tomorrow."

That's the extent of the message.

That night I dream a strange dream. I am being pursued and find myself chased, by one man, into a large white room, a room without windows and doors, save for that one door that led me in. I run across the walls in search of an opening, my arms flailing at the solid partitions in the hope of finding some weakness in the structure, some give that might lead to an escape. All the while this one man stands by the door laughing. I am hoping for a miracle, divine intervention to instantly create another opening.

This awakens me. I'm in a cold sweat. I feel a presence. I hear breathing. I hear a voice. I'm awake. I know I'm awake. I can't make out what's being said, but I've heard this voice before, don't know where or when, but it is familiar and even comforting. I can't even make out the language. Is this English? Is this Arabic? Is this Hebrew? I think it's Hebrew. Am I hallucinating?

There's a mirror up ahead and it reflects the passing shadow of a man. If this is so, then he is exceedingly tall – tall, thin and bearded.

I get up. By this time all voices and fancies are gone and I am determined to go back to sleep and make no business of all this; maybe I am hallucinating. Most likely, yes, hallucinating; I am trapped in the supernatural intoxication of this place. People come here and stand by the door to greet the messiah who is expected at any moment, and here is where the End of Days is expected to begin, throngs already in attendance upon the cliffs, ready to jump. I've been seduced and entranced. This is where visions happen, some true, some false.

I stagger to the bathroom, stagger back out, and here against the wall, by the door, is a cane, or rather a staff, with a carved inscription that begins, in the Hebrew, with the words, "Adonai yevarecha veyish merecha." I know this. This is from the Book of Numbers, the priestly blessing of Aaron to the people, that goes, "The Lord bless you and keep you; the Lord make his face shine upon you and be gracious unto you; the Lord lift up his countenance upon you, and give you peace."

Was this here all along, this staff? Is it in every room of this hotel? Did I miss it when I first checked in? I phone the front desk and ask and they think I'm crazy and I'm beginning to agree. I persist. No, I'm told, never heard of this, a cane with the priestly blessing. Could the previous guest have left this behind? SIR, this is Israel. Our people clean every room meticulously. You must be dreaming.

Maybe. Maybe so. Yes, maybe.

It's near sunlight and I get dressed and walk over to the Western Wall, the Kotel. It's all lit up, bathed in floodlights. I say a prayer for my Christian mother, my Jewish father. I present a note to the Wall that Arnold Coffey gave me, and tuck it in between the cracks and among a million other petitions, along with one of my own. I say the sh'ma – "Hear 'O Israel, the Lord is our God, the Lord is One," and with all that, even with all that,

I am still not sure if I can be counted as a believer. I still lack faith.

I don't know. I just don't know. I wish I could be as sure, as fervent as those around me who are really going to town in their devotions.

I am an American. Thus I prayed for America. I am part Jewish. Thus I prayed for Israel. I also threw in a prayer for all the good people anywhere, just in case I missed anyone. Personally, I don't know who is good, who is bad. Wait. I do know who is bad; not so sure who is good. But that's me. I can't always separate the two. Let Him sort them out. Does He know? Does He know, and can He (like Santa Claus) tell who's been naughty and nice? I run a newspaper. I see no evidence that the Almighty makes any distinctions in divvying up his blessings. In fact, from the script of newsprint rather than the ledger of Scriptures, often enough it appears that the wicked get the better half of His blessings.

But that's just me operating under the cynicism of a journalist whose gods are the Associated Press and Reuters.

These people who are so devout, whether Christians or Jews, what is the secret of their faith? What do they know that I don't?

Back at the hotel I shower and shave and get ready for what's coming, and it is odd that I take such care in my grooming, as if my life depends on a good hair day. I brush my teeth and use the underarm deodorant as if this will count and score points. I even go for the aftershave. I know I'm being ridiculous but it's the routine. Joel, my son, doesn't shave yet, but he uses the Old Spice just like Dad.

* * *

"Ready?"

That's Ibrahim, but without Avraham.

In the car, a beat-up Subaru, there's the driver who calls himself Ahmed. Next to him, as we take off, sits Ibrahim.

I'm in the back with Suliman. We zoom away and it's a beautiful day in Jerusalem but there is no taking the temperature of these men. They are silent but their eyes are eyes of resolve. Past the cobblestone streets and the shuks and the minarets we begin climbing and I know this only from sensations because I've been blindfolded. Suliman does this in one sudden move, and quite violent. He seems pleased with himself. There's some chatter among them now in Arabic. Between all that I make out the words "America...New York...newspaper... Internet...Kahane." Obviously that piece got in and got out.

We're driving over some flatlands now and I hear gravel, children, women, occasional gunfire. I smell the stench of tires in flames. We're passing from village to village apparently, possibly Gaza, which is now fully in control of Hamas – if indeed this is Gaza. Most likely it is. (In Gaza, Samson, blind from the betrayal of Delilah, prays that he may regain his strength to die with his Philistine enemies, and literally brings down the house upon their heads.) I am prepared to be slain at any moment, whatever the whim of these men. I hear the roar of a crowd in the distance and when we reach the scene of this clatter I sense that we're getting closer to our destination. The crowd is upon us now and the driving is slow. I don't know what they're shouting, these mobs.

Then it all subsides. I am forced out of the car and, unsure of my footing, trip, stumble and nearly fall. Suliman and the rest of them find this humorous and chuckle. One of them says, "America," and I say (finally we speak) "fuck you bastards, it ain't over." Suliman removes my blindfold and I am led into a one-story brick building that reminds me of a high school gym, and perhaps it is or perhaps it was, and now it serves as some kind of headquarters. There is but one entrance, no other doors, no windows. It's empty except for the walls that are festooned with photos of jihad massacres, or glories, depending on your point of view.

Now I am alone in a corner room that is bare except for one desk, two chairs, and a plastic bag. A man enters business-like, unceremoniously. He is wearing a keffiyeh. He is probably in his 60s, short, thin, unimposing, bearded and, as it turns out, soft-spoken. I am expecting a lengthy conversation. After all, the point of it is to hear his complaint against my newspaper, the Manhattan Independent, in order to win the release of Phil Crawford, primarily, and/or, to exchange my life for his, secondarily, or perhaps I've got it backwards. So I am expecting to hear him out, this mullah, if indeed it is Sheik Salaman, the man who was to serve (or to pose) as Phil Crawford's friendly contact so that Phil might have access to Hamas from the inside and provide our newspaper with a scoop bonanza.

Yes, from the start nothing was mentioned, openly, about this exchange, me for Phil, but it has always been so obvious.

He speaks.

"We have your number," he says in perfect English.

(Rumor had it that Sheik Salaman had been educated in an American university and became radicalized, a born-again Muslim, by our freedom in excess; depravity, in his eyes.)

"I don't understand," but I think I do.

"We have your number."

"Truly, I do not understand."

"Do not play the fool."

"Where is Phil Crawford?"

He nods. I follow his eyes to that plastic bag.

"His number was up."

"Why?"

"Do not count leaves on a tree. Praise be to Allah."

He gets up, leaves, is gone, I check the bag, it's Phil, Phil Crawford all right, his head. Praise be to Allah.

* * *

What kept me from killing this man when it was just the two of us? I kept pondering this on the trip back home and even later, into my sleep. I had HIS number right there, right then and there, and there was nothing to stop me, even in those few minutes, nothing, not even the likelihood, the certainty, that I'd be struck down in return. I was a goner anyway, so there was nothing to lose, even, as it turned out, they never intended to do me in. I was to serve as their messenger.

So I could have sent my own message.

But the answer is simple. There'd be no gain from weeding out this one, single, individual. They keep on coming and the supply is endless.

Chapter 38

The arbitration panel, also known as the ethics board, was meeting here in our main conference room.

Arnold Coffey said, "They're setting a trap for you."

I knew that, and I knew that the moment I left Gaza bringing myself home instead of Phil Crawford. Why is he dead and why am I alive? This, this hearing, was supposed to be about my dispute with anchorman Kevin Rod Rodgers, or rather his dispute with me over my (unprovoked?) assault upon his person, in any case, a question of ethics, but we all knew that this was bait for a bigger catch. Rodgers was the back story. Phil Crawford was the headline.

Three of them were seated at the front table, two men on either side of a very angry, very pissed off woman. This was Bessy Larkin Berlitz, the main judge, or arbitrator. She was in her 40s and attractive, former editor and later ombudsman for the Cincinnati Sun-Herald. She let it be known straight out that even though this was no formal trial in a formal courtroom (no lawyers), this was serious business. Journalism itself was on trial.

Due to all this informality, any witness could speak up at any time.

Rodgers' evidence against me was based solely on that footage that showed me slugging him.

"For no reason?" said Ms. Berlitz.

"For no reason," said Rodgers, checking his watch.

He had already alerted the judges that he had an evening

newscast to get out, and I said I had a newspaper to get out, so we were assured that this would be quick.

Rodgers testified how he'd been out there, in front of Pat's Gym, just signing autographs, when, behold, I stepped up and nailed him.

"Quick question," said Ms. Berlitz. "If found guilty, what would you recommend for sanctions?"

Quick answer. Rodgers wanted me banned for life from any newspaper.

The most they could do, this panel, was fine me, fine the newspaper, and recommend universal suspension. But recommend was all they could really do. (That does not sound like much, but it is plenty. It's about guilt among your peers and shame among your public. You've been disgraced, shunned. It's about a blacklist.)

"You, Mr. Garfield?"

"I have nothing to say without those missing eighteen seconds of footage."

"What would that prove?"

"That Mr. Rodgers' goons..."

"Mr. Garfield, please."

"Mr. Rodgers' bodyguards..."

"I have no bodyguards."

"Mr. Rodgers' associates. They were attacking a woman after she insulted Mr. Rodgers. I merely stepped in to defend this woman."

"What was the nature of this insult, Mr. Garfield?"

"She called him an anti-Semite."

"Is that correct, Mr. Rodgers?"

"That is correct," said Rodgers.

"That is correct? In other words," I said, "Mr. Rodgers admits that he's an anti-Semite."

"No! I was answering a direct question."

"Are you accusing Mr. Rodgers of being an anti-Semite?"

"Why not. What the heck."

"Sir, you do not seem to be taking these proceedings very seriously."

"I'm here."

"We've been warned about your cavalier attitude."

"Now I've been warned about your attitude, Ms. Berlitz."

The judge to her left asked why this hadn't been settled by a simple apology.

"Because," I said, "Mr. Rodgers never bothered to apologize to me."

"This is ridiculous," said Rodgers. "I'm the injured party."

"We have also been warned about your sense of humor," said Ms. Berlitz. "Be advised that this is no joking matter."

"I'm not joking."

"Who was – who is this woman who issued the insult against Kevin Rodgers?"

"Marta Geller," I remembered.

"Why isn't she here?"

I said I didn't have the time to look her up, though I knew, thought I knew, that she had filed charges against Rodgers, but then gave up, or something.

"So you don't have a witness."

I said I did; that goon sitting next to Rodgers.

"Please, Mr. Garfield."

(I did not offer up Rodgers as a hired gun for the Saudis, a paid foreign agent, my knowledge and revelation of this being the origin of this grudge.)

"This is not about him," said Ms. Berlitz. "This is about you."

Well, that straightened that out. I likewise did not remind the assembled that, in this mega-corporate world of ours, Ms. Berlitz's newspaper was owned by Rodgers' network.

That wouldn't be any help. But I did repeat that 18 seconds were missing that would positively exonerate me.

Rodgers insisted that there were no 18 seconds on the lam. No such thing. I was dreaming. I'd been making it up all along.

I said there were, there were 18 seconds of missing film,

and that I knew the cameraman, the photojournalist, who shot the film.

"You have his name?"

I gave her Waji Halid.

That would be my LA buddy and friend to the stars, Wayne.

"That's ridiculous," said Rodgers.

"Why isn't he here?" asked Ms. Berlitz.

I said I didn't have time...

"You said the same thing about this woman, Ms. Geller. Seems you don't have much time for this panel, Mr. Garfield."

Not when it's so lopsided, I said, resorting to one of Rodgers' favorite phrases.

I did say that I looked up Waji Halid and that he confessed, but wouldn't talk.

Rodgers said of course he wouldn't talk because he never confessed and because there were no 18 seconds of missing footage.

"We don't do such things," said Rodgers in his adopted British accent.

This led me to those five minutes of missing footage in connection with the Mohammed al-Dura Gaza Incident that was flammable deception from start to finish, so flammable that it even ignited a war. I said TV, Rodgers and his network especially, omitted anything that would slant a story their way. I gave it good about media manipulation, since we were all gathered together on ethics, after all. I don't know why I threw all that in. I was a goner anyway. So what's the difference?

"I shouldn't have to listen to this," said Rodgers.

"Would Mr. Halid be willing to support you?" asked Ms. Berlitz.

"I doubt it," I said.

(Maybe he would. He started coming around there in LA.)

"Well you'll have to try."

"I'll try," I said.

"Yes you will," said Ms. Berlitz.

Again she reprimanded me for being so cavalier. "Your career may depend on the outcome of this case."

So it kept going, back and forth, until Ms. Berlitz called for some character (or lack of character) witnesses.

Paulette Hammerman was quick to deliver me as having been "entirely indifferent" to the fix Phil Crawford was in. "He didn't seem to care."

Ms. Berlitz took my side here, and asked how this was relevant to the case at hand.

"This is within the context of Jay Garfield's general attitude and behavior," said Paulette. "He didn't seem to care if Phil Crawford lived or died."

She conceded that I didn't seem to care about myself, either.

So there – it's about Phil Crawford. Soon (I guessed) Rodgers would be forgotten altogether. That whole business was so slim.

Minerva Watson and Peter Brand chimed in about my heavy hand as managing editor. "Insensitive," said Minerva. "Tyrannical," said Peter.

Peter had more. "There have been rumors in the newsroom about Jay Garfield and Lyla Crawford."

"Is this our business?" asked Ms. Berlitz.

"Phil Crawford was my friend," Peter testified with some emotion. "It's my view, shared by others, that Phil was sent out to Gaza to get killed."

"Who sent him out to get killed?"

What a set-up!

Peter Brand points directly at me. "Jay Garfield."

"Recess."

* * *

I walked over to Nat Sherman's tobacco shop on Fifth Avenue to buy myself a meerschaum pipe for $850. I had bought a meerschaum when I first got promoted to managing editor so if that's how it all began this is how it should end. Let this excess, this splurge be a further sign of my indifference and recklessness. The pipe was a beauty, long-stemmed, deep bowl, for a long smoke, and from the looks of things there'd be plenty of long smokes. Meerschaums were royalty. They aged with the man and, as they burned gracefully from white, to pink, to red, to golden brown, they defined the man, were the picture of him, in all his ups and downs, his flaws and glories.

We are still inhaling the smoke and ashes of 9/11 but people stepped wide when, outside the tobacco shop, I lit up my $850 pipe.

"Jay?"

"Lyla?"

She'd been at the hearing and would be returning to testify. We walked together. There hadn't been much of that, togetherness, since I'd been back these five weeks. We'd kept a distance due to – due to everything. She was convinced, finally, that Phil was still among us, in spirit, and cursing us from the grave. She wasn't the same. We weren't the same. Something happened. The coolness began when we both agreed that, especially now, post Phil, we'd be walking targets for gossip, billboards for our sins and conspiracies. We were, no doubt, being watched. Lyla was especially skittish. (Already the tabloids had her tagged as the LOVE GODDESS.)

There'd been no trysts since my return. Not much of anything. She'd lost weight, not through dieting, and she was a step slower off her usual tempo. We were not to speak of the overdose when she heard what happened to Phil and what, obviously, lay in wait for the two of us. I knew about it because I was the one who rushed her to the hospital, St. Vincent's, where she'd become a regular guest, taking herself there, when I wasn't around, for the migraines.

Finally, we were strangers all over again, practically.

"Someday," she said, "we'll get it back, start fresh."

"First this," I agreed.

"Yes, this," she sighed.

I spared her the details about my adventures out there and she wanted no part of all that anyway. She had enough going on. She had even said, when I first came back, "Don't tell me. I know. I know enough." What was it like when she first heard? I didn't want to think about that, either. Wasn't this exactly what we wanted? Yes, sure, of course. But it is not always good when you get what you want.

Would she have been happier if this were Phil, here, and me, there, with my head lopped off? No, certainly not – but it still didn't work out as we had it planned.

Actually, all of it did go according to plan, and it was still awful.

Nearing the building, she said, "We'd better arrive separately."

"Right."

"Jay, I still love you."

* * *

Sam Cleaver spoke up in my favor, saying, "Jay Garfield was a dream editor."

Was?

Stu Greenwald testified that, to the contrary, I had been "reluctant" to send Phil to a place where he might get killed.

Ben Hawkins – about my overall performance as managing editor – declared that he had "no complaints."

Thank you, but not much of an endorsement. That's what we say about a dog when we've finally got him housebroken.

No complaints. Hmm.

Next – Lyla.

"You must still be in mourning," said Ms. Berlitz in (mock?) sympathy.

"Yes, this is painful."

"Those are terrible rumors..."

"Yes."

"Which can only add to your despair."

"Yes."

"But those are the risks of journalism."

"Oh yes. Yes."

"I'm sure you must be shuddering at those rumors."

"Yes I am."

"Those rumors that couple you with Jay Garfield...who, let's be plain, is not on trial for this."

"Of course not."

"But Jay Garfield did..."

"Ms. Berlitz, Jay Garfield did what he had to do...he went after a story...and then he risked his own life to SAVE my husband..."

"Yes, yes, yes. We know. But you know the rumors. You surely..."

"Are there any more questions?"

"Just this. Did you support Jay Garfield in his decision to send your husband out there where reporters repeatedly get kidnapped and even assassinated?"

"Phil wanted to go. Phil insisted."

"So it wasn't your idea."

"It was Phil's idea – Phil was a journalist."

"Thank you, Mrs. Crawford."

Waji Halid? Wayne? Yes, that's him, all the way from Brentwood, but for me or against me?

"I have the entire taping," he said.

"Please," said all three examiners.

Yes, please, roll film, and there it is, black and white, – Rodgers' bodyguard shoving the lady, and down she goes, and here I come to the rescue.

Could not have said it any better myself!

"That about does it," declared Ms. Berlitz. "This evidence is irrefutably in Jay Garfield's favor."

She asked Rodgers if he had anything to say.

"No," he said.

"I thought not. Manipulation of this sort paints us all with the same brush. This is awful, this is sickening."

Rodgers and his network loyalists were ready to shove off. "Not so fast," said Ms. Berlitz.

"Oh?"

"You owe Mr. Garfield a private and a public apology."

* * *

Really, I don't know what's going on anymore. Is it still the same out there, or has it gotten better or worse? One day I intend to pick a number and find out. I don't watch television too much anymore. I don't watch it at all anymore. I do read the newspapers. That's not true. I read only one newspaper, The Daily Racing Form. That's all the news I need, back here in the backstretch where the horses come first. This is sweet.

One day I'll check back. That'll be the day when everything is settled, which means, I guess, that'll be the day. But what am I missing other than the latest genocide, assassination, roadside bombing, hostage-taking, rape, murder and all other acts that define us as members of the human race? In here we keep all that out. Sometimes I reflect over how silly all of it was, the pursuit of news, the heat of life from deadline to deadline, the grieving over a typo rather than the bloodbath within the headline, or like Lyla and her J.D. Salinger caper. Chasing Salinger, I have come to believe, is a metaphor for our (elusive) pursuit of nirvana. Catching one is as fruitless as catching the other. But it was fun, fun while it lasted, and maybe it will still happen, the Salinger scoop. If anyone can do it, it's Lyla. (Was any of this legit? Lyla was not one to be easily duped. I still expect something to come of this. I did get that e-mail from someone claiming to be Salinger – Salinger willing to cooper-ate and sit for an interview with Lyla – but it would have taken time to get all that authenticated, and besides, I didn't care that much anymore.)

Around here people don't know who I am, or rather who I was, and that suits me fine.

I, Jay Garfield, was King over the Manhattan Independent, a great American newspaper with worldwide influence. I acted in grand style. Whatever my eyes desired I did not deny them. I did not deprive myself of any kind of joy. Then I looked at all the things that I had done and the energy I had expended in doing them. It was clear that it was all futile and a vexation of the spirit – and there is no real profit under the sun. Futility of futilities, all is futile. (Still true today as it was 3,000 years ago).

Today I am a hotwalker. I walk horses for Kuana Banks and soon I will become a groom and one day I will become a trainer. My home is the backstretch, my travels are the racing circuit.

That was some terrific verdict that came from that ethics panel. We won. But beware even of triumphs. The slide began with Rodgers. Rodgers made amends. This he did. He showed those missing 18 seconds of film and confessed that he'd been mistaken (without conceding the slander). He apologized – but, reminded the world that there was still "a cloud hanging" over me, and Lyla, about Phil Crawford. He made sure to get that in. Clever bastard.

The rest of them picked that up and what had been a victory turned into a drubbing. The sniping began with Rodgers all right, but it morphed and soon plagued from all over. Lyla got the worst of it, as she kept being headlined as a "temptress." I got a good part of it, too, of course I did, as a powerful two-fisted managing editor who had conspired, along with Lyla, to have her husband slain by proxy.

Kahane was implicated, even though dead. Israel was implicated, even though blameless. The demonstrations began outside the building of the Manhattan Independent but soon spread to rioting here, there and everywhere. I wasn't fired. I quit. Or maybe both. Ken Ballard and Ben Hawkins, they both wanted me to stay. I had done so much for this newspaper, excuse me, so much good, some bad, sure, but so much good. Really, said Ben Hawkins, they're making you out to be a villain when you're actually a hero. You went out there and offered up your life in exchange for Phil's. Can't figure it out.

Given the chaos, better I should just leave. This, from me. For the good of the paper. Ah, for the good of the paper. This, from Ben Hawkins. I guess that's what it comes down to.

We wish you the best, Jay. Really.

Lyla, too.

Oh, Lyla and me? We're splits. Even after Phil's death she got an e-mail message. Signed...Phil. Spooky. Yes, anyone could have done that, impersonated his e-mail identity (as with Salinger), but too spooky. So we could not be seen together. Someone is watching. Ironic. She refused to see me because by seeing me – that could spell my doom. Those were the terms of the message. This time the perishing would be mine, if I so much as touched her again.

She also had to leave the Manhattan Independent, and also "for the good of the paper." She is now editor (actually assistant editor) at a small publishing house. It's a start. She always wanted to start all over again. She was fired from the Manhattan Independent but still had some blessings in reserve to go out dignified, as resigned "to pursue other projects." But people in the business knew the code, and the disgrace. It all came down on her at once, including the suicide of Trevor Kent, the author who got that horrific review in her pages and on her watch and because of it committed suicide, blaming her by name in his farewell to the world. Lyla accepted the blame, harshly, and that alone aged her as I saw for myself when we met up outside that cigar shop. She told me then how apparent it was that Phil's curse was still upon us.

She wept when we parted. She would always love me. I would always love her. No regrets. But she was spooked by that e-mail that seemed to come from the grave.

She was spooked by the death of Trevor Kent who had died on her account. (I'd never persuade her that this man had troubles separate from this.)

All of this was supposed to bring us together and keep us

together. Now it keeps us apart?

Midda Kenneged Midda. Measure for Measure. God evens the score. He punishes you with the same sin you had in mind for someone else.

Like when Pharaoh started going about slaying the firstborn of the Hebrews. God said, okay, take this. I will slay the firstborn of the Egyptians.

Midda Kenneged Midda.

You have become so Biblical, she says. My reviewers always panned books that were too Biblical.

I've become a believer.

So have I, she said. God evens the score. He evens the score all right. He sure evens the score.

Let's not get too cynical. That's what got us into this.

He was evil, Jay. We did nothing wrong. He deserved to get what he got. It was you or him.

Small comfort.

I have the memories, Jay. Do you?

All of them.

That's our revenge.

Yes, I agree, that's our revenge.

Even here in my seclusion there's news from the newsroom. Paul Westman – the man who came to us like a ghost from another generation – has died, and he died with his boots on, journalistically-speaking; keeled over at his desk atop the typewriter. That's the way to go if you have to go and for this man there really was no place. Who knows if he really died like that, sounds entirely too poetic, but fitting. No one attended his funeral and that too is poetic. What a shame that he could sell none of this poetry while he was still alive.

Three months have passed and I write this in Kuana's tack room, after all the hotwalking and all the hosing have been done. I await the day when I am qualified to become a groom. That's the next step. One day, after I pass the test, I will become a trainer. This is very big. Trainers lead good lives.

They are harbored from the world outside. In fact that's what the rest of it is called – the outside.

That's why I am inside. Isolated and insulated and even sedated. I don't want to know what's going on out there where now even machines, the cash registers say "have a nice day" to save people the trouble of being polite. Other than the horses, I don't care. I am quite happy. I am up four in the morning and am at the shedrow by five. I live inside the grounds. They have apartments. Not fancy, not the Waldorf. I have no enemies. I have one regret.

I never got the chance to thank Waji Halid, Wayne. He came all the way from Brentwood, California to speak up for me. All of it happened so fast that I never had the chance to thank him. He is Muslim. So they are not all like that, are they? I hope he does not think I am ungrateful. He is Muslim and he came to speak up for a man who declared himself a Jew. So not all of it is futility.

I understand that he did lose his job on account of taking my side. So there is no justice. I understand that Peter Brand the snitch was fired or suspended by Ben Hawkins. So there is some, some justice. Ben Hawkins? Ben sold out Jerusalem along with me into the bargain. Nothing personal. Really, nothing personal. Business. You understand, don't you? Yes, I understand.

I have a dream.

One day I will be there in Louisville, Kentucky and when they sing *My Old Kentucky Home*, weep no more my lady, one of those horses prancing so proudly and gorgeously under the May sunshine will be mine, my horse, a horse that I trained, and all my friends will be there in the stands to root home Mr. Beethoven – that's the name I've already picked out – and there he'll be, Mr. Beethoven, galloping to the wire ahead by 31 lengths.

I get goose bumps dreaming that dream. I know it will happen, and when Mr. Beethoven crosses the finish line I can just hear Lyla, standing next to me, saying, "I'm not crying." Waji Halid will be there and so will Jimmy Smokes, along with all the rest of them who were with me and even those who weren't. That's a good dream. I'm in a good place. In here I feel safe, quite comfortable, nearly content. Full contentment is impossible but this will do. Out there – that's not my world anymore. I'm giving it back. Take it, please, and be quick.

*   *   *

But now this...months later. Lyla has been calling. Every morning now, that's her on the phone. She keeps making up excuses, like had I really given James Joyce a chance...like what he writes on page 143 of *Ulysses* about J.J. O'Molloy having died "with a great future behind him." That, she says, is such a great line – and so appropriate! To us, of course, and to me, specifically. A great future behind him. How perfect, she says, sounding quite like her old self, verging on the Lyla when she was Lyla. On that same page of *Ulysses*, she says, there is this line – Gone with the wind. The copyright is 1914, about a generation before the movie.

Do people know about this? she asks excitedly, literary sleuth that she is and so thrilled when happening upon a gem.

Do people, she asks, know about that line – with a great future behind him? So compact in its restrained power; it implodes.

She asks if I appreciate this as much as she does, and I do, yes I do, and even more, I appreciate her love of language, the music of a thought perfectly expressed. This is charming in a world rushed along by clatter and it is charming that someone can stop to love a phrase amid the pandemonium, a simple but majestic phrase lost in the depths of literature, and it is charming that this excites her so that she must share. She needs to share this windfall.

She thinks people care about things like this, and this too is charming, and lovable, and noble, because nobody cares.

I know what she is trying to do by bringing up Joyce and all the rest. Bring me back to life. She thinks I'm dead. She thinks I died leaving a great future behind me. I can tell by her voice that she has recouped, or perhaps only regrouped, and wants us back, curse and all. She thinks I died and went to the race-track, heaven, to me. Though not really, about this being heaven. This was not the plan. The plan was that after I'd been immensely successful, old and successful, a revered old news-man like Walter Lippmann – then I'd retire to a second life, as a trainer. This is not the case.

Another time she calls to ask if I'm doing any reading at all. Yes, the Daily Racing Form. She chuckles but says that that is not funny. I must stay in touch with the world. Have I read Jonathan Delancy's latest novel? That's the novel that's got the literary world doing flips and orgasms. My answer is that I tried, and there probably is a novel in there someplace, but too many words got in the way.

Same old Jay, she says,

I never hired reporters without making them read "The Killers" first. That too is brevity and simplicity that implodes.

I gave up on literature too soon, she says. That's where you'll find all the answers; not in journalism, not in the latest news.

The difference between the two types, between Lyla and me, Lyla embracing the infinity of Literature, me being the dead-line-to-deadline newsman (once upon a time), is that one seeks truth, that's Literature, that's Art, the other is in pursuit of lies, that's journalism when it's on the job. Amid my own transgressions, I did the job. That's what got me exiled. That's what happened.

She wants to know – How could we have let it get this far?

Heroes will always disappoint – remember?

We're essentially bad from birth onward, according to Machiavelli and anyone who's been around. That's what makes journalism. That's reality spoken from the lips of literature.

Thanks to bad behavior newspapers will never die and if circulations dip and if newsprints run dry, for the latest on how poorly we're behaving we'll switch to the writing on our computers.

That's how we're taught, not by the virtues of the saints but by the manmade mistakes that preceded us. (We never learn, of course.)

The Bible? The Hebrew Bible, at least, is all about bad behavior, beginning with the headline: EVE TEMPTS ADAM.

Or – GOD TO SODOM: DROP DEAD.

It also gives the weather: FLOODS IN THE FORECAST – NOAH BUILDS ARK.

Some call it the Bible but it's just good reporting.

Literature and journalism are in the same business. Euripides may well have been the first tabloid journalist in his telling of Medea and how she went about murdering her own children, filicide. That's literature, yes, but it's also going on today (Andrea Yates?), so it's still tabloid. (Do all writings, from Homer to Stephen King, speak to us beyond the obvious text but in code? We may not be aware of it, but we're being sent messages. The handwriting is on the wall and on the page of every book.)

Am I seeing anyone? she asks.

She's been asking this more and more.

I see lots of people.

Come on, she says. You know what I mean. Are you seeing anyone?

I say – Can't you stop being a girl for a minute?

She gasps. That is soooo sexist!

Aha.

I've got to come down there, she says, and knock some political correctness into you – hit you upside the head with a 600 page book.

I've given up on women.

You've plain given up, she says. You know who you sound like?

Who?

Sam Cleaver.

Really.

Exactly. He quit. You accused him of being a quitter. He quit again? Sam Cleaver quit again? Back to the novel, huh?

Well, that is his defiance and this is mine.

You've lost the will to fight.

No, I called it plainly, having lost the skill to equivocate and sugarcoat. This headline did me in: THE KORAN HAS ARRIVED AND IT HAS COME TO DEVOUR THE BIBLE. That headline was the beginning and the end for me. Everything else, what happened in between, was just commentary. From there on I was dead man walking.

I had tried to change the world but instead the world changed me. But I'd do it again. I was no quitter.

Neither was Sam Cleaver. He just got fed up. He just told the world to go fuck itself. Likewise. His destination is literature, mine is Santa Anita.

I loved you, she says, because you were a fighter.

She asks if I am afraid because there is a fatwa hanging over my head – and yes, this also happened, a contract for that headline, and of course, for Phil Crawford.

I should be afraid of a fatwa? Sweetheart, it's not personal. The fatwa is against all of us.

This is when she says, "I'm coming over."

Over the past few weeks she has been hinting at something – something about phone calls she'd been getting from Ben Hawkins, maybe wanting me back, or something, but she'd been good to my word, that my phone number here in the backstretch was not to be given out (I had already dumped my cell phone), not to anyone, unless it was about a horse. Otherwise, no phone calls. Nothing from nobody. If she betrayed me on this, I threatened that I'd never have wet dreams about her anymore...except for that time I had her up against the car.

"It's too soon."

"If anything, it's getting to be too late. I'm coming over."

"They won't let you in, like that other time."

"Oh they'll let me in all right."

Yes, she wouldn't need a press badge. Lyla had legs.

* * *

Meanwhile, as I wait, wait for Lyla, I muck the stalls. I use a big rake. A man in the next barn also uses a rake and his rake is much bigger. His name is Hiram Berker. He is an assistant trainer, tall, athletic, weather-beaten, around 35, a stem of straw always dangling from his mouth, a man from Hazard, Kentucky, very tough country. He's been on my case from day one.

He keeps saying I look familiar. He'll amble by as I'm mucking away and just glare at me.

This bothers Kuana, too. This is his barn and it is bad manners for horsemen from one barn to impose themselves upon another man's barn. This is not only bad etiquette but also falls into the category of spying. But Hiram Berker only says that he is trying to place me. Then one day in the track kitchen, as I'm sitting there alone after all the mucking and hotwalking and hosing and bandaging has been done, sitting there alone over a hot cup of coffee, here he comes and, leaning in, so that I can smell his liquor breath and see his green teeth, says, "I know you."

"Oh?"

"You're the guy, right?"

"Yup."

"You're the Jew."

Okay. That's that for a while. For a while that's all there is. That's fine. That's settled. That's quite all right. Perfectly understood. I know who he is and he knows who I am and that's fine and quite all right. I know his baggage, he knows mine. A few days pass and it's about eleven in the morning when all is quiet and people, horsemen, are resting up for the afternoon, the morning's been done.

I am resting like this on a lounge chair outside Kuana's tack room, relaxed and satisfied, when Hiram Berker eases on over, his walk too purposeful, his grin too familiar, and says he's just come from the back gate where there's a woman trying to get in and using my name. I nod and thank him and tell him I know who it is. I start to get up. He says, "That's some pretty lady."

"Thanks," I say.

"Pussy," he says, smiling, rolling that straw around his gums as he smiles, and keeping his balance, I notice, on a rake.

The raking's been done.

I shake my head to let him know that not all women are pussy, definitely not this one. I put on a very relaxed demeanor, but I know what's going on.

"Wouldn't mind some strange pussy," he says. "Nothing like strange pussy."

Now I stare at him, eyes narrowed.

"She a Jew?" he says. "Never had Jew pussy."

This bothers me very much. This is not supposed to happen among horsemen. This defiles the backstretch.

I ask him to put down that rake. Instead he lifts it up and comes at me with it and in a snap he's got me cornered and begins using the rake as a sword and as I duck and swirl I can't get in, get in to box him, because he's got that rake, which gives him distance, strategic depth, and with that rake he proceeds to cut me up, up and down, with a thousand steel-pointed fingers. I am already bleeding badly, manage to get hold of a broom, which I use as a lance, and now we're going at each other back and forth, swinging wildly, my harmless broom against his lethal rake, and it is no contest. I must get inside.

I wait for his next wild swing – a high one – and when it comes, finally, I dive in, head to belly, the momentum of which makes him lose his grip, and as the rake falls, I've got him, I've got him boxing, and now it's my turn, and as I set him up, prop him for my combinations, left, right, uppercut, then again, and again, and again, and again, and again, he is defenseless, though most of the blood is still mine, the rake having done all that, but as I set him up and trounce him he is every son of a bitch from the day I was born...and now, now that I've got him on the ground, pleading, I continue to flail, something in me has snapped, when finally a group of them lift me up and off.

He is unconscious. The track ambulance arrives and smelling salts bring him back. They take him some place I don't know where and don't care.

I am driven off to first aid. My cuts are bad.

The nurse says I am one lucky horseman that none of those spokes got into my eyes. She begins to wash me off. It takes a while. I am bleeding all over. The nurse says if the bleeding doesn't stop I will have to be taken to the hospital. But she is managing. Security arrives. They'll need a statement. Witnesses have already given their accounts and seemingly I'm in the clear. They saw it all, from the beginning.

* * *

I am reclining on a hospital-type bed as the nurse begins to patch me up. I keep my eyes closed. This is painful.

I open my eyes and here's Lyla.

Lyla is smiling.

"That's more like it," she says, beaming, but she has aged.

She's trying to pretend nothing happened. Plenty happened.

I hear the nurse tell Lyla that I need rest.

"He'll be fine," says Lyla.

I'm not so sure.

CPSIA information can be obtained at www.ICGtesting.com
Printed in the USA
BVOW04s1815171214

379849BV00001B/28/P